Annihilation by Appointment Only...

A Love Story

Book Four in the Sanctuary Series

By, S. C. Williams

ISBN: 1491003758
ISBN-13: 9781491003756

Other Books by S.C. Williams

Sanctuary
Mad Lavender
Starman Heart Stargirl

Acknowledgements

Firstly, thank you to the Starman Hunters, who went searching for the actual locations described in my books. This stalwart group would show up at book signings with proud photos of themselves lying on sidewalks or arms spread in a classic "ta-da" pose or even triumphantly kneeling at the site, like the athlete having just made the winning touchdown. They are very nice people, very fervent in their desire to find evidence of fantasy in the real world.

They are not at all stalker-ish, I assure you.

I have suggested in the past that the names of such stellar people should be used frequently. Their names are likes talismans, nice names that should be used when naming, say, a favorite gold fish or pet schnauzer. May I suggest you use names, such as Stephanie (a personal favorite), Brad, Ann, Phil, Kathy, Frank, Carl, Lisa, Renee, Simon, Curtis, Jason, Jen, and Margaret?

These are all perfectly nice names of perfectly nice people who all have a touch of whimsy and quite possibly are magical creatures.

I'm just sayin'.

Yes, the locations are real and so are some of the characters. I am not kidding you. Some of this stuff actually happened, or, to put it more eloquently: in my real life, the line between fantasy and reality is blurred, to say the least. This has been both a gift and a curse. But wait, I digress. This is not about me, it's about you.

I do particularly want to thank as well as apologize to certain individuals with the names Curtis, Margaret, and Jason. Let me thank them for letting me steal bits and pieces of their personalities, as I adore them so and just had to immortalize them in several books. Let me also apologize to them by inferring that they actually possess the characteristics of the characters who represent them. They have been trying to live down their fantasy reputations for years now. Oops.

It's a funny thing. You think you have carefully drawn a character and thus intend to make it behave exactly as you wish it to. Yet when it gets down to the actual writing, something very odd happens. You think you are going to write "plan A," and the character rebels. In a very firm voice inside your own head, it says, "No way, Ray," and such. Instead, it tells you what it really wants to do. It deviates from the well-laid path you set before it. It does whatever it pleases, throwing all ideas like plotlines and character development out the window. Resigned, like every mother when confronting a tantrum-prone toddler, you let it do what the hell it wants. Within reason.

So apologies, Margaret. Marissa is you but not really. You are much, much nicer. Sorry, Jason. Jacob is conflicted and you are not. And, Curtis, Ben is way too stoic for my taste.

I take no responsibility for what Jacob, Marissa, or Ben do. They are their own creatures and simply will have to bear the consequences of their actions.

Well, you have to read this, don't you?

Enjoy.

S.C. Williams

Contents

Prologue

I am a chronicler of tales. I am a writer. I am also known as Noel, The Professor. I am currently writing a tale that, when published, will be categorized as "fantasy," when, in reality, it should be listed under "non-fiction/biography." For this is a tale about an actual family, living comfortably in the hills of San Francisco's East Bay and what happens to them when a baby gargoyle falls out of the sky one dark and stormy night.

The story is true.

It is a fairy tale only in that fairies are actually in it. For they exist, you see. So do gargoyles, trolls, dragons, and elves for that matter. As well as the mysterious Others, a sort of magical police force intent upon regulating the amount of magic actually used by Fairfolk. Too much magic and the whole thing blows up, Fairfolk and humans alike.

As I write, I am sitting at a perfectly normal kitchen table, looking outside the back door to a perfectly normal deck. I am in a nice house situated atop a windy hill, with views of the San Francisco Bay. Nothing terribly unusual about it, except for the fact that sometimes, fairies hang out on that very deck.

Interesting group, those fairies. Their methods of transport from their abode to my deck vary.

Although they certainly can fly, using their sparkly and iridescent wings, what they really need is some sort of creature to protect them from hungry raptors and such along the way. At times, they have used Bob, a cat of mysterious origins. But lately, they have been using these overly large rainbow-colored lizards. The lizards love fairy magic. They absorb it and are nourished by the ambient magical leakage. It makes them grow huge and shine in an array of weirdly metallic colors. Contrary to what you may think, this is not cute. It makes them look garishly dangerous. I would not like to make one of those shiny lizards angry.

In return for this magical hit, they provide easy transport for the fairies, who ride these miniature monsters like cowboys and cowgirls—that is, if cowboys and cowgirls were about twelve inches tall, wore loud and sparkly outfits, and sported translucent wings. Like that.

Other times, gargoyles have visited this backyard. They rarely come inside, as the house really isn't designed to accommodate their large proportions and their very *expressive* (code word for *destructive*) wings. You see they are about eight feet tall and their wings span maybe twice that. Big guys those gargoyles.

There has even been a dragon or two in the yard. Times I don't really care to recall as I was once considered an entrée item for one of them.

That will be a difficult chapter to write, I tell you.

I sigh at the task set before me. It is daunting, to say the least, for there is so much to tell and so much that I have personally experienced that I have lost all objectivity in structuring this story—or stories...but I do my best. For this is a cautionary tale of sorts, written for any future hapless human who may fall into such circumstances as I have. All of these notes and records, now strewn across the kitchen table, may well help some other human who may find himself thrown into such chaos as has befallen me and my associates.

My table includes all the usual things a writer needs in order to write. My vital writing supplies are as follows: a laptop computer, a caffeinated beverage of some sort, candy for sustenance, the occasional adult beverage, and notes. Only my notes are a little out of the ordinary. They include etched dragon bones, delightfully illustrating stories of Fairfolk life—usually cautionary tales warning the viewer of annihilation by the Others should too much magic be used.

I also have parchment sketches made by the elves, one in particular named Mad Lavender. She used to be a person and now is an elf having a very fascinating life. There are more sketches by an elf named Nebbin—an unusual name for a very unusual elf. His drawings were quite different from Mad Lavender's. Hers had all of the emotion while his had all the objective detail. His were more careful, technical, and precise. Between the two of them, I am able to flesh out clearly what life in the elfin realm was truly like. That will be an easy chapter to write. Lots of detail right before me to draw from. Literally.

At the moment, I am alone. My companion—once known as Sleeping Guy, but now we call him Kenneth—is gone on some sort of mission for The Family. For when they call, we jump. They called. And he did. I will be filled in later on the secretive nature of this mission. For now, I am blissfully alone and able to think my own thoughts and perhaps write a coherent paragraph or two about what happened to that very family after their brush with magic.

It is a big tale. True to the formula of fairy tales, it is full of hope and danger and even a war. There is the eternal conflict between good and evil. Although in the fairy realm, who is good and who is evil is sort of a moving target. Sometimes, the good are bad and the bad do good. Sort of a situational ethics thing with Fairfolk. They definitely subscribe to the ends justifying the means. Hence, it is a bit tough to determine the black hats from the white ones. But I shall try.

True to all fairy tales, this one will have a happy ending—or many happy endings, depending upon how this all turns out. For as I write, the story has not yet wound down to a conclusion. It is still unfolding. But all things considered, I have hope that all will end well.

Regardless of the outcome, I am a good chronicler and I shall tell you all. I am sure there will be a happy ending. I anticipate it. All signs point to it. In the fortune cookie of life, I read it. That's how it's supposed to be, right?

Texting: One, Two, Three...

"...So, in conclusion, I can think of no other course of action but to neutralize the area." Nervously, he smoothed the front of his toga—an old-school uniform that operative Others wore when at Other Residence, or as the new Elder Other called it, Home Base.

"You mean plan C," the Supreme Elder Other flatly corrected. Her silence telegraphed her displeasure at his not adopting her new terms. Irritation sizzled in the air. The operative paused, stunned at his superior's vehement reaction.

"Er, yes. In your vernacular, plan C." Struggling to deal with the demands and yes, even the new jargon established by the new Supreme Elder Other, the operative stammered, trying hard to avoid the steely gaze of his new boss, and wondering for the millionth time, *Why oh why did **she** get this job?*

"First of all," she started, voice rising as she hovered above the end of the desk (she often hovered, as her diminutive size made it impossible for her to be seen while seated in the massive chair), "you never read my text I sent you about slowing down the neutralizations, now did you?" Her green leathery wings snapped in irritation, causing her to bob in the air in a rather

1

unladylike fashion. Her icy look was softened only by the soft cascades of fiery auburn hair gently wafting around her. She floated at the end of the large desk, a dreamy vision but for the fire in her eyes, the wicked blue scar on her cheek, and those lethal green wings.

Her cold condemnation was wasp-like, stinging. He winced as her words rained down upon him. She was fierce and intimidating despite her tiny size and her penchant for high fashion. He could not understand her passion for all things "Internet"—a human invention and therefore a thing of lesser magic. He had, naturally, ignored her edict about using cell phones and Internet connections, as all decent operatives should. Or so he thought.

He was not the only operative to strongly object to her new regulations. Imagine being weighed down by such a thing as a cell phone! A ridiculous human invention, with its many buttons and complicated numerics, when simple scrying would do the same thing. No, rather than contacting the Elder Other via a nice smooth pool of water or a glassy sheet of morning ice, *she* required the field operative Others to press a series of buttons and speak into this small box-like thing, called a cell phone.

And where, may I ask, does one carry this object when togas do not have pockets?

And that's not all. She also sent messages via this big box. A computer. Of course, all Others were literate, but lately (last few millennia), they preferred messaging through a series of mental pictures, which was easier and more eloquent than words.

Now operative Others were required to look at the nearest stupid box daily and get their orders from *her*.

And let's not even get into an actual face-to-face meeting with her. She *never* gave you her full attention. She was constantly consulting this cell phone as well as a box-something called a laptop (which was a funny term considering the entire apparatus certainly could not fit onto her lap). Her "lap" was the size of well, the cell phone, and this laptop was many times larger than that.

She also had to change the location of Other Residence, that is, Home Base, from its perfectly acceptable location in the woods near a small town up in Northern California to the suburban winemaking valley of Livermore.

Livermore. What kind of name is that for a town? It sounds like a regenerating organ.

Now, everyone acknowledged that it made sense to locate discreetly near human habitation in order to quietly tap into some of the human magical reserves, or in their words, *electricity*. That way, less magic would be used in basic residence operations. After all, it doesn't bode well for others to cause a magical rent in the big net of life by using tons of magic when they are always punishing Fairfolk for doing that very thing.

But Livermore? *What is with that name anyway? Only humans would be silly enough to confuse a town with a body part! As if one liver wasn't enough. They want liver more! Humans. Ridiculous!*

But this place was what she had chosen, specifically to lure her errant father, a renegade who should be put down immediately rather than be rewarded by coming home to the place of Others.

She relocated there because it was close to her home site, which was now being occupied by humans who actually knew of our existence. (Blasphemy in itself, yet somehow, that too was accepted.) It was also chosen because of our ability to blend into the surroundings. Our place looks just like so many others out here on the edge of the human town—largish storage building blending into the landscape like so many other barns and, in the case of Livermore, wineries.

The question is: why couldn't we just stay where we were before? There was nothing wrong with it. It had an adequate access to the electrical magic that humans cleverly devised.

This was just one more of the many things that rankled this Other about the new Supreme Elder Other.

But there were so many more complaints.

Like the new punishments. *Punishments!* he thought. *We are above such things, being that we* are *the ultimate authority.* He sniffed in disgust as she apparently consulted her cell phone yet again in the midst of his meeting. As she pressed buttons, making texts, as it were, he pondered the new regulations involving punishments.

The ultimate humiliation for disobeying this particular Supreme Elder Other was the issuing of red, yellow, and green cards—and not in that order. If she so chose, she could make an example of you by issuing a yellow card, a warning not to continue in the offending behavior, or the dreaded red card, ultimate punishment for repeated bad behavior.

The yellow card was, of course, a misnomer. It was her term for punishment bestowed. At first, quite a few operatives were running around in yellow card status—that is, she turned our nice white togas into a bilious yellow. No matter how many replacement togas you had, all of them were permanently yellowed.

God help you if you incurred her wrath to the extent of receiving a red card. Then, not only was your toga red, but your entire epidermis became scarlet-hued. Many an operative in the red- or yellow-card status had a lot of explaining to do to Fairfolk who encountered him or her in that form. The entire intimidation factor was lost as the perplexed Fairfolk began peppering the disgustingly-hued Others with questions like "Fly too close to the sun?" and "Fall into a vat of pee?" etc.

Reform and repentance was seen in the form of a green card. It meant you were following the plan and were on the mend for past errant behavior. It was just as bad as a red or yellow card. The only good thing about the green-card status was that eventually the color faded from your skin as well as your clothing. Eventually.

All things considered, working for her is an utter nightmare, he thought.

After the lengthy review of his mental list of complaints, he began to realize that she was done consulting her phone and was waiting for a response. From him. *Oh dear, what was the question?* He worried. Perhaps it was written in his cell phone. He fumbled with the device, looking for help of any kind.

She had finally lost all patience.

She flew up into this face, hovering mere inches from his nose. He had, like many operative Others, adopted a human form. He knew that in the world of Fairfolk, the human form was the least intimidating and therefore the least stressful when an Other, like himself paid a call to errant Fairfolk, to intimidate or exact punishment.

However, in this case, he wished he could, for just a moment, revert to his original gargoyle form. At least he wouldn't feel so frail and weak in front of this most imperious creature.

He sighed. In the end, he thought it wouldn't matter if he were the size of a full-grown dragon. She was the most powerful creature in the entire Fairfolk realm, diminutive size or no. The air around her fairly prickled with latent magic.

"Hello…Other! You have not read my daily texts, correct?"

Aha. That was the question. "Oh yes. Wait, I mean no, that is I *do* read them, but you see, this cell-box-phone thing doesn't fit anywhere on my clothing and so I don't always carry it—" He demonstrated by trying to tuck it into the belt around his waist. It fell through to the ground. He picked it up, smiling weakly, hoping she got the point. She did not appear to be amused. He began to sweat.

Good, she thought. *He is nervous. Maybe he will treat his Fairfolk a bit more kindly knowing what they must go through when he visits, carrying such notions as total annihilation.* She tried a different tack.

Hovering in front of him, she slowly rotated, letting him get a good look at her gown; it was her newest creation. An iridescent golden sheath made from fish scales, topped by a crown of baby's breath in her glowing auburn hair. She thought it was a good look for a chief honcho. Gold is such a power color.

"Do you know what I am?" she asked sweetly, fluffing her hair for emphasis. At this moment, she looked demure, like a stunning young fairy girl. Or a flying Barbie doll.

Uh-oh. This is a trick question. There are no right answers, he thought. Bravely, he ventured a satisfactory reply. "Why you are the Elder Other. The supreme power in the fairy realm. You control the fate of all Fairfolk, large and small. You are—"

"A fairy." She interrupted.

"Yes. Quite. A fairy queen and also The Supreme Elder Other." He hoped he had answered correctly.

Perhaps not. He watched her slow and freeze midair. It was a very difficult thing to do, requiring her magic to hold her entire body weight aloft and upright. I mean, have you ever tried to lift your entire body weight while continuing a conversation? Her wings paused, stopping their gentle movements. Pure magic held her aloft, yet her demeanor remained calm, serenely sweet.

Suddenly, she lost her young, innocent air as her gaze turned pure steel.

"Operative Other, do you know *why* I retain my fairy body rather than adopting a rather generic human one as so many Others do?"

"Well, it, uh, of course, becomes you. But. I think, well, perhaps, it is your prerogative to choose any shape you wish." He was hopeful his slightly wheedling tone would appeal.

It did not. She replied in short, angry bursts, piercing him on the spot with her flashing, angry eyes. She looked at him with utter disdain and frosty condemnation.

"I was once a fairy. Then, a human. Then a fairy again. I have come to love my fairy form. Even this—" She pointed to her bluish skin and a scar on her face.

"...a reminder of all I have been through due to a chain of interference by incompetent Others."

He winced yet again, knowing the insult was intended for him.

"I am The Supreme Elder Other and the Supreme Fairy. A Fairy with a capital **F**. Do you know what that means?"

"I, uh, er—"

"It means don't *F*- with me. Ever."

"Oh yes. Of course. I fully intend to read my daily texts. So I guess that means we will defer neutralizing the area that I monitor."

"It was in the text."

"Sorry."

"And next time you want to talk annihilation, make an appointment."

Beauty Must Suffer

She held her imperious stance as the cowering operative backed out of the room. Once the door was completely shut, the Supreme Elder Other Marissa plopped down in a most unladylike fashion on top of the desk and asked in a tiny voice to the empty space, "How did I do?" In that moment she sounded more like a young girl and far less like the Supreme Elder Other.

In the far corner of the sterile, white office stood a scrying pool. It was the only interesting object in the spare and antiseptic room. A necessary holdover from the previous Elder Other, who preferred surrounding himself with arcane and rather dusty objects of Olde Magik. His taste ran to carved gnarled wooden desks, crystal balls, and even a messy, noisily intimidating raven perched on the chair back. Considering the unsanitary nature of a nasty familiar like a raven, she quickly dispensed with the clutter, the bird and the mess when she moved into the office, preferring basic white and modern décor so as to show off her latest fashions of the day.

The scrying pool, a.k.a. birdbath, had to stay. It was one way she was able to communicate with her mother, who was in the building nearby feverishly searching for her father via her own scrying pool. It was simply easier to use the medium her mother was using to, in effect, quickly see what her mother was seeing in the continued search.

A tiny dust mote, bobbing in the air near the water, zigzagged across the office, growing in size as it approached the superior's desk. What once was a lazy speck of dust hovering gently across the room, slowly expanded taking on a neon-green color and quickly dwarfing the dimensions of the plain bare office. Finally, a full-sized green gargoyle rested on the corner of her broad desk. His wings draped over the side and wafted gently, happy to be their full shape again.

"Awesome. You scared the shit out of him." The big green gargoyle smirked.

"Yeah, I feel kinda bad about that...Not really." She chuckled, absently scratching where the fish scale dress gently chafed. "I mean, this way, he will tell everybody that I mean business about stopping this random and unnecessary neutralizing. Maybe it will buy us some time while we look for Dad. I mean, I can't have them going around zapping areas he might be hiding in."

"Mari, we have been through this before. I agree," the gargoyle replied and with one large talon, gently moved her hand away, putting an end to the incessant scratching. Lately, he had been worried about her, noticing how she had adopted annoying new quirks—absent-minded scratching, cuticle picking, or even tugging on her perfectly coiffed hair—a byproduct of the stress of the job. He worried about his adopted sister. Yet he knew how she hated pity. He treaded softly.

Smiling, he continued, "Intimidating operative Others into submission is our only way at this point to find Dad now that he has gone renegade, before the hunting parties do. Otherwise, you know what they do when they catch renegade Others…"

"It makes me sick to think about it," she said scratching resumed. "I am just glad I have my shape-shifter gargoyle brother Enjie to lend a hand along with some extra magic. You made me look massively badass!"

Warmly, she smiled at her faux brother. He smiled back, although the effect of a smiling gargoyle is about as warm as meeting a smiling shark— all pointy teeth. He thought, *Man, when she smiles, she could charm the birds from the trees!*

She thought, *Man, he could use a toothbrush!*

"You go, girl. And by the way, I told you—quit calling me Enjie. My name is En——"

They both looked down at the laptop as it pinged, alerting them to a new visitor.

"Who is it, Seen?" she asked, speaking into the microphone on the monitor.

"Your brother, Supreme Elder Other," Seen replied through the laptop.

"Seen. Are you the only one out there besides my brother?"

"Yes, Elder Oth——"

"Seen. Shut up with the 'Supreme Elder Other' crap, OK? It's just us kids now."

"Yes, Elder-Queen-er, Mari. Ma'am," he added. Lamely.

"Just send in Jay." Mari sighed. Seen was the most literal person she had ever met. And he had absolutely no sense of humor. *Doesn't get a joke to save his life.* But he had utmost respect for authority—even if it was pretend authority like Mari's. But somehow, he was loveable. And loyal. All in all, he wasn't so bad. Just a little nerdy.

She watched her cool, iridescent-blue gargoyle brother stroll in, gently compressing his wings as they scrunched through the door. The office door was extra wide to accommodate the size of Fairfolk creatures, but even this door was a bit of a squeeze for her massive brother.

"Hey," his sister said.

"Hey. Nice get-up." Jay walked in. He strolled in, all eight feet tall, happy to greet his one foot and a half inch tall sister. Despite their obvious differences one could tell by their common jargon and tone that they were somehow related.

Today, he was full-on gargoyle. Must be he knew that his adopted brother Enj was going to need to feed after this stint in Mari's office. Shape-shifting and lending Mari some of his magic was a very draining exercise even for a master magician like Enj.

Probably going with his gargoyle brother to lend support until he replenishes his energy, Mari thought. Jay was like that. Always trying to make people feel well, even if it meant accompanying his bro on a gross gargoyle feed.

Jay saw that his sister was in full commander-of-the-troops mode. *I wonder if she knows how tough she really is? She doesn't really need Enj's help to be strong,* he pondered, proud of his kick-ass sister.

He flicked his talon at his sister's greenish, leathery wings. They snapped back in greeting. Everyone knows you have to befriend the person *and* the wings. Mari's tiny gargoyle wings liked Jay. He wrinkled his nose pretending to take a whiff in the direction of his little sis.

"How come you smell like sushi? Forget to brush again?" Jay mocked his sister. After all, someone had to take her down a notch every now and then.

"Thank you, Jay. And no, I do not smell. I had these fish scales deliberately dried and perfumed before they were made into this fabulous gown."

"Must be your breath then."

"Get out of my office and be useful." She sent a warning zap of magic toward his head. Jay ducked as his wings waved off the tiny assault, not the least bit offended at the fairy's rebuke. She blew on her finger, holstering her imaginary magical gun.

Jacob changed the subject. "What's Mom doing?"

Marissa shrugged. "What is she always doing? Scrying, drawing, and matching the images to maps. She is determined to find Dad before the search party finds him."

"Anything?"

"You know, she keeps seeing rocks. Boulders, serpentine rocks, so she thinks he still is in California. Granite too. These odd rock formations all clumped together."

"Weird. Serpentine and granite together?"

"Yep. Mixed together, on the same boulder, even."

"What's up with that? I mean, I guess I don't know much about geology, but that sounds plain weird," Mari asked.

The brother and sister moved toward the scrying pool to take a better look at what their mom was seeing.

"Oooh. Yeah. You know what that means?" Enj interrupted the two. Previously, he had been picking at his talons while lounging on the desk. His grooming suddenly stopped at this curious and telling news. They looked at him, uncomprehending.

"What?" they both asked.

"Well, I am not entirely sure, but the granite could be the person and the serpentine the outfit."

Accustomed as they had become to the strange and unusual in the Fairy Realm, this proved incomprehensible to Marissa. "Who wears a serpentine rock dress?" she asked, thinking that a) it would be ugly, b) too heavy, and c) perpetually wrinkled, so euww.

Instead of answering the question, Enj told his family, "Let's call Seen in. He's the best tracker we have. Maybe it's time we send him upriver."

Safety in Numbers

The previous Supreme Elder Other spent a lot of time lately contemplating the demands of his old job, that is, the one Marissa currently occupied. As it was his favorite topic, he mulled over his strategy in retiring. Specifically, he recalled the series of events leading to his naming the fierce little fairy queen Marissa as new Supreme Elder Other.

To say there is only one Supreme Elder Other was to stretch the truth. Oh, as far as anyone else was concerned, there really was only one, until he or she retired and then another took his or her place for the duration, or until he or she (literally) burned out. Using too much magic can do that to you.

Elder Othering required tremendous amounts of magic and allowed for very little downtime. The job of the Elder Other was to assess the information given him or her by the operatives, or Others out in the field, and, if there was a dangerous amount of magic used in any particular region; then give the final OK for, well, total devastation of a race or even total geographic elimination.

Neutralization was required if there was an area of dangerous energy buildup. Usually, it meant an area where way too much magic was being spent.

The entire magical network was threatened until that area was mended and magic was dispersed. It was either neutralize and excise the area or risk the entire magical net collapsing. It was an ugly job, but someone had to do it.

Once an area is neutralized or even annihilated, it's the Elder Other's job to make sure the event takes on a natural tone, appearing to humans as though some catastrophic natural event had caused the devastation. This can be in the guise of, say, a hurricane, tornado, earthquake, or even a flood, although there are really infinite combinations of the above available in order to convince humans that it is not an unnatural event. To that end, the concept of "global warming" was introduced. The Elder Other was particularly proud of his "global warming" invention, which had taken on a life of its own, once humans began to actually believe in it. It became great cover for any number of neutralizations that occurred in order to fix breaks in the magical network.

This process of balancing magic and covering for neutralization events, however, takes great skill, imagination, and creative use of magic to keep the two worlds from knowing each other, even as they coexist. It is a draining job, causing a high degree of job stress for Elder Others. Quite literally, burnout can and has happened to other Elder Others. A perilous job, that of Supreme Elder Other.

On the *other*—ha ha—hand, there are certain perks to the job. For instance, a Supreme Elder Other is allowed to manipulate time just a tad, ostensibly to more effectively observe the magical realm. Actually, this Elder Other drifted in and out of the year just to ensure he had a steady supply of goodies only available seasonally. Let's just say, wouldn't you love to *always* have a steady supply of Quarterback Crunch ice cream (fall flavor only at Baskin Robbins) or Girl Scout cookies? To say nothing of McRibs from McDonald's and pumpkin spice lattes from Starbucks.

That's what I am talking about, he said to himself, savoring the heady aroma of cinnamon spice, before taking a long and satisfying sip of the delectable coffee.

Burnout is the real problem. It is an exhausting job, as much personal magic is used when mending the small tears in the magical net that holds this earth together. That's a constant job with almost no letup.

And then there is the issue of the large amount of magic needed for the infrequent but necessary neutralizations. That damn nearly kills a Supreme Elder Other every time. It can take weeks to recover after an event. And yet, the next day, there is always someone else reporting in asking for magical repair work.

Hence *the Ingenious Solution.*

The Ingenious Solution

Well, actually, Ingenious Solution Number One. This was to get his two closest cronies, magic them to look exactly like himself and rotate the Supreme Elder Other job among the three men. That way, two would be off relaxing while one was working his ass off. Just when it seemed too much to bear, shift over, next guy punched in. No one was the wiser.

The field guys, the operatives, never noticed slight differences in speech and behavior from one faux Elder other to another. They usually were so intimidated by the rank and the office that it was all they could do to report in and flee the room as soon as possible.

The office itself was designed to distract. Between being chockfull of gadgets and gizmos of Olde Magik and the squawking, pooping raven, visitors did not notice much detail about the Elder Other aside from the basics: long white beard, requisite spectacles, long gown embroidered with ancient runes, and a few missing teeth for added interest.

There were a few wise guys who gave the Elder Other the occasional stink-eye or at least the suspicious squint. Bob, for one. That guy was a wily one. *Too bad he despises authority, else he would make a great*

successor, the Elder(s) mused. Crafty, slick, smart but with a decent heart, he flatly turned down the job as Supreme Elder in training. Instead, the Elder Other put him on recruitment. Boy, had he brought them some great candidates unconventional to be sure, but times were changing.

Time to be flexible.

Which sort of brings us to *Ingenious Solution Number Two.*

Bob, in his job of recruiter, brought in this little motley group that called itself The Family, as potential Other recruits. He brought them mostly because they didn't fit in anywhere else. But eventually, the Elders came to realize that each had remarkable talents.

First of all, the mother was an elf and was quite talented at scrying. It had a lot to do with her visual and artistic skills. She could pretty much pinpoint an operative almost anywhere in the realm. Just give her a clear pool, parchment, writing implements, and something called an aerial map, and she was all set. She also had powerful magic which she used rarely as her sense of control was a bit shaky. Last time she used her magic in an uncontrolled environment she nearly blew up a forest. She was deemed to have latent talent worth exploring.

The son was comfortable in both human and gargoyle skin. He traded off regularly as it suited him. Now, he didn't just adopt some pale, bland, androgynous humanoid look that was so popular among many operatives. No, his human form was real, distinct, and could pass for any human person walking down the street on a sunny day.

His gargoyle form was this deep, mysterious, and very stylish blue. And he had, what humans called "big guns." So he was a somewhat studly young gargoyle on the verge of massiveness in adulthood.

And yet, his strength was in the healing arts. He wanted to derive a new way to mend the tears in our magical net, to balance the use and misuse of magic by redirecting rather than excising. And he wanted to come back to an area after neutralization to help heal the broken. Very interesting concept. Jacob was a great thinker with deep and unconventional approaches. This was sorely needed in the Other world.

Also, he thought some of the operatives had mental health issues. The Supreme Elder Other was convinced that he was right.

The remaining "brother," perhaps the greatest find of the family, was no blood relation at all. He was a young gargoyle, a common green with decidedly uncommon abilities. He became attached to this family when one of the operative Other's previous *ingenious plans* went terribly awry.

At any rate, he identified with this family and went where they did.

This green Gargoyle was an interesting chap, smart and a bit of a rule breaker, but the Elder Other chose to chock that up to youthful exuberance. What was so amazing about this one was his tremendous magical capacity. His shape-shifting abilities were simply stunning. Imagine condensing every molecule that comprises your large, badass self into the space of say, a marble. He could do that with ease. And not leave a big shadow behind. His potential was enormous, and the Supreme Elder Other(s) chose to have him close by for further observation. If this unconventional family had to come along with him, then so be it. They all could join recruitment. After all, you never knew what abilities one had until he or she was tested. And in recruitment camp, they certainly were tested.

Speaking of testing, the last two in the family had tested the constraints of recruitment, as well as the Elder Other's patience.

The girl was the aforementioned fairy with odd gargoyle wings. She was, despite her size, ferociously stubborn but with great magical talent. One of her biggest skills was her glamour.

No, not *glamour*, as in glamorous, although she would love you to think of her as such. No, her sense of glamour hearkened back to ancient Celtic days, or as the Others call it, the Golden Age.

Back in the Golden Age, the Celtic priestesses recognized glamour as a magical talent. It was the ability to manipulate through personality and guile, with just a touch of magic. It was the action of taking one completely opposed to your cause and coercing him or her, through charm or otherwise, into surrendering utterly to your will. Mari, the fairy girl, had it in spades. And she didn't even have to "egg" to get her way (old fairy joke).

She also possessed a boatload of magic, which she used with great style.

But then there was the thorny matter of the father, Ben. Fully human. Intractable, suspicious, and completely immune to the subtle manipulations of anyone in the magical realm save his own family. He came along into recruitment as a measure of protection for his family. As such, he refused to take on his original form, that of a gargoyle; instead, he stubbornly hung on to his human body—flaws and all.

He was a concern to the Elder other(s) from the get-go. His constant taciturn wariness belied his unwillingness to acculturate. And before he turned renegade, the Elder Other(s) noted his growing bitterness as the rest of his family became adjusted and bonded with the Other world, while he most assuredly did not.

An Other tutor was present at Ben's big moment of defection. Apparently, he had had enough of the small trials and tests the Other recruiters were putting the family through. He became irate when several members of his family were *slightly* injured. He himself had been bitten by a poisonous snake but was unfazed by that. No, it was when his family placidly accepted the danger they had been subjected to that he had, what the Other tutor described as a *psychotic break*. Using his full magical abilities, he cured his own snakebite poisoning and simply vanished, after staging quite a tantrum.

Going renegade incurs the *ultimate punishment*. It meant that a recruit knew the full extent of the magical powers available to him or her and then chose to be completely alone, acting without counsel or supervision. Anything could happen with a renegade. Potentially disastrous for the entire magical realm.

Renegades were typically hunted and then brought before the Supreme Elder Other for the ultimate punishment...

In this case, however, the remaining family members begged the Supreme Elder Other (well, actually all three Supreme Elder others, since they nagged each one incessantly in succession) for clemency, promising that the renegade Ben couldn't possibly do any harm. Thus, the Supreme Elder Other(s) decreed that while hunting parties would be dispatched to look for the human Ben, they would defer capture and punishment pending further investigation.

"Pending further investigation" is the Elder buzz phrase for they didn't have a clue what to do. After all, Ben didn't seem particularly harmful, just pissed off. To excise him would have devastating effects on the rest of the family. And each had such delectable magical gifts that it would be criminal to waste them.

After much deliberation, the Supreme Elder Other (well actually, all three Elder Others) concluded that he (they) had one heck of a dilemma on his (their) hands.

Plus, they were just flat-out tired. Despite the rotating nature of the job, all three of them were beat, especially after being hammered constantly by that Family to save their renegade Ben.

And so, after endless discussion as to the fate of the renegade and the potential devastation to the family, the Supreme Elder Other(s) determined precisely what "pending further investigation" really meant.

It meant they were going on spring break. To Las Vegas. And from that, they derived *Ingenious Solution Number Two.*

Ingenious Solution Number Two

This required devising a way to have a substitute Supreme Elder Other while the real three stooges were AWOL. The trio had a lengthy consultation on this issue over McRib sandwiches, washed down with pumpkin ale, followed by a hefty serving of Thin Mint cookies.

They had to pick someone who was a natural leader without actually wanting the job for his or her own personal gain. There were plenty of operatives waiting, hoping, and yes, conniving for the opportunity to be named Supreme Elder Other in-training, or SOEIT (pronounced SoBeIt). They were quickly crossed off the list. Too thirsty for power and a bit too eager to neutralize.

Actually, Bob would have been great— specifically because he didn't want the job. But he said he already liked his "gig" and declined. Again. Finally, all that was left of the talent pool were the members of that motley crew called The Family.

Enj, the gargoyle, had perfect mastery of the magic and seemed an ideal choice. But after much discussion and more Girl Scout cookies, it was decided that he functioned best as "wingman"' to another. But whom?

His brother Jay possessed a brilliant mind and adequate mastery of magic. And he was terribly reluctant to destroy. In fact, he wanted to fix more than excise. His fatal flaw was he hated detail. He assumed everyone a) knew his or her job and b) would actually do his or her best to execute that job. With Fairfolk nature being as it was, that was simply not the case. The Elders worried that although he would have the best intentions at heart, he simply wouldn't mind the store while they were gone.

The mother was, as they say, out to lunch. She was obsessed with finding her husband and simply could not function well without him. It was as though only a part of her was there. The other part was with her most troublesome renegade spouse. No amount of fresh lavender (which she was especially fond of) or potions or elvish herbs could rouse her from this perpetual fog that the absence of her mate caused. Very annoying, as she was extremely talented in her own right. They had witnessed her use of magic nearly destroy an entire forest, when she was only going to light things up a bit. Great raw talent. If only she would focus. Which she seemed unable to do so, since her husband had left the scene.

Clearly, the fairy girl, Marissa, had to be interim Supreme Elder Other until they returned. She had the most organizational skills of any recruit ever seen. She even suggested conduct charts with green, yellow, and red cards to be given to field Others for behavior. Most amusing.

And she had previous skills. She once was a tre-mendously successful fairy queen, saving her clan from destruction and then coming back later to beat them into submission, er, *suggest* ways for them to behave better.

She magnificently annoyed, cajoled, and even harassed the Elder Others like *no other* in the matter of her renegade father. It was impressive as to how such a small package could send even the Supreme Elder Other scurrying down the hall at the mere sight of her. It was only when until the little fairy came laden with gifts for the Elder's colon health (as bathroom breaks were their favorite excuse to be rid of her) that the Elder Other(s) knew how to address the problem of the Family while pondering the pending further investigation.

They decided that she of all people would be the perfect pick to run the shop while they were gone for all of the above reasons. She would spiff up and organize the place, as it were. But they also knew that she and the Family would not allow any neutralizations to take place until they were sure where the father was and if he was safe.

She did ask them upon agreeing to take on the job, if she could make a few *small* changes to the operation. Since she was literally the queen of the organization, they agreed. A little cleaning up would do the place some good. Besides, they were tiring of mopping bird poop off the backs of their capes. After all, the bird wasn't really a familiar, just an annoying prop designed to distract.

Astonishingly, her first act of reorganization was to relocate the operation to a busy town in the middle of one of Northern California's wine regions. While they applauded her very good taste in wines, they really thought a more remote location would do much better. Hence they had found no fault with the previous choice of a sleepy ranching community at the Northern California border.

The needs of a Home Base (as she called it) are rather simple—privacy, access to electricity, and a place in which a few large, boxy buildings would blend easily into the landscape. This is why they usually chose a place on a remote farm road and arranged the buildings to look like barns or storage facilities.

She explained that the location was intended to draw her father in. After all, he was a winophile and perhaps he might wander over to this area in search of a really good Meritage. And the barn-like structures certainly fit in with the rural nature of the place. There was adequate electrical availability. All in all, they couldn't really find any fault with the idea. She felt they should know so that when they were through pondering their "pending further investigation," they would know where Home Base was. Plus, they could get some really good wine cheap. Clever girl.

Certainly then, nothing could go wrong by putting this ad hoc family in charge while they took a brief sojourn to recharge their batteries in this charming land called Las Vegas. Right?

Rockstars and Other Misnomers

Ben thought a lot about what it meant to be human. Lately, he had amended his thoughts to what it meant to be a magical human. All in all, he liked being human. He felt very comfortable in his middle-aged dad-skin. And he had no desire to go back to his original gargoyle roots.

Or at least that was what they told him, that he once was a gargoyle and gave himself up for sacrifice to save his gargoyle clan; that he once could fly, and that he ate lots of raw meat on the hoof.

Bullshit, he said to himself. *I only like my red meat medium rare. It's my wife that likes her beef mooing.* Oh, but at the thought of his wife, his musings turned very dark. A big, gaping echo-ey hole opened up in his heart every time at the very idea of her.

And then he would get ticked-off. Big-time. Because as much as he loved her—human or elf or whatever—he was pissed that she had chosen the world of the incessantly creepy Others over him. To say nothing of the jeopardy their children were in. It was like the three of them, well, four if you counted the stalker gargoyle Enj, just drank the Kool-Aid and joined the ranks in lockstep. Since he couldn't protect them he had no choice but to take a stand against them all and leave.

Fact was, he couldn't stand by and watch as his family put themselves in peril for the sake of these Others—these magical gamers who played with the lives of humans and Fairfolk alike.

And by the way, he thought, *screw them all to the wall if they think humans are lesser beings.* After all, without magic being handed to them, humans had created societies and technology and an app for almost anything, even Angry Birds.

So yeah, he was totally justified for leaving them all behind.

But was this forever or just for now?

This was the point in his deliberations when his thinking wandered back to his wife and children, even Enj, and how much he loved them. Then, they went right back to how pissed off he was at all of them for staying with the Others and not leaving when he did. Then, he would return to how much he liked being human. Well, human with magical abilities. But are you truly human if you could do magic?

Hence, the internal dialogue about the human-ness of being human. It started as a distraction from the spiraling dark thoughts about his family and then morphed into a possible solution for quieting these thoughts.

Which brought him to the inescapable conclusion as to why humans were such a noisy bunch, surrounding themselves with cell phones and computers and TVs and music and traffic—you name it—the more noise, the better as far as humans were concerned. Why? You ask.

Because then they don't have to think these angry, circular thoughts. It's the quiet that brings these random and deep notions to the surface, rising up from the silent depths like some dark leviathan, threatening to drag one down into the abyss of deep depression. Quiet was his true enemy.

Which was why it was a pretty dumb idea to hang around with trolls.

He literally stumbled upon them on his angry walk several weeks after telling his family off and quitting Other school. Up until then, he had been roaming around like some hobo, avoiding human habitats and preferring the deep, rugged coastal range. He made impromptu campsites for himself, warming himself with a good, old-fashioned campfire night after night and scaring off the local predators by magiking a barrier to keep them out as he slept.

Food was no problem, as he generally hunted a bit of rabbit, zapping it with a tiny magical "bullet," thereby causing little concern for attracting undue attention. And McDonald's was virtually everywhere. When he grew tired of nuts, berries, rabbit, and the occasional stray chicken, he would venture into the nearest fast-food restaurant present a "Special Free Gratis Coupon"- entirely made up by hand on scratch paper, but magiked to feel authentic to the worker—and ordered at will.

It was on one such day east of the Coastal Range and into the Sierras when Ben, loaded down with bags of Happy Meals, ran into one. Literally.

Easy to do really as they don't move much.

Ben was happily guzzling down a second liter of Coke, when he heard the call of nature—that is, he had to pee.

Juggling two Happy Meal bags in one hand and the Coke bottle in the other, he realized in order to complete the act of bladder voiding, he would have to free up his hands. The large granite boulder nearby looked like a handy table.

However, the top was rather rounded and neither the Coke bottle nor the bags wanted to stay upright. So he plopped them unceremoniously there, after using a teensy bit of magic to flatten out the bumpy top. Several large chunks of the greasy green rock peeled off, revealing sparkling granite beneath.

Ben shrugged at the odd agglomeration of strata and commenced the process of urinating while being vertical. As his back was to the rock, he failed to notice a little eye open near the base. He did, however, hear a very audible grunt and then a "Damn it."

This naturally entirely disrupted his previous activity. And, despite being startled and not a little bit frightened, he paused long enough to tuck away and zip up properly to greet whoever was damn it-ing.

As he turned toward the sound, the first thing he noticed was that his lunch/dinner was strewn on the rocky ground and spilled Coke was seeping down into the sandy dirt. The second was the big boulder was gone. Third, right beside where the big boulder once was, stood a large, shambling, very dirty block of a man, stretching and shaking out his legs.

His head was very square, and he hadn't much of a neck. *Kinda like when the kids were little and Jay would pull off the heads of Marissa's Barbie's. I tried to jam them back on*, he thought. *Barbie never looked the same after a beheading*—no neck.

His shoulders were very straight and broad. The rest of his body was large and lumpy. His big, bulbous toes looked like fat river rock, and his face had an unfinished appearance, as though a sculptor went on a permanent break after roughing out the basic eye, ear, nose, and mouth locations. Slashes and gouges comprised its general features.

He had hair, which was visible when the big guy ran his thick fingers through it, dislodging bits of dirt and the hapless weed that had attempted to root in it. Ben stepped back to avoid the shower of debris that rained down through his fingers. He thought to himself, *Rocks. The guy is wearing a suit made of rocks. This guy might possibly be a rock.*

The back of the suit was missing, revealing the gnarly gray skin of his back. The sleeves were barely hanging on to his arms. As he was feeling the tattered remnant of his missing suit and scowling, Ben reasoned this was the source of his "damn it."

"Uh-oh," he said to the big guy. "It appears I blew up a part of your suit."

"Yes, you did."

"That sucks. I am so sorry. I thought you were just a big rock."

The big talking rock man was astounded. This stupid magical human actually thought his suit had a mouthpart that *sucked!* This thought left him completely speechless. He sat back down, hoping to settle into a nice, pleasing rock shape again and meditate on the amazing juxtaposition of the words *sucks* and *suit.*

"Hey," Ben said to the new boulder shape that the dirt man had just become. "Come back. I'll magic you a new outfit, OK?"

The new boulder was silent. Sullen. The quiet around him felt annoyed, like it was waiting for him to leave.

In fact, oppressive and disapproving silence was all around him, not just from this big pouting rock but emanating from other largish boulders situated around as well.

Ben then took a long look at his surroundings. Sure, he was up in the high Sierra Mountains, where granite boulders abounded. But here, the granite boulders were all about the same size and looked as though they had been placed in a large circle, which if you looked closely, had a cold and old fire pit in the center. It was like a fairy circle on steroids. Or Stonehenge, without the nice tall monoliths. Just large and lumpy granite and serpentine boulders arranged eerily in a circle. Giant and certainly deliberately placed. But who would or could place thousand-pound boulders in such a way? No human could; that was for sure.

Ben felt quite certain that in the days of old, any local Indian tribe would quite wisely have avoided the place. Ben—big, stupid magic human—walked right into it, peed among them, and busted up a perfectly nice stone jacket. To say nothing of the sticky Coke dribbling at the feet of a few more.

No wonder the very air felt disapproving.

"So," he said settling against one of the rocks and then, realizing his gaffe, getting up again. "There's a bunch of you. It's a confab of some sort, and I busted right into it. My deepest apologies." He bowed low to the original dirt man rock.

"I'll just clean up my mess and be going. Awfully nice speaking with you." More silence. Crickets chirping.

At this point, Ben had become a tad annoyed. After all, these were the first magical beings he had been able to talk to in a very long time. It reminded him of how lonely he really was, and he did quite nicely apologize for the Coke and peeing incident.

To be fair, they didn't smite him or bite him or threaten to magic him into oblivion. So that was a good sign. Perhaps they could be friends. And he sure could use the noise. Dark, depressing leviathans had been threatening his disposition all day. He needed something to tamp them back down to the depths where they belonged. And yet, they refused to talk to him.

This made him peevish. He waited long enough, staring at stupid, unyielding rocks, until he felt very foolish. *Time to go,* he thought.

Rudely, he said, "See ya—wouldn't want to be ya!" He picked up the trash, stuffed it in his pack, and wandered off, continuing eastward toward Lake Tahoe.

Marvelous. They all sighed with exquisite pleasure. Their collective meditative minds instantly changed focus from "sucking suits" to the deep and luxurious question of why a bumbling, fragile, magical human wouldn't *want* to actually *be* a glorious and impervious troll. They were aware of his departure but only vaguely. Their new mantra was "*See ya/not be ya.*" The theoretical concept of humanness and trollness with a dollop of magic thrown in was too irresistible to turn their minds from.

This could take days to work out. They would remain in this state as long as they could, or until one of them felt hungry or experienced some other bodily urge, which required tending. Then they would revert to their lovely, if somewhat blocky, humanoid forms to hunt, eat, sleep, possibly rip a few musically inventive farts, and then settle back into a meditative state once a new group topic was introduced.

Fabulous life, really. Oh, they toiled now and then. They were known to be great metal smiths, retreating to the secret depths of the mountains where their forges were. They used the cover of thunderstorms in the mountains to mask the din of metallurgy. But that kind of work was only done for trade. They had no need for such things themselves since mental pursuits were their highest need. They traded with metal only when they ran completely dry of the mental.

They traded their goods for songs, news, and tales of new excitement abounding in the fairy realm.

And boy had they been treated to some really good stuff lately. On a recent trade, they were informed of a strange and fragmented story of a human—imagine, human!—family that had turned the entire fairy realm upside down with the notion of their equality and worth.

They also learned that a new Supreme Elder Other was installed. That it was an extremely fierce and gifted fairy queen, who was, in their opinion, far too smart for the job. After much meditation on that matter, they concluded that they were in no peril. After all, they used very little magic and kept entirely to themselves, save for trade. They concluded that they were safe but that the rest of the fairy realm had best mind their P's and Q's. ("P's and Q's," being derivative of the phrase "pints and quarts" from the British fairy realm.)

That particular phrase was the subject of a vast group meditation wherein British fairy culture was explored, including the satellite subject of "odd idioms." The troll clan concluded much from that particular mind-think, like, for example, the ancient

Celts actually still have a great influence in fairy society and that the Brits drink a lot, that bunch.

Ah, those were the days.

But now, this bumbling, magical human unceremoniously plopped, or rather peed, in their midst. Although the suit mussing and the bladder voiding were serious slights to be sure, the new concepts he introduced in his short contact with them were wondrous. And he didn't even want any metal for it!

This man bore looking into.

But not now, while they were embarking on a new and fabulous meditative journey. Best to send some young and antsy- (*antsy*, a derivative of "ants in your pants," colorful phraseology and quite true for some trolls) -young troll or two to keep a few sets of eyes on him.

Ed was summarily dispatched to keep track of the man's whereabouts.

Which brings us to the subject of landslides. Ha. A troll's favorite joke was the often-seen roadside sign saying, "Beware of Falling Rock." Falling rock. What a joke! Rocks didn't *fall*. Well, yes of course they did. On occasion. But really, most of the landslides in the Sierras were actually a band of trolls picking up and roaming a bit before they settled in for a long meditative stretch somewhere else.

The only real falling rock had more to do with troll bathroom humor than with actual inert mineral agglomerations tumbling about. This made the cautionary signs even funnier as though they were an indication of where you might find a large pile of troll poo (which looked just like crumbly pebbles. Remember that next time you run your hands through loose rock).

Troll humor was your basic teenage bathroom stuff. It was a good foil for the highbrow intellectual banter they were used to. A good fart joke was the perfect break in an endless discussion of, say, the origins of the universe or which came first, the fairy or the egg.

Roaming trolls and falling rock aside, it was determined that young and frisky Ed would not miss the current engaging groupthink. Quite probably, owing to his youth, he would rather nose around after this curious human than hang with the oldies.

Well, Ed was a young one, so were Fred and Ted—Fred being the girl in the group. Trolls weren't terribly fussy about names. After all, their greatest moments came when they were in a group mind-merge. The singular version of themselves was far less interesting. Hence, names were given very little attention. If they rhymed, that was rather interesting, but if they were applied to the wrong gender, it didn't much matter.

If Ed was given a job, you could be sure that Ted and Fred would tag along. The three of them were the local troll youth. They had not yet learned the high art of patience and sustained meditation, so they were the only ones who would not be disappointed in missing out on a long stint at group mind-think.

Besides, they were really pains in the ass—always fidgeting and rearranging themselves. And they could not sustain a long group think without erupting in a flurry of giggles over basic bodily functions— i.e., farting. To say nothing of Ted and Fred and their constant sibling bickering.

So it was really a gift to the group to let Ed, Ted, and Fred be awarded the job of *tailing* (funny rock joke) the magical peeing human. They were actually pretty good at it, quietly moving through the rocky terrain despite their large size. They, being trolls, were adept at simply freezing and blending into the rocky landscape at will.

This, of course, inspires paranoia in the heart of the one being tailed. Imagine the feeling of being followed and yet, when you turn around, not only is no one there, but the terrain looks vastly different. Rocky outcroppings appear behind you when you would swear that you just walked through a flat stretch. Very disconcerting.

Ah, the troll games of the randy youth—scaring and confusing the bejeezus out of weary hikers. Ed, Ted, and Fred had a great time playing tag (another geo-joke) with hikers. This time though, they had to keep track of the peeing man. Without getting too close. Fred (the girl) especially would not like getting her dress peed on. In fact, it would actually piss her off to have her clothing befouled. Don't ever piss off a troll. Ever.

Many a natural hot spring came about through emergency measures pertaining to an angry troll. During a stint with a furious and fuming troll, the troll clan would submerge said irate troll in an icy mountain pool until the ire wore off. The steam was incredible. Although an angry hot troll certainly was helpful to have around on a chilly winter night. Better than a toasty campfire, they are.

But this day was not the day to irritate a troll. And it was also a day not to play tricks on the lone hiker. It was simply a day to discreetly follow, watch, and try to learn what this magical man's true purpose was, besides bladder voiding in their territory.

So, at a respectful distance, the three troll teens quietly followed magical urinating human until he reached a small clearing where he chose to settle in for the evening.

Ben was very aware that he somehow was being watched. There is a unique sensation that overcomes you when there is a magical presence about. It is somewhat more than a simple tingling feeling, although that is one of the signs. No, it really is a feeling that a) you are being watched and b) that someone is secretly having a great big joke at your expense. It makes you feel 1) paranoid and 2) like checking your various buttons and zippers for proper closure. He picked up this ability at Other school. One of the few useful tools he had obtained during that period in his life. He found himself grudgingly grateful for that and the ability to use his magic at will. Besides those two gifts, he had no love for his stint with the creepy Others.

This feeling was making Ben very irritable. It was also driving him crazy to have to wonder which boulder was an actual inert piece of matter versus a poser of the troll kind. At least that was what he supposed them to be.

At any rate, he decided to flush out the pretenders as it were.

Finding a shallow field with an old depression in its center, probably once used as a fire pit, he chose to make camp for the night. He gathered a few smallish granite rocks to ring the fire pit, kicking several largish boulders along the way for good measure. Finally, with great force and no magic whatsoever (a macho, *Don't mess with me* gesture), he rolled a rock near the fire pit, for a nice seat by the soon-to-be toasty fire before the chilly Sierra night fell.

Dropping his backpack by the stone seat and rummaging through it until he found the remains of an old granola bar to momentarily assuage his hunger, he sat and thought, long and hard, about the short conversation he had had with the presumed troll/boulder.

After some chewing and more deliberation, he decided to light his fire for the evening. The sun was just beginning to set, and dark comes fast in the Sierras. In the midst of his campfire preparation, he deduced two things from his encounter; first, the act of blowing up one's clothing and the subsequent peeing appeared to create a big reaction. Second, his brief conversation was a bit one-sided, in that Ben spoke and the troll seemed astounded at his words.

But was it his words or simply his choice of words that astounded the troll? If it was colorful language, involving phrases such as *sucks* and the like, well, by cracky, he could entertain the landscape all night with catchy phrases.

Besides, he was kind of lonely and it might be fun just to try talking out loud for a change—even if there wasn't much of a reply in return. And it might keep the lurking depression monster at bay, at least for one more night.

After a bit of harrumphing and clearing of pipes and such, he began, "So I'm talking to all of you sentient boulders out there...Great crowd tonight. Thanks for coming...So how you all doing?"

The air around him was quiet. Even the crickets stopped their chirping. The feeling was one of expectancy, as though they were waiting for him to go on—whoever *they* were.

"Well, I for one have had a great day. A flippin' fantastic day. For example, I found magical creatures to talk to, share my Coke with, and generally pee all over. It was a bonding moment." At a loss for what to say next, gibberish seemed the natural course. His inner fifteen year old child took over.

"Speaking of pee, do you know how many ways there are to describe the act of urination? Countless, I would imagine. Here are a few that come to mind: *whiz, piss, piddle, pee-pee, tinkle,* and of course *wee.* To say nothing of the odd phrase like: *go to the john, take a squirt, shake the tree, go number one, leak the lizard, bleed the bladder, break the seal, drain the main vein, pee like a racehorse, see a man about a horse, free Willie, hang a u-ie,* or possibly *golden showers,* which, perhaps, may have a slightly different meaning—"

"Ooh, I love 'whiz,' but my favorite is 'leak the lizard.' It has such nonsensical clarity!" a gravelly, slightly feminine voice said from the tree line a few yards away.

"Fred!" another rough voice whispered in the shadows of the growing dark. "We're supposed to be tailing the peeing man, not interacting with him." And then, the voice appealed to a shadow in a different direction from the darkness he had just admonished as though it was speaking to another person. "I told you we shouldn't take her. She never shuts up!"

"But his words are so gloriously colorful," the female voice protested. "I wish I could bundle them up and wear them as a cape. A wonderful verbosity of Technicolor pee-ness swirling around me!"

"Verbosity isn't even a real word, you gravel for brains. And 'pee-ness'? Really?" Ted weighed in, annoyed as ever by his sister Fred.

"It absolutely is. When we get back, we'll settle it with the Wordmaster. And then I am going to kick your—"

Ben decided to intervene. As a father, he had had quite a bit of practice distracting squabbling siblings. And that was exactly what they sounded like to him. "Well, kids, now that you are fighting in front of the company, you might as well come out of the shadows and introduce yourselves." Ben was delighted that his urination diatribe had had the desired flushing out effect after all.

The crunching sound of tumbling rocks and, in the faint evening shadows, the sight of showering sparks as the rocks shifted together and then melded into living flesh was all that Ben could discern. Soon, largish rocks at the periphery of trees rose and stood, becoming three distinct individuals.

They approached the human. Try as he might in the evening light, he couldn't really distinguish between their facial features. The only real difference was that one seemed to be wearing a dress, while the other two seemed to be wearing pants-and-shirt ensembles. The fabric looked more like gravel bits woven together. They even refracted light as they neared the fire. *They really are wearing rocks*, Ben marveled.

"Take a seat," he said. "I've been dying to talk to someone."

"Ooh, do you have new stories for us?" the dress asked.

"Is that what you want?'

"Oh yes!" the troll juveniles cried.

At last fresh stories that only we would have! The youth thought.

Ted asked, just to be sure, "Is it a new one?"

"Brand spanking new!" Ben said.

"Ahhh!" They sighed. 'Brand spanking." *A new phrase to decipher.* Their minds began to chatter amongst themselves.

Brand spanking…Is that a reference to spanking a human child at birth? Ted silently asked the two.

Shuttup your noisy brain, Fred responded to her brother. The only audible noise in this exchange was a slight shifting of rocks as the three fidgeted ever so slightly. Ben just waited until this curious, muted fidgeting subsided.

Sssh, Ed thought to the both of them. *The man is getting ready to speak out loud. Save those thoughts for later,* Ed mutely admonished the brother and sister.

This conversation was happening in front of the man of urination, all without his knowledge. This was think-speak, a method of group communication perfected by the outwardly quiet and taciturn trolls. A chatty bunch really, once you got the hang of thinking on their wavelength.

The man cleared his throat from the granola bits.

"Are you guys ready?" They nodded in unison and began to arrange themselves around the campfire. Ben waited for them to settle and then began, "Oh, I've got a helluva story for you. It starts like this…"It was a dark and stormy night…"

And so Ben, the magical peeing human, regaled the three young trolls all night long with the complete, unabridged and epic saga of the human family who trespassed into the fairy realm subsequently turned it on its head, and even kicked some of its magical ass. By the end of the night, and as the dawn spread its glowing rosy light over the three rapt and crouching trolls now fully entranced by the human father, it was agreed upon that forevermore magical peeing man would have a new name:

"Rockstar".

Shenanigans in Sin City

It's best to keep moving when you unexpectedly appear in a busy human environment. A large crowd is the ideal. Just pop in and keep on walking with the mob. A human might suddenly notice you to his or her right, for example, but reasons that you sped up from behind to match his or her stride. And humans are always so busy looking ahead to their particular destination that they often neglect to see what is right next to them. Besides, it's Vegas and they are usually so distracted by the pretty lights and the endless cacophony of sounds that they hardly notice anything else.

So the three Supreme Elder Others, known to each other as Demetrius, Albert, and Arthur, began their spring break in the heart of the Vegas strip, amid a loud group of drunken revelers. Besides, hanging with humans was the perfect way to eavesdrop and find out where the action was.

Las Vegas was quite accustomed to crazy costumes during Halloween weekend. The gentlemen chose that time of year because of the availability of Buffalo Bill's Pumpkin Ale, as well as the latitude humans gave to eccentric behavior during that particular time.

They were old, the three of them, but they were canny. They knew that their detailed lack of knowledge about the specifics of human customs and dress would cause undue attention at any other time. Not this season though. In the casino, there were normally attired individuals to be sure, but there were also a great number of Cleopatras, witches, pirates, jungle animals, and even a great many called "Elvis." So a few old guys in togas didn't particularly seem out of place.

Togas were the uniform of choice at Elder Residence. Certainly floor-length ones were worn beneath the ornately embroidered capes Elders routinely sported. However, the embroidery on the capes contained actual runes, which if copied correctly ignited real spells. So the three gentlemen prudently left the capes at home in the event some humans chose to copy their outerwear designs and inadvertently blew themselves up.

"Arrgh," Elder Demetrius said as a young lady dressed in a pirate costume stepped on the hem of his toga. She was wearing perilously high heels and had apparently lost most of the bottom half of her skirt. So when she tripped on his hem, she was more inclined to keep the remainder of her skirt covering what it could rather than taking care not to spill her drink.

So the drink spilled, and Elder Demetrius nearly lost his wrap.

Elders Arthur and Albert rushed to help the girl. After all, she was scantily clad and might injure herself on the hard walkway should she fall. Demetrius seemed perfectly capable of repairing his wrap without any help whatsoever. Besides, what fun was that when you could aid some charmingly tipsy wench?

The girl took a look at the two elderly gentlemen dressed in Roman clothing, holding each of her elbows, and giggled drunkenly. "I know...You're Zeus! Ooh—" she said, looking at the holder of one elbow, and then turned to the other. "You're Zeus too. Wait..." she said, thinking drunkenly and slowly. "You're Zeus squared!" She laughed at the two gray-bearded men, their long, white, wispy hair floating softly at their shoulders. Their togas were draped elegantly from their thin, bony shoulders and dragged a bit on the ground.

"Yes, yes, come along now, gentlemen," Demetrius said catching up with them after his brief pause to straighten his own clothing. "The young lady, I am sure, has people to aid her in her quest to, er, possibly find her lost clothing." Demetrius tapped his two friends warningly on their backs. They released their hold on the girl as she stumbled into her group of girlfriends, waiting and giggling at the sight of the Halloween revelers and the three old Grecian guys who had caught their drunken friend right before she face planted on the sidewalk.

"Thanks, Grandpas!" they said almost in unison, as they towed their stumbling friend away. They all were very tipsy, bordering on drunk. They were hell bent on taking home an epic story from their weekend in Vegas, and the three old guys didn't look very promising.

"Ah the folly of youth," Elder Bert (he liked to be called Bert rather than Albert) mused watching the reveling crowd move off.

A taxi rolled up to the curb. The driver, a large matronly woman, had been slowly making the crawl up the strip, looking for random groups of males to offer a ride. They were her best bets for the real business of her cab. These old guys looked pretty promising.

"Guys need a ride?" she hollered through the passenger window.

"Lovely!" Demetrius replied, astonished at the hospitality of the citizens of Las Vegas.

"Where you going?" she asked to the men on the curb.

Arthur looked around, desperate to find a name of somewhere to go. The bright, flashing lights made it all so terribly confusing. "Er" was all he could come up with.

Bert stepped up to the cab, hoping to sound worldly, "Well, my dear, do you have any suggestions?"

He knows the code, the cabbie thought. *It's going to be a great night.* "I think I know where you fellas want to go. Hop in."

"Splendid. You are an ambassador of sorts to this place?" Demetrius inquired after settling himself in the front passenger seat. The two A's, Albert and Arthur, got in the back, grateful to be off their feet for a while.

"Sure, sure, Momma ambassador, that's me. In fact, I have a few *ambassadors* that could *escort* you around here for the evening."

She eyed the men in the back seat for their reaction. They seemed curious and pleasant. She continued, "Would you like to see some pics of my ambassadors?"

Demetrius furrowed his brow, unsure of this word *pics*. He turned to Bert for clarification; Albert enjoyed thinking of himself as the expert in human jargon.

"Ah, 'pics' is short for *picture*, a form of scrying that hum—I mean, children like to use." (*Children* was the code word for humans.)

"Oh, I don't got no kids in my pics. That's not what I do, boys. But I got some plenty young enough, just barely legal."

The largish matronly woman handed Elder Demetrius a binder of sorts. The kind pages could easily be added to or removed from. Each page contained a photo and a name of a girl. The names ranged from "Candy" to "Kitty" and the like. The *girls* ranged in age from twenty-somethings to much older, as evidenced by the style of hair and clothing in the photo. Some (the older photos, now turning yellow and losing their color) showed ladies in puffy-skirted dresses bending at the waist and showing a bit of frilly underwear. They were all pouting or blowing kisses to the viewer. Others had angry looks. There was even a very ferocious-looking black lady in a leather bustier and not much else. That one was called "Honeysuckle." In short, the cabbie had an entire binder of hookers for the gentlemen to peruse.

"Hmmm," Demetrius said after viewing an exceptional photo of a young lady in a much-too-short cheerleading uniform. He handed the binder to the riders in the backseat to take a turn. "Are these serving wenches?" Elder Arthur asked.

"Sure, they'll serve you. Just about anything you like," the woman cabbie said, sizing up the guys in the backseat. *Hell*, she thought. *They look so old and feeble, one of my girls could snap them like a twig if any one of them gives her any trouble.* But first things first…

"You guys got any money?" she asked, slowing her drive down Main Street to almost a crawl. She was ready to dump their asses in a second if they didn't have any green or anything to trade.

"Ah, funds. Yes, I anticipated this problem," Bert replied, digging into a deep fold of his toga. This was his secret pocket, which held any number of things. Presently, he pulled out a large gold pocket watch. He handed it over to the cabbie, who took it one-handed as she continued negotiating the busy street.

She held the watch up and inspected it closely. It certainly looked like the real deal. She had seen plenty of jewelry in this cab, presented by many a busted-flat fare. She knew just the right pawn shop to take it to, one that gave her a small commission for her trouble. Then, after that, she planned on taking them to one of her favorite casinos, so that they could either improve their investment or lose it altogether, in another "commission-based" drop-off.

Either way, once she extracted her cab fare and the several kickbacks, she would make decent money on this fare. And if they were lucky enough to win a little, they would have her card to call for some "serving wenches" later on.

"Listen, fellas, let me help you out. You need cash and I know the place that will trade good cash for this piece." (She handed it back to Demetrius for safekeeping.) "Besides, if you want some serving girls for a party, that'll cost you."

"How much to get the party started?" Bert asked, ever the practical one.

"Two hundred to walk in the door."

"Well then, we are at your mercy," Elder Arthur said.

You bet your ass you are, the cabbie thought.

"Just stick with me, and I'll help you out. I have done this for plenty of *others just like you*," she said in her best grandmotherly voice. Only this grandmother had the raspy voice of a chain-smoking lumberjack. Nonetheless, it seemed to delight the three old farts.

"Others?" Demetrius said. "There are *Others* like us around here?" The three began peering thought the dusty cab windows as though they could spot one of their own walking down the busy sidewalks.

"Sure! All the time," she said, perplexed but pleased at their intensely happy reaction. "I'll take you right to them. But first, let's take care of the little money issue."

"Do carry on, good woman. It was a happy day when we met you," Bert said. The gentlemen all nodded in agreement. The cabbie nearly wet her pants with greedy glee.

Yep, it was going to be a great night.

* * *

"*Wheeeeeee!*" a tiny voice shrieked from inside the dollar slot machine.

"My turn! My turn!" cried an older man, long in beard and wearing a floor-length toga while yelling into the coin return at the machine's bottom.

"Arthur, I asked you not to speak to the machine in front of the children!" he said in a most stern voice, usually reserved for chiding hapless Others-in-training. He also used the code word for humans, as they were up to their necks in people. His partner, another older gentleman, similarly dressed in Roman clothing, whispered fervently in his friend's ear.

The three men really liked the slot machines. They were bright and noisy and spit out money, which was very important in the human world. The dollar slot machines were the best, having the most helpful young serving ladies, who would be happy to bring you more of your favorite ale. And quickly. Just as long as you continued putting money back into the machines.

At this hour, one of the three elder gentlemen was presently miniaturized inside the machine, having a wonderful time figuring out how to make more dollars come out. Apparently, he was taking a ride on the wheels that spin inside the metal box.

Elder Bert had learned quite a lot during his ride inside the machine—like how there were three different wheels that spun around each time you placed a dollar coin into it. They stopped randomly, and if the same pretty pictures ended up lining up in the window, then dollar coins would fall out. By taking rides on each wheel, which consisted of merely hanging on the edge of a picture as it spun around, you could get marvelously dizzy. Almost vomitingly so. Very exciting.

Also, each picture had a tiny weight attached to it. The heavier the weight, the more likely it would stop on the viewing screen. The ugliest pictures and even the blanks had the heaviest weights. All you had to do was to find the prettiest pictures (thus having the lightest weights) and hang on tight. Using the weight of your own body, you increased the odds that the same pretty pictures would show up matching in the frame.

Now, one of the three wheels already had a weight attached to the prettiest picture, so the Elder didn't have to worry about that one. A little magic added to the weight on the second wheel made it so that he would only have to ride one wheel at a time in order to ensure that all three pretty pictures continued to line up in the viewing screen.

It was easy, fun, and a very wild ride.

But even the best times do have an end. Elder Bert was quite perilously close to vomiting, and if he was actually going to do so, he had better have a damn good reason, like drinking more alcohol first. He hadn't figured out how to drink inside the metal box, so he decided his turn was over.

Also, the machine was running low on dollar coins.

"OK, I'm coming out now," his voice peeped, tinny sounding through the change tray. "Ready?" he asked.

"Ready," the two other gentlemen replied.

It was just a blur really. First, there were two old men at the dollar machine, scooping up the heavy coins and emptying their load into the large plastic cups the lovely young servant girl brought them. Then there were three of them—for just a fraction of a second. The third gentleman whispered quickly, gesturing and pointing at the machine. The other two nodded sagely. Then, quick as that, another blur, and then there were two.

Elder Demetrius had chosen to take a turn inside the machine, just to test the ride. Bert and Elder Arthur remained outside of the machine. Arthur preferred to remain large and upright, so as to maximize the amount of drinking he could do. After all, you couldn't drink much being inside the noisy machine, so what was the point in being in there? Bert was tuckered out from his wild ride on the inside and was anxious to get another drink. Demetrius was the methodical one, very interested in the mechanics of a machine that spit money at them. He would be in there quite a while it would seem.

Back in the control room, a worker gestured to his supervisor. The supervisor walked over to his bank of screens. "Wach you got?" he asked, ready to radio security.

"I'm not sure," the man said. "Check out the guys in the dresses." He hit replay in slow motion.

Seen Finds His Peeps / The Early Years

Seen, the elf, was an odd one to be sure. He was named because of his large and somewhat protruding eyes. Elves are an extremely economical lot, not wanting ever to waste magical energy, or any energy, doing things that involve extra effort. And that includes how they name their own. If an elf child has some particular characteristic that is unique, then that's what they name him or her. Hence, Seen and his big eyes.

This is, in fact, how they named the human-made-elf Lavender—not because she had lavender sprouting anywhere out of her, but because the only thing that calmed her down was the smell of lavender. And, they thought she was a bit crazy. So, her name became Mad Lavender. Mad Lavender, whose real name is Christina, now resided at Home Base. She was desperately trying to find her renegade husband. It was making her a little bit mad for sure. Crazy mad and angry mad. So Mad Lavender, her elfin name still applied.

That's just how elves roll.

Elves are a very crafty and useful lot. They figured they could use this elf kid called Seen and his big eyes for sentry duty. After all, big eyes see a lot, right? So they put this young loner at the perimeter of the elf realm to do a little watching out after dragons, humans, and other pests that might want to stroll in. That was how Seen spent most of his formative years—alone and watching.

He was in his teens on that day, many years ago, sitting on his favorite rock, deep in the canyons and zoning out (it was after all a bit boring to be by yourself all day long), when he made a very interesting discovery—that, in fact, his eyes were special. Or maybe it was his brain. Or both. At any rate, he really could see what others could not.

It started with a simple exercise. One which evolved from the pure boredom of sitting still all day long. Stage 1 was simply sitting quietly, eyes closed, focusing only on his breathing. He slowed his heart rate until he took a breath only after long intervals. Inside and out, he was completely still. After a very long while, during which even the birds confused him for a perch, he was ready. When he was in the quietest state, he then proceeded to stage 2.

He liked to think of stage 2 as the detached stage. It was almost as if he could disengage from his body, leaving it quietly at rest for a bit while the rest of him floated around somewhere. At first, it was quite disconcerting to look down and find that he was somewhere up in the treetops hovering over his still body.

Then, it was just fun. It was like taking a trip away from yourself. He liked the feeling of being up in the trees with the birds and the crazy zigzagging insects. He could feel as they zoomed through his invisible self, unaware that there was a floating young elf in their midst. Because there really wasn't a floating young elf in their midst, only a wispy suggestion of one—a spiritual signature with no physical substance, while the rest of him waited patiently below for him to come back. He felt like he could hang up there for hours.

There was only one drawback. He couldn't go very far. He felt like he was attached to his physical body by a tether that was only so long. Once he stretched it to its full length, there was nowhere else to go. He was anchored, as it were, to his solid and waiting body below and couldn't venture terribly far from it.

Soon, the treetops began to grow boring to the young elf. There was only so much you could do up in the trees without a real body. And he had explored the entire breadth of his reach. Besides birds, bugs, and some interesting spiders, the canopy of the forest was really rather dusty and dull.

So onto stage 3. He came up with stage 3 one night in his cot in the youth dormitory. It was a restless night for him. The constant giggling and rustling from his fellow youth reminded him of his loneliness. He was pondering the depths of his disconnect from the rest of the clan when he thought that maybe there were others like him, floating about. If only he could see them. Then he wouldn't feel so very lonely.

Seeing was the key. And he was rather good at seeing things. So if he could just alter his meditation to keep his physical eyes open, he might just see something or even someone new. Possibly even friends.

Friends. It warmed him in the chill of the night to think of secret friends, friends that no one else had, friends who could be seen by virtue of his excellent and prominent eyes. *Yeah, that would show them,* he thought.

He couldn't wait for the morning when he would be dispatched to his lonely post. There, he would begin the grandest experiment of all—to see things that no one else could. And to finally have some friends.

He began his journey to stage 3, the seeing stage. This stage, however, was not without its drawbacks. For one, it was very hard to keep your eyes open without blinking. And if you happened to get a speck of dirt or, god forbid, an actual bug in your eye, then the attempt was over. So he had to train himself to blink, ever so slowly, and after a long interval, in order to take care of the basic physical needs of his eyes without breaking his concentration.

Also, his spiritual self tried very hard to break free and take its daily constitutional float above the treetops. This was not what he wanted to happen at all. Seen figured he needed all of his resources, physical and otherwise, to remain in one place in order to try to see beyond the usual. Having part of himself hovering somewhere else would certainly dilute his concentration as well as his energy.

The solution was rather simple. After much trying and failing to rein in his wandering spirit, he finally ordered it to stay put. And it did. Simple solution really. Before beginning stage 1, he matter-of-factly told his inner self that the reins were short and there would be no roaming about during this time.

Oh, his inner self said. *So you want me to stay home?*

Yes, I do he answered himself.

Well, why didn't you say so? it replied.

Shh, he said. *Time for us to see what we can see.*

OK, it said. *Mum's the word.*

I said, "Shh."

Oh, right. Tick a lock. His psyche mimed locking up its lips.

Are you always this chatty? He asked his inner self.

Sure, it answered. *I am the entire reason why you can't get to sleep at night. Busy, busy me.*

Do you mind? He reminded it.

Sorry. Going dark now. And his inner self just powered down and got very quiet, much to his great relief.

Getting to stage 1 with his eyes open was impossible. So for just a little while, he had them closed. Finally, when his breathing grew very quiet, and there wasn't even a speck of an idea floating in his head, he opened his eyes.

Keeping his gaze soft and his body very still, he focused all of his energies on what he could see just in front of him. The usual suspects emerged a tree, a rock, the edge of a trail, dust motes floating softly in the air, and a glint of sunlight piercing the deep gloom of the trees.

He concentrated on seeing them without studying the details. He focused, not on identifying the things in his line of sight—the rock, the bush, the tree but rather noting their general shapes. Eventually, he ignored their shapes and concentrated on the light and dark of his vision. He perceived the shadows and sunbeams that made up his view. Deciding to concentrate on the negative light— the shadows—he began to see different densities, different values in the shadows themselves.

Slowly, he began to see that there were shadows within shadows, areas of darkness that seemed to have a life of their own. And in these shadows he saw the barest beginnings of shapes, shapes that moved through the trees—inky, sinewy forms that were not created by a rock or a tree or any other piece of the natural landscape. These were shadows that moved on their own accord.

These furtive shadows had a life of their own. They were large and fluid and seemed to be moving to their own mysterious cadence. Soon, they flowed out of the murky gloom of the trees and tentatively surrounded him and his rocky perch. They were all around him. They felt very foreign to his world. And yet, he supposed they had been there all along, ignoring us as they moved in the courses of their own fluid existence.

What are these things? He thought as they lapped softly at the base of this rock. *Are they creatures, or are they something more elemental? Is it magic itself?*

He sat in awe and wonder at this amazing substance as it flowed around and over everything—rocks trees, hills, even him. It swirled languidly around him, as though it was testing this new creature, pausing and sending soft, tingling probes into his skin. It felt foreign and yet so familiar. He wasn't frightened, however. For it seemed very nonreactive to its environment, and its touch didn't hurt much, just tingled a bit.

Seen relaxed at the contact and just let this mysterious substance move about its business. He studied this amorphous mass and tried to memorize every facet of it. He wanted to rethink this entire experience after he came out of his meditation, to review it later in minute detail. It glistened in its luminous darkness, fluid, like silvery-black drops of oil on water.

But for now, he was tiring. He had been sitting very still for a very long time. And, although he had been slowly blinking, clearing his eyes every now and then, they were very tired and strained, so much so that he just had to rub them.

Carefully, he raised his hand from his lap. The hand made an eddy in the substance and seemed to attract more of it to it, as though it was following the hand's movement. He raised his hand to eye level, noticing the substance's midnight iridescence as it surrounded his outstretched fingers.

He couldn't really help himself and cannot even remember why he did what he did next. He allowed a tiny spark of magic from his forefinger to touch the substance, just to see what would happen. He really meant no harm.

Suddenly, the substance flashed a brilliant white where the magic had contacted it. There was a silent explosion, and then a gaping hole in the substance where the magic had been. On the ground beneath it lay ashes, which quickly dispersed in the air. The entire flowing mass for as far as he could perceive, trembled and shook from the tiny impact. Soon, after a trembling moment of aftershock, it seemed to right itself, resuming its languid flow.

Seen had understood then what this was. It was the magical net that surrounded all things. He knew when he used magic that a tiny tear had been made in the net. It was small enough to be easily repaired by the adjacent mass. *But if too much magic was used, what a great hole there would be!* Seen thought, shocked at the image.

Slowly, he stretched and shook himself to full consciousness. As he awakened from his meditative slumber, the image of the amorphous net faded away. The memory did not. At the end of the day, as he made his way back to the elf clan, he thought about how he could use this new and startling knowledge.

Well, you didn't make any new friends today, his inner self sadly reminded him.

It's OK. Until I do, I still have you, he said to himself, happy to have someone to talk to, even if it was just in his own mind.

And Seen did make friends. Many years later. As an adult, he grew a strange pair of green gargoyle wings, because of unusual contact with a powerfully magical young gargoyle. This further alienated him from the elf clan. Ultimately, it proved to be a benefit to him and his quest to feel what it was like to have friends.

He met up again with this family during their escape from a dragon-caused canyon fire. It was then he began hanging out with them. No, not stalking the family as Marissa the fairy declared, just hanging with them. But his actions drew him closer to a strange human family, and they eventually accepted him into their own hodgepodge clan of magical creatures.

Well, now you have friends, it congratulated him one fine day as he sat in the front office of the Supreme Elder Other Queen Mari of the fairy clan, otherwise known as Marissa.

Sort of, Seen replied, still longing for a true best friend. The family needed him and trusted him; that was for sure. After all, he was beginning to know more of their secret, private lives, but he still was a bit separate from the heart of things. As though he was always the last to know what was going on, an afterthought, almost.

Best you can do for now, it tried to comfort him.

Until I find real friends, I'll never know what it's like. Seen sighed to himself.

What? It was baffled.

To have a best friend, he said.

I am your best friend, his psyche pouted.

Not the same. I want a best friend that doesn't already know what I am thinking.

Seen smiled to himself, vowing never to disappoint this motley crew, his new family, while he kept his two good eyes searching for that elusive best friend.

Orders from the Commander in Chief

Seen's computer pinged its usual singsong tone, indicating that Supreme Elder Marissa wanted him. "Yes, Supreme Elder Other ma'am?" he said into the big box. He liked his computer. There were a lot of things his big eyes could see and read and study while "surfing the Net" as Marissa called it. Seen did that a lot in between screening visitors to his boss's office. He especially loved the Google.

This time, however, Marissa wanted him in the office, which was already filled with two gargoyles—the closest things he had to friends. Why, they even let him feed with them on occasion. *Yes, that's probably what they want,* Seen thought. *They want me to accompany them on a gargoyle feed.*

He entered the office, head bowed in observance of the Supreme Elder. Marissa noted his obsequious pose and snorted in irritation, wings flaring in mutual annoyance.

"Seen, it's just us. I told you a million times, there is no need to bow and scrape when we are together in private. So straighten up and listen. We need you to go on a special secret mission," she said with great authority.

Uh-oh, Seen thought. *They are banishing me from their midst!* "What did I do wrong Supr...Elder, Oth, oh, I mean Marissa, ma'am?" Seen scoured his memories, wondering what he did to deserve such punishment as banishing. He wrung his hands. His green wings drooped. The gargoyles, Enj and J, noted his demeanor and stepped in to soothe his feelings.

"No, dude, there's no worries," Enj said, hands outstretched, patting the air in front of the poor elf as though to calm the distress radiating out from him like ripples in a lake. *Jesus,* Enj thought, *even the air around him is agitated and depressed.* "Look, we need you to track someone down for us."

"Yeah," Jacob said, "and only you can do this."

"But there are Others-in-training that are skilled trackers," Seen pleaded. "Let them take charge of this matter. I am needed here to screen your visitors and to watch the Google in the computer box. These are very important jobs that only I can do. You told me this," he appealed to his boss, who had been bobbing in the air above her desk, hands on her hips, a bit miffed at his protestations.

"Am I late?" a new voice asked. Christina, or Mad Lavender, as she was still called on occasion, entered the room, softly closing the door so as to deter eavesdroppers.

"Mom, please explain to Seen here what he needs to do and where he needs to go. He seems *reluctant* to obey me," Marissa said in a she-who-must-always-be-obeyed tone.

"No, no, not reluctant, ma'am," Seen hastily interjected, entreating his boss's mother to understand. "It's just that I am, for the first time, happy. Happy here with all of you, and I don't see why I need to go away. That is, unless I have done something inadvertently wrong. At which case, I will hasten to correct my—"

"Seen, just chill," Enj placed a large hand on the elf's bony shoulder, effectively halting the poor guy's tirade. The elf's wings folded aside to accommodate the proximity of the large gargoyle. They liked him. After all, it was Enj's errant magic that had created those wings in the first place. They felt a bit beholden to their maker and would always obey his wishes despite what Seen may want. In fact, they were ready to fly off on whatever mission Enj sent them on, regardless of any protestations of their owner. "Let Momma Christina fill you in on what she knows. I'll help with the rest."

Christina led Seen over to the scrying pool—an indoor birdbath carved from very old stone. It sat in the corner of the otherwise bare and sterile-looking office—an ornately decorated thing from another century, or perhaps millennium. Chiseled from smooth obsidian, the carved designs showed constellations, clouds, and a myriad of stars. It certainly looked arcane and was created in such a way as to help the scryer to get into the right calm and meditative mind-set to see the images reflected in the water.

Seen looked without trying to see. That, he knew was the first step. In fact, scrying was very similar to the meditating he had done on his own as a lonely child, in the woods. And that, he recalled, had certainly had a surprising outcome. So he was ready for whatever the water would show him. "Just think about my husband, Ben. You know him," she prompted Seen. "You helped him out of the dragon fires that day long ago. Imagine anything you remember about that day as long as the memory includes Ben. Then see whatever the pool will show you."

Seen thought hard about the troubling day when he first discovered he could fly. His new, renegade wings flew him right into the path of some warring dragons, which were fighting over a potential mate. The female dragon had encountered Seen earlier that day, pegging him for a tasty postmating snack. It was traumatic and frightening. The hapless elf eventually dropped right into the burning fields right below the warring male dragons. It was there he found Ben, Marissa, and Jacob, lost and close to perishing in the smoke and flames. Seen quieted his thoughts and narrowed them down to his memories of Ben and the Family. His memories came like photographs in an album, pages turning slowly as he drank in the details his memory provided.

He saw Ben first, sooty, sweaty, and smelling of ashes. Seen held that image of Ben and fire and smoke in his mind. He imagined the vision of the rumpled and dirty Ben as a fully dimensional image—turning him around and in profile in his mind. He began to fill in the details of his clothing, as he remembered them in great detail, including how the backpack was slung low and heavy off his shoulder. Just as he pondered the question of how many pockets were on the man's shirt, the surface of the pool began to shimmer.

Small ripples played across the water. Quietly, so as not to disturb the surface of the scrying pool, the whole group carefully moved to see what Seen had conjured. The image began to take shape, first in shadowy colors of gray and green. Eventually, details emerged. First, large boulders appeared. They were most of the hues of gray in the image's foreground. In the background, greenish-black conifers speared the achingly blue sky. This was the green and the gray of the image. It appeared to be sunrise in some remote mountains.

A small glowing smudge was in the lower left corner of the scene. This looked to be a campfire tended by a crouching human. His back was to them, but he appeared to be gesturing, as though he was in the act of telling a big story. Only it was a performance for no one but the rocks and trees. The family didn't have to see his face to know it was Ben. His broad shoulders were deeply familiar to them. They took a collective sharp breath among themselves as the shock of recognition set in. It was the way he shifted, crouching and rolling from foot to foot in his excitement, as he told his tale. This not only told them it was their dad/husband, but that he was really wound up about something.

"Is he talking to himself?" Marissa asked. She hovered above the pool, careful not to disturb the watery scene with the vibration of her wings.

"Oh, my poor Ben! He's gone crazy," Christina said, her heart aching for the lone man. She reached out to him, barely missing the water before Jacob gently moved her hand away. Instead, she patted the edge of the stone, gently caressing it over and over. A poor substitute for the real thing.

"So Dad has lost his mind?" Jacob asked.

"Nah. He found his audience," Enj said smugly, happy his theory about an earlier scrying of Ben was now confirmed.

"Ah," was all Seen could say, nodding sagely at the green gargoyle. His wings began to quiver in excitement about the journey to come.

"Uh, seriously, he is talking to the trees," Marissa reminded them, concerned about her father's mental health.

"Not trees, the rocks," Seen said.

"Oh, that's *way* better," she said dubiously.

"Calm your bad self, Supreme Leader" Enj smiled at her, dropping into an easy banter, indicating all was well. "Dudes, he is talking to a bunch of rocks that are surrounding the fire. But they're not really rocks. These guys are really diggin' his story, so they settled into a boulder shape in order to give him their full attention. Those rocks..." He pointed his sharp talon. "...are a bunch of trolls."

"Lovely," Marissa said flatly.

"Oh, thank god he is not alone," Christina said. "I mean look how remote and rugged this is. He could get hurt or die out there by himself. He's not much into camping, you know..." Christina's control began to crumble, her emotions taking over by degrees as she contemplated one scenario after another with danger that could befall her husband in the wilderness. Before she could become full-on hysterical, Enj led the group back to the big desk to review some of the drawings and maps Christina had been drawing. Only Seen stayed by the scrying pool, watching and studying the image with nearly unblinking intensity.

"See," she said, rifling through the many sketches she had made, tossing several aside, thinking them useless. "The images don't flow. They never show me any landmarks that I can tie into topographic maps. He could be anywhere in the mountains. Any mountain range, any state, I don't know. I just can't—"

"Mom, relax. There's a lot of information we can get out of these drawings. We've done this kind of guesswork before," Jacob said, reminding them of how despite all odds they had found their mother. Marissa and Enj nodded in agreement. "Let's just make a list and see what we've got." Jacob worked to focus his mother so that they all could make logical assumptions about the whereabouts of their dad. He kept his hand at the small of her back, a calming gesture that helped her slow down and start again from the beginning of her drawings.

After a lengthy discussion regarding types of rocks and the altitude at which coniferous trees grew, with much help from Google, Enj summarized. He ticked off his facts using his enormous claws. "One," he said, "he is high up in the mountains. We know that because the sky is so blue—no smog—and the trees are the ones that grow several thousand feet above sea level. And B—"

"I hate when people do that," Marissa muttered, interrupting his list of the facts.

"Hate what?" he asked, annoyed at the interruption.

"Confuse their lists One, two, three with A, B, C."

"I didn't do that."

"Yes, you did. Listen, Enjie, I heard everything you said. You just said, 'One,' and then said, 'B.'"

"I don't care who you are Supreme Dictator; if you call me Enjie one more time, I'll—"

"You'll what?" she challenged flying right up to his face. Everyone else was forgotten for the moment. The two of them, nose to nose, a great magical beast and a tiny, powerful fairy queen—sparks began to fly between them. The air was charged with the heat of the impending battle. Both were breathing rapidly and for some reason, unwilling to stop the fight.

"Christ. Tip over the birdbath and hose these two down," Jacob said to no one in particular. Seen was blocking said birdbath, still raptly studying the unfolding images, so the threat was an empty one.

Jacob was baffled. He had seen his best friend and his fairy sister work so well together as a team and just about equally fight like cats and dogs. There really was no telling which fairy or which gargoyle would show up on any given day— the crazed ones or the chill ones. *What is with those two?* he asked himself for about the millionth time.

"I think I can find him," Seen murmured to himself, still studying the images in the pool, thereby quelling any more bickering. Surprised, the group halted all conversation. They gave the strange elf, bending over the scrying pool in the far corner of the room, their full attention.

The family rejoined Seen at the pool, Christina edging her way through the big beasts to be the first to stand next to the elf. Seen's wings moved aside to make room for her. "Thank you," she said, ever respectful of any Fairfolk wings. Wings always remember such courtesies and in so doing, would treat her kindly in the future.

The view had changed. The image was strange and blurry. If one stared hard, the original landscape, campfire, and man were still visible. But only barely. Superimposed over that tableau was a swirling, sparkling, dark mass of mist or fog. "Seen, what is this?" the mother asked.

"Oh man, this is way cool. Dude, you rock!" Enj said, smiling hugely, exposing his sharp and deadly incisors.

"Anyone besides the big green asshole care to explain this?" Marissa said, still miffed at the beast.

Hovering at the edge of the scrying bowl, she squinted and angled her head to best view her dad, hoping to keep an eye on him despite the foggy mess surrounding him.

"I believe it is the magical net surrounding all of us," Seen explained. "I learned early on that I could see it if I wish to. It is the ether in which all magic resides. When in balance, it flows and moves all around us. But when magic is used, small gaps appear, even the color changes somewhat. Eventually, the net repairs itself and all is well. But sometimes, when too much magic is used, it thins and stretches like a pretty soap bubble, threatening to pop, until it can repair itself or until someone comes to repair it.

"I have found that when you use magic, it changes shape and color. It swirls just so. See?" he said, pointing to the mist swirling around the very large boulders by the fire as thought it was attracted by them. It was stronger in color, more iridescent, nearly greenish in hue by the boulders, less so by Ben. And nearly neutral gray everywhere else in the scene.

"We know Ben is here in the mountains closest to us," The Sierra Nevada's," Jacob said helpfully, not realizing the name was only relevant to the family.

"I can follow that mountain range with these drawings Mad Laven—uh, Christina has given us. Then when I am close, I will follow the shape and color of the magical net to specifically locate your Ben man."

"Oh, I do love you!" Christina said throwing her arms around the elf, wings and all. They allowed this owing to her earlier good manners.

"I knew you were the man, uh, elf for the job," Enj said.

"Ditto," Jacob agreed.

Marissa frowned, seeing a flaw in the beauty of the plan. "But who will stay and be my secretary?" Christina gazed at her girl, while still drawn to the image of her husband in the water. She was fascinated with the actual sight of this net that caused them all so much grief. And yet, despite the interesting images in the scrying pool, her daughter needed her help. She stepped closer to Marissa and away from the scene shimmering on the water. She smiled at her fierce daughter. "Well, I can work a computer. And I am certainly not afraid of you. So let me have the job. I'll keep the pesky Others at bay and maybe teach you a thing or two about good manners," Christina said archly, nodding in the direction of Enj.

Marissa blinked, considering this proposition. "Well, I suppose so, but you can't start ordering me around. I already get enough of that from these two guys." Marissa pointed in the direction of Enj and Jacob.

"So that's cool then. Hey, Seen, when can you start?" Enj asked. Seen's wings twitched madly in excitement, ready to fly him out of the room at the gargoyle's bidding.

"Very soon, I would say, judging by these." The elf pointed with his thumb back toward his very antsy wings. Inclining is head toward his shoulder, he asked them, "But may I please use the lavatory first?"

Lust among the Vines

"Now that we are on the way to finding Dad, I think it's time for a little party. Mom, cancel all my appointments and get some wine. Please," Marissa added belatedly.

"Wine in the morning?" her mother admonished.

"This is what I am talking about," Marissa complained to Enj, of all people. She began picking at a pesky cuticle. Pretty soon, she would pop the offending finger in her mouth and chew the hanging piece of skin off. Before she could do any more damage to herself, Jacob batted her finger away. Before she could retaliate, Enj stepped in between them, talking all the while to Momma Christina in a soothing, conciliatory tone. It was for everyone's benefit.

"Momma Christina, you have to understand that when she is at Home Base, she is the supreme boss. Her word must be obeyed," Enj said, attempting to soothe the ruffled feathers of the mother.

"That's right," Jacob agreed. "So here is your first job as secretary. I mean, if your boss doesn't mind." Jacob looked at his sister, eyebrows arched, angling his head toward their mom as if to say, "*You know how she is. Just go with this, OK?*" Marissa shrugged her shoulders in silent acquiescence. He continued,

"And, since we are right in the wine country, maybe you can get some of Dad's favorite Bordeaux blend as a gift to bring him. You know, as a reminder of the good times we've all had together. Seen could tuck it into his backpack and take it with him."

"Oh," Christina said, considering the idea of a conciliatory gift. After all, she wasn't sure how upset Ben still was at all of them for choosing to remain at Other School, rather than follow him. A bottle of wine might help smooth things over—or at least begin the process of smoothing things over.

She reasoned that at this point, the remaining family members were stuck here. Marissa had to remain in charge to keep Other operatives from tracking her husband down and giving him the ultimate punishment. And her daughter needed Jacob and Enj to stay and help her. Although Christina could accompany Seen on the tracking down of her husband, her inability to fly would only hold him back.

Besides, someone should stay here to keep an eye on these kids. Wine at 10:00 am. Jeez-its!

All parties in agreement, Christina left the office and tracked Seen down near the lavatory down the hall. She directed him to wait until she could get some wine for him to take to her husband. This did not set well with either Seen or his wings. They all were ready to go. Right now. Even Seen's talonned hand twitched in irritation.

Soothingly, for she was a mother and knew how to calm an irritated youth, she led Seen back to the reception desk and clicked on an interesting website for him to navigate. Heading down the hall toward her art space, she pulled the cell phone from the pocket of her tunic and dialed up Sleeping Guy, the student living in her human home.

Sleeping Guy and the Professor had taken up residence in the family home—the big house at the top of a windy hill in the East San Francisco Bay Area, as caretakers, while the Family was presumed to be "away." As far as the neighbors were concerned, Christina was dead, having perished in a freak electrical accident up by their pool, Jacob was away at college, and Marissa was in some sort of rehab. They had all assumed Ben had joined his daughter for some extended family counseling. After all, wasn't it terrible how the mother was killed—right in front of the family? When the firemen arrived, they surmised that Jacob was so close to the event that the sparks had burned all the clothing off his body. A teenage girl seeing her mother killed and her brother naked would need a lot of family counseling to get over that.

The truth was Christina had given herself in trade for the safe return of her son in his gargoyle form. She became an elf. Later, Marissa had been permanently turned into a fairy in order to be saved from some nasty fairy poisoning. And all of them had been recruited by Bob, the family cat, into Other School. That is, until Ben defected and became renegade.

Sleeping Guy and the Professor had been drawn into this web of lies having discovered that Marissa was attempting to go to college with Jacob as proxy. Eventually the student and professor saw through the ruse and discovered Marissa the fairy, sitting on Jacob's shoulder the entire time in class. Whether they liked it or not, they were a part of the conspiracy to keep the world of Fairfolk secret.

They also did a great job cleaning the pool and mowing the lawn, in addition to collecting the mail, returning phone calls, and paying the bills from the family checking account, which had a considerable balance. Ben saw to that prior to his leaving the home and their affairs in their care.

At first, the two men loved being right about the strangeness of the area. They loved having credibility to their notions of seeing strange things "out of the corner of their eye." They felt vindicated in being right in their theories about the existence of "things that go bump in the night," or more precisely, "things that go bump when landing on your deck."

In time, it was clear that the housesitting arrangement was going to be more or less permanent. It was a bit tedious, being stuck there. Although occasionally, they would be summoned by one of the family for a special job. That job usually involved going over the blackberry bushes and yelling at the fairies to do their work the way Marissa had taught them. Not fun being the bad guy with fairies. They buzz very annoyingly at your head when they are vexed.

Sometimes, however, they were summoned to Other Home Base or Other School, which was very conveniently located over the hills in the Livermore Valley. That usually was very interesting. Also, they generally coupled their errand with a quick trip winetasting at some of their favorite local wineries. Well, why not? Besides, they always did their best writing after a few snorts of their favorite cabernet sauvignon.

The other job the Professor had been given by Christina was to write the epic story of this house and the sanctuary it had become to Fairfolk. They were using actual interviews of the family, as well as Christina's notes in her journal. They also had something else called "Nebbin's Notes" for reference but aside from the copious drawings, they were hard to read unless magiked from elvish runes to the English language. And seeing as how they were usually mad at the local fairies (and vice versa), they had little magical interpretive help from that front.

The cell phone thing was a tremendous improvement from past communication devices. Thank god, they didn't have to put that damn yellow purse on their heads and yell into the leather bag to talk to Marissa. So humiliating. Besides, the damn bag was getting smelly from the sweaty heads contacting the suede lining. Gross.

Originally, each member of the family chose a personal item with which to communicate back to the human world. When it rang, buzzed, flashed, or (in the case of the purse) glittered, it was like ringing the Professor and Sleeping Guy up. To answer it, you had to speak into it. Hence, wearing the purse like a hat so that you could see and hear Marissa, whose face was located at the bottom of the bag. So when the idea of communicating by cell phone came up, they were all for it. Everybody got a nice new one. With apps and everything.

Sleeping Guy was out on the deck this fine fall morning, watering the basil in the big pots, when the cell phone rang—rather, it sang to him in a song of his choosing. His latest favorite song was by a band of angry Englishmen. It was a wailing and irritated sort of tune recorded probably after a long night at the local pub. Sleeping Guy liked it. The song said everything pissy he ever wanted to say to someone but was too chill to say.

He fished the phone out of the front pocket of his tatty jeans. The caller ID said Mad Lavender. He liked her. She was nice. And she was Marissa's mommy. He always heard that if you crush on a girl, get her mom on your side. That was what he planned to do.

Oh sure, Marissa and he had their differences— she was sarcastic and bossy, and he was chill. She was magically powerful, and he was just a guy. She was a fashionista, and he was still wearing the same jeans from the year 2000. And she was about five feet shorter than he was, sporting green leather wings. And then there were the tattoos, which is to say, he had a lot of them and she hated them.

Minor differences really. After all, they shared a big secret about the existence of Fairfolk. Certainly, many successful relationships were based on far less, right? Anyway, he had been working this angle for a few months now. So when Christina called, he was ready to help her however he could and then some.

"Hi, this is Kenneth."

"Yes, I know," Christina said. "That's why I called you." She was patient with him. He was nice in a clueless sort of way.

"Um, yeah. So…what's up in magic land?" he said.

"Oh, not much," Christina replied, dissembling. She yawned. She always yawned before telling an untruth. The fact was, there was a lot going on. She toyed briefly with the truth. Things like, *Yeah so, Marissa is drinking at 10:00 a.m. Jacob can't figure out what creature to become. I am lost and useless without my husband, and yeah, he has run away to the mountains, talking to rocks.* She thought the better of it. "I actually need for you to come to Home Base and run a little errand with me."

"Ooh, magic stuff?" He wondered if finally, they would let him roam around the base camp. After all, maybe he would run into Marissa. He looked down at his attire. His favorite red T-shirt was now pink from multiple washings over the many years he had worn it. The jeans were (he thought) fashionably torn, so they were probably OK. But flip-flops? Were they allowed there? He wriggled his bony white toes, wondering if he could tactfully bring up whether there was a dress code or not.

"No, no," she advised. "I just need you to pick me up at the entrance. We need to go winetasting. I have to do a pickup for the family."

"Oh." Disappointed, he drew out the *oh* to a two-syllable word. Sort of like oh-huh. Then, he added, "'Kay. So I will meet you at the driveway?"

"Right," she replied.

"Anyone else coming with us?" he asked hopefully.

"Nope, just me. Oh and I might not look like my usual self. So I'll just get in your car when you drive up."

"Who will you look like? I mean, how will I know it's you?"

"Don't worry. Marissa is outfitting me to look like some yuppie woman out for the day, trying to get a little wine buzz. You will be my driver, all right?" she asked, but it was understood that he would do whatever she asked, no matter what. That's what happens when you crush on a girl. You are a slave to the family. "Can you come soon?" she asked sweetly, adopting a slightly higher voice than usual. This is the little-girl trick most women employ at some point or another, in an attempt to make the guy feel strong and capable and totally biddable. It's a form of glamour that has elements of old magic in it.

"Sure," he said magnanimously.

Naturally, he fell for it. He finished watering the potted plants on the deck, wound up the hose, changed his faded pinkish shirt for another tee in a somewhat better condition, and headed off to Livermore in the family sedan. All the while, he kept thinking of his latest ploy to see Marissa and gain her favor. She was such a tough one. But he was relentless in his laidback way.

This new tactic he had devised just might do the trick. It appealed to one of her better qualities—that of protecting the ones she loved. Over and over, during his drive, he imagined how the encounter would occur. All of the scenarios ended in her bestowing tiny kisses all over his face and thanking him profusely. She then would give him her undying gratitude, offering to magic herself into being a human girl again, so that they could live happily ever after. *Yeah, that's the ticket*, he thought, smiling to himself.

He took the last Livermore exit off the freeway, headed toward the vineyards, and began the slow, winding drive around the vast plots of cultivated land. Vineyards and olive orchards grew in between the wealthy islands of luxury homes. These were rather small pockets of neighborhoods that grew where some previous farmland had been. The prior farmer gave up the ghost and settled for a wad of cash instead of the daily toil of farming. Seemed like the prices of homes depended on the proximity of the cultivated vines to the lot. The closer your back-yard was to the orchards or grapes, the more valuable it was. *Weird*, sleeping Guy thought. Because the closer you were to the cultivated fields, the more you were exposed to fertilizer, pesticides, dead leaves, busy farm workers at 5:00 a.m., etc. *So why would you pay more for that?* he wondered. Well, he was not a very materialistic sort and did not understand words like *status, image,* and *cache.* So the concept of elegant vineyard living simply didn't appeal to him.

He traveled past the tony neighborhoods back to where it truly was farm country. Making his way down a tiny country road, he began searching for the right gravel drive. The road was dotted here and there with a few one-story farmhouses. Spotting the unobtrusive dirt road, he made a right up a slight uphill grade, approaching what appeared to be a farmhouse and barn, surrounded by rows and rows of lush, purple grapes. The grapes themselves were not like table grapes; they were tiny, dark, and had a frosty sheen on their skin. Despite their tiny size, they looked plump and nearly ready for harvest.

Blackbirds appeared from the depths of the neat rows of grapes, circling the approaching car. They alternated between their odd game of tag they played with his vehicle and flying in and out of one of the rafter vents of the barn. Sleeping Guy knew they were actually a form of sentries for the Others.

Additional security came in the form of magic. Sleeping Guy had felt the aversion to the place when he first turned up the drive. It was designed to keep people out, especially the tipsy sort, always looking for the next tiny winery to do some tasting. He felt the Charmers at work and ignored the irritable, itchy feeling it always gave him. Eventually, a "farmer" came out and stood in the middle of the drive, looking as though he had just left his work in the field. His hair was mussed, and he sported a worn baseball cap. He was an Other-in-training—rotating sentry duty being a requirement of the job. "Help you?" He asked, blocking the path of the car.

"Mad Lavender asked for me. Also, is Marissa home?"

Marissa? the Other thought. *Dear gods, she would pluck his head off if she knew he referred to her in any way but Supreme Elder Other!* His features did not register his surprise at the human and his shocking knowledge about Home Base. His key words, *Mad Lavender* and *Marissa* were enough to let him pass.

The only response the Other made to the human was to shrug his shoulders at the question of the whereabouts of Supreme Elder Other and to step aside, allowing him passage into the Other realm. Sleeping Guy wound his way on the gravel road around the back of the farmhouse and parked in front of the big barn doors. As soon as his engine cooled and stopped its post drive ticking, the barn door rolled opened wide enough to allow a woman to pass through.

The woman did not look like the elf woman known as Mad Lavender. Although this woman had pure white hair like the elf, hers was cut into a stylish bob. She wore tight blue jeans, and a frilly white blouse, cinched with a wide cowboy belt. Her chandelier earrings dangled and swung gently at her neck. Despite her white hair, she had a youthful look to her, and a very tiny, fit body. The only flaw to this country-chic style, were her suede boots. Flat and with no heal, they sported leather thongs that wound their way up the boot to the top of the calf. They looked like they were homemade, clunky and awkward, but definitely not in a shabby-chic style. Just clunky and awkward. It spoiled the image somewhat.

"Hey," she said, "it's me Christina, or Mad Lavender, or whatever the hell I am called today." She laughed, sliding a lock of hair away from her face, correcting the fashionable but impractical coif.

As she opened the passenger door and climbed in, Sleeping Guy still couldn't get over the transformation. "What happened to the regular you?" he asked.

"Oh well, I couldn't exactly go as my usual self. I mean, the winemakers would shit their pants if a cat-eyed, pointy-eared elf walked in! So I magiked my face back to my original one. We can do that, you know, since we are Others. Still, I used only a little bit of magic, so I am on the timer. Can't last too long, or I revert back to my scary elf self when the magic runs dry!"

Christina smiled briefly at the student and then settled into the passenger seat, buckling herself in while taking in the scenery. She looked out the window at the beautiful valley they were in. She rarely had the opportunity to get out of "the office" since she spent most of her time scrying for the lost Ben. The break in the action felt good for a change.

Returning from her reverie, she added, "Oh and you know Marissa; she wouldn't let me out of there without the appropriate outfit. I balked, however, at the high-heeled cowgirl boots. Bad feet, you know. So I opted for my usual elf shoe wear...its weird though..." She paused, looking down at the outfit.

"I only used enough magic to change my face. The elf body is the same. My human body could *never* squeeze into these jeans. Sheesh, now I know what a sausage feels like!" She giggled, adjusting her pants legs, pulling them down to relieve the pressure from sitting.

Sleeping Guy sat quietly in the parked car. He let her run on until she had no more to say. When there was enough of a lull, he shyly asked, "Um, is Marissa home?"

"Oohh," Christina said, understanding dawning upon her. "Well, she is always around, but she is very busy saving the world, you know. I'm pretty sure she can't break away right now."

"But it's important."

"How important? I mean is everything OK at home?"

"Well, sure. It's, uh, about the fairies and stuff."

"Are they OK? How are the family? You know, baby Hummer, Eedle, and Otib?"

"Look, everything is fine. I just need to talk to her, all right?" This was the closest he came to being snippy with her.

"All right, all right, I'll call her." She wriggled in the seat, reaching into her back pocket to retrieve the cell phone. The ring tone was audible despite her holding the cell phone to her ear. Sleeping Guy heard the Supreme Elder Other, Queen Mari, answer with a tired, tinny-sounding voice, "Whaa-at?"

"So, hi. It's Mom. Oh, you already know that. Funny. Anyway, Sleeping Guy—"

"My name is Kenneth," He interjected somewhat more forcefully than usual.

Christina eyed him, wondering about his present state of mind. She continued, "—and I are outside.

Before we go, he wants to tell you something important about the fairies."

"Are they all right?" Marissa asked worriedly.

"Apparently fine. He says it's important though."

"You know what—Seriously? Oh, I'll be right out." Marissa clicked off. Christina smiled sheepishly at Sleeping Guy, hoping he had not overheard the impatience in her daughter's voice. "She's coming." Sleeping Guy nodded, leaving the car to stand by the barn door.

He fidgeted, waiting for a glimpse of the fairy queen, pondering upon which amazing prom dress she would be wearing this day. He was shocked then, at today's choice of attire. Leather. Leather tank top and a leather miniskirt. Her feet were bare, and in an odd juxtaposition to the severe and simple leather outfit, she had tiny rows of daisies in her hair. She looked like she was a flower child on the way to a heavy-metal rock concert instead of a head honcho, running the organization. She didn't look terribly happy, either.

A large bumblebee tracked her head, attracted by the color of her red hair as well as the bright flowers tucked in the tendrils. She paused midair, stared down the bee saying, "Are you kidding me?" The bee, realizing his egregious error, buzzed off. If you listened very carefully, you could hear a faint, "Zorrry, Queen Marrrri," as he sped away in great haste.

She took stock of Sleeping Guy. It looked to her like he had cleaned up a bit from his normal attire. The T-shirt seemed somewhat new. At least the rock band it advertised was more current. But the jeans were a hot mess—so tattered that they seemed held together only by good intentions. And the faded and tacky tattoos. It looked to her like they came from Tattoos-R-Us. Oh, he was a nice guy, all right, but so weird and too needy for her liking. She liked them feisty. Like Enjie. *Eeuuw*, she thought. *Now why did I think that?*

Sleeping Guy noticed her scrutiny. Subconsciously, he began pulling his shirt sleeves longer, hoping to cover some of the tattoos she found so objectionable. He pulled his favorite sunglasses off and folded them onto the neckline of his tee. He wanted her to see his eyes. *They are the windows to the soul,* he thought. And today, maybe he would bare his soul to her. "Uh, hi, Marissa. How's it hangin'?" he said, unsure how to start. He was rolling slightly on the balls of his feet. It was yet another nervous gesture he always made in her presence.

"Settle down, Kenneth, and tell me what's going on with my fairies."

"Oh, sure," he said, willing his feet to stay still.

Christina smiled softly while viewing this little drama from the safe confines of the car. She felt sorry for Sleeping Guy, knowing he had absolutely no chance with her daughter. *Maybe I'll get him a nice bottle of wine to take home,* she thought. Small consolation for being turned down by Marissa, but a comfort nonetheless.

"Yeah, so, there's these developer guys that want to build on the vacant lot up by the pool. You know, the one that has the fairy realm on it."

"Really, Kenneth. Do you think I don't know my own backyard?" Marissa was becoming impatient and worried now that her fairies might be in great jeopardy. They had no real defenses against big bulldozers. "Where are they in the building process?"

88

"Well, when I was out cleaning the pool, I saw surveyors up there. They were putting up the sticks and plastic flags. That is the beginning stages, but it is a sign that they are totally serious. Anyway, I had this idea…" He looked away, trying to make the next few sentences as clear and concise as possible.

"Yes? Please, make it snappy."

"Right. Well, I thought, you know, those lizards that Eedle accidently turned into shiny rainbow colors? You know, the really big ones?"

"Eedle didn't do it; her baby did," Marissa corrected. "The lizards were assigned to take care of the little prince, but then no one took the time to feed them. The only thing they could do to survive was to absorb some of the baby's magic. It kept them from starving to death. But it changed them. For good."

"OK so, yeah right…The lizards got big and shiny and rainbow colored. Anyway, I thought if I made a few calls to some local environmental groups and told them a new and rare species of Gila monster lived on the land, no one could build there. It would be protected. Forever. And the fairies would be safe."

"Not a bad idea, Kenneth," she said his real name in a kind and supportive way this time, instead of using it for shock value as she usually did. "Have you talked to the fairies? Because you have to get them to watch out for the Eco-Nazis when they start tramping all over the place. They will have to know and provide cover, keeping the scientists out of their actual dens. Also, they can't hurt any of the lizards. That would be bad form, I think."

"Yeah, yeah. I'll square it with the fairies before I make any phone calls. And if we say the lizards are endangered, then they can't take them away and hurt them, right?" Sleeping Guy was about 99 percent sure this plan would work. He would make that 100 percent before he started anything. It would be disaster if this went wrong and damaged his relationship with the beautiful and badass looking fairy.

"Talk to the fairies first, then work something out." She turned midair and began to fly back to the barn. "Oh," she said belatedly. "Good job, dude."

Well, it didn't exactly turn out the way he had hoped. No kisses and promises of undying gratitude. Not even a soulful look. But she did call him "Dude," a decided improvement over "Sleeping Guy." And she actually said his real name several times without using it like a mallet. This was a definite improvement. He liked "Dude." That was nice.

"Let's go, Mr. Dude. I am on the clock here!" Christina called out of the open car window, impatient to get going. A lot of people, including Seen, were waiting on them to get the job done.

The Fine Art of Wine Scamming

Winetasting in most regions in California is a delicate dance between the pourer and the taster. The pourer is there to inform and sell. He or she is neither your friend nor bonded to you in any way, despite what you think is your exceedingly charming nature. He or she sells wine. Period. The taster, however, may be one of three types: the drunk, the snob, or the happy wine aficionado.

Drunks are just there to drink as much wine as possible. They play a game with the pourer. They will pay the obligatory tasting fee, of course. Then they will try as hard as they can to scam extra pours. Success comes when they get the pourer to give them a little more than the usual amount especially from the better wines under the counter. Those wines are ones not on the tasting list, but available if the pourer a) knows you and/or, b) believes you to be a big spender. Pourers take the chance serving the drunks the special wine, in the hopes that, in their drunkenness, they will shell out the big bucks to buy it. The drunks are loud, obnoxious, and hog the counter, never giving an inch of space to new people walking into the wine-tasting room.

The snob is there for his or her own personal entertainment. He or she is there to show everyone in the listening vicinity how smart he or she is and how staggeringly stupid you are about viticulture and enology. Including the pourers. Snobs will gladly pay the obligatory winetasting fee. That is their golden ticket to abuse the pourer. They will then scoff at the choice of glass for the varietal. For example, they would die if given a pinot noir wine in a chardonnay glass. Horrors. They ask penetrating questions about appellation and the merits of foil versus wax tops—to say nothing of the endless debate over using plastic versus cork. And don't even get them started about the sulfite process!

Why do they ask such things? They don't care about the answers. They don't even know half the answers themselves. They derive pleasure in watching someone squirm, or better yet, stutter in their reply. That means they have won in the dominance-submission game. These are the same people who never let someone merge in their lane. In the end, they may or may not buy wine. It just depends on how much sucking-up the pourer does to them.

And then there are the happy wine aficionados. They like asking questions. But that's because they really want to know. They love a certain type of wine, having almost an emotional bond with it. They know a lot about that particular varietal—it's their favorite friend. They are open to trying new varietals as long as they get to have a taste of their old pal first. Most important, they buy. Some come into the winery looking like old farmers and cleaning ladies. Others come in driving their midlife crisis luxury autos. They really span the spectrum of type. But what they do have in common is a love for the wine and an appreciation of the process of getting the grape from the vine to the glass.

Pourers like these guys. These are the Holy Grail of customers. They buy. A lot. They let these people go in the back and taste wine futures right from the barrel. They get secret food pairing suggestions. They get to taste a lot of wine—even after they protest that they have tasted enough. They are treated like royalty. Pourers kind of bond with these types, at least insofar as they try to recognize them when they come back to visit.

This is the pourer's dilemma when a new taster first comes into the tasting room. He or she undergoes a subtle process of trying to determine which category the taster falls into: drunk, snob, or happy consumer. So when Sleeping Guy, a twenty-something grungy type, sporting aviator sunglasses, and a chic older woman with platinum-silver hair came in during the late morning one fall day, the pourer was confused. Were they a cougar couple, looking for a quick buzz prior to an afternoon tryst? Or was the young man the designated driver for his mother/ aunt/cousin, looking to let her hair down midweek? Both would put them in the category of drunk.

Yet, they both had warm, open smiles and immediately thanked the pourer for allowing them an early visit to the tasting room. This politeness immediately took them out of the category of wine snob. The pourer breathed an inward sigh of relief. He really did not want to deal with that sort first thing in the morning. He tried to imagine the nature of the relationship between this odd couple and made some rather instantaneous assumptions.

Here's a thought. They don't appear to be related, yet they seem to know each other very well. Perhaps, he was her future son-in-law and they were winetasting for a big wedding reception. Then the keys to the winery were theirs. The pourer would do anything in that case to please them. It could mean a ton of sales for the day. In that case, the pourer would go home that night with the owner's hearty thanks and a small fortune in wine as gratitude from the winery owner for a job well done. A pourer's fantasy.

In the case of the white-haired fashion plate and her scruffy young friend, the pourer opted for the happy wine aficionado on a mission. Possibly the future son-in-law and wedding reception scenario. That one seemed to fit best.

"Are you familiar with our winery?" This was the standard opening line for the pourer. It helped him know where the customer stood in the information department.

"Why yes," the woman answered. The young man wandered around the room, checking out the T-shirts for sale with snappy wine slogans. "This is my friend's first time here," she gestured toward Sleeping Guy, who now was squinting at the barrels trying to figure out what the chalk marks and dates meant on them. Wine code. It seemed more interesting than the silly wine banter that often goes on in tasting rooms. She continued, "This is my husband's favorite local winery. Mine too. We just love your Estate Cab, you know, from the grapes on the south side of the winery. And aren't we lucky to have you open so close to harvest?" she said brightly.

Christina smiled warmly, looking directly into the man's eyes. Yes, she was using glamour on him. She needed to have him biddable since she was about to buy a lot of wine with no cash whatsoever. She went on for a bit, knowledgeable about how long in the barrel the various varietals were aged. She expressed her deep appreciation at the length of time the wine-maker chose in order to get that lovely mouth finish that all of his wine had. All the while, she stared deeply into is eyes, fairly mesmerizing him with her soft and pleasant words.

Dimly, the pourer thought, *Is she coming on to me?* But then no, it didn't really feel sexual. And she mentioned a husband. Now whether that meant grunge boy was her future son-in-law or some designated driver, well, that remained to be seen. It simply felt like she was someone very important thanking him for his brilliance in choosing to work at such a fine establishment. It made him feel special. He wanted to impress her.

Magic is a wonderful tool.

In time, she and the pourer tasted all the best wines, Sleeping Guy having declined to drink so early in the morning. Now, for his tastes, had it been a joint, well, that would have been different. But wine before noon felt weird to him. Everyone has their standards apparently. Eventually, Christina had chosen a case of the best that the winery had to offer.

The pourer moved over to the cash register station and totaled the purchase. "That will be four hundred dollars even," he said.

"Oh, but what about the case discount?" Christina gently asked.

"Oh right, I forgot. Three sixty."

"And I forgot to tell you I am a member of the private club." Christina pulled a sheet of drawing paper from her rear jeans pocket. On it, she had drawn a lovely cluster of grapes. The caption said, "Friends of Woody." (Woody, being the name of winery dog). Christina held the sketch toward the man, continuing to bore a hole through to the backs of his eyes.

The pourer squinted, turning the page over and over. "I'm not sure," he said terribly confused.

"Oh wait, I forgot." Christina removed the page from the man's hand and turned her back to him. While she was out of his view, she waved her hand over the sketch. It glowed bright and sparkly and then faded into an official-looking certificate, complete with border designs, a stylized grape cluster, and a tiny image of the winery dog along with fancy script writing. The writing read over and over "Free free free free…" She handed it back to the pourer, who took it and without further question, accepted it as payment in full for the case of wine.

Sleeping Guy completed his browsing of the winery and joined the two at the register to help heft the case and pop it into the trunk. Christina thanked the man profusely as they hurried from the tasting room.

"So will he get in trouble when the boss finds there is no three hundred sixty dollars in the till?" Sleeping Guy was very worried about the karma of this transaction.

"No, I erased the receipt and its cash register copy. Unless they do a complete count of the stock today, they will never know that the wine simply disappeared. Besides, this is a family winery. We have seen over the years many a family member pop in and take product at will. If they do a count, they will just assume the wife took it. The certificate will fade in a few minutes into a blank sheet of paper. Eventually, he will wonder why it is there and will toss it out."

They were almost at the car when Christina said, "Oooh, I forgot one thing." She wandered off to the surrounding vineyard and walked through the vines until she found just the right spot. Holding her hands high, she whispered an incantation. There was a brief flash, and then the world settled back into its everyday sound and smell.

"What did you do?" Sleeping Guy asked, looking around to see if there were any noticeable changes.

"Oh, I just ensured they have a great harvest this year. They won't believe the sugar content. And no bugs." Feeling her karmic debt was repaid, they headed to the car.

The pourer rushed out to see what the flash was all about. "Hey, guys, did you see tha— hey, *what is wrong with your face?*" He was horrified. Her magic time was up and her features returned to their elvish state. The magic she used while at the winery temporarily exhausted her resources, so she hadn't the ability to re-magic her face back to human form. There she was, in her stylish outfit, with cat eyes and pointy ears poking through her long white hair. "Shit, shit, shit," she muttered.

Sleeping Guy, having stowed the wine in the trunk, assessed the immediate problem. Hurrying over to Christina, he pulled his sunglasses from the neck of his shirt and quickly popped them onto her. The pourer blinked, wondering if he really did see her eyes look so funny. Too late now, they were covered in dark sunglasses. But her ears! His eyes wandered to the tips of her ears, marveling at how pointedly inhuman they were.

"Hey, over here," Sleeping Guy whispered conspiratorially while pulling him away from the elf. The pourer allowed himself to be ushered away, yet he couldn't take his eyes off the strange woman. Christina hastily got into the passenger side of the car, locking the doors and praying that they could get out of there without any more incidents. "Listen. I know you saw the ear thing she has. She tries to hide it with her hair. I guess the wind took care of that, eh? Look, she hates for people to notice. It's best if you look away. She feels bad enough as it is."

"What is **wrong** with them?" he asked, perplexed and still a bit alarmed.

"Unfortunate ear piercing incident. Ever heard of keloids? She has 'em. In spades."

"Oh my god, the poor thing. Can't she have surgery to fix them?"

"Keloids, man," he reminded. "Bulbous scarring every time she gets cut. Surgery would probably make 'em worse."

"Oh my god. And she is so engaging. Such a shame."

"You got that right."

"But wait. Wasn't her hair much shorter when she first came in?"

"That's just the hairstyle, man. Look, I don't get women's fashion and probably neither do you." Sleeping Guy shrugged his shoulders and winked conspiratorially at the increasingly baffled pourer. "It's some ponytail thing that she tucks into the back of her blouse when she wants to sport short hair. She must have freed up her hair when she was in your vineyard."

"OK…" the confused pourer replied, trying to absorb everything that had just happened.

Sleeping Guy escorted the pourer back into the winery with more sad stories about disfiguring scars and the unfortunate piercing decisions of Christina's fictitious misspent youth.

He quickly returned to the car and backed out of the parking lot, spraying gravel and dust in their haste as they hightailed it out of there. Christina watched the winery recede in the side mirror and began to chuckle.

"What?" Sleeping Guy asked.

"Shit, I am just glad I kept my little elf shape instead of trying for my big mama human body. That would be a trick if I shrunk to this size. My clothes would have fallen off, and I would be a funky, naked elf standing outside in the vineyard for all the world to see. Not pretty." Sleeping Guy left that alone. That was one of those comments that had no right answer. Plus, she was his crush's mother. Didn't do to dwell on things like her nakedness.

"Regardless," she continued, oblivious to his inner commentary regarding her potential nakedness "I have to get back to Home Base quick and see to it that Seen has this wine to give to Ben." Just saying his name out loud like that made her feel weak and shaky. Between the use of magic and her emotional turmoil, it had already been a very big day for Christina/Mad Lavender.

The pourer returned to the safety of the wine-tasting room. All was quiet. He tried very hard to sort out what had just happened. Leaning against the counter and staring out the barn door to the vineyard, he struggled to recreate the events of the morning. But the memory kept slipping away every time he tried to pin it down, like errant puzzle pieces that didn't seem to fit. In the end, he decided that the Estate Vintage they just had tasted better get its alcohol content rechecked. It must be way too high. For it had resulted in a mild amnesia. Maybe they should rename it Date wine.

The Thrill of Victory and the Agony of Vegas

"So you see, *gentlemen*, we always comp our big winners with the best our casino has to offer. Step this way, please, to our special guest suite." The man was substantial in size and oily in demeanor, resulting in a subtle, violent nature. It seemed as though being pleasant was an effort for him. As if his true nature, his more comfortable skin, was that of a vicious bully. That his polite words were only a facade to the monster within.

He loomed massively above the three frail old men in their diaphanous togas, their thin, white ankles peeking out beneath the folds like fragile toothpicks. In contrast, the big man wore a shiny greenish suit, which stretched tightly across his massive chest. His shoes looked soft and, expensive, with crepe soles that seemed designed for quick pursuit. The three wizards were baffled. The man said nice enough things but seemed very threatening somehow. It was in part, due to the coldness in his eyes and the constant flexing of his hands, as if he couldn't wait to hit something. Or somebody. His words did not match his demeanor; neither did the room they had been escorted to.

As soon as they had won the big jackpot for the second time, the serving wenches disappeared and their luck ran out. The big man appeared and escorted them and their buckets filled with casino chips. Their entourage suddenly included two security guards, who appeared seemingly out of nowhere. *Magic?* Arthur whispered to the wizards as soon as the guards showed up. Demetrius and Albert simply shrugged their shoulders in reply. There suddenly was too much commotion to sort out magic from the mundane. All they really knew was that they were being herded quite quickly somewhere.

The three were escorted past the slot machines and though a plain door set flat against a busily wall-papered hall. It wasn't just any door, or any hallway. This one seemed hidden, away from the flow of the general public. You would never know the hall or the strange door in the middle of the hall were there, unless someone had pointed them out to you. And the door itself had some sort of mechanism that let it open only if one possessed the proper badge. Big Man just waived his badge by the seam in the door, and it popped right open. Just like that. The wizards noted the magical access while they were led down a blank and dingy hallway (no pretty lights or decorations) and into a plain, spare room. It contained little: a sagging couch and a table with a few mismatched chairs. The only item of any interest was a mirror that stretched across one entire wall. Well, it was interesting, only in that you could look at yourself rather than at the rather Spartan furnishings.

Big Man sat in the sturdiest of the chairs. This placed him at an advantage as the wizards had little option save sitting on the ratty couch. It made him appear taller than they, even while seated; they seemed scrunched, touching shoulder to shoulder in a pathetic heap. The two security guards placed themselves at the door to prevent a hasty exit. All three wizards had their buckets on the floor by their feet—the only shiny and pretty decorations in the dismal tableau.

"Comfy?" the big man asked.

Arthur used this as an opportunity to request, "Any serving wenches in this part of the inn?"

The security guards said nothing but were grimly amused. They tried to conceal a few slight smirks. Their fidgeting was quickly silenced by an icy look from the Big Man.

"Let's talk about how you won. We have seen it all and aren't fooled by your Three Stooges act." Big Man got down to the heart of the issue. Actually, in his own way, he was stalling. Getting down to the point for him meant hurting someone. And since he hadn't yet resorted to that, well, this was just stalling. He needed time for the techs to remove and take apart the slot machine to see how it had been tampered with. Once they knew they could proceed with his preferred option of communicating with his fists.

"But I thought we had been very clever with our ruse." Arthur was very confused. They had thought they had covered all contingencies and were fitting in nicely with the human realm. Bert nudged his cohort in the knee with his own, hoping the clueless Arthur would just shut up for once.

"Uh-huh." Big Man smiled. This was going to be easy. They were spilling already. "What was this *ruse?*"

"Demetrius, you tell him." Bert turned to the presumed ringleader of the three. After all, it was

Demetrius's idea in the first place to have rotating Elder Others and in Bert's mind, he was therefore responsible for all that subsequently occurred. Demetrius shifted uncomfortably on the couch, adjusting his toga for modesty's sake, unsure exactly, how to begin. His thoughts were rapid and disjointed regarding the matter of humans. It was difficult to pull together a reply, considering how his thoughts bounced like crazed hummingbirds inside his head.

Normally, they would divulge absolutely nothing to mere humans. The trouble was that these humans had already displayed a form of magic. They had two guards magically appear out of nowhere, and then the Big Man had magiked a door open. The three wizards already understood from their past encounters with the pesky human family that some people did possess a form of magic and that humans seemed more capable of understanding about the magical realm than they had previously thought. *What to do? What to do?* After a bit of head scratching and belt adjusting, Demetrius began, "Well, you see, we just wanted a little vacation from Other Camp. So we came here. Since it was your dress-up crazy holiday, All Hallows' Eve, we thought we had a better chance of fitting in. So we picked this time and this place. Plus, there is the added possibility of pumpkin ale at this time of year, so naturally, you see, this was the perfect opportunity for us. The problem was that nothing seems to operate in your realm without the magic of currency, that is to say, money. So we had to obtain some. Elder Bert here…" At this point Demetrius smiled at his partner in crime at the end of the couch. Bert smiled hopefully at the Big Man while pulling a thick, gold chain from his pocket. It was a backup item he thought useful in trading for currency, in case the gold watch was not enough. "...had the foresight to provide materials, which we traded for your currency. A sturdy, woman-like carriage driver was kind enough to help us make the trade for money as well as brought us here to obtain more through the clever use of your mechanical gadgets. Imagine a game that gives out your pretty chips. I mean, just spinning round and round on those dials was enough fun for me, but money as well? My, when one thinks of it, one would think *someone* was being a *very generous* host in this establishment!"

Demetrius smiled warmly at the Big Man. His partners smiled and nodded as well. Bert gave the Elder the high five for so masterfully distilling the events of the last few hours in such a concise fashion. "Back at you" was a bit clumsily returned owing to the fact "high five" was a new move they had just learned from Jacob and Enj. This gesture sorely needed more practice. But Bert was such a trendsetter; he always tried the new and unusual just to say he had.

Big Man had about had it. His patience was all but worn out with the three old men as he watched them attempt to correct the bungled high five by redoing it. There was a brief discussion among them about whether the hands simply slapped at each other or if they grasped in a brief handshake. Arthur attempted to high-five himself. He missed and nicked his own jaw. Big Man reached across the span and slapped their hands away, growling, "Shut up!"

There was stunned silence. The wizards were speechless at the thought of such gratuitous violence placed upon their persons. They watched as

Big Man took several deep breaths, in an attempt to regain control over the situation. "Tell me how you tampered with the machine. Just tell me that." His tone became quiet and menacing. A dread chill crept over the room—especially so for the men in dresses. They felt their skin creep and nether parts shrink.

Arthur looked hopefully at the Big Man "Ooh, very good! Scary magic. Tell me, have you thought about recruitment? We could use your particular magical intimidation at Other Camp."

"I. Am. Not. Going. Anywhere. And neither are any of you. Until you tell me how you fixed the machine."

Bert answered, since he had the most experience inside the mechanism. "Oh, we didn't fix the machine. It wasn't broken. Not at all. We simply rode the wheel thingies. A marvelously nauseating experience, wouldn't you say so, gentlemen?"

"And how did you ride the wheels?" *Now we get to the heart of the matter*, Big Man thought.

"We simply magiked ourselves very small. Now we only did this one at a time, mind you. We certainly did not want to hurt the interesting, rotating mechanism. We went round and round and round and—well like that, until it was someone else's turn inside. Thrilling actually, right boys?"

"Oh assuredly so."

"Lovely ride."

"Worth the wait."

"Especially so with the lovely serving wenches and all that ale."

"Yes, by the way, any of those lasses in this part of this inn?" Demetrius asked the security guards hopefully once again. The guards became very busy studying their feet.

During this entire exchange the security team had been fidgeting in earnest. The guards couldn't wait to see what the Big Man would do next with these yahoos. Besides the fact that they were all loony tunes, the old men seemed so child-like, so unaware that they could very well become another of those tragic missing persons cases that happened much too often in this town. The Big Man was presently inspecting his nails, quietly pondering his next move.

The way he saw it, were several problems with these wackos and their stories. Well, obviously they were either escapees from the Alzheimer's home, or they were great cons—maybe both. The first problem was that they had mentioned a taxi driver. She dropped them off there and would be one to know their whereabouts. That was not good, a living witness to their last known location. And it didn't do in this town to take a driver out. A cardinal rule around there was to take good care of the transportation trade. They brought in suckers like these guys, which in the usual case meant good business for the casino. So now the police had a credible witness should the three go missing and the authorities started asking around.

The alternative was to turn them over to the police, which, in a way, was good, as long as the casino could show evidence of machine tampering. But it was also bad. It brought up the second problem with these wise guys. The publicity around a casino manhandling three old guys in an advanced state of dementia would definitely turn off the retiree trade.

And the flocks of old coots and their ubiquitous tour buses did a lively trade around there. Imagine what the senior groups would do if they knew this casino treated old guys so badly. They would cross this stop off their tour list; that was what.

That was the problem with involving the police. Everything seemed so public.

A soft knock broke the tension in the room. One of the security guards opened the door a crack, briefly spoke to the person in the hall, and then gestured to the Big Man. He rose heavily from the chair and went outside to speak to the messenger.

"Machine's clean," was the message from the tech.

"No way," Big Man replied. "That slot hasn't delivered such a payday in years, much less two times in one day. There's got to be something."

"We checked, man. No abrasions or nicks inside the gadgetry. No signs of magnets or weights being added. Not even any sign that an apparatus had been inserted up the channel. Nothing. Looks clean of dust and grime even. Like someone wiped it inside with a dust cloth. Fully functional and assembly-line new, that's what it looks like." Big Man looked back at the old guys wedged into the couch. Presently, Albert was wiping a smudge off his tunic, generally tidying up the dusty cloth. He turned back to the tech in the hallway.

"How long have we had that one in service?"

"Years, man. It shouldn't be that clean, but it is."

"Yank it."

"Will do. But what about the video?"

"Well, what about it? Tell me exactly what you see." Big Man was stalling, thinking, trying to figure the best move for the casino—the one with the least amount of exposure.

"Well, a couple of times, there are three guys in the picture and, then there's only two and then there's three again. Like that. Oh yeah, sometimes the shot is super blurry, and then it clears up again. Also, it looks like the guys are talking at the machine. Yelling at it, even."

"Everyone with a jones for slots yells at their machines. They think they're dating it. Nothing new there…Take the video camera out of service. Put in a new one. Could be defective."

"Just like that? You gonna give them a pass?"

"What do you want me to do?" he yelled. Then realizing he was in a hallway and could be heard outside the passageway to the casino lounge, he tried to quiet himself. Big Man ran his meaty hands through his short hair, ruffling it and causing a slight dent in the gelled arrangement. He sighed. "The only thing we got is a bunged-up video that tells me one of them disappeared, crawled inside the machine, and give it a nice cleaning. You want to tell the bosses that? Do you? I didn't think so…Shit. Sounds like we gotta let 'em go."

Big Man reached the door to the holding room. He turned to the technician and added, "Get these guys a cab. Sounds like Lola May brought them here. Call her. Tell her to keep an eye on them. If they even go as far as walking into a casino on this strip, they're mine. Tell her our deal with her is off if I even hear about these guys again. I personally will take care of her and them if there's any more trouble. You got that?"

"Yup," the tech knew at these moments, the less said, the better. Big Man dismissed the tech and turned to reenter the room. A one-sided conversation was taking place. The wizards were asking the security guards lots of questions about serving wenches. They weren't answering. The old men, undaunted in their queries, changed tactics and began asking questions about where they might find pumpkin spice lattes—the full-fat kind. There was a flicker of interest from one of the guards who seemed to be prepared to respond. However, he quickly resumed his stoic demeanor as soon as he realized Big Man had entered the room.

"Gentlemen, I believe you were asking for a bar girl? A serving, uh…?" Big Man paused, trying to recall the words.

"Wench. A serving wench" Bert said, ever the linguist.

"OK. A wench. Well, I have called you a taxi. I think it's the same gal who brought you here. She can take you to a place where there are lots of wenches. Unfortunately, there is a slight fee."

"We have lots of your pretty chips; I am sure that will suffice, will it not?" Demetrius asked. Ever helpful, Arthur held out his entire bucket to the Big Man.

Big Man shook his head no, not wanting to be on videotape cashing in a bucket of the casino's chips. "Sadly, no. But I am sure that lovely gold chain will pay the fee for my call to secure transportation for you." Big Man held his hand out to Bert, who quickly fished the heavy gold jewelry out of his pocket. Delighted that he had brought a smile to the scary man's face, he asked, "Can we do anything else for you before we go?"

"Let's get a few things straight." Big Man tucked the chain into his suit pocket and patted the heavy weight of it gently as if to assess the value of it by its heft. "You did some funky weird things in my house today. We saw it but can't prove it. These nice security guards are going to help you cash in your chips, for a small service fee," he said, winking at the guards. They smiled back at him, for the first time dropping their serious demeanor. "...then I want you out of here. For good and forever. And don't even think of doing this hocus-pocus in any other casino on the strip. Because if you do..." He paused, leaning into their collective faces. "I will personally track you down, put the smack-down on you then leave you in a heap at the doorstep of whatever loony bin you broke out of. Do you understand?"

Much enthusiastic nodding all around. The gentlemen helped each other out of the sinking depths of the lumpy couch and after much toga rearranging, left the room with the security guards in order to cash in their chips and find the sturdy carriage driver waiting outside.

It was all smiles at the entrance of the casino as the three wizards made their goodbyes. The security guards each got c-notes for their troubles. This was not lost on cabdriver Lola May, who now saw that the guys were loaded with cash. As the guards made their way back into the casino, Elder Demetrius paused and reminded the gentlemen, gently chiding them for their lack of good manners,

"Fair trade, gents?"

"Oh, yes! Horrors, what were we thinking?"

"Quite so. Although we did clean the inside of their machine!" Arthur offered.

"Where are our manners? Cleaning the machine wasn't nearly enough!" Demetrius reminded. "It was a lovely afternoon. I think the rules of fair trade say we should give them a wee bit more than just a simple house cleaning."

All three raised their hands high, preparing to leave a small magical token of thanks for having had such an entertaining time in the casino as well as for the wenches. Bert was thinking primarily of the fun when the machine binged and clanged upon winning. Demetrius thought of the Big Man and how angry he would become, over nothing really. *Depression, it seems. Perhaps,* he thought, *something exciting would cheer him up.* Arthur thought of lattes. The pumpkin spice ones and how the security guards seemed to like them too.

The three wizards held their hands aloft, closed their eyes, and murmured their own separate incantations of thanks. There was a momentary blinding flash, and then all hell broke loose. Machines began pinging, bells ringing on all of the slot machines. Players screamed with joy, holding out hands, buckets, even ripping off T-shirts and turning them into makeshift sacks, in an attempt to catch all of the pretty chips that were simultaneously pouring out of every machine on the floor of the casino.

Big Man was rooted in the center of the gaming floor, stunned at the impossible scene happening all around him. He was beside himself, not knowing which machine to disable first. He was left turning around, and around, witnessing the disaster take place in every direction, unable to choose a direction to act. It was all chaos and mayhem. Security guards came running from all directions, closing in on Big Man to await his orders. Two security guards found extra-large coffees in their hands, unable to remember where or how they came to have them.

Upon hearing the uproar, the wizards smiled and nodded at each other from outside the casino. "Job well done!" they said to each other. "That should make them all happy," they agreed.

Their cab driver, however, was not convinced that all was well inside the casino. "Hey!" Lola May hollered at them from inside the cab, "Sounds like trouble. Let's get you out of here!" She was anxious to get these guys and their wads of cash out of harm's way, quick before security carted them off to the twilight zone. They scurried into the cab, and she sped off as quickly as traffic and the streaming hoards of pedestrians would allow. "You guys OK?" she asked while maneuvering her way through traffic.

"Oh, perfect. Everything is just perfect," Arthur said. "Any way you can find us some serving wenches now?"

"I know just the place for special guys like you." Lola May smiled looking in the rearview mirror at them. It was going to be a very good day after all.

Smoke and Mirrors

"Marvelous tavern, wouldn't you say so, lads?" Bert was soon feeling mellow and expansive. The room was dimly lit and full of smoke from competing cigars. The Elders were seated at a tiny table that abutted a wide, elevated ramp, which awkwardly bisected the length of the room. This made table service difficult, as there were no shortcuts across the room. The serving wenches had to maneuver all around this ramp, juggling their trays of food and drink around the tightly arranged tables. There was little leg room, as most of the cramped tables either abutted the ramp or were snuggled next to semiprivate booths along the perimeter of the wall. A curtain covered one end of the ramp. Upright brass poles were situated randomly along the length of the platform.

The food was, if not wonderful, at least in ample portions. Lots of it was fried. That was good. Fried food tasted so good with the lovely cigars the tobacco wench provided. Ale was everywhere. Alas, no pumpkin ale, but lots of other options, which they were partaking in quite freely. Strangely, they were made to pay each time they were served rather than waiting until the end of the evening. No matter, they all had wads of cash stuffed in the pockets of their gowns. And in a pinch, Bert probably had more jewelry hidden somewhere inside the folds of his gown.

The lights dimmed. The other gentlemen in the tavern began whistling and stomping their feet. "Will there be a reel?" Arthur asked, watching to see if fancy footwork was required.

"No, no, I believe the entertainment will be musical, perhaps a quartet." Bert looked around, assessing the noise level of the room. "A very loud quartet."

The curtain on the far wall fluttered. The men in the room held their collective breaths, waiting for the vision behind the curtain to appear.

Suddenly, she was there. A scantily clad young woman with a depressed attitude, strutting energetically down the ramp, her lady parts nearly exposed and jumbling wildly. "Oh dear," Demetrius said worriedly, anxious for the young lady's reputation.

The other two wizards watched in awe as the young woman performed feats of athleticism they had not thought possible with the human form. This nubile creature made very good use of the several poles strategically placed along the ramp. She was by all accounts quite fit and flexible. All the while, she seemed utterly unconcerned about her various fleshy parts hanging out most inappropriately.

"I had no idea one's back could bend in such a way, did you Bert?" Arthur was agog.

They all were. She strutted off the ramp but was soon replaced by another barely attired young woman. One by one, each performer was bold in her (lack of) clothing and her angry, pouting poses. *They seem so sad*, Bert thought. *And cold*. "Someone should magic them some decent clothing before they take a serious chill," Demetrius suggested.

Dimly, the old men had vague remembrances of the true meaning of the dancing and the jiggling parts. But that was a millennium ago and none of the gentlemen had any inclination to go down those old roads again. So they focused instead on alternative explanations for the curious behavior of the angry amazon-like females.

Other patrons were waving dollar bills about, trying to get the dancers' attention. This was absurd to the wizards. These girls didn't have pockets to hold the money. Besides, the other wenches on the floor were better at taking food orders. The pathetic creatures on the ramp had none of the little pads and pens the usual serving wenches used to take down orders. And they seemed so pouting and angry that it was unseemly to ask them to take an order. In short, these nearly naked, depressed wenches were absolutely useless for anything important.

"Perhaps they are on display for adoption purposes," Arthur suggested.

"Brilliant!" Demetrius replied, taking up Arthur's train of thought.

"Oh, I see," Bert said, for once, slow on the uptake. "So you are saying that they once had nice sturdy wench jobs, but now are too weak and poor (hence, no clothing) to do anything useful. So they are paraded around up there on that walkway, hanging on these poles like trussed geese in the butcher's window in the hopes that someone will pity them and take them home. Well, how sad!"

"And the gentlemen here are waving money around bidding for them. My, isn't that nice of them," Arthur commented, smiling benevolently at the men in the audience, imagining them to be kind benefactors to the poor.

"We should get one."

"Oh, yes, we should."

"We will feed her the finest fried foods and ale, and we will magic her some warm clothing. It will be fair trade for the lovely time we have had in this tavern."

"Yes, let's. But just in case, shall we ask Lola May, our carriage driver, what the rules are for this transaction? We certainly don't want to stand out peculiarly in any way, now do we?" They agreed with Bert that fitting in was key. They adjusted their togas, brushing the cigar ash off their laps, so as to look more presentable and fit in with the crowd. Stroking their beards thoughtfully, they decided to leave the lovely Tavern of Waifs (as they dubbed it) and went out to the curb to speak with their driver about how to transact an adoption.

Lola May was waiting outside the gentlemen's club. She would wait all night if necessary. The cabbie was not going to leave these guys for anything—at least not until all that cash ran out. Screw the other fares for the evening. The three old men were a gold mine. And after they got their buzz on in the gentlemen's club, she knew just the "wenches" who would satisfy whatever itch they need scratching.

They tumbled into the back of the cab, smelling like spilled beer and nasty cigars. One burped quietly behind his hand, adding to the odoriferous miasma hovering inside the vehicle. "Pardon," he said.

Whew, the driver thought. *Smells like they are ready for my girls. Time to take out my binder-o-babes*, as she referred to it. "Boys, ready for some fun with my gals?"

"Well actually, we wanted to talk to you about that." Demetrius leaned forward, talking to the back of the cabbie's much shellacked hair. *A helmet for protection*, he thought, peering closely at how the strands of hair were somehow welded together by a glue-ish substance. *We are so lucky to have her to keep us safe. She thinks of everything!*

"You guys want to look at my picture book again?" She pulled the book out from the glove box on the console. Handing it off to Demetrius, she drove aimlessly around while the gentlemen made their pick.

"Are these waifs for adoption?" Albert asked, hoping to clarify the situation.

"Oh, I get it. You guys like the sugar-daddy role. Fine, fine. Adopt away. Rent 'em even. Buy only the parts you want! Ha!" she barked a big laugh, cracking her own self up.

They murmured among themselves at the options available. Some of the pictures looked faded, as though the color had been bleached out of them over time. Those waifs actually were clothed the most. Poufy skirts, maid costumes, ruffles, and lace were the costumes du jour of the faded photos.

"Too well off," Arthur suggested. "I mean, just look at the layers of clothing on them!"

"Yes, yes. In order for us to really help one of the truly underprivileged, we need to find the one with the least amount of clothing," Demetrius said, rifling through the binder, unable to clearly focus because of the quantity of ale they had just consumed.

"Here, let me," Bert said, taking the book to study the pictures more closely. Lola May watched the three men closely from her rearview mirror. Even though they were studying her book carefully, they didn't seem exactly hot to trot. It was more of a clinical review. It wasn't the first time she had wondered about the quality of her girls. Some of them were definitely on the verge of retirement. And the ones who were nice and young weren't exactly Grade-A prime. More like B-minus. That was how she got them so cheap. She sighed inwardly, hoping someone in her binder would float their boats.

"Ah. Here's one!" Bert handed the book over to Demetrius. Arthur leaned in to check the waif out.

"Yes, so little clothing!"

"Straps of some sort. That's all that's left of her gown!"

"And so angry looking!" Arthur was a bit concerned about that.

"Well, wouldn't you be angry if they made you sleep in a stable. It's an outrage!" Bert heatedly defended his choice.

"My apologies, Bert, but I don't see any animals about her person. I mean, it's not exactly as though she could hide a pig in her pocket. She doesn't have a pocket, don't you know!" Demetrius was confused.

"But you see, she has a whip—a crop of some sort. I am sure that's all she has to fend off the encroaching farm animals crowding in the stables with her. Poor dear." Bert was fully engrossed in the amazing tale he had spun by making a few important assumptions about the wretched thing. Since he was usually so savvy about things human, they all agreed.

"Let's adopt the shepherdess!" Arthur handed the book back to the front of the cab to Lola May. She one-handed it onto her lap and saw the photo of the lean, hard-bodied black woman with a towering afro. She was dressed in thin straps of leather, studded with metal; holding a whip in one hand and a riding crop in the other. She had a decidedly fierce look to her, as though her picture alone could beat you down in staring contest.

Lola May was stunned at the choice. The S & M queen, Honeysuckle? Her? Dear god! But then it did make a sort of sense. None of the usual types seemed to interest them. Maybe their tastes ran a bit kinky. At any rate, of all of her girls, Honeysuckle could handle herself best in the weirdest situations. And these guys were off-the-charts weird.

"Fine, gentlemen. But I warn you, she don't give no group rates."

"Oh, that's fine. We only want one waif."

"Say what?" Lola May was getting more confused by the minute. She actually had to slow down her driving to try to decode what these guys really wanted. Granted, they were being circumspect. That was part of the trade. But these guys were really out there in their requests.

"One waif at a time—no groups." Bert was a little confused himself that she would think they would need more than one waif. *Mercy, it would probably take all three of them their best efforts to turn this one lost lamb into a healthy, dressed, useful wench.* But then again, this carriage driver had many concurrent responsibilities—driving, guarding her fellow travelers and finding homes for foundlings, all at the same time! *No wonder this simple request was baffling to her.*

"So you are saying that you only want Honeysuckle and that you will all take your turn one at a time with her?"

"Well, I would say we each have special gifts we could provide her. Wouldn't you say so, Demetrius?" Arthur was attempting to be helpful again. Actually, it had been a while since he had contributed anything of value to the party, and he felt it was his turn to speak.

"Fine then. One at a time. She'll sort out the fee. Let me call her on my cell." Lola May pulled a tiny cell phone from the ample cleavage nosing its way out of her Hawaiian shirt. She discreetly wiped the sweaty phone dry and began to dial with her long thumbnail while driving one-handed. It was a trick she had perfected over many years of cruising this strip. Drive-dialing while somehow avoiding hitting the ubiquitous random groups of pedestrians who never crossed at the intersections was a mad skill.

"Hey, its Lola May...uh huh, yeah. Right now. Three of them. Nah, don't worry; they're like, uh..." Lola May paused, studying the wizards in her rear-view mirror, in an attempt to find the right words to characterize these guys. "Amish. Age-ed. Aged Amish guys, I think...OK. Meet you at the motel in five." With that, the cabbie hung up on her girl.

The wizards knew she was talking on a cell phone to the waif. Marissa, the new interim Supreme Elder Other, had tried to introduce them to this piece of human magical memorabilia before they left on vacation. Try as they might, they couldn't get the hang on all of the buttons. Besides, their raven would wreak havoc on it, periodically stealing it from them when they weren't looking in order to peck it to death.

Really, they were so glad to put that damn crow into retirement. Between the noise and the random excrement and the destruction, it was too much sometimes. Marissa told them she would put it to work doing sentry duty outside Other Camp. *Good riddance*, they all thought, concurrently reminded of the crow and its destructive idiosyncrasies.

The cabbie brought them to a motel situated on a street several blocks from the strip. It ran parallel to the major street, but in an area just far enough away to be seedy and tired looking- bereft of the usual glitz and glamour of the casinos on the main drive. The sound of airplanes droning overhead was loud enough to get you to look up about every fifteen minutes, as they were very close to the airport landing strip. The planes loomed overhead and dropped out of the sky from the mountain range, quickly losing altitude as they made their final descent right over the motel.

The parking lot was peppered with a sparse selection of much-used cars and trucks sporting rusted truck beds. The cinderblock structure boasted two floors—the ground floor and the "penthouse" level. Owing to the fact that the motel was in the flight path of the airport, the word *penthouse* strictly applied to the second floor—the highest they could build without causing a collision with the incoming flights. The entire structure was painted a utilitarian grayish color in that high-gloss enamel designed to highlight the bubbling, flaking paint layers underneath.

Lola May double-parked in front of the U-shaped building by a sign on the wall that said "Manager." She seemed quite used to this parking maneuver, quickly sweeping her hulking vehicle to within inches of the front door. It was as though she had performed this feat hundreds of times before and could navigate the U-turn without any conscious thought.

And, in fact, that was exactly correct. She had not performed this feat hundreds of times—rather, she had done it thousands of times before. This was her equivalent of a bunny ranch. She had a standing arrangement with the manager. He held several rooms just for her and her trade. A flat fee was paid every month for that privilege. Her job was to "check in" using a fictitious name, apprising the manager of the type of patrons arriving for the day, hour, night, whatever. That way, he knew what to expect and when to call in housekeeping after the booking. The room would be left unserviced during the stay of the gentlemen, even if they were there more than one night. He didn't want his staff to inadvertently walk in on some hijinks taking place. Lola May's girls would leave the door ajar after the event, as it were. That was a sign to the cleaning staff that all was clear to enter.

They also could call him should there be an out-of-control customer. There were only a few times he had had to intervene; his nightstick and brass knuckles took care of most of the rowdy fellas. After all, if there were funny things going on, it was usually handled by a swift knock to the back of the head. Rarely were the customers facing the door, and therefore, they were easily surprised by the wily old manager. The girls were very grateful for his protection as well. They often showed him their thanks in very generous and kind ways. Hint: they didn't bake him cookies.

Lola May informed the manager that Honeysuckle would be entertaining three Amish gentlemen, inclining her head to the old men waiting patiently in the back of her vehicle. The manager took a look through his dusty front office window to size these guys up. He knew he wouldn't have any trouble with them. Sure, there were three of them, but, jeesh, they were old and this was Honeysuckle. She came with her own weapons. And they were Amish. He could see that for sure because of their long hair and beards. They sure dressed funny too. Didn't Amish guys wear weird clothes and make quilts? Yeah, these guys would be easily handled by the Amazon queen called Honeysuckle.

The cabbie installed the three wizards on the second floor, or the penthouse, as she called it, with strict instructions to wait there for the wench. When they inquired about the adoption fee, she just shook her head, telling them that the wench would negotiate all of that.

The motel room wasn't much of an improvement over the special guest suite they had been escorted to at the casino. It had the same drab, slightly seedy quality that the couch and mismatched chairs in the previous room had had. It too had a mirror along the wall opposite the lumpy bed. The bedspread sported a jaunty flame pattern of beige and green. It had a funny smell and had an unpleasant crispy feel when one sat on it.

"Oh, the poor girl. To think she has to stay here," Demetrius said, sizing up the decidedly inelegant surroundings.

"Now, don't be judgmental, Demetrius. After all this may be a big step up from the stables," Bert tried to put a nice spin on things. *But really*, he thought, *it is rather cramped and dismal in here. And there is in fact a peculiar, odd smell about it. Perhaps just a little magic would spruce things up.* "Let's give this a make-over!" he suggested to the men.

This, they all heartily agreed to. It would be good for her to see how they wished to welcome her to her new home. Besides, it would be so much nicer if they had comfortable chairs to sit on and perhaps a gaming table like at the casino. Arthur strongly suggested thrones for the three of them, but that was nixed owing to lack of space. Instead, they agreed on plush comfy easy chairs with lovely tufted footstools. And the bed, well, what an atrocious thing for the waif to sleep on! Now she might not think it was too bad, being a marked improvement from the stables and all, but they thought something tall and canopied would improve her lot in life considerably—with pretty velvet covers and satin sheets.

At first, they had no idea what to do with the privy. And the smell. They did, however, wish to improve the cleanliness and the pervasive tinny odor it gave off. Remembering Mad Lavender and her penchant for her namesake, they decided bundles of fresh lavender tucked in the corners of the room might calm the waif's agitated nerves. And new towels would be nice. The big ones that wrapped all around you twice would do just fine.

Bert carefully closed the blackout curtains for privacy's sake. Each wizard took a corner of the room, Arthur was given the duty of the privy. They took their positions and, raised their hands. The room grew blindingly bright and, then faded to the usual murky daylight.

The transformation was stunning. Lush, brocade draperies hung heavily against the freshly painted yellow walls. They thought a Tuscan look of jewel tones would be welcoming for the lass. The bed was tall, its canopy reaching the ceiling, and draped with purple velvet with green and rust-colored tapestry pillows. The carpet was soft and thick, the kind that just begged for you to slip off your shoes and squiggle your toes into the ample plush pile. "Come see, come see the privy!" Arthur cried, so excited to show off his creation.

It was a thing of wonder. Arthur had stretched the limits of space and elongated the privy to include a water basin that sported a waterfall of fresh water filling it. The flooring was a stone mosaic set in a fleur-de-lis pattern. A rock wall covered one side with an ornately framed mirror in its center. Large lavender and rosemary (Arthur's personal favorite herb) shrubs grew in piles of gravel in the corners of the room. Songbirds sang in the branches of the brush, trilling along with the lulling sounds of the waterfall. In the corner stood a large claw-footed tub, fresh with warm, soapy water and floating rose petals.

The commode was an actual throne. Well, he really wanted one and got it after all. It had a lovely ornate tassel mounted from the ceiling that when pulled worked the flushing mechanism. There was gold gilding and (where practical) soft padding with tufted velvet pillows. It was a thing of wonder.

"Er, Arthur, not to criticize, but do you think perhaps the privy is a wee bit too big for the place? I mean, it really requires a continual flow of magic to keep it expanded beyond its original dimensions." Demetrius tried to be kind. After all, Arthur had done a fine job on such a pedestrian site.

"Oh dear. She will never be able to manage the magic necessary when we are gone, will she?" Arthur pursed his lips and blew out a rude sound in vexation. "Ah well,'" he said waving his hand as though to say good-bye to the bathroom of wonder. In an instant, it reduced down to its original proportions. The flooring retained its regal mosaic, but the birds disappeared. The shrubbery shrank to the size of floral arrangements sitting on the marble counter. The rock wall and waterfall basin remained, now only a tiny miniature of their previous grandeur. The tub sat glumly in the corner, as though pouting from its newly petite proportions.

The throne however remained the same. Arthur glared stubbornly at his cohorts, arching his bushy eyebrow darkly, daring them to object to the royal chair. This was as extreme a pique as Arthur could muster, as he normally was most amiable and compliant. But really, he firmly believed, in the matter of the bathroom, anything that would enhance one's output, as it were, should be allowed.

There are a fair number of magical Fairfolk that suffer in the excrement department. Trolls, for example. I mean really, you try being frozen into a stone for several millennia and then turn into flesh to try to evacuate you inners. Not easy waking up all the internal processes necessary to accomplish the job. They suffer, often in silence. And fairies. It's a little-known fact that owing to their atrocious and unhealthy eating habits, they endure a variety of intestinal disorders, a lot of which would be cleared up if they just would stop drinking so much mead and eating spoiled food. A throne is just a nice comfy spot on which to park oneself and deal with those types of thorny voiding matters. One *should* have one's very own throne if it would help the matter along.

Along those lines of thinking, who knows what manner of bathroom accommodations the waif had living in the stables? The least she should have was a lovely padded and gilded seat on which to think deep thoughts. Arthur was determined to let the poor creature at least have that.

"Fair enough, fair enough, dear friend," Bert said placatingly. After all, his compatriot rarely took a stand. And this, although it seemed to take up a lot of space in the small room, was not a matter on which to argue. Let the wench have a throne, even if the only time she felt queenly was when her bum was hanging out.

"Well, lads, what now?" They were touring the redone room, touching the lovely accessories, rear-ranging a pillow or two as they went, until they ended up at the small gaming table. They parked themselves in their comfy ergonomic chairs and stared at one another, waiting for an idea. "We could while away the time playing cards?" Bert inquired, fishing in the depths of his hidden pockets. Eventually, he retrieved a candy wrapper and, something furry and lintish, which he disposed of into another pocket after making a disgusted face. Eventually, he fished out a set of antique playing cards. These were thick, made of a type of pressed board, and decorated in gold filigree. The suits were Elizabethan in nature, all the queens looking like they suffered from receding hairlines. The kings and princes looked sinister, with thin, pointy goatees, which looked like they would be painful upon contact. Despite the ruffs and jewelry, they were a sorry-looking bunch. Nonetheless, they were quite usable as playing cards. Bert shuffled the thick cards and began dealing them to his friends.

Outside the motel, a small, older-model German car pulled into the lot, right below the outer stairs to the second floor. It was a gray, nondescript vehicle that appeared to be, although dated, quite well maintained. A woman stepped out wearing a long khaki raincoat. She had a scarf on her head and had large dark glasses resembling safety goggles. She wore very high heels that strapped up her leg, the tops of which disappeared somewhere in the raincoat territory. A duffel bag was slung heavily across one shoulder, and she tilted, ever so, to accommodate its weight.

Ascending the stair she dug into her coat pocket for the room key. As she reached the darkened alcove at the door, she quickly dropped the duffel, pulling out a large horse whip and riding crop. These she placed in her left hand while she maneuvered herself out of the raincoat. The glasses were dropped in the bag along with the wadded-up coat. Her hair sprang out in all directions once she pulled off the scarf. It seemed to want to eject from her head in protest at having been forced into scarf submission. Once the duffel was zipped and her outside clothes were securely stowed, she straightened, adjusting the many leather patches and skimpy straps making up her strangely lethal-looking teddy. Placing a whip in each hand, she softly jiggled the key in the lock, getting ready for her big entrance.

Surprise was pivotal. Although it did not sound as though the TV was on (that was always the best for masking the door-unlocking sounds), she did hear the gentlemen talking rather loudly about "the rules."

She'd show them the rules all right. She began speaking before the door was fully opened.

She used her dominant voice, big, black, and in charge; she threw open the heavy motel room door. "What's your game bitches?" she barked.

There was a brief pause as the gentlemen beheld the sight that was Honeysuckle the dominatrix standing before them.

"Well, it's Whist right now, but I am quite sure we could use a fourth!" Bert said, smiling.

"Holy shit on a stick!" she cried, dropping her whips, her act all but forgotten as she surveyed the newly elegant room.

The Big Bang Theory and Other Fantasies

"Stay with me, Enj. Remember what they taught us in Other School?" Jay was pacing in the weeds. Enj, Seen and he had just finished a feeding. Enj needed to eat after working some big magic with Marissa, and Seen needed to fuel up before leaving to find renegade Ben. Jay went along with them in his gargoyle form because he knew his pals liked a wingman during feeding. You kind of lose yourself in the gore and tend to ignore your surroundings. Good to have someone with his wits about him to watch for trouble while you gorge on fresh venison.

There were certain perks about being an Other. Being able to change your form was one of them. Even though they all were technically Others-in-training, they still were allowed to magic themselves into any creature they chose. It was considered a type of practiced skill, since a bit of Other spying had to go on in areas of intense magical usage. It helped them to find out who the culprits were. Careful of that familiar, or perhaps that ever-present squirrel. They just might be an Other in disguise, attempting a magical audit of you.

Enj generally stayed with his Enjie-gargoyle look. Jacob split his time between gargoyle and human. Seen was just Seen, worried that if he changed his look, he might be forgotten. At least this way, with his elvish body, leathery green gargoyle wings, and a decidedly gargoyle hand, people would remember him.

The three had just finished a big feed in a remote field in a rural part of the coastal foothills. These consisted of rolling, golden hills, dotted with oak and manzanita. The elevation was higher than the Bay Area, as they were at the foot of the Sierra Nevada mountain range, a series of mountains that bisected the length of California. The land there was too low to be in the snow line but too high up for much in the way of habitation. The major population in this area consisted of some hearty cattle, who quickly skedaddled as soon as they caught the scent of the three predators, along with herds of mule deer. So by process of elimination, venison was on today's menu. The equivalent of gargoyle fast food. They ran fast, they caught them quickly, and they scarfed them down easy. Really fast food.

Enj and Seen were feeling the usual post feeding remorse. All they really wanted to do was to clean up in a nearby creek, allowing the tumbling icy mountain waters to flush away the remains of the dinner that they all wore. But Jay was on a roll. He wouldn't let them leave until he had told them his entire chain of thought. He strode up and down the tiny alpine meadow, waving his hands for emphasis and fluttering his wings in his excitement. He thought he might have found a way to avoid all of this annihilation business and wanted to run it by the two smartest people he knew.

"It's been in front of us all along. I mean, I can't believe no one else has connected the dots before." Jay wiped some blood off his cheek, waving a horsefly away. His wings slapped it down, midair. The fly dropped dead, landing heavily on the ground. The wings high-fived each other by knocking their tips together.

"Hurry up, dude. I am gross." Enj sprawled on the dry grass, belly firm and hard, filled with dinner. His hands were sticky, the blood quickly drying in an unpleasant cakey way. He really couldn't think when he was all icked-out like that. But when Jay was on a roll, there was no stopping him. He and his sister were a lot alike in that way. No matter how long this took or how many flies accumulated on his scaly skin. Enj had to tag along for the ride. Seen quietly hunkered down in the weeds, listening carefully to the blue gargoyle. He was honored to be included in this most important discussion, especially since Jay had indicated that he might play a pivotal role in testing the theory.

"So, in the beginning," Jay resumed his line of thought.

Enj groaned. *This is gonna be a long one.* He sighed to himself. He crossed his sticky arms and used them as a pillow as he lay face down in the dirt, preparing to endure however long this was going to take.

"Nice, Enj," Jay chided. "Anyway, so in the beginning, there was no annihilation, right? Just a bunch of Fairfolk running around using too much magic. The magical net got wonky in spots—"

"Developed a bubble, a blister if you will, threatening to burst, creating a large leak in the net whereby all magic would run out," Seen added in an attempt to be helpful and thus speed things along. He was feeling the need to get going and couldn't for the life of him figure out why Jay needed to discuss this right now.

"Right, so they all realized something had to be done to mend this big, honking magical zit. But the real question is, do you pop it or just a dab a little Clearasil on it?"

"Must we do this? A zit? Grotesque," Enj mumbled into his arm.

"Clear-a-what?" Asked Seen.

"Never mind, just listen. The Others here at camp tell us we pop the zit; we annihilate everything and everyone in the area to release the pressure, right? That's why everyone is so scared of us. They think we are friggin' magical Grim Reapers. They hate us. They fear us."

"We never get invited anywhere——" Seen complained. Jay just looked at him, pondering briefly, the depths of his nerdiness. Presently, he continued, "But what if we just have to treat the area—a little magical ointment to take down the swelling? I mean, the original Fairfolk didn't annihilate anyone. Sure, some people had to give up their magical abilities, become human and leave the area, but that was it. Isn't that way better than blowing everything up?

Besides, when you blow up an area, you then have to magically camouflage the place so humans don't figure it out. Isn't that adding even more magic to an already unstable location?"

"Yeah, but, if that's true, why hasn't someone else figured it out before?"

"Ooh, ooh, I know!" Seen said, raising his hand in the hopes that he would be called upon to answer.

Both Jay and Enj paused quizzically, wondering what world this guy existed in.

"Yes?" teacher Jay said.

"Because it's all about power! The Others need to maintain their power over all of us to make sure we obey. The bigger the blowup, the scarier they seem. That's ultimate control. So why do the easy thing when something big and showy would make more of an impact?"

"Yeah, but if this is true," Enj sat up, now fully invested in the conversation, "they take big risks with our very existence by over magiking an already weak area. That's just wrong."

"I told you some of these guys have mental issues." Jay smiled, happy that his friends were trying the new theory on for size.

"So what do we do about it now?"

"Well, we test my theory. We identify an area where too much magic is being used. Then, instead of creating some sort of catastrophe, we remove the magical culprits from the area to see if the net will repair itself. Maybe take away their magic, even. We really have nothing to lose. If it looks like it isn't working, we can just go to plan B—annihilation. This requires that Mari, you Enj, and I work together on this. We'll quietly see what's what with our plan."

"And my special role?" Seen asked, sure that once again he would be left out in the cold, or at worst, given a token job on the pretense of helping. A pity job. He could smell pity jobs a mile away. It was what always happened to him.

"You have to find Dad and bring him home safely. Then we are going to use your special seeing powers to monitor the magical net for areas of weakness.

You would know before anyone else if Houston has a problem," Jay explained.

"Oh, Houston is fine," Seen said, in the hopes of clarifying. "Although I am a little concerned about Las Vegas."

"Figure of speech, man, figure of speech," Enj clarified. "But seriously, if you think Vegas is using too much magic, maybe we could try our theory there."

"Vegas might be good," Jay said. "But Seen, you job is to find Dad."

"I shall," Seen said standing up and dusting his pants off. He straightened his shoulders, looking most sincere and geeky, having been given a very important task in the great scheme of things. "First, I will clean up; then I will track your father using my vision of the net. I will look for areas where magic is being used. And then I shall focus on searching those pockets. I will keep checking one by one until I find where he and the trolls are. Meanwhile, I will be practicing my seeing skills so that I will be ready to experiment with you when I return."

Seen was amazed. These two were treating him like an equal, actually giving him a critical job in the mission. His heart swelled to bursting in his chest.

Steady, boy, his inner self cautioned. *They might be playing you for a fool.*

Oh, just shut up and get out of my head, Seen curtly reprimanded himself.

Well, really. I am going dark now, and I may never return. So quickly you replace me with real friends. Remember, real friends can be fickle. I, on the other hand, have always been there for you. Just a warning…

Seen shrugged off this inner dialogue of nagging doubts and prepared to complete his very important mission—that is, finding Ben. His wings grew anxious. They were terribly impatient. And really, they had been good for so long, waiting to fly free. They sensed the elf's excitement, noting his rapid heartbeat.

This kind of inner emotional turmoil was highly unusual for their dour elf. His wings began fanning him, urging him in the direction of the stream. Cold water might snap him out of it, they reasoned. Failing that, they planned on slapping him. He staggered off along the edge of the meadow, his wings waving him along, parachuting him over to the water. They were as anxious as the elf to get the search underway. Perhaps then, after a brief dunking in the chilly waters, the excited young elf would be rid of the vapors he seemed to be experiencing. Wings are so helpful in a pinch. Or so they thought.

The Friendly Skies of the Sierra Nevada's

It was glorious soaring in the clear, crisp mountain air, so close to the treetops. Seen was flying at a rather low altitude to best search for areas of magical disturbance. From the ground, he looked like a peculiar elf dangling beneath an enormous set of leathery wings. If one peered closely, the elf's right hand was visibly larger and deadlier in appearance. His right hand had claws which hung heavily in the air, dragging against the wind. His left hand looked harmless and soft.

But if one was a human, the mental image would instantly scramble to resemble a large, ungainly turkey vulture. The human would dismiss the image, perhaps shuddering slightly while thinking of what kind of carcass that large thing was in search of. Fortunately, there were few humans in this part of the mountains. It was too remote for habitation. The railroad didn't even cross this part of the range.

Granite boulders seemed to sprout up from the rocky slopes like gigantic Easter eggs. Pine trees and conifers of all sorts were the vegetation of choice. On a warm day, the heat from the sun and the rocks would scent the air with the perfume of the pine oil. The streams were icy, consisting of runoff from the higher- altitude snow melt. The water rushed noisily over the boulders, making spectacular waterfalls as it hurriedly sped away from the ragged slopes toward the placid rivers far away in the flatlands.

Besides the geography and the gentle swirl of the magical net as it languidly poured over the rocky terrain, there really wasn't anything of interest to see. Occasionally, a territorial bird of prey would dart from the tree line, aggressively swooping toward Seen in order to warn him off from its nest. But that was about it. The search eventually grew boring. Seen began to look for a place to make camp for the night.

Suddenly, he noticed a change in the net. It stretched thinly over an area, as though it had lost some of its magic and was vainly attempting to cover the same distance with less of itself. It didn't exactly constitute a bubble or blister in the net, but it was interesting nonetheless. It was obvious that some magic had been used there recently, and the net was working to repair itself from the activity.

He landed with a slight stumble, owing to the uneven ground and his cumbersome backpack. The wine bottle sloshed heavily inside the bag, slightly squashing the rest of its contents. He had landed in a small mountain meadow, flattened by some past glacial migration. Millennia ago, large glaciers cut their way through these mountains, leaving exposed layers of rocks and making deep cuts through the uplifted range. In its wake, it had left rubble—huge boulders were dragged along the bottom of the ice floe, scouring the ground and making deep rents in the earth.

Although eons had passed since the last glaciation, the wild and untouched land seemed like it had been freshly scored from a newly passing glacier.

Seen righted himself as he landed; his wings billowed out behind him to stop his forward momentum, which would have smashed him into a large rock. He steadied himself against the granite, quietly surveying his surroundings. It was quiet, but not unnaturally so.

The birds were still and silent, assessing whether this new intruder was friend or foe. But he was aware of their presence, nonetheless. All of his years as a sentry made him acutely aware of the creatures of all sizes in his midst. Small things—large ants, tiny mice—scurried, disturbing the pine needles as they searched for places to hide from the elf. Anything bigger than themselves they considered dangerous. And he was plenty big to their frame of mind. A cricket sprang closer to him—acting as sentry for all other creatures in the vicinity. Seen ignored it, allowing it to hop away unmolested. It reported to the population hiding in the brush that this was not a serious predator. A doe ventured quietly from behind a tree. Picking up the faint scent of the venison Seen had just eaten, she quickly fled back into the dense brush so as to hide her young. *Not a predator?* she chided the cricket. *You should smell the deer he has just eaten. He is virtually wearing it! We really need to get a better sentry*, she amended.

Seen sat down to survey his surroundings. Besides the usual animal activity, (and he was rather sad that as a by-product of being a hybrid elf/gargoyle, deer were now afraid of him), he did not sense magic being presently used there. But it had been. Recently.

This, he knew because the ground was so disturbed. It was as though large boulders had simply picked up and walked away, leaving the raw and loamy earth they had sat on exposed, new, and reddish against the rest of the dark ground. *Trolls*, he thought.

He stood, and while viewing the pattern of the raw earth, he noticed that a small campfire had recently been made. Ash and the remains of charred logs, piled in a pyramid shape, showed that the fire had burned hotly not too long ago.

In the interest of recycling, he made a fresh fire where the old one had recently burned, using the remaining fire material. He hunkered down by the fire, his wings spreading like a loose blanket around him. He rested, idly pondering which direction to take for the next leg of this journey. He had a feeling he was close to the dad, so the next phase of the search should be fairly short.

Since he was done searching for the day and technically had nothing to do, he decided to kill time in his favorite way: meditating—or rather, meditating in such a way that the magical net thought he was ignoring it. It seemed easier to read when Seen pretended not to be staring. As though it were a shy and demure creature, not really liking being in the limelight. It only glowed brightest when fully ignored.

So Seen sat, concentrating on his breathing. Slower and slower did his rate of breathing go, until it was simply a few soft breaths every few minutes. Eventually, when it seemed as though he scarcely needed to breathe at all, he opened his eyes. And there it was.

Although he could naturally sense the net around him, this was a completely different view of it. This was the spectacle of the net he never tired of seeing. It was a swirling, vibrant fluid, moving all around him. It undulated thickly in the air, briefly eddying around a living creature, say, the errant grasshopper, testing it for wholeness and magical capacity, before it moved languidly to its next subject. As it left its evaluation of the insect, the grasshopper rubbed its legs together, in order to remove the skittery itchiness the magic had left behind. Soon, it flowed thickly, slowly savoring its favorite creature in the alpine valley, Seen. It gently caressed him, petting his hair, flowing like a viscous, sparkling meringue down the length of his wings. It tickled. It tingled with energy.

Not long ago, Seen had thought this was the closest thing (besides his busy mind, his witty alter ego) he had to a friend. After all, it interacted with him. It seemed to acknowledge him. It kind of liked him, in that it didn't zap him or otherwise spark him uncomfortably upon greeting him. No, it was really a very pleasant thing encountering this net. And back then, a pleasant encounter was the best he could do for a friendship.

But now, there was the real and distinct possibility that he was on the verge of having real friends, friends who would actually talk to him and do things for him, like accompany him on a feed. Jay was really very kind in that way. Very nonjudgmental. That must be friendship, yes?

And now he had a mission, a job to do for his friends— one that if successfully completed, would greatly please Jay, Enj, Lavender/Christina, and even Queen Mari. Oh, if only he could find the Dadman Ben and bring him home. He felt he was close.

Very close to finding him. What a wonderful world it would be for the lonely little elf boy, once doomed to sit on a solitary rock for all of eternity. His quasi-friend the net would show him the way. His world seemed so much fuller now that all of these possible real friendships were on the horizon. Who cared if the deer no longer liked him? They were just fast food anyway.

His inner psyche pouted as Seen pondered the possibilities of true friendships. *Careful,* it warned. It waited. It hoped the best for Seen but wondered when the pain of rejection would come, as it almost inevitably did.

Oh, shut up and get out of my head, Seen snapped at himself. His psyche snorted (metaphysically) and then went dark. It was in a big snit.

The Art of Squatting (without Injury to One's Bum)

The laughter was uproarious. Much knee-slapping, along with the requisite farting (which always came as a result of any physical activity) continued for some time. That is until one or two trolls would amble off to a suitable private spot for bowel evacuation. It was their special time.

Let's just call it what it is: troll constipation. An unfortunate by-product of long periods of inactivity and stone-like rigidity, which wreaks havoc with one's innards. It's why trolls are thought to be so scary. The sour expression of intestinal distress that you see is not really an indication of their general disposition, just a temporary moment of discomfort.

And why do fairy tales place them under bridges and in dank caves? Well, those are prime potty spots. It's not one bit funny when one is interrupted in the middle of a very necessary moment requiring intense concentration. Hence, the notion of grumpy trolls under a bridge. The Brothers Grimm should be ashamed to forever document such private moments in a shy creature's life.

When the man, Rockstar Ben, came into their lives, they just couldn't stay still for any length of time. They would hear some inventive colloquialism from the human about things such as "snooze you lose" or "push comes to shove" and just had to ask lots of questions. He would elaborate in some colorful and enigmatic way, pause and then deliver the "punch line" (another new phrase from the urination man). This would send them into spasms of belly laughs. Now, when one hasn't pottied in a few millennia and one then spasms with laughter, well, the whole activity tends to prompt first, farting and then, well, you know.

As cerebral as trolls are, they are rendered speechlessly hysterical over the act of gas emissions. It just cracks them up. Literally. It's a necessary yin to the yang of intense group thought. In short, the crude physical humor brought a sort of balance to their intense intellectual ruminations. Plus, farts are just funny sometimes. To most people. Besides, everyone is much happier after a good evacuation. It makes one feel light on one's feet and gives a certain jaunty spring to one's step. And that's a mean feets for a thousand-pound troll.

All in all, it was a great day when the teens, Ed, Ted and Fred, brought Rockstar Ben into their fold. He loved having someone to talk to, and they were delighted with his bold and impertinent ideas about the importance of humanity. Plus, he made them laugh, which brought the farting, which brought on the bathroom activity. And it was simply a good and necessary thing. Everyone benefitted.

He seemed so starved for interaction. He even tolerated Ed, Ted, and Fred, who the rest of the group thought were generally annoying. After the first night when Ben regaled the teens with the epic story of Sanctuary and the human family, the four of them strolled back to the troll circle like a posse of old friends. Rockstar Ben was nestled like a small, squishy meat sack between the three lumbering goliaths. They were so companionable, so easy with each other.

And the banter. It started the minute the four entered the circle. It was at first astounding. The adults were awestruck at the plethora of fabulous new words introduced by the man in the first few minutes he graced them with his presence.

After that moment of stunned amazement, the first fart sounded, followed by a giggle. Then an "oops" heralded a chorus of toots. All decorum was lost, and they just fell apart, forming mini-land-slides as they collapsed in laughter. Eventually, they magiked themselves back together, living and whole, to introduce themselves to the man. Then most of them slunk off to go potty.

Once refreshed, the trolls went about taking care of the basic nourishment needed to maintain their fleshy forms. Several went off to hunt their dinner. This comprised of magiking themselves into stone-like rigidity until some unsuspecting large creature (bear—they love bear; it tastes so meaty and lasts so long) ambled by too closely. Then the troll un-magiked him- or herself so as so spring, felled the beast with his or her club, and dragged it back to the circle. Should trouble develop and the bear decides 1) not to expire immediately or 2) fight back, other trolls in the party would add their efforts to the fray. Eventually, it all worked out. The trolls got dinner and some lucky troll babe got a nice new fur coat to wear while she was in an ambulatory phase.

Other troll duties included checking in with the smithies in the heart of the mountains to see if they needed a break from the heat and the fire. Making metal tools and glass windows for the Fairfolk (mostly elves) was hard and laborious work. Fortunately, there were always elves present in the mountain helping the trolls and maintaining the able workforce should a troll choose to take a break and settle into a nice rock shape for a day or two. This could be terribly hazardous, as fires can go unattended. It has sparked many a fire in the high Sierras.

So the safety crew, elves who never sleep (dour and predictable elves), were always present to lend a hand. And to supervise. They didn't talk much though. You never knew what peculiar colloquialism might send the trolls into happy meditative reverie (boulders). So the elves agreed that it was best not to talk much to those guys. No stimulation, no interaction. It was just fine for the dour elves but kind of boring for the trolls.

What the elves were particularly good for was communicating with the *trolls on outside terrain* (acronym, TOOT, a favorite subject for trolls). So through some very nice scrying baths, the elves responded when the trolls on the outside terrain, or Tooters, woke up, said hello, and asked if anyone needed a break.

Everyone took a turn in the mountains. It's kind of a rotating job, which allowed each troll to have equal amounts of fun in the wilderness as a Tooter and a turn at the forges. It was on the way to his rotation that one troll caught up with a certain gawky flying elf. Life was never the same for either of them after that first encounter.

How Mommy Lost Her Bad Self

This gig just wasn't what she thought it would be. Oh, working for her daughter was fine. But Christina just couldn't shake that unsettling feeling that she was neglecting something important, a vital task that she had to do. It made checking Other emails and scrying for signs of her husband's whereabouts seem so insignificant—a distraction from her real task.

Emails and messages from Others were so ridiculous with their total lack of understanding about the fundamentals of texting. They were so disjointed and misspelled to the point that the autocorrect function went crazy trying to provide a fix, eventually shutting down to take a nap. Christina usually spent most of her day deciphering what the heck they were saying. In the end, it was usually something mundane and trivial, like "What time is the meeting?" Only their texts came in "WWWWhat im is the mtetnjgl?" All day long, she untangled their garbled questions and then returned them clearly and succinctly, only to be rewarded with a reply that came in like "Dow e neeed to ear the usual togA today//?" Really. It totally made sense that Marissa blew her stack at these yahoos on a daily basis.

And now that Seen was tracking Ben, there really wasn't any urgent need for her to use the scrying pools. Her efforts of pouring over topographic maps, trying to match what she saw in the pool with actual geography, were suddenly unnecessary. That left her with little to do each day that seemed in any way important or vital. It frankly made the day boring. And where Christina was concerned, boredom was soon replaced by anxiety. Considering the state of her family and the looming threat of annihilation of her spouse, she had plenty to be anxious about. In fact, she had a whole shopping list of worries, which if she took the time to properly dwell on them, would bloom into a full-fledged anxiety attack—complete with the shakes and nausea.

Terribly distracting from her real job. *Whatever that is*, she said to herself for about the millionth time. Besides, she had just about had it with the nearly constant bickering between Enj and her daughter.

Their squabbling was a daily occurrence. One minute, they were chuckling conspirators in some shenanigans thwarting an Other from getting too close to the search for Ben. Then the next, they were arguing bitterly about something, usually trivial. Ridiculous. Somehow, Christina had morphed into the great conciliator, trying mostly in vain, to resolve each conflict.

I think they like to fight, she concluded this day. *And, if that's the case, then I am so done solving their issues. Done. Over. Out...But then what do I do to fill my day?*

Her frustration about being irrelevant in resolving the Ben situation was increasing, almost to her breaking point. Each day they had no word from Seen about the whereabouts of Ben made it worse and worse. Cell phone reception was terrible in the mountains, so most of the time, it was impossible to reach the elf.

And the weirdest things were happening when she attempted to scry. Instead of seeing images of Ben or even Seen, all she saw when she looked into the water was her own face reflected back in the water. Her breath would make small ripples across the surface, breaking up the image so anxiously looking back at her. She wondered, *What is happening to me? Am I losing it? Have I already lost it?*

A general pall followed her wherever she went. It was almost palpable. Even the Others-in-training, with their persistent questions, began to avoid the office. Marissa and Enj were so involved in their own daily dramas, they never noticed much more than her increasing quietude. Jacob saw it but was at a loss as to what to do. *Besides,* he thought, *maybe it's a woman thing, a female -cycle thing an Eeesh!* It was too gross to think about since it was most likely about his mom and her female organs. So he left it alone.

Christina, for lack of anything better to do, sat, peering into the depths of the basin, her own image mockingly returned by the water. Pondering her loss of scrying ability, she thought, *I have to get back to the basics of scrying...I am off track. I am doing things way wrong. But where did I begin...? And where did I go wrong?*

So she tried to recall the basics of scrying. It all starts with a question a specific question—and in reply, the water gives you the answer. Simple as that.

The problem is that her recent attempts to see in the waters were muddled by several questions, reflecting her jittery lack of focus. She couldn't really simplify them into one. *Where is he? Why did he leave us? Is he alive? How do we find him? Will he come home willingly?* And mostly, *Does he still love me?*

It was that jumbled mess of questions that she projected into the water. Her face was its only reply.

It's broken. It won't talk to me, were her first thoughts. Then, panicked, she concluded, *I have nothing, no skills to offer since I can't even scry.* She sat in the stark corner of her daughter's office staring at the blank wall beside the ornate water basin. Why was the basin so stubbornly silent?

After a time, she thought that maybe the water was, in fact, still talking to her. What if the answer to all of her questions was herself? What if the water was replying over and over to her many queries with the same answer? "What if—", and "Why doesn't—" and "Will he—?" were all solved by her—Christina. Hence, the only reply was her own image. If the solution to finding Ben was Christina herself, then how did she find him? Her desperation to do something, anything, to get out of this funk made her go deep within to find the truth. She absently chewed on a snaggy cuticle as she mused:

Maybe all of the answers I already have. I just have to think them through...

Where is he? Well, *we know he is in the mountains, probably the Sierra Nevadas. Possibly in a region he already knows. Hey!* She thought in a light bulb sort of epiphany, *I think I know where he is! He would gravitate to an area he knows well.* She remembered the last few vacations they had taken with friends up in the Sierras, when they had lived a normal life, before gargoyles and elves and dragons and fairies, *oh my!* She finished the little ditty sadly. He liked it up there. Even said he could live up there. Great golf courses. *We joked back then about how remote it was and how the kids would never live with us if we moved there. No shopping for Marissa and no schools for Jacob. But as a couple, we would love it. No, I don't need to see the magical net to track him. I'll start with where I know and trust my instincts from there...*

Why did he leave us? *Because I was stupid and didn't want to keep us all as safe as he did. Because I was in love with the idea of having magic and power that made me feel like a bigger, badder version of myself. Because I forgot to be a united front with him on the very important issues. Because I didn't even want to talk about his fears for our safety. Because I am a selfish ass.*

Is he alive? *I think I would feel it if he weren't. I think I have to have faith he is still walking among us.*

Will he come home willingly? *That depends. On me. If I can convince him to.*

Does he still love me? *Oh, hell if I know. I just know I still love him and feel like an empty husk, not whole, and without an anchor, without him here. So I have to go with that and see what happens.*

How do we find him? *Well, if the water is any indication it will have to be my doing.*

And, *I am going to have to find him myself.*

Christina felt she had the beginnings of a plan to find Ben. But first, she had to find her badass old self in order to make this happen. The real question was, where was her old badass self who had the courage of ten men? Where did the old Christina go?

She had once been fearless and beautiful. She had once felt bulletproof and even reckless. She had once always been the first to try a daring new adventure (and thankfully, lived to tell the tale). She once turned heads when she walked into a room and got the full attention of anyone she spoke to. She once had her glamour on twenty-four/seven, regardless of whether or not she had a good night's sleep.

In short, she once was in her twenties.

Time and common sense eroded some of those once was-es. Back then, everything seemed black-and-white, easy to sort through—quick choices, easily made. In time, black-and-white faded to shades of gray. Suddenly, everything seemed nuanced in "yeah, buts." Uncertainty became the rule of the day. Uncertainty led to concern. Concern became indecision. Indecision morphed into fear. Fear crept into decision-making in the guise of "good sense and maturity." And fear was an insidious houseguest, a ubiquitous squatter, happy to set down roots in the mind and heart of Christina. It gradually took over all the spaces within her, until the answer was always "*No*" and "*I can't.*"

And so she sat, a fifty-year-old white-haired woman, once, an artist called Christina, now more often than not called Mad Lavender. There she was, brooding in the corner of her daughter's office, paralyzed with fear, afraid to go find her husband and afraid not to. It made her feel weak and useless and the littlest bit angry. *How do I get out of this funk?* she asked herself, regarding the water in a distracted sort of way.

The waters began to shimmer, forming a new vision for her alone to see. A flat, featureless vista appeared, a blank sort of land, spreading outward to a pale horizon. The sky in the image dominated everything. Huge roiling clouds billowed in the air, always moving, collapsing in on themselves only to form anew in ever- changing monstrous shapes. *Why are the clouds so angry?* she wondered.

Anger. *Hmm*, she thought. *Maybe, that's my answer. Anger. I will use that to motivate me to get up and find my husband. I am angry that I have let so much time pass before I went after him. Disgusted at myself for becoming this weak, dependent creature. And sad that I let myself grow old before I could have my happily ever after.*

Well, this is a fairy tale I live in, isn't it? Then I **demand** *my happily ever after. Even if I have to go out and get it myself... especially if I do!*

And so it was that the tiny seed of anger motivated her to get up and move with purpose out of her daughter's office out to her own desk. She picked up her cell phone, and before she lost her tenuous hold on her newfound courage, she punched in a very familiar number. "Hi," she said. "It's me... Well, not so fine... No, no word. Listen, I know you hate to be in the office, but you are the only one I trust. I need you to sub for me while I go on a secret mission... No, nobody knows. So you have to keep quiet about it, OK? I'll tell you when you get here... Yep. Thanks a million... See you soon."

And then she dialed another familiar number. "Hi, it's me. Get the car gassed up, and bring a change of clothes. Oh, and an extra pair of sunglasses. We are going for a drive."

Meanwhile, in Marissa's office, the basin was still churning and frothing. The waters were especially agitated, continuing to display images of thunderclouds and the corresponding dark shadows cast upon the gray plain. The message was meant for the Seer. And that Seer had left the room. Regardless, the images would be played over and over until the message took. The basin felt it was that important to impose its will on the Seer—unprecedented and yet understandable. After all, that thing had been in use for several millennia and had absorbed plenty of magical essence. At this point, it nearly had a life of its own. It was only a matter of time before it began to operate using its own directives. And in this case, the Seer was particularly obtuse. Hence, the basin was taking matters into its own hands, as it were.

The soft murmuring of the Seer as she spoke into the little box seemed to indicate that she understood the message. She had to move. She had to leave the premises, not frozen in fear but motivated by anger, if necessary, in order to accomplish the goal of finding her mate. It seemed the Seer was finally acting toward that goal. Satisfied the message was understood, the waters in the basin settled down into their usual placid form, vision erased, now that it had finally done its job getting through to the stubborn old woman.

Bob Is Such a Sucker for an Angry Woman

That darn Family made his crusty old self go all squishy inside. He just loved how they turned this staid and rigid magical hierarchy on its head. They broke rules. They made up plans on the fly. They cheated the system. And it all turned out good. They were the best recruits he had ever had. Also, they had, up until then, survived the many trials imposed upon Others-in-training, plus a few they never imagined.

And Queen Mari, what a tiny, badass chick! A little young for his taste, yet she had the wisdom and maturity to know when the rules were just flat-out stupid. Even her brother was working on a whole new take on death and destruction to the magic takers (his term for those who overused magic and threatened the net). He loved them all, from feisty curmudgeon Ben, who questioned everything the Others threw at them, to Enj, their biggest fan and the coolest gargoyle he had ever met. Christina was a work in progress, yet even she seemed like a very deep well—the depths of which had not been plumbed. Like the rest, she too had big magic and was far more powerful than she gave herself credit for being.

And now that very elf/woman had summoned him to be in on some secret caper she was cooking up, one that even her own daughter, the Supreme Elder Other, didn't know about. He couldn't—no *wouldn't* resist such a call, even if it meant coming back to Home Base, because now he would be in a position to shake things up himself. Queen Mari would certainly be on his side, not like the previous Supreme Elder Other, with his creepy long robes and his squawking, shitting crow— and the mess in his office, all of the arcane wizard stuff looking like props from some Hollywood horror movie. Yes, he had recently installed a flat-screen TV in his red caboose perched on a hill in the canyon by the Family's home. He had since watched a lot of old movies and a lot more of *Judge Judy*. The llamas would guard the place while he was gone. Maybe catch a few episodes of *Wild Kingdom* while he was out. He thought all of this *Judge Judy* stuff would help him in this little caper up at the camp, making pronouncements and judgments and whatnot.

Bob needed to use only a little magic to transport himself back to Home Base, since he was in the form of his favorite animal, the cat. Bob the cat appeared on the desktop in the little ante office that Christina temporarily called her own. She briefly wondered what Seen would think about leaving the job to crazy, insane, and when in human form, completely pierced and tattooed Bob. But it really wasn't an issue now. As much as Christina cared for Seen, she needed her husband more. Nothing else mattered at this point.

Christina looked up from her computer, having consulted Google maps for the route to where she was headed, only to find this enormous multicolored cat sitting next to the keyboard.

"Hey Bob." he smiled at him, her heart warming to how quickly he had gotten there without knowing anything about the job, yet already fully committed. Her "hey Bob," conveyed her gratitude and the depth of affection for the guy in a way that no other words could.

Bob growled or purred or sneezed in reply. It was sort of all three at once, as though he was a cat trying to speak human. Impossible. As she turned away from the keyboard to address her partner in crime, her fingers brushed against the buttons, accidently deleting the map page. "Shit!" was her response. Bob purred. This office hadn't seen a shit in many an eon. He loved this Family. "Sorry, Bob," she said sheepishly.

"The first thing I am going to do is install a quarter jar for this desk." Bob said, suddenly very big and human and sprawling across the desktop. His method of magic was particularly subtle, having been honed to perfection over the centuries—no flashy lights or popping noises when he changed form. Just a small whoosh—an insubstantial waft of air, and there he would be, large and skuzzy and human-ish. His legs hung awkwardly off the table, swinging from the momentum of the instantaneous magical change.

"Sorry, Bob," Christina said again, leaning slightly back in her chair to accommodate the looming largeness of the lanky, spiky-haired, living, breathing tattoo that was posing as a human. "I guess you don't like swearing in the office, huh?"

"Nah. I could give a shit about that. I can't stand all of the apologizing you do. Cheeses, someone says it's cold outside, and you even apologize about that. I could make a lot of money off of you and your stupid 'sorrys.'"

"God, Bob, I am so sorry—wait, no, shit! I have no idea how to talk to you, god damn it!" she spluttered to a finish, nearly chuckling at the absurdity of the topic. If she weren't so damn depressed, she would have had a good laugh with him about her foibles. Now they just seemed a hindrance to her immediate objective—which was to bring Bob up to speed and leave before Marissa or the boys found out what she was up to.

"So anyways, what's this caper all about?" Bob asked, ignoring her temporary discomfort at speaking without somehow working an "I'm sorry" into the mix.

"Well, I need you to cover the desk for me while I'm gone."

"I gather that. How long will you be away?"

"Hopefully not too long. Just long enough to find Ben."

"Do you have a bead on him?"

"Well, yeah, at least I think so. I mean, I know the general direction he is at. And I am pretty sure I can guess which direction he went once I get there."

"'K," Bob answered, regarding the black nail polish on his long fingers. He chipped one, and it kind of pissed him off. Little things like that irritated him—big things, like annihilation, not so much, but get a scar on your favorite tat or chip a nail, and God help anyone in his flight path.

"OK? That's it?" she cried, pacing a bit in her general agitation. "I mean, you aren't even going to ask me why, or where he is, or what I am up to? You are not even going to try and talk me out of it?"

"Nah. I'm good."

"But wait. I have all these really good lies to tell you. Then I was going to break down and tell you the truth. Maybe cry even, I don't know. For sure, I would have thrown in at least four or five 'I'm sorrys' just to make you laugh. I mean it was an epic story, and you don't want to know even a little bit of it?"

"Not really." He yawned for good measure. The he popped back into his giant cat shape, in a liquid sort of way. She found him still draped over the desktop, this time in a much smaller and cuter form. He thought that maybe a nice cat nap would change his disposition about his chipped nail.

"This is why I sort of love you, Bob," Christina said, finding it way easier to talk to him like that when he was in his kitty shape. Bob purred in reply, circling counterclockwise on the desk until he had found the perfect position to plop down on some pages, while still eyeing the computer screen.

"Now, listen. This job is pretty easy. You divert a bunch of these Others and especially the Other Hunters far away from Marissa. And really far away from where we are searching for Ben. He's actually around here," she punched back up a Google map of the High Sierras, close to Truckee in the Lake Tahoe region. "I sent Seen up to track him, but we haven't heard from him for a while. He hasn't scryed me recently, and his cell phone apparently doesn't have coverage, so I am going up there myself."

Bob made a small chirping sound, a sort of question, Christina thought. Guessing what it might be, she answered, "No, nobody but you will know where I am." Bob growled his displeasure.

"OK, OK, I was thinking about taking Sleeping Guy with me east, towards Lake Tahoe. Actually, I was thinking about leaving him here when he brought the car, but I think that would only piss Marissa off more than usual. And that would **not** be fun for you. So yeah," she decided, "I'll take him with me."

Bob blinked at her, his big kitty face relaxing into a sort of feral smile. Thinking she had satisfied his concerns, Christina quickly went through the tasks associated with the job. As she was winding down and readying to leave, the door opened and an Other-in-training, toga mussed and looking rather rumpled from his travels, meekly stepped in.

"Mad Lav—uh, er, Madam Christina, I was wondering about the schedule...You see, I have trouble with basic toga tying, and it takes me longer than usual to ready myself in the morning, so I thought—"

A loud hiss erupted from Bob, the new monster on the desk. He rolled out of his lounging position and into attack mode— upright, paw raised, black claws outstretched (one having the tiniest chip in it, white nail gleaming through), teeth exposed, grimacing in fierce anger. The Other quickly backed away from the desk, looking at Christina for help. "Sorry. He's in charge now." She shrugged.

The young Other turned and fled the office, vowing from then on to figure out his issues all by himself. Christina smiled at the retreating young man. "Good job," she said to the cat as she exited the room.

"You just said it again. That'll be a quarter for the jar, ma'am," the tattooed man replied.

"Let me just work on getting some spare change. I'll do that after I find my husband, save his life, and settle the family. Oh, by the way," she remembered. "I am leaving you with almost a full case of wine under my desk. For emergencies only," she warned him, in case her tiny little daughter decided to imbibe. She had just indirectly put him in charge of doling the alcohol out. Judiciously, was the implication, as her face suddenly became very stern and mom-like.

"Only a partial case? What? Did little elf momma get into the sauce on the sly?"

"Uh, no. I actually gave some to Seen to give to Ben when he sees him. Sort of a peace offering. From me. He'll know what it means."

"Oh, great," Bob said. "Because alcohol always fixes an emotionally volatile situation." He fixed Christina with a withering look.

"Bob, why don't you leave interpersonal relations to me? I think I have it covered."

He would have flipped into his badass cat form, hissed in reply, maybe even raised a paw in defense. But this was Christina, and she probably would have responded with ten more "I'm sorrys," and he just wasn't in the mood.

Terrorizing Others sounded much more fun.

This Bud's for You

It took slightly longer than usual for Sleeping Guy to make his appearance. Christina paced outside, just inside the vines, the scented grapes almost heady in the aroma that said, "Harvest me now! I am full of sugar and about as fat as I'm ever going to be." She thought that the lush foliage of the fruit would conceal her whereabouts should Marissa or the boys step outside for air. The blackbirds were putting on quite a show, dive-bombing among the fat grapes and gorging themselves on the sweet fruit. Normally, this would be cause for great consternation among growers. But, here, the grapes were just for show. Besides, it was fair trade to let the birds feed in return for the sentry duty they did so well.

Finally, the big SUV made it up the drive. Not seeing Christina, Sleeping Guy honked, lightly tooting the horn so as not to draw too much attention. It was enough, however, to startle the birds from their feast. They began making their way en masse toward the opening in the barn rafters, to alert the staff. Christina hurried out from among the vines and waved the birds off. A few may have made it inside the barn before getting the signal to stop. It couldn't really be helped. She made her way as fast as she could to the passenger-side door, hopping in before he had a chance to shut off the engine.

"What's the big rush?" He smiled sloppily.

"Just back out of here. I'm in a big hurry."

"Ooh, sounds serious" He chuckled with mocking gravity. The gravel crunched loudly as he turned the car around to head back downhill. A few Others, dressed like farm workers, looked up from their supposed trimming, noting Mad Lavender's human assistant quickly speeding away with Mad Lavender herself as passenger. Thinking nothing was out of the ordinary, they returned to their faux labors, basking in the sunny day and the fresh air while they basically did nothing constructive.

Christina punched in the location of the High Sierra golf course that she knew her husband liked. It was north of Truckee, near Lake Tahoe. As she busied herself with getting the directions, she didn't notice at first, how loopy Sleeping Guy seemed until several cars honked at him for driving too slow. She looked up from her GPS and gave him the kind of long and hard once-over that only a mother can. "Are you high?" she asked in a tone that said, *You **are** high, and you are in so much trouble!*

He glanced over at her, laughing at her crazy cat eyes, distracted ever so slightly from the actual question. "Well, gee, I guess I just may be a **tad** toasted, yeah." He stretched out the syllables to make it appear he had given the answer a great deal of thought.

"Shitballs!" she exclaimed. "Pull over. I am going to have to drive."

This was an epic moment for her. Driving was an issue for Mad Lavender. Firstly, as she was now a smaller version of her human self, the car felt proportionately too large for her. Her sense of space was off, and the mirrors played havoc with her vision. They gave her a funhouse version of distorted clarity, where everything seemed quite clear, yet she was unsure how close things actually were.

To say nothing of the fact that she had plainly and simply been out of practice driving. It is a skill that comes naturally for some and not so much for others. Christina was always in the not-so-much category, preferring to have Ben do the big driving. Being an elf for so long had deprived her of any driving time at all. And now she was stuck with a drugged-out driver and no way to get to Truckee but by herself. Panic began to seep in; her old nemesis, fear, exerted itself to the fullest.

"No," she said, at first to herself, softly. Then, "No" much louder both to herself and to Sleeping Guy. "I won't let you get us pulled over. I am not going to sit here worrying about if you are going to kill us outright or attract the attention of some passing CHP by driving recklessly. That's all I need for the police to spot the weirdness that is me. And I won't call attention to us from the Others by magiking myself into being human while you drive. No, there is only one answer to this problem. Pull over at the next off ramp. I am going to drive. Carefully and soberly. You navigate. Got it?"

"Oh, this ought to be fun," Sleeping Guy muttered, having heard how notoriously bad her driving skills were purported to be. They were the stuff of much merciless teasing in her family. As a mother, she had always seemed capable in so many ways yet so inept in this one.

He pulled over near the Altamont Pass. It was a strange off ramp, built for a large development that never came to be. It looked like a sad ghost town, a community that never had a chance. Bright and shiny new lampposts showed the hope that once was for the now-empty place. Those lamps were put in to illuminate hundreds of new and sprawling homes, whose presence never came to pass. Now they lit up plots of land, worn orange flags staking the subdivision, hanging limp and defeated in the empty fields. Consequently, the place was very quiet, with little or no traffic—the perfect start for a nervous driver.

The two got out of the vehicle and switched places. She didn't turn the ignition until she had adjusted and then readjusted the mirrors, moving the driver's seat forward until her tiny belly almost touched the steering wheel.

"Ooh, Granma takes the wheel," Sleeping guy said noting her 10:00 and 2:00 hand positions and erect posture.

"Shut the f- up!" she snapped back nervously.

As she pulled away from the curb, she began to instruct him on his duties. "You are going to help me change lanes, got it?" he nodded briskly, realizing she meant business. "You are going to watch the GPS and help me navigate this drive, right?" Again, furious nodding. "And you will not space out or fall asleep, OK?" He started looking at her a bit fearfully. He had never heard her bark orders in this way. Why, she almost sounded like her daughter. Snappish. *Ah, that is where Marissa gets it from*, he thought with both dawning realization and the beginnings of a newfound respect. "Because if you do any of those things, I will zap the shit out of you with my magic fingers. And I don't know my own magical strength. I have been known to blow things up with these bad boys." She waggled her fingers at him. "Now, give me that extra pair of sunglasses, and let's go." She took a deep breath, trying to feel as fierce as she sounded. One thing was for sure, no one or nothing was going to get in the way of her finding Ben. Not even herself.

After the first twenty or thirty white knuckled miles, she began to relax, just enough to ask a few questions. Sleeping Guy was on full-alert status, realizing how much assistance she really needed. It was as if she were a brand-new driver and it was driver's training school. A driving instructor's job was definitely one career he would *never* apply for, he decided. *So not a chill gig*, he thought.

"So why were you high? Did we have a party at my house?" she asked, as though the answer had better be an emphatic "*no.*"

"No way, dude. We don't bring anyone home. That would be seriously whack. You never know what magical menace might show up. Big N-O on that one."

"Sooo, you get high all by yourself? That's really sad."

"That's not it at all. Jesus." He bristled. Even if it was Marissa's mom, he hated to let her think he was some sort of loser loner. "If you must know, it's medical marijuana," he declared importantly, in a tone that said, "Now don't you feel bad for me?"

"What? Are you sick?" she said with the teeniest bit of concern, edged in skepticism. After all, he didn't look particularly ill.

"No, dude. I have a chronic issue. Pain. I need it for pain management."

"Who broke your arm?" she asked in jest.

"Well, I did. It was a skateboard injury."

"Skateboard. Where did this happen?"

"Up at the college."

"The college. Up on the hill, surrounded by precipitously steep roads? That is where you decided to skateboard?"

"The very one."

"Who in their right mind tries to skateboard at that school? Well, never mind," she stopped herself, realizing that *he would*. "No wonder why they call you Sleeping Guy, you are always stoned."

"Well, no shit, Sherlock. What? You didn't know?" he asked incredulously.

"Listen, son, the seventies were a long time ago for me, OK?"

"Yeah, well, the way you are driving, you might do better with a toke or two. Might make you chill out, you know?"

"That's enough from you, sir. Why don't you be constructive and tell me which lane to be in at this interchange. I can't figure it out."

"Relax, Momma. What would happen if we took a wrong turn and got a little lost?"

"I am already lost enough with you. I don't need to get stranded in the land of bubbas with only you for assistance."

"Come on; you got me and GPS and your magic. Between that and your feisty temper, we could get out of almost any scrape."

"Really?" she asked dryly. After all, a pep talk from a stoner really doesn't carry much weight.

"Really," he replied stubbornly, offended by her lack of faith in him. Fully lucid now, he was determined to show her he could be a real help in this caper. Maybe, just maybe, it would further his case in wooing Marissa.

Seen Goes Native

The strange elf was spotted long before he actually noticed the troll clan. It was on a potty stop for one of the trolls making his way to the underground tunnels in order to take his turn at the forges. There he was, under a train trestle, taking his time at a very difficult evacuation when he noticed something at the tree line flying slowly and deliberately. It was an odd creature, part gargoyle and part elf, making methodical sweeps of the alpine valley.

This annoyed the troll, who had thought he had finally found a spot of total privacy for his epic bowel voiding—well, epic in that he hadn't gone in years. And he needed time and quiet in order to achieve this act. It made a troll almost want to be igneous permanently. But then, he sighed to himself, all the fun he would miss. After all, the human, Ben the Rockstar, was so engaging to interact with. So sadly, he had to put up with the uncomfortable and slightly humiliating aspects of his human form in order to have fun with the man. It was for Ben's sake that he subjected himself to the bowel-moving ordeal under the bridge.

Absently, as if he were nonchalantly expecting a bus, instead of terrifically anticipating a poop, he surveyed his surroundings. This was his way of avoiding the urge to strain—acting like he didn't care, like his bare and slightly rocky bottom could hang out all day long for all he cared, disconnected from the act like it didn't matter when it most assuredly did. So he pondered the view. Then he looked up. That's when he saw the goofy flying elf. *Crap*, he thought, chuckling to himself that he made a funny despite the unwanted interruption. Pulling up his baggy pants, he came out from under the trestle to meet whoever it was that had the nerve to disturb a good poop.

Seen did an aerial double-take, noticing the large troll as it emerged from the train trestle. He swooped down in a wide arc to land awkwardly in front of the blockish creature. Silently cursed himself for the lack of cool in his landing, he thought that it always went that way when he wanted to impress someone. His wings compensated for his awkwardness by majestically flaring out in their leathery grandeur. The troll eyed them briefly, returning his gaze to give the scrawny elf his full attention. Feeling a bit cocky and irreverent (which he attributed the influence of Rockstar Ben), he felt like acting in a rebellious manner. He dispensed with the usual formal Fairfolk greeting. After all, this was an unconventional elf, requiring an unconventional hello. Besides, he couldn't wait to try this new Ben-ism out. So he greeted the elf, "How's it hanging?"

"Oh dear," Seen said, quickly checking his pants to see if there was an egregious breach of etiquette involving his private parts. Relieved to find everything buttoned up, as it were, he addressed the troll. "I'm sorry?"

"What's shakin' bacon? What's the scoop, poop?"

"Have you been talking to humans?" Seen inquired, incredulous. He had heard all of those lines before from Enj, who had heard them from Jacob, who shared them with his family. Thus, his first thought was *Humans.*

"How'd you know?" the troll asked shocked as well that this strange elf had dealings with people. It was one thing to think a troll in his rock form could have easily heard those things. But there was no hiding the strangeness of this peculiar elf so that he could safely interact with humans.

"Know what?"

"What what?"

At the point of total confusion, Seen's inner self was on its last nerve with the nerdy Seen and began to direct him. *Relax, he's trying to act cool. Just like Enj and the kids do. And since he knows these words that are not the vernacular of the magic realm, he has probably gotten them from a human. And since he wouldn't talk to just any human, it probably is a magical human. It is probably the same magical human we are tracking. So start over; be respectful and try to get him on your side.*

"Right," Seen said.

"Right what?" the troll asked now irritated at this odd thing. The nerve of him to waste his valuable bowel time with this inane talk.

"Er, right. You asked how it was hanging. It hangs on the right." Seen looked down at his pants front, with a shrug and a smirk.

"Ooh. Funny. You made a funny. That is very good." The troll decided to like this elf. He made a funny. He couldn't wait to let the others in on that one.

"Yeah, I know a bunch of funnies, let me tell you." He lowered his voiced, conspiratorially. "I know a lot of funny things. Uh, funny, *human*-type things." Seen looked at the troll to gauge his reaction.

Suddenly, the troll became suspicious, anxious that this strange elf would somehow spirit away their new human friend, Rockstar Ben. His protective mode kicked in.

"Well, I don't know anything about humans except what we hear from stray backpackers. They hike and hike and hike, breathing hard. But the female humans usually are the talkers. They usually whine. But sometimes they say funny things. That's how we know human funny things." The troll knew he was talking way too much to be believable, but he was on a roll and couldn't get off the elaboration train.

"OK," Seen said, backing off a little. *New tack,* his inner self barked.

"I know some human things from living close to their abodes. I hear things being a sentry and all." Both were lying badly and knew it. Trying to dig himself out, Seen attempted to be helpful. "Not to be rude in any way, but I noticed I interrupted you. You were under that structure trying to, get, er, privacy?"

"Yeah, so?" The troll was annoyed that the gangly elf should bring up such a delicate subject before they had even traded names.

"Well, er, being close by to humans and all, I noticed they do certain things that might help with the problem of, well, moving things along, yes?"

"OK, I get you. Now what about it?" The troll was actually curious about some human method of bowel accommodation. It was something he had never spoken to Rockstar Ben about but would certainly bring up when he returned to the trolls on the outside.

"I heard," he whispered conspiratorially, "that if you sit down cross-legged and twist your torso, you squeeze toxins from your body, it helps the process of elimination." Seen demonstrated by plopping down cross-legged and twisting his upper body, rotating at the waist. The troll sat down in the dirt mirroring the elf's strange position. There he sat for several minutes in deep concentration until he had the strangest feeling. With a "huh" and a look of surprise, the troll quickly got up, heading down to the spot under the trestle, taking advantage of the twinge that foretold relief was at hand. *If this works*, he thought, *I have a friend for life*. It did, and he does.

"Hey!" the troll called out from under the trestle, finishing up a long overdue task. "What do humans call that move anyway?"

Seen smiled at the now friendly tone in the big fella's voice.

"Yoga," he replied.

"I gotta hear more about that shit," the troll said in his best Ben imitation.

I found him! Seen smiled to himself, recalling that Ben used that phrase all the time.

I Ain't Playin' Wich You

Honeysuckle, having dropped her whips in the shock and awe of seeing the transformed hotel room, stumbled over said paraphernalia as she entered the luxurious abode. Her shoe skidded on the thick carpet, the strap from the riding crop tangled in her six-inch heel. The old gentlemen rose in unison from their card game, anxious to help her before she fell. Bert arrived first, gently taking the prostitute's elbow as he guided her to the edge of the canopied bed. He nudged the door shut with his shoulder while moving her from the doorway.

The woman made no sound as she was being ushered toward the bed. Instead of sitting (as the mattress was very high), she opted to hold on to the bedpost. And hold on she did—as though for dear life. Wordless, her mouth made little fishy movements, opening and closing as though the very act of breathing was suddenly difficult.

Well, really, she made a lot of sounds, but few of them were actual sentences. They were *what-the's* and *who-the-hells* and *uh's* and *oh-my-god*, but nothing that made any sense. And her eyes. Dear lord, Arthur was afraid they would pop right out of her head. Demetrius was further concerned about her neck; she kept swiveling her head back and forth, taking in the spectacle of the lush room, as though she might injure herself from whiplash. Suddenly, she looked down at the thick velvet coverlet she had been directed to. Realizing that she was crushing the expensive velvet, she jumped away, only to wobble in her heels, nearly falling again.

"Calm yourself, dear," Demetrius said gently approaching her. *As skittish as a colt*, he thought to himself. *I shall speak softly to her until she shakes off her nervous agitation. And use perhaps some soothing music; a harp will see an end to her spasms.*

A warm cloak will settle her, Albert thought. *She must be jumpy from the shivers in that remnant of a gown.*

Pumpkin ale is what she needs, Arthur thought. *That always makes me happy.*

In an instant, and after a bright light accompanied by a soft popping sound, a harp appeared in the corner of the now very cramped room and began to play itself. Bert, who had stood when she entered the room, now had his arms full of yards and yards of fabric, which he tentatively draped around her shoulders, clasping it at her neck with a fine silver brooch. Honeysuckle was too stunned to flinch, allowing this to happen. She was on sensory overload and had resigned herself to standing (albeit in a very wobbly fashion), mouth agape. Music was softly playing from the harp, plucked by invisible hands. Arthur placed a mug of some sort of alcohol in her hand. Her gaze dropped to it, and she saw that it was possibly beer. *Good, I need a drink*, was her first coherent thought. She chugged down most of the ale. Then she had her second coherent thought...

"I ain't paying for all this!" she said faintly. Slowly, her courage gathered. *I am Honeysuckle the Dominatrix, and I am in charge*, she scolded herself. *Get a frigging grip, girl!* "I ain't paying a **damn dime** for any of this!" she said much more forcefully, gesturing expansively all around the room, spilling the remains of her beer.

The gentlemen were stunned. They watched this magnificent creature with her wiry hair wafting in the air, trailing the movement of her head almost as an afterthought. Her lady parts were mostly covered now by the voluminous cape, but her lean and muscled legs were rigid with anger. It was as though her body was speaking as loudly as her words. Each one hardly knew which to respond to. They only knew that she and her anger filled the sumptuous room. There hardly was any space left for the three wizards. For the second time in twenty-four hours, they felt frissons of fear and the accompanying nether parts' shrinkage. It was the most action those parts had seen in millennia.

Then suddenly, she changed her demeanor completely. Her eyes narrowed, and a sly smile played on her lips. She walked to the ornate dresser, placed the beer stein on it, and began peering intently at her reflection in the mirrored surfaces, especially those hanging on the golden plastered walls. She carefully paced the room, looking behind the wall hangings and mirrors.

"You boys are punkin' me, aren't you?" She smiled hopefully to look good in the hidden cameras she felt sure were mounted somewhere in the room. "THIS IS A SHOW ON TV; I KNOW IT!" she exclaimed. "A magic show! Oh, you had me good for a while." She wagged her sharply filed nail at them.

"But you know, I was not born yesterday and this is Vegas. Anything can happen here. And it does. So where are the cameras?"

"Cameras?" Demetrius looked at Bert, but the knower of all things human was dumbfounded. He began searching the many hidden pockets for something. Perhaps a camera-thingy had fallen into one. He began retrieving the usual pocket flotsam that he carried. Nothing looked vaguely like this camera item, whatever that was. It was Arthur who solved the riddle of the camera.

As Bert dug desperately in his pockets for something that could be called *camera*, Arthur had far more limited options. He pulled out of the folds of his toga the cell phone Marissa had given them. "Camera?" he asked helpfully.

"Oh, I get it. YouTube!" She grabbed the cell phone, looking for the message icon to see what had been videoed. Instead, she saw only message after message from someone called MariQueenB. They didn't even reply back. Just her messages. Simply worded little things. They said things like, *"Cool,"* *"No worries,"* *"I got it,"* and the longest one was *"Have a nice vacay."* There wasn't the slightest indication that someone had filmed this for mass distribution. "Wait," she said. "It must be some other app I don't know." Sadly, his phone had very few icons and none seemed remotely able to video and send.

"Well, what the hell?" she said, looking around yet again, at the accommodations for any indication of a camera.

The wizards calmly watched as she searched the room, touching the fabrics and the carved moldings and then gasping in surprise when she saw the bathroom. They heard the flush of the commode, harrumphing among themselves as they wondered why she did not at least close the door. But using the commode wasn't her mission. She just wanted to test if it really was a functioning bathroom. She emerged from the bathroom, both hair and cape softly trailing behind, calmer now but still baffled by it all.

"I know. I got it!" she cried. "A reality show. This is your new crazy series where they plunk you guys down in some totally awkward situation and watch with hidden cameras as unsuspecting regular people have to try and cope with your asses, right? But where are the cameras, the production team, the people?"

"Let's review, shall we?" Demetrius sought to get their adoption back on track. This waif obviously was both angry and confused. Perhaps the ale had been unwise after all. "First, there simply is no room here for pets, livestock, or people as much as I know the stable may have once been your abode."

"Whach you talkin' about?" she asked.

"Asses. You mentioned asses and stable hands and there just isn't any practical way to keep them here. I am sure you understand."

"Uh—"

"Next," he said, ticking some imaginary list off his long and gnarled fingers. "You mentioned **regular** people. Well, that's exactly what we hope to attain for you, my dear."

"Most assuredly," Bert agreed. "Absolutely," he added for emphasis.

"Would you care for more ale?" asked Arthur.

"Oh, I think beer isn't gonna fix this weird shit," Honeysuckle replied. She suddenly felt vaguely insulted. "Regular people"? She was regular all right.

It's these Amish guys that didn't look too main-stream. Time they heard about it.

"Look," she said, "I may be confused, and I may be shocked by this weirdness, but I am Honeysuckle the Dominatrix. I handle all kinda weird. I know weird. I get paid for weird. What I don't know is how all this shit got here. And maybe I don't care—except if we are on TV, then I want it to be cable. They show good soft porn on the cable, and I could work that angle just fine. If not, I am guessing you stole this shit. Which is weird cause I thought Amish guys are good and..." She strode up to the three brandish-ing Arthur's cell phone. "...don't use cell phones!" She smirked as they registered surprise at her accusa-tions. "So I aks (pronounced "ax") you again, what's your game?"

Arthur sank down on the soft bed. Which was difficult owing to its elevated height. He then sort of jumped up onto it and sank down into its downy vastness. He sighed. "I guess the jig, as it were, is up. We have no cameras. There are no other people. She knows we are imposters." He discreetly dabbed his moist eyes with the edge of his toga, tipping out the contents of his pocket. A tightly wadded fat roll of one-hundred-dollar bills fell out onto the carpet. Honeysuckle, never being one to steal, and always one to earn her bank, bent down, picked up the wad, felt its weight, and experienced a profound sort of awe as she handed it back to its rightful owner.

Her instantaneous analysis of the immense wad of cash was that it was real. It smelled like money. Specifically, it smelled like casino money, having a bright bouquet of cigarettes and stale drinks. And it was a lot of money. Maybe, she thought, she should stick around a little longer to see what these cagey, cell-phone-carrying, spindly legged, possibly gambling, poser-Amish magicians were all about.

"Now, Arthur, don't get soppy," Demetrius chided. "We don't have to go home just yet. And I am sure this young waif will treat us kindly and not tell on us once she understands why we have improved this abode just for her."

"Wait, what? This is all for me?"

"Why yes, dear. We chose you from the carriage driver's book of waifs. And we deemed you most worthy of all of this. It is entirely for you so as to save you a life in the stables." Bert smiled encouragingly at her. This seemed to calm her a bit. Thankfully, he thought, her fit of pique had subsided.

Honeysuckle was incredulous. They didn't really mean to steal all this for her? Did they? They hadn't even had a date with her yet. But if they *did* mean to give all this to her, well then, she could hock all this stuff and make big bank. She looked down at the big silver clasp at her throat. Shit, if that thing was real, she could make a butt load of money off the jewelry alone.

Suddenly, she didn't much care if they talked weird, stolen this stuff or even if they weren't Amish. All she really wanted right now was to finish the date and get them to leave so she could take this room apart and sell every damn thing in it. Maybe if she treated them all real good, they would even tip her from that big wad of cash the old crying guy had. This could be it for her—her way out and onto the life of the green.

Honeysuckle was all business as she addressed the old guys. "Now, fellas, let's reconsider the situation.

In the end, we all just want to get down to the business side of things. The other matter of where all this came from is just small stuff. And I never sweat the small stuff when I work. That's your job. To sweat. 'Cause that's what I do. And, honeys, that's just what I'm gonna do to you. I am gonna make you sweat good..." She smiled a very feral and wicked smile. The wizards all shrank back a bit, wondering what the waif could possibly mean by that!

Groupies, You Gotta Love 'Em

"So you see, it's really a big love story. On so many levels—" Seen explained as the troll, Ed, led him back to the encampment, toward Ben. They strolled companionably through the dense pine forest, taking a small deer trail back to camp. The trees were immense, the canopy starting way above them, allowing for easy travel through the thick trunks. Their footfalls were quiet owing to their skills at traversing trails without being noticed. On the other hand, an elephant could tramp though those trees unheard as the thick pine needles dampened all sound.

Both were deliriously happy with their new-found friendship. It was mutually satisfying in so many ways. Ed was hearing huge nuggets of fun facts about Rockstar Ben. The epic story Ben had told them left out all kinds of details, including the family-love-story angle Seen was suggesting. Hell, he and the clan would sit and ponder that one for decades. Also, it gave him a reason not to get to the forges anytime soon. After all, he had found the odd-looking elf, and it was his duty to escort him to the encampment. So yeah, he got a reprieve from underground work, and a reason to get back to the happening scene at camp.

Seen was reveling in the fact that someone thought he was cool—in the know, part of some inner circle. It made him feel important and looked up to. Well, as much as a large giant rock man can look "up" to a smaller elfin creature. Seen's inner psyche was pretty happy as well. It kept cuing him on snappy lines and crazy human idioms that entertained the troll to no end. It felt needed. Often, the story would be interrupted by the troll mouthing a phrase, as if to commit it to memory for later. Both Seen and his inner self felt very validated.

Sometimes, the story would morph in an entirely different direction as Ed would ask for clarification of a word or the origins of a phrase. Seen would be only too happy to comply. He was proud he had used his computer skills well as Supreme Elder Other Marissa's secretary, often "Googling" a word or baffling phrase himself. *The trolls would do well with computers,* he thought. *The word* Google *itself would give them hours of entertaining pondering.* Eyeing the massive size of Ed's fingers, he amended, *keyboards might be a problem though.*

They reached the small clearing in the woods, the alpine meadow punctuated by a strange outcropping of boulders curiously set in a semicircle, alongside an ashen fire pit. Ben was nowhere in sight as he was off foraging for greens—something he thought the troll diet desperately needed. The trolls were unusually glad to see Ben leave. They had so much to group-think upon and wanted to sort it out for future ruminating. So they took the opportunity of his brief departure to settle into pleasing rock shapes and meditate on many Ben things.

Ed approached Ted, kicking the base of the rock corresponding to an ample rump. "Dude." he said in his new Ben lingo, "Get up. We have company. This is one of Ben's peeps!"

At that, the boulder made a grinding sound as the top half swiveled slightly, exposing a crouching figure with one eye opened. The eyeball scanned the elf from toes to head, stopping briefly at the sight of the unusual leathery wings. The figure then unfolded, making the sound of tumbling gravel as it changed to the color and texture of a lumbering, dirty Neanderthal. The other figures shifted slightly, aware that two individuals had invaded their presence, electing to wait for Ted to determine friend or foe. Waiting was what they did best. Waiting and meditating. Sadly, not shitting.

"You do not look like a dude Ben would be with." Ted was highly suspicious. His teenaged sense of societal pecking order had kicked in. Teens, even Neanderthal teens, always sense where someone fits in the social order. This elf with his crazy wings and bulbous eyes looked like the kind of elf that even other elves wouldn't want to be with. He looked sheepish and nervous. The wings were attractive though, in the way they twitched aggressively, but other than that, no. Unless… "Say, you aren't the tragically magiked elf that saved Ben and his family from the dire flames at the dragon battle, are you? Because if you are…" Ted didn't wait for Seen's answer. He had to be the one. "Hey, everyone. Get up. A character from Ben's Epic Saga is here to greet us! Get up! Wake up! The story is here! It's happening right now in our midst!"

Seen was shocked to be the center of so much attention. To say nothing of the gravely unsettling feeling of seeing so much rock tumble and change all around him. It made him want to crouch, taking cover from what should be a terrible avalanche. But no. Trolls are very tidy in their metamorphosis, spewing very little in the way of pebbles as they shift from rock to living creature. After all, with so many other trolls in close proximity, a messy transformation could mean putting someone's eye out. They had learned over the millennia to be very careful in transition.

Soon, he was surrounded by a group of very large, very thick lumbering things. They all sort of resembled one another and, other than a bit more upper torso covering for the females, there was hardly any way to tell male from female. They surged close to the elf crowding to see his wings and study his features for future reference. Seen cowered in their presence. His wings snapped angrily at the intrusion into Seen's very personal space.

"Back off!" Ed shouted. "You are giving him creepings."

"The creeps, you mean," Fred said. "You are such an idiot, and you never listen to how a phrase is being said."

"Oh yeah," Ed hotly replied. "Well, I listened right good when this elf told me how to make a proper shit. And…" He smiled smugly. "It worked."

"Ooh," the crowd said, impressed.

"Ah," someone else said.

Toot went someone else, who later asked, "Might I have that information sooner rather than later?"

"Of course," Seen said, proud to be of service, even if it was in the defecation department. "But first, I have a package for Rockstar Ben. Some wine from his lady," he added lamely. He tried to speak in the terms the trolls used for what they referred to as "The Epic and Tragic Saga of Rockstar Ben."

"Ooh, will it make for a happy ending?" Fred asked hopefully. Currently, she was obsessed with all creatures living happily ever after. She was bothered that this saga didn't quite yet have an ending. She most desperately hoped it would turn out well. Alcohol sounded like just the ticket to make it so.

The Siren Song of Bacon Bits

"Look, I really don't care if you are hungry. I know we are almost there. But I haven't found a place where I can park without being seen. Maybe just around this block we can find a spot more private than the main road." Christina was tired of driving. All of this concentration was giving her a headache. And she probably was as hungry as Sleeping Guy. It had been a long while since she had really eaten anything of substance. Seemed like the closer she got to finding Ben, the hungrier she felt—for a lot of things, it seemed, when she thought of her husband.

Sleeping Guy was starved with a capital S. He had been outrageously hungry since the Altamont Pass, and that was hours ago. Plus, he was post-stoned worn out and full recovery required food. It was a wonder he didn't weigh five hundred pounds with the way he could scarf down the chow. Metabolism. He used his best, most-convincing tone of voice to get through to Marissa's mother. It bordered on whining, but at this point, he didn't care.

He had worn a lot of hats so far on this road trip—been passenger, driving teacher, navigator, and scolded child. At this point, the scolded child won out and he was flat out perishing for a burger and fries for sure. And maybe a frosty freeze ice cream dipped in chocolate. Oh, yeah, his stomach reminded him, don't forget onion rings. With barbecue sauce. This was all too much. He burst out, "For craps sakes, can't you magik yourself a teeny bit to look normal so we can stop. Pul-ease!" He stretched out the word *please* as if his very life depended on it.

"Fine." She sighed. "I guess a little bit of magic this far away from Home Base won't hurt." They pulled into the next diner they found. It was located on one of the side streets that peeked out through the thick stand of pine trees.

The town was typical for the mountain region, just a meandering thing poking out now and then through the trees. There were enough buildings to entice the tourist to drive down the little streets. On this road, there was a motley shamble of homes, cabins, junk stores, diners, and tourist shops that boasted tumbled rocks and beaded Indian belts. A Smokey the Bear sign told you what the fire danger was for the day, and realtor billboards boasted of the best listings for the vacation cabin you always wanted (to clean).

This road was wide, allowing for street parking. The diner was called something only known to the locals, as the neon was partially out. Filling in the gaps, it seemed to read "Tasty Cantina's," and yet it also could have been "Fantastic Blinis." Maybe not. They pulled alongside the café, pondering the name of the sign. The parking lot adjacent to the eatery was packed earth, showing the tire treads of big trucks. Truckers are always a good sign. It means the food is quick, hot, and plenty of it. Probably pretty good as well. They pulled into a space and, turned off the motor.

As the car engine ticked down quietly from its trek, they noticed the sound of birds, big scrub jays from the sound of it, squawking high up in the pines. There was another sound. A soft roar of water telling them a stream was nearby. It smelled like piney heaven, and it felt peaceful. Tasty Cantina's' or Fantastic Blinis, notwithstanding, they both felt the need for a bit of refueling.

Sleeping Guy looked away, out the passenger window as though to give Christina some privacy in making her change. She let go of her death grip on the wheel, took off the sunglasses, and closed her eyes. Her hands made small twitchy movements in her lap, like they were at a keyboard, typing in the magic spell. After an almost audible pop, he looked at her. She was back in her gray hair bob, with her designer jeans and frilly shirt, along with her clunky suede lace-up boots—the same outfit she had used winetasting. She smiled sheepishly, "Rerun outfit. Sorry. Without Mari, I am at a loss as to what to wear."

"Do you know you say 'sorry' a lot? For no real reason."

"Sorry." She smiled arching her eyebrow, daring him to remark.

"Uh, so, anyway, let's go in. No, wait…" He paused, grabbing her elbow. "Do you have any money?" he asked her, knowing full well she probably did not.

"Oh damn. No, but I can make a coupon real quick."

"You know, forget your magic coupons. That got us in a lot of trouble back in Livermore. When you called for me to come and drive you, I took the precaution of bringing the credit card and extra cash. So it's on me. Well, actually, it's on you since this money is basically your money from back at the house, and—"

"Forget it. I get your meaning. Let's go eat and pay like normal people."

The diner was a cavernous place of vinyl flooring and randomly placed banquette tables. The chairs were a bit better than the folding kind but not by much. They were mismatched and seemed to have had previous lives in thrift stores and old homes. Despite its hodgepodge appearance, it was clean and tidy. The back of the diner was a very noisy kitchen partially covered by a half wall. Lots of action was happening back there. Waitresses hung out at the half wall grinding fresh coffee at the counter and bantering with the two fry cooks. There appeared to be some sort of flirting happening. Loud laughter came from one of the waitresses, who was trying too hard to be noticed by the shyer of the two cooks. She poked and kidded him while he went on with the commerce of cooking for the customers. A faint smile played on his face, so maybe she was getting through to him after all.

A few regulars hung out in the corner of the room, newspapers spread out on the table in between plates of food and large ceramic coffee mugs. Several other tables were populated by foursomes—men mostly, garbed in casual cotton slacks with button-down shirts and baseball caps that read any number of swank golf courses. Golfers, intent on fueling up before their rounds, all dressed similarly in order to conform to the course dress code, while around them wafted the heady perfume of suntan lotion.

Christina and Sleeping Guy came in, catching the eye of the less flirtatious waitress. "Anywhere you want to sit, hon," she said addressing Sleeping Guy. She came over quickly, menus under one arm, carrying two coffee mugs and a large carafe of coffee. "Welcome to Nasty Nina's. Coffee?" she said, not exactly a question, more like an order.

"Uh, sure," they both replied, despite the fact that breakfast time was long over.

It was good. It had just been brewed and tasted like the beans were fresh ground. "Yum," Christina murmured. Sleeping Guy made happy sounds as well, once he loaded his up with sugar and milk from tiny metal containers that were already on the table. As he looked at the menu, she looked at what everyone else was eating. Breakfast. That seemed to be their specialty. And it smelled good. Like bacon. And cheddar cheese. And butter. The waitress stood by waiting for them to decide.

"OK, I'm in," Christina said. "An omelet for me, with grilled onions and a side salad. Spinach. That comes with bacon, right?" she asked the waitress.

"Oh yeah," she answered. "In the omelet and in the salad. You want a side of bacon too?"

"Why not. And toast too. Sourdough," Christina answered.

"That's a lot of food for such a bitty thing like you."

"You have no idea." Christina smiled handing her back the menu. Tiny elf-sized Christina still had the appetite from when she was human and a bit more substantial. Besides, magic was making made her hungry.

"Metabolism sucks," the waitresses countered, tugging her top down a wee bit to cover her own hips. *I've had way too much bacon on a daily basis,* she silently chided herself.

"So here's what I want," Sleeping Guy said, suddenly and uncharacteristically all business. "Hamburger with everything, medium. Fries and onion rings, with a side of barbecue sauce, and a chocolate shake. Oh, I'll keep the menu in case I want to order dessert." He held on to the menu, placing it on the table next to his silverware.

The waitress rolled her eyes, another one who could put it away without gaining an ounce. Life just wasn't fair.

As she put in the order, the two discussed their next move. "You know, now that I feel like we are close—he's around here somewhere. Maybe at this point, I can scry him so we can narrow our search."

"Scry. What manner of arcane weirdness is that?"

"You know scry. Usually, it's with water, but really, you can use almost any object familiar to that individual to try and locate them. Before Marissa instituted the use of cell phones at Home Base, we used to use items of our own to actually communicate with you guys back at the house. Remember? That was scrying **and** communicating. Mine was a pen, and Ben's was a golf club and Marissa's was a purse, and—"

"Yeah, I get it. Who could forget Marissa big yellow purse?" They both chuckled, remembering the little fairy's wicked joke in using the purse and how silly the men looked talking into its depths. "So why water?"

"Water is a universal substance. It is literally a part of all of us. So we use water when we don't have a specific items belonging to that person," she said, looking at the ripples in the coffee. "Now, say, if Ben made coffee for a living, I would be able to use this here to locate and maybe even talk to him. But he doesn't, so I resort to the universal element. Water.

"I am sure the creek nearby has a somewhat calm pool where I can try to locate him. If we are lucky enough to see some big landmark in the image, like giant boulders or falling rocks and such, then it's easy. We simply ask some local, 'Hey you know how to get to the massive falling rock formation?' They tell us, and we go find him."

"How about a demonstration?" Sleeping Guy asked. Easily distracted, he was still stuck on her coffee analogy. "That waitress over there makes coffee. And she probably knows every chipped coffee cup in the place. I bet for sure she would know well that very coffee cup you hold in your hand. Try scrying her." He wiggled his eyebrows conspiratorially.

"OK," she said. "But just for a sec. I don't want to use too much magic and lose my, uh, persona, if you know what I mean." He nodded. Smiling he leaned forward across the table to see how the process worked.

She carefully set the cup down before her on the table. As the hot drink settled, ripples smoothing to stillness, she closed her eyes and hummed a little. Or at least that was what Sleeping Guy heard. It was actually a vibration, soft and sure, coming from deep within her. The surface lost its blurry reflection of the ceiling tiles and began to change. Colors and shapes swirled in along the top of the liquid until they settled on a shape. A human shape. A woman, hair pulled back in a head band, revealing the tired but friendly lined face of their server. She was in the midst of filling the grinder with fresh beans when she paused, as though the scrying was calling her. She had a faraway look in her eyes, as if she were remembering something from long ago. Her Fairfolk origins had linked her into this scrying, and by instinct, she was responding to the magical call.

"Ask her something. See if she'll talk to us," he suggested, leaning as close to the cup as he could, table width notwithstanding.

Christina thought for a minute and then spoke softly into the cup. "Golf courses. Tell me where they are around here."

The waitress whipped her head around, startled at hearing a question from presumably the coffee-maker itself. She scanned the room, wondering if a customer had called her. She had distinctly heard a question asked of her. *Must be crazy acoustics in here today,* she thought. Looking carefully at the crowd, she eliminated the golfers (they would already know where the courses were), the locals (they could care less about golf) and turned her attention to the mother/son couple waiting for their meals. Maybe she heard them asking about golf. *Yeah from across the room? Weird.* She thought. *Probably gonna be a weird kind of day.* She headed over to them.

The older woman quickly took a sip from her coffee, thereby breaking the spell. The waitress approached, putting on her friendly face to the big-order couple. "You guys need anything?" she asked.

"Well…" the young man said, smirking as though there was something really funny just said, "we were wondering where the *golf courses* were around here."

"That's weird. I was just thinking about them myself," she said, feeling a general odd vibe about these two. "There are two right down the road that way…That's where those guys over there are headed." She gestured with her chin toward the noisy table of golfers. She paused for a moment, then added, "And then there's the creepy haunted one up the hill."

"Ooh, that one. Tell us about it" the stylish white-haired mom said.

"It's all dead grass now. You can't play it. Was gonna be a planned ritzy development with luxury homes all around the course. Then the bottom fell out of the real estate market. The golf course was abandoned, and the few homes that actually got built are now in foreclosure. It's a weird place. There's all these crazy American Indian statues there and an honest-to-god ring of standing stones they built the course around. Here's the spooky part." She leaned forward, talking conspiratorially to the two. "Right after the development went bust, someone must have come by and knocked the boulders down. Just rubble where the big rocks once were. It's kinda a big mystery around here what happened to the stones. At any rate…" She shrugged. "…no one's gonna be playing that golf course anytime soon."

"Cool," Sleeping Guy said.

We got him, Christina thought.

Fireworks over the East Bay

"WHAT DO YOU MEAN HE'S GONE?" Marissa shouted into the phone as it lay on her desk. It was on speaker as she spoke to the Professor. The sentry raven had just informed her of the family car arriving at the barn, her mother getting in, and the car subsequently leaving the base camp.

This resulted in her checking out her mother's desk, only to find Bob the cat napping away on top of the computer keyboard. Well, actually he was only in part on the keyboard. The rest of his multicolored, furry largeness was spread out on the desk. She angrily buzzed the cat, flying close to his furry head. His first instinct upon waking was to swat at the flying thing. He quickly checked his claws however when he noticed it was Supreme Elder Queen Marissa. He sat up, at attention and on his best behavior. This was followed by furious licking of his fur. A cat's way of saying, *I am so embarrassed I almost snagged your outfit, and let's just put it past us, shall we?*

"WHERE IS SHE, BOB?" Marissa shouted.

He flattened his ears at the force of her fury and did his best at shrugging an "I don't know."

"Come into my office," she growled. "And close the door behind you." Knowing that the only way he could do that was to have opposable thumbs, this was her way of getting him to become tattooed-guy Bob. The human form of Bobness would get her far more specific answers than the kitty version, whose repertoire of communications ranged from meows to grrs and purrs. Not enough specifics for her.

Bob suddenly changed, filling the chair in a sprawling, leisurely way opposite Marissa at her huge desk. He yawned, dissembling. *A universal trait of liars,* she thought, to yawn before answering. *My brother and half the operatives do it all of the time.* "Spill it, Bob."

"No clue, Elder Other," Bob said, inspecting his right arm, checking out his neat new tats.

"You know something. Tell me. Or do you think I won't use the entire power of this office to get it out of you?" she threatened in a soft, deadly sort of way. All the while, she hovered, over the desk in a swaying sort of trajectory. Back and forth, she moved, as though her wings were attempting to soothe her by rocking to and fro. It wasn't working.

"Nah. I know you would do anything for your fam. That's why you are keeping the Others away so your peeps can find the Dad-ster. Mommy is just away doing her part."

"What part? She can't do anything but scry. And that's right here." Marissa gestured to the birdbath in the corner of the room. Bob briefly looked at it dismissively.

"She had a lead on him, all right, just like the rest of you. Just like your buddy Seen. But she knew that finding him isn't the same as bringing him back. She figured she would be the only one who could convince him to do that, being the wife and all."

"I could do it. But I am stuck here, doing this gig, and—"

"Oh, let's not get all Freudian about who Daddy loves best." Bob straightened slightly in his chair, firmly addressing his queen. "You are here, keeping the world from being blown up by those idiot Others-in-training. That's a huge job that only you can do. Let Mommy do her part, 'K?"

He rose from his cockeyed position on the chair, unfolding his lanky legs from the armrests.

"Wait!" she said. "I'm going to phone home." That was when she keyed in the autodial on her phone to ring the house she grew up in. The Professor answered. She imagined him holding the phone in one hand and nervously flicking his swoop of hair from his forehead with the other, while pacing back and forth. This was his go-to nervous gesture. As if the tone in her voice would get him into maximum crisis state. *Or at least it should*, she thought. It did. He was pacing and hair flicking. She yelled, "*Where is Sleeping Guy?*"

He answered, "He got a call from your office to meet your mother. He's gone."

This was followed by her yelling at the top of her tiny but powerful lungs, "WHAT DO YOU MEAN, *NOEL*, THAT HE'S GONE?"

Her anger was palpable and immediately felt by every creature at Base Camp. *Uh oh*, was the collective thinking of the moment. The birds outside of the barn squawked in unison, agitated at the state of their queen. They rose from their gorging on overripe grapes and circled the air above the vines. "Not good, not good," they cried in distress to each other.

"Tummy's full; let's roost," said one lonely voice in the flock.

"OK," they all replied, immediately settling back on their perches in the vines. Crisis forgotten.

Crap, she actually used my name. And not in a very nice way. I'm in big trouble! "Uh, er, I guess that's exactly what I mean." The Professor looked out the back door while Marissa went ballistic on her end of the phone. He gazed out to the peaceful deck while she ranted. How quiet it seemed in contrast to the din on the other end of the phone. And it all started right here.

Outside was where the amazing story of this family had begun—a stormy night, a baby gargoyle, a human mother rescuing a crying creature from the winds. Now, the daughter is some sort of all-powerful queen, the family is away in fairyland, and his life was constantly harried by mischievous fairies. And all he really wanted to do was live in a quiet place and write the story of this family. Not easy. *I guess getting screamed at by the temperamental daughter is a small price for the story of a lifetime. To say nothing of the fact that I finally have the answer to my eternal questions of what is exactly out there,* he mused to himself as she ranted on the line. Finally, he knew it was his turned to speak. Heaving a heavy sigh, he said, "Look, as soon as I hear from Sleeping Guy, I will call you. Yes, and I will tell him to get his bony ass and your mother back to base camp or Home Base or whatever you call the place." He cancelled the call, hoping not to anger her any more that day.

He resumed his place at the kitchen table, laptop open and pages strewn about its surface. Besides his story notes, there were copious handwritten notes and drawings on parchment. These were the elf drawings made of the strange elf Mad Lavender (Christina's name when she resided with the elves). They were done by Lavender's elf mentor while she stayed in the elf clan. In addition, there were drawings made by Christina herself.

Christina's drawings, detailed and full of squiggly lines and hash marks, contrasted sharply with the other elf drawings. His were composed of short, forceful strokes all in a dazzling display of economy of effort and minimal use of ink. As the drawing tells the personality of the artist, he could read Christina's well. Hers told of intensity of focus, bordering on obsession. Over and over, she drew in a particular spot on the page until she had rendered it completely (some would say, rendering it to death). There was a certain fluidity in her style, as though each image on the page was connected by one continuous line. *This is a person who sees not just the thing but its relationship to objects around it.*

The other elf's drawings, while meticulous, were done with a measure of economy— once the general lines were there, he quickly moved on. *This person probably is a more impatient sort,* he thought. *Dispassionate, disconnected from his feelings. His drawings are cold, precise, and accurate.* He compared the two artists' drawings side by side, pondering the persons behind the images, hoping for details to flesh out these characters in his story.

His laptop blinked patiently at the right. Curiously etched dragon bones acted as paper weights for the growing stacks of pages on the left. Book writing for the Professor was always a messy business, especially when compiling a story from a variety of sources. In this case, the sources included those in an elvish language, which was a bitch. It was necessary for him to create in such a disorganized environment. It followed his line of thinking—a zigzagging process where somehow everything was pulled together in the end.

And yet, the effort was worth the trouble. Even being yelled at for no good reason by a queen fairy was a small price to pay for the story of a lifetime. Also, let's not forget the fact that this little gig freed him from the relentlessly boring job of teaching. Thank god that tedious chapter in his life was over.

He sighed again, thinking of that seemingly endless time in which he taught, tested, and graded, only to begin again once the current crop of students finished the class. Teach, test, grade, again and again, an endless cycle of passing time, until he no longer was a brash and bombastic young professor. By the time he had left, he had become a tired, jaded sort, whose language was heavily salted with equal doses of nostalgia for the seventies and derision for the current era. *A curmudgeon*, he thought. *I have become a curmudgeon.*

Funny, I don't feel much like a curmudgeon anymore. Even when that feisty Queen Mari is yelling at me. I feel..., He paused, looking for just the right word to express his present state of mind. Then he had it. *Alive. I feel alive.*

Energized, he moved the piles of papers aside, shook his forehead free of offending and irritating locks of hair, and began to write.

Talk about Feelings, or How to Torture a Guy

"Dude, I like your whole concept. It seems so, I don't know, *precise.* Whereas the total annihilation route seems so, you know, wasteful." Enj, the gargoyle, reclined on the edge of the dry, rocky mountain overlooking the city of Las Vegas, Nevada. It was daylight, but the city still glowed from the endless display of neon lights and glitter.

Squinting, Jay tried to see only the energy fields swirling around the town like Seen did. He wasn't quite as good as the elf, but was getting better with practice. The blinking neon lights of the glittery city weren't much of a distraction as they formed the background to the moving mass of energy. What he was looking for had little or no color. The swirling, misty magical elements were darkness itself, silver and black, flowing like India ink on the surface of water. The magical energy poured like shimmery liquid around the buildings and through the streets of the town.

There, off to the side, was an area of magical damage. A blistery bubble on what would otherwise be a smooth surface of shimmering energy. The bubble appeared to have swollen to bursting. And it was a rather large area, encompassing one of the casinos and a flat, sprawling building that looked like a motel. The two gargoyles, Enj and Jay (Jacob in his gargoyle form) viewed the area with concern.

"If we could figure out who is causing the misuse of magical energy, maybe we could just relocate the offending Fairfolk and hope it all heals by itself," Jay said, squinting hard to see what Enj saw. He had not quite mastered the art of seeing energy the way his other pals had. Enj said that was because he was handicapped by his all-too-frequent human form. It was as though when in man-shape, you began to forget about magic. And Jay equally split his time between human and gargoyle forms, as it suited his needs. That seemed to affect how well he could see magic, even as a gargoyle. What he saw was a filmy sort of substance snaking its way like pale fog through the city below. To him, it was faint in comparison to the rich and subtle hues that Enj was seeing.

"Being human a lot of the time makes it harder for you to see it," he had explained one day to his friend, to which Jay had replied, *"So you are saying I am a retarded gargoyle."* Enj had heartily agreed. Swearing and cussing each other out ensued, until one conceded the superiority of the other's insult. It was a game they played while dealing with serious issues like life and death and their sister, Marissa—which could be a topic of life and death all in itself.

"Soooo," Enj said still studying the magical boo-boo. It was time to broach a most delicate subject, the gargoyle thought. He was stalling, trying to say just the right words, words he had never said to himself, much less to his adopted bother, but words that had to be said.

"What?" J replied. "Spit it out; I haven't got all day. Worlds to save, you know." He gestured to the bustling city beneath them and its big, blistery bubble of magic.

"Well, it's about Mari, uh, Marissa. Supreme Elder Other Queen and all."

"I know who she is. She *is* my sister, you know. And our boss."

"Well, that's it!" Enj said, sitting upright. His friend had put his talonned finger on the problem. In a nutshell.

"OK, in English please."

"Look, Jay, I don't want to be weird and I truly don't want to change the dynamic"

"Dynamic? Have you been hanging out with Seen again? Dynamic, sheesh."

"Well, I have," Enj said, stung by his wingman's criticism. "Seen taught me how to read the magic like I do. It's a mad skill, and I like it. So does Marissa." Enj smiled at the recollection of Mari praising him for finally being able to see the magical net. A tough skill to learn. Even for an Other. But it was her praising him that pleased him most of all.

"Euww. I really hate the way you just said, 'Marissa,' right now. If I didn't know better, I would say you have become fond of her. And not in a familial way. If so, I will have to kill you." Jay sat up, looking closely at his friend, trying to read the subtle expression on his big, scaly gargoyle face. Enj looked away, uncomfortable with the scrutiny, wondering how much to tell his friend about his feelings for his adopted sister—*their* sister. After a few awkward moments, Jay put it all together. "That's what you meant when you said I had it in a nutshell!" He stood and began pacing the rocky slope, piecing the conversation pebbles together into one big avalanche. He turned to his friend, who sat very still on the ground, watching his pal, his brother, hoping what came next wouldn't ruin all that he had in the way of a family.

"You like her. You really like her. You want to— Oh gag, I can't say it. **You** say it. Tell me the truth." Jay planted his feet squarely on the slope, hands on his hips, steeling himself for what was to come.

"Yeah, yeah," Enj said, rising to face his gargoyle brother. "I like her, OK? I can't help it. It just sort of happened. And now, I can't deal with it cause she's my sister, sort of, and my boss and well, your sister to be sure. Then there's the matter of the parentals finding out, and I can't handle **that** at all." Enj's wings began to twitch. They were very agitated at their owner's distress, even lifting him a bit off the ground owing to their highly charged emotional state. Enj looked back at them and said, "Hello, we are in the middle of a conversation here." They came to their senses, as it were, and gently lowered him to the ground, facing Jay. His friend sighed, exasperated at the situation.

"Well, shit, Enj. What do you want me to say? I mean, if she had to hook up with anyone, I guess I'd rather it would be you. But the real question is why? I mean, it's my sister and you **know** how she is."

"Yeah, I know. But do you? I mean, yes, she is your sister and you grew up with her, but in a way, I kind of did too. I was outside looking in, watching how you guys were as a family and all. I know you say she can be a bitch sometimes, but to me, that just means she is strong—a leader. She has a lot on her shoulders and isn't even legal drinking age in your world! She takes care of the big picture while still protecting her family. She never said no when they asked her to take on the job of Supreme Elder Other. And she is smart. Really smart. Her magic skills are the bomb, you know that. Besides, she is cute."

"Oh. You did **not** just say my sister is cute."

"She is. She has all these fashion statements that suit her mood. Glamour, I think it is. It's a kind of power."

"Yeah, I know. Funny, she doesn't even know how cool she can be. So, yeah. I guess I get it a little," Jay conceded. "Theoretically, I can understand, but the thought of the two of you actually hooking, up—that just grosses me out. Plus, have you thought that you two are different magical species? You are hugeness itself, and she is, let's just say, height challenged."

"That's what's cool about being an Other, we can use our magic to change ourselves." Enj smiled at his friend, grinning. "If I can compress myself to be an itty-bitty dust mote, I sure as hell could become a fairy for her."

"You—a fairy? She doesn't egg, or have you not heard."

Enj tried another tack. "Or I can be a guy like you."

"A human guy?" Jay asked, wondering, if Enj became human, what kind of guy he would look like. Probably a little like Sleeping Guy. Kind of laidback but—"No tattoos. She doesn't do tattoos. And you have to clean up your act. You can't look too casual, or she will think you are skuzzy." Jay thought of her numerous criticisms of Bob and his grunge look. To say nothing of his tattoos. She just hated them.

"I'll take that into consideration," Enj said, smiling. In guy speak, he figured this was as good of an approval as he was going to get. He exhaled a deep sigh of relief. "Whoo-ey. I am so glad that's over!"

"You and me both," Jay replied, attention back on the blistery magical owie down below.

"I guess the only thing now is to see what the parentals think about this odd turn of events."

"Parentals?" Jay looked at his friend. "We don't even **know** where Dad is, and Mom is checked out half the time. I wouldn't worry so much about them. It's Marissa you need to worry about. Big-time. She is going to kill you when she finds out you love her."

"Love her? Wait now. I didn't use the 'L' word."

"You love her. You want to marry her," J said in a singsong-y way.

"You are a putz. A prime, grade-A poser gargoyle. A brainiac, geek, nerd bomb."

"Shut up, you incestuous pig. I am going to find Dad and let him magically kick your bony green ass."

"Butt wipe."

"Ten-year-old."

"Weenie."

"You win," Jay said, unable to come up with anymore insults that day. His head was still on the topic of Enj and Marissa sitting in a tree, k-i-s-s-i-n-g. "Now can we please get down there and save the world?"

They rose gently up into the sky and began their descent down the mountainside toward the motel.

* * *

A lone backpacker, climbing up the mountain, was looking for a perfect spot to shoot the neon spectacle of the glittering city. Even during the daylight, Las Vegas had a sort of brilliant aura that glowed. As he trekked up the steep terrain, he distinctly heard, "You have shit for brains," followed by "At least I know better than to date my sister!"

Glancing around, he saw there was no one for miles around. *A stray hot-air balloon?* he wondered. But when he looked up, all he saw were a couple of large red-tailed hawks dive-bombing each other. And yet, when he spotted the same two from the corner of his eye, they seemed bigger than mere birds, more like alien creatures with big leathery wings, swooping up and over each other, playing chase in the sky—only for a second. Looking directly at them, he saw that the glare of the sun had only created the illusion of winged aliens. They were just a couple of large raptors.

So where did the conversation come from? He vowed from then on to eat a better breakfast before hiking and to definitely cut back on the ganja.

Will the Real Honeysuckle Please Stand Up?

"Come on, boys," she ordered, flicking the whip in their direction. "Let's play. Now you all take your clothes off. I'm gonna get all you Amish guys in a lather!" Honeysuckle had retrieved her fallen props and began working the three old men. She wore a wicked smile, which she hoped would encourage them to play S & M games with her. In her mind, she had other S & M games of her own to look forward to. She said to herself, *Let's go, fellas. Get this train down the tracks and finish right quick. I have other things to do with that big wad of cash you are gonna give me.* Outwardly, she was all about them and the business at hand.

The three wizards were dumbstruck. Gobsmacked. Gaping-fish-mouthed, especially at her order to get undressed. "You want us naked?" Demetrius asked timidly.

"Oh yeah!" She smiled even wider as though better to eat them.

"In a lather?" Arthur asked. "Like horses?"

Honeysuckle growled suggestively at the idea. *Horsey? They like to play horsey? I think I got some stuff in my bag for that,* she thought.

Bert started with the shock of understanding the very big picture she was painting. "Ooooh, I see," he said. He gestured for the two Others to confer with him. Whispering, he told the exactly what he thought she was up to. "Oooh" was the joint response. And then "Ugh."

"You mean you want us to angrily conjoin with you?" Demetrius was aghast at the thought.

"Uh-huh," was her reply. She gave them her best, feral smile for emphasis.

"But we don't—" Bert said.

"We haven't—" Demetrius stuttered.

"Not for ages!" Bert continued.

"I forgot how," Arthur concluded. "Does anyone remember how?" he appealed to his brethren. Head scratching all around, with murmuring that included phrases like, *Well, I think,* and *you have to wash first* and *No, no, you wash after.*

Honeysuckle was perplexed. How else was she going to earn that big wad of cash in the dumb one's pocket? Maybe this was just a game. "You like games, boys? I can play which you. Just give me the down-low on what you want to play and I'll roll with that."

"No rolling!" Demetrius emphatically stated.

"I thought we already covered that," Bert whined, a bit frightened of their waif's rather ferocious tone.

"Games, you say?" Arthur asked hopefully. "We do love a good game of Whist!"

"Whist," she said flatly. She had one hand on her hip and the other with the whip dangling. She notched one long leg outward as if striking a pose. Actually, this was her thinking stance. "That's like cards, right?" They nodded enthusiastically. Cards were nice, they all agreed. Cards were so much safer than her whips and her scary spiky shoes. "You tell me you wanna pay me money to play cards? That's it?"

"Oh. Are we to pay you too? I thought this lovely home was all you needed." Demetrius was baffled by her. Imagine wanting silly money when this luxurious domicile would get her out of the stables. That alone should be enough.

"Remember, Demetrius, the nice people at the gambling facility? They liked our money. And then our carriage driver? She liked money too. Oh and at the place of wenches and ale. They *really* liked the money we were giving out. Maybe that is just the custom around here. To hand out lots of money to all the people you meet." Bert, ever the social scientist, made the suggestion in the hopes of fitting in better. Honeysuckle was aghast at the thought.

"Oh now. You ain't just gonna give money to random fools. No more, no how. From now on, you are going to give it to me, got it? I am your, uh, waif for the duration. And waifs need money, honey. Lots of it."

"Oh, well then, by all means, take this," Arthur offered the much-coveted bank roll to her.

"That's just fine. And I thank you kindly," she said taking the cash and stashing it in her big carry bag. "Now if you will excuse me, I'll be on my way." She smiled sweetly as she stashed her props along with the nice new cape they had provided in her bag. Honeysuckle retrieved the trench coat cover-up and began shrugging it on. The wizards' faces adopted a rather crestfallen demeanor.

"Our waif is leaving home!" Arthur wailed.

Golly, it made her feel bad. Like she had disappointed her Johns. Up to then, she had never disappointed a date. *Well, they weren't really Johns,* she reminded herself. *I didn't do nothing for them.*

Then it's like stealing, her conscience scolded her. *And you do not steal. Stay a bit, and earn that bank,* her good angel chided.

Inner turmoil over, she addressed the three sad Amish magicians, "OK, we can play a game. But my game."

"It doesn't involve conjoining, does it?"

"Or pain?"

"Or torture?"

"Or nudity?"

"Oh, honeys, my game doesn't involve no con-join-ation. Or nudity. In fact, there is a rule—a dress code, and that definitely involves clothing."

Well, that sounded promising, they all thought. Anything that didn't expose or threaten their male regions was probably all right. They nodded agreeably at her suggested game. Whatever it was.

"But..." She paused and smiled in that not-so-sweet way she sometimes did. "...my game does involve some pain and torture."

"Oh dear," Arthur said. "How much?"

"A fair amount," she admitted, digging into her bag as she spoke. "But it will get better the more you do it. Well, sometimes, it gets better, sometimes worse."

"And this game is called?" Bert hoped it would be something within their realm of understanding. Perhaps, he thought they could mitigate some of the pain and torture she had alluded to with magic, if only they knew what it was.

She pulled some pants and a very proper-looking shirt out of the duffel bag. It looked like the kind of clothing that provided a vast amount of coverage for her body. The pants seemed long enough to cover the entire length of her very long legs. And the top looked like the sort some of the Other sentries wore outside at Base Camp—short sleeved and collared. She dangled the apparel in front of them.

"This is what I wear for my game. You gonna have to get some duds like this too. It's a rule. My game of cruelty is called *golf.*"

Never Piss Off a Film-Noir Gargoyle

"Careful now," Enj whispered, peering around the corner of the building. While Enj was acting the super-sleuth, Jacob was standing in the middle of the parking lot, out in the open, openly ignoring his friend. Enj, the uber-stealthy spy, was mimicking what he had seen oh so many times on TV; hanging on to the edge of the building, scoping out the façade in a not-so-sly way. The problem was that it called attention to himself. A lot of attention. But seeing as how he was a magical creature and therefore one to be largely ignored by humans, his stealth skills were a bit rusty.

Jacob, now in his human form, figured no one would really look at him if he was out in the open, ostensibly watching the airplanes descend over the building as they landed on the nearby runway.

"Enj, you are a putz. Come out here and help me figure out where the center of this magic ouchy is."

"Well, if you insist. I just hope we don't get fingered." Enj reluctantly left his position and joined his friend in the middle of the lot.

"'Fingered,'" Jacob said, arching one eyebrow. "I don't think so. I think you mean 'collared.' Whatever

'Fingered' meant in those 40's movies, it presently has another meaning entirely, my friend. Best not use that phrase too often."

"Oh, my bad." Enj smiled. Only this time, his smile wasn't the usual toothy feral beastly gargoyle grimace that Jacob had become all too familiar with. This one was a simple, easy smile of a young twenty-something human. Enj had decided to come out to the parking lot, copying Jacob. He made himself into a human creation.

His hair was a tad too long, brushing his fore-head in a Justin Bieber-ish sort of way. But his clothes said surfer, beach dude—faded jeans, white T-shirt under a baggy plaid shirt was the uniform of the day. He had the easy swagger of a swimmer—an athlete. Instead of being buffed, he was lean tall, and very tanned. He had a long aquiline (aka, beaky) nose, which made him look rugged and slightly danger-ous. "Where did all the bronzing come from?" Jacob asked as soon as Enj transitioned to human form. Everything else about him looked pretty authentic, but the skin tone was very weird. It made his green eyes sort of glow. Or perhaps that was just a bit of his magical self leaking out through his eyes. Hard to tell. *At any rate,* Jacob thought, *his skin is off. Like a spray tan gone bad.*

"*The Bachelor,*" he said, proud that he was still up-to-date on his TV shows. "All the girls and guys are tanned. It's a young thing," he concluded, so happy to be in the know.

"The Bachelor? You look like a cast member of *Jersey Shore.* Tone it down a bit, would you?"

"Oh, sure," he said, closing is eyes and willing the color to visibly fade. "That better?"

"Yeah, now you look like some laidback surfer stoner. The way I imagined you." Jacob smiled. It was still a bit orange but much improved from before. His pal was a bit taller than he, yet they looked like they belonged together in the way that close guy friends tended to. They dressed, walked, talked, and acted similarly. Jacob currently was sporting about the same outfit as Enj (Truth be told, Enj copied him a bit)—T-shirt with an opened short-sleeved, button-down shirt draped over faded jeans, and slip-on loafers, all looking very well worn and abused. Jacob's current hairdo involved gelling and spiking. He wore black- rimmed glasses and looked rather retro cool. A definite hipster. The glasses framed his bright-blue eyes, making them sparkle. But perhaps the sparkle had to do with his magical abilities. Hard to tell. Nonetheless, the human shape was one that he slipped into like an old shoe.

Hair is a very personal thing for guys. Clothes not so much. The only thing that differentiated the guys was the hairstyles. Enj's loose, haphazard style wafted in the shimmering heat coming off the paved parking lot. Jacob's wouldn't have moved if it was hit by a hurricane, owing to the magic of hair gel. In that way, the two were different— that and Jacob's black-framed glasses.

"I can't tell which room this is coming from. What should I be looking for?" Jacob asked, squinting, trying to imagine what the source of the magic trouble would look like. Rays? Smoke? Lightning bolts? This was where his skills at seeing the net failed. He depended on his friend for the answer.

"Nothing. It should look like nothing," Enj said. Seeing Jacob's confusion, he tried to point it out to him. "I think the source should look like a void in the flow of magic. Like the energy wants to flow away from it. And so, think of it like a misty net with a big hole. Then see if there is a buildup of the net all around the edges. A thickening as if it had been pushed away from the hole. See? He pointed to a room at the top level of the building. There. I think someone is in there doing magical shenanigans." What Enj saw was a blistery magical bubble with a black dot at the top of the curve. Jacob just saw a hazy smear. *Oh well,* he thought, *I go with the master seer.* Being blind to magic was frustrating for Jacob. Good thing he had his wingman to help him through.

"I guess I can see it, now that you explain it." But, really, to Jacob, his perception of the net was like smudges on his glasses. He was just agreeing with Enj to move things along. *Hell, if Enj says so, then it's probably true. He may not know the difference between collaring and fingering, but he knows his magic.* He looked at his friend. "Let's go up and see who's home."

"Wait. We have to have a plan," Enj insisted, holding his friend back. "Like in the movies. You knock and step away. I say, 'Room service,' and then we bust the door in, OK?"

"Not OK. Not really OK in any way, dude. Have you looked at this place?" Jacob gestured to the worn and shabby exterior. "This is not the kind of place that has room service."

Enj tried again. "Telegram, then. We knock say, 'Telegram'; and then—"

"Yeah, if we lived in the nineteen twenties, then yeah. Otherwise, no. Listen," he said looking at Enj, his pal in a human package. "Why don't we do it like we learned in Other School? Let's magic ourselves into elements. I'll be wind, and you be dirt. We sneak in under the door, and then bust their asses."

"Oh yeah, I forgot." He smiled, remembering all of those tedious lectures about suddenly appearing and scaring the offenders. "We've been so busy ignoring the rules we forgot basic training. You know the helpful stuff like how to surprise your targets." He thought for a minute and then added, "But can I be wind? It would make my hair look so bitchin' when I transform back into a human. Your hair is so stiff it wouldn't make a difference."

"OK. I'll be dirt, and you be wind. When we get under the door, we appear like *whoosh*. But in our human forms just in case any civilians are around. Got it?"

"Yep. That's the plan, Stan."

The two ran up the steps and approached the doorway, which was set back in a recessed nook. The nook gave them enough cover to turn into the two elemental forms they had chosen. A small popping sound was followed by a tiny flash of light, the kind you see on your windshield as a car passes by on a sunny day, temporarily blinding, but of no real consequence. Blink and it's gone back to normal.

A tiny whirlwind swirled outside the door. A pile of white sand puddled at the doormat. Slowly, the grains began to snake their way through the gaps in the cracked weather stripping at the bottom of the door. The tornado (Enj) waited patiently for the sand to make its entrance. It was taking a lot longer than tornado thought it should. So he hurried things along by blowing the last of the pile through the cracks under the door. Much to the surprise of the occupants, a small sandstorm erupted in their room. Well, one of the occupants was surprised. The other three looked at the blowing pile and said collectively, "Uh-oh."

The drapes and tapestries on the wall tugged against their mountings, the air whipping around the room until even the heavy velvet coverlet began flapping about. Eventually, the tiny windstorm subsided, and two young men appeared in the center of what was once a tiny, dusty tornado. In a none-too-smooth gesture, they stumbled forward, attempting to look grave as they tried to adjust their clothing, setting it to rights after the wind tore at them. *How do the Others do it and keep their togas on?* Jacob wondered, trying to shake the last bits of sand from his spiky hair. He pushed his glasses up the bridge of his nose to get a good look at the magical offenders.

"Shit!" he said, when he saw who it was.

"Shit," Enj said, when he saw who it was.

Then they both said, "Huh?" looking at each other for explanation as they saw not one but three nearly identical Supreme Elder Others before them. "Who the hell is this Poindexter and Ashton Kutcher, and *how the hell* did they get into my room?" Honeysuckle demanded.

"It's the boy" Bert said to Demetrius, who nodded in agreement. "But who is the other one?"

"Ooh! I know! I know!" Arthur raised his hand, waiting to be called on. "It's his adopted gargoyle brother. Look, you can see it in his eyes. All green-y and gargoyle-y and just oozing with magic!"

"Nicely done," Demetrius said, coming closer to inspect the human form that the gargoyle had devised.

"So authentic," Bert complimented.

"Funny skin color, though. A shame really. Just a tad too dark," Demetrius added.

"Watch it now!" Honeysuckle warned, making sure there was no slur against dark skin color. She was so confused. This magic stuff had gotten way out of hand with people popping in and out and such. It was like some crazy Chris Angel stunt, except that she was sure now there were no cameras around. And these young boys looked like a whole pack of trouble. They probably would want her to work for her bank, as opposed to these old guys who just wanted to play golf. The game had definitely changed and she was going to have to deal with it. She decided to take charge of the situation. Fake it until she could make it. Out of here. With her money. And the cape. And the silver brooch. She liked the brooch.

"Now, look. I don't know where you all came from, and I really don't care. This is my house and my trick, and I don't want any more than I can handle right now. So you boys call up Lola May and ask her for the book. She'll tell you how you can get your own party started. Go along now, and scoot. The old boys and I gots things to do." She began to herd them toward the door, using her crop as a prod.

"No, wait. You don't understand," Enj said, sidestepping this large and slightly scary black woman. Her six-inch heels looked lethal, and that weird costume, or lack thereof, wasn't at all sexy to him. It was threatening. Jacob dug his heels into the thick carpet in order to prevent this Amazon from herding him out of the room. He gave the wizards a very hard look. "Have you told this huma—I mean, *civilian*, what you are all about?"

His tone was definitely churlish, as it seemed to him that these guys— guys he once thought were singular and definitely not plural, guys who had once seemed very scary to him and now just seemed bumbling, should have known better than to cause all this trouble. The three wizards stood there, sheepishly shuffling their feet, adjusting their robes, knowing that the jig was, in fact, up. They would have to come clean and maybe even suffer consequences for their little adventure away from Home Base. Possibly even the ultimate consequences—they had before always been on the giving end and not the receiving end. It did not feel at all pleasant.

Demetrius, the original Supreme Elder Other and the one who devised all of the Ingenious Solutions sighed. Looking far older than the untold age that he was, he admitted, "It all seemed so manageable at the time. We were simply going to take a little time off. That is, myself and my two substitutes. We just wanted to have some fun and then return to relieve your sister of her duties. It was all so simple. Until we tried to fit in with humans—"

"And their quaint customs regarding money and games and unfortunate waifs," Arthur finished.

"We really tried to behave," Bert added. "But there was so much we had to do, fair trade and all, while aiding this destitute orphan. It was all based on good intentions and not just wanton use of magic. Surely, you understand." Their explanations were met at first with a stony silence. And then it was Enj, laidback Enj, who erupted in a torrent of angry words. The old men hung their heads, knowing that they deserved at least this tongue lashing. And probably a good deal more than that.

"And yet, the same could have been said for Christina and her family. We all were well intended, trying to follow your rules of fair trade after she returned me to my mother. But you in your *great wisdom* choose to sacrifice Christina, make her a damn elf, basically trashing the lives of the entire human family, which, by the way, while I have your attention, why oh why would you throw me, a baby, to the wolves—I mean humans in the first place?" Enj said, getting all fired up now.

"Oh that was a misguided plan of a truly incompetent Other. He has since been demoted to sentry. We are much more selective in who we choose for recruitment now. We have Bob to help us!" Demetrius was very quick with this answer. They had all deeply regretted the hasty actions by several very incompetent Others.

"Fine. Wasn't your plan. But what followed for the humans was pure shit. Wasn't any kind of picnic for me either, by the way. I always felt caught between two worlds." He thought back to his times watching the human family go through the commerce of their lives, bonded in some way, yet very much apart from them. Until just recently, that was his life - being disconnected from both worlds.

He spoke softly in a tone that was beyond fury. It was rage. "It all turned to shit. War, strife, wayward dragons—all because you chose to punish someone for misuse of magic." Enj was just getting warmed up, pacing the small space in the entry of the room. He began ticking off items on an imaginary list as he processed this situation. "You gave Marissa, the nicest girl in our realm…," (All the men registered some surprise at that assessment.) "…the truly crappy job of running your realm while keeping the rest of the Others from finding Ben. You had no idea how to resolve the Ben issue, so you dumped it on a teenage girl. A height-challenged bitty fairy had to pull the load that the three of you couldn't. Spineless of you. Then, you split up into three people—,"

"Well, we were always three people, just taking turns at running things," Arthur tried to clarify.

Enj gave him a withering look and continued his rant, "So you scammed all of us in the realm into thinking there was just one of you while you perpetrated three times the magical trouble down here, including, the involvement of a human woman, which I have no clue what to do with that. But by rights, I know what we should do with you. Your rules. Your consequences."

Jacob interrupted, placing his hand on his friend's shoulder. The touch shocked Enj a little, as human skin was so much more sensitive to touch than Gargoyle scales. The slight shock was enough to briefly dampen his anger. But the rage continued to simmer beneath the surface while he allowed his brother to speak. "Listen, everybody," Jacob said addressing the crowd. "We aren't here to blow anyone up. But we need to get out of here soon because you have made this place unstable. It just might explode without any of our help."

Honeysuckle was terribly confused with all of this talk about magic and dragons and teenage fairies and such. One thing she did know was an angry dude when she saw one. Despite his laidback style, the surfer dude looked like the kind of guy with a long fuse. When it was lit, watch out. Besides, they had been talking about blowing up things. *Terrorists!*

she thought. *They've come to blow up Vegas!* She slowly, so as not to attract attention, began zipping up the items in her bag, trying to plan how to get out the door and escape from this volatile group. "Listen, boys, I spent a lot of my life not telling secrets that my Johns, er, friends, had. I have lived a long damn time in this town just because I don't tell secrets. So I will just keep this one under my hat." She patted her afro, briefly wondering what kind of shape it was in after the bizarre windstorm had blown in. "And be moving along." She gathered up the rest of her things, clutching her bag to her chest like a would-be security blanket and edging toward the door.

"Sorry, sister, but you aren't going anywhere. Unless it's with us." Enj restrained her by grabbing her arm, just firmly enough to show his strength. The dominatrix had spent a lot of her time assessing just how strong her customers were. She could tell right away this one was tougher than he looked. She stopped, knowing he wouldn't let her go without a fight. Of all of the times she had wondered if a John was going to do her in, she thought that now, at this moment, her number was up. And she was so close to qualifying as a professional golfer. *I guess dreams don't really come true, do they?* She sadly thought.

"Could we all just calm down. I have a plan that doesn't involve blowing things up. Just a little sacrifice is all." Jacob gently moved Honeysuckle and Enj away from the door and toward the window. She was only slightly relieved to know they weren't planning on exploding anything. On the other hand, it all sounded like they were involved some seriously shady business that she now knew way too much about. She probably wasn't going to be able to leave this room. Ever.

Pulling the heavy drapes aside, he gestured for the three wizards to look at the view. "Can we just focus now on the magical net?" he asked them, watching their perplexed reaction.

Bert asked for clarification, "The ether? The magical essence?"

"Yes," Jacob said, impatient for them to really look.

"Oh, we decided not to do that whilst on vacation," Arthur explained. "We shut down that ability so as not to distract our self from having fun."

"Well, flip the switch and start looking. You have made a big, bad mess out there!" Enj barked, still smoldering and on his last nerve with these guys.

That was when they looked and really saw the world outside their window. Looking down, they saw the fluid silver and black of the net of energy, the magic that is all around us. They tracked the net as it slithered up the wall and toward their window; it took a sharp turn, veering away from them, leaving a gap in the liquid flow. A big gap. Tiny sparks flashed where the magic was repelled.

"How did we not feel that?" Arthur asked. "I always feel when the magic is thin."

"We chose not to. We chose to have fun instead. And now we have threatened this realm," Demetrius explained, realizing they alone had to bear the consequences of their thoughtlessness. The three old men looked at each other, realizing the gravity of their situation. Each of them then understood that they had to accept the price of their fun. Demetrius addressed the two young men. "We bear the consequences of what has been done to the ether. We are ready. Do what you must."

Honeysuckle wandered over to the window, wondering what all the fuss was about. She squinted, trying to see magical mist or misty smog, or whatever the hell they were all so amped up about. "I don't see nothing, except an afternoon thunderstorm comin' in. That's all."

Jacob followed her to the window. "Good. Very good. The lightning strikes will cover some of the magical flash," he murmured. He was finally going to test his theory. "Look, guys, I, well, we..." He included Enj, who was standing apart from the group in a pout. He really wanted to smite the hell out of these old farts, for a lot of justifiable reasons, but knew Jacob was about to thwart his plan. "We think that annihilation isn't really necessary. Maybe all we need to do is remove all magic from the area, permanently. You give up your magical essence to the net and hope that is enough for it to heal itself."

"One of us has to give up our magical essence?" Bert was horrified.

"No, not one. All three of you," Jacob replied.

"And become human? I think I'd prefer annihilation," Demetrius said.

"Annihilation is too good for the likes of you. You are not calling the shots here. We are." Enj stepped forward, still massively pissed off. Yet, somehow, he knew justice would be served. A big slice of bitter retribution, and he was going to be the one to do it. "Step back," he said to Honeysuckle, raising his arms high.

The dominatrix scurried to the corner of the room, behind the gaming table—the furthest point away from the old men. Clearly, this pissed-off beach bum was directing his anger at the old guys. Thank god he didn't include her in his wrath. After all, she still had that wad of cash in her bag. She hoped that didn't implicate her in any way. She crouched as low as her stiletto heels let her, waiting for the other shoe to drop.

With a great whoosh, it felt as though the air had left the room. A bright flash, a gust of hot wind, and a thick drumming sound in their ears were the after-effects of Enj's act. Honeysuckle blinked hard, trying to get her eyes to recover from the flash. Soon, she could see clearly.

The first thing she noticed was the furnishings. The opulent accommodations were gone. The sad room with the crusty linens and the dirty walls, was back. The canopied bed was just a lumpy, well-worn double bed like it was before. No more birds singing in the bathroom and the fresh smell of a fruit orchard was gone. Musty vapors and something else best not thought of wafted from the commode. Just like always.

The three magical Amish guys lost their luster and now looked like old men. Crouched and, wrinkled with long, white beards swaying slightly in the aftermath of the change, they looked tired and lost. Enj had dressed them in baggy pants and flannel shirts. In a brief moment of concern for their welfare, he outfitted them in dark sunglasses, in the event the bright flash might permanently hurt their eyes. *The better for them to see what they have become,* he thought—old, helpless, and decidedly mortal.

There they stood, in the center of the shabby motel room. Crones with shades. Honeysuckle took one look at the three bearded men and exclaimed, "Oh my God. ZZ Top is in the house!"

Enj moved to the window to see if this had had a good or bad impact on the bubble. "Jacob, what does that look like to you?" Jacob moved around the guys to try to see what Enj saw.

The magic was moving better up the wall but still showed signs of sparking and instability. "Probably takes a while for the essence of these guys to cover the wound," he concluded. "At least I hope so."

"I still think it's a good plan to get out of here right quick. You have a car, ma'am? Because you and these guys need a ride," Jacob asked the hooker.

"Yes, but I **never** have passengers in my car," she protested. "It's an eighty-nine classic BMW, and I worked damn hard for it. Besides, I gots things to do and best be on my way. Seems like you fellas got some serious connections. Maybe you can get a ride for the gents."

Damn, thought Jacob, *she's not cooperating, and I have to get her to get with the plan—whatever that is,* he amended, realizing at this point they were making things up on the fly. *I can't use big magic to con her. Not a good idea right now, right here. I am just going to have to do it the hard way. Maybe a little magic and a lot of coercion.* In other words, he was going to have to use Glamour on her. *God, I hope she doesn't mistake my glamour for attraction. The worst-case scenario is if she thinks I want to have sex with her. I am so done having sex with beasts,* he reminded himself, thinking of his disastrous and embarrassing attempt with a female gargoyle. *I just want a nice, normal human girl,* he told himself for the umpteenth time. *Not this crazy sex warrior.*

Marissa is so much better at this than I. Where is she now when I need her? The idea of him (average Joe) and her (massive scary Amazon) coupling was too much. *She probably would pick her teeth with my bones after. Eeesh.* He could really use some pointers from his sister right now.

But his sister wasn't there. And this wasn't her job to resolve. Steeling himself, he prepared to act the part and accomplish this goal. He hoped it would get them all safely out of this room and far away from the magical anomaly storming outside their room without giving mixed signals.

He got right up in her grill, inches away from her face. This was disconcerting as she was so beast-like and so very tall in those wicked stilettos. Still, he had to make this work. He stepped even closer so that they were eye to eye or possibly eye (his) to nose (hers). Looking up slightly, staring deeply into her liquid brown eyes, he gave it just a dash of magic to seal the deal. "Ma'am. Forgive our being so impolite. In all of the excitement, we haven't formally met. I am Jacob, and you are?"

She stared long and hard into his bright-blue eyes. *They're so glittery,* she thought. *Just like neon.* Her voice took on a soft, breathy tone as though she was speaking from far away. "Honeysuckle, well, actually no. Uh, I mean Betsy. Wait, it's Betsy. For real. My real name is Betsy, after Elizabeth Taylor. My momma just loved Elizabeth Taylor. She named me Elizabeth, then shortened it to Betsy," she replied in her dreamy sort of voice.

"Betsy. So nice. Honeysuckle isn't really who you are, is it?" He cooed softly at her, thinking, *Relief, relief, relief. She isn't a sex warrior after all. Just Betsy. Whew!*

"No, Honeysuckle is what I am on the job. I don't even talk the same when I am not at work."

"I thought so," he said to her quietly, as thought they were the only two in the room. Just two old friends bonding over secrets and memories. "Betsy," he said again like it was the greatest name ever.

Honeysuckle smiled a happy, toothy grin. *He likes me. He really likes me. He likes Betsy, not Honeysuckle.* This was the first time she had really smiled since entering the room. It lit up the place. Her teeth were brilliant blue-white giving her a slightly horsey look. But it was, overall, a sweet smile. So different from the thundering angry dominatrix she purported to be. Actually, that one big grin dispelled the whole frightening image she had worked so hard to portray. Now, she just looked like some all-American girl, playing dress-up in someone else's ridiculous clothes.

Oddly, she chose this moment to pull a black rubber band off her wrist and all the while never breaking her eye contact with Jacob, smoothed her wild afro back into a tight ponytail. It hung low at the nape of her neck, bursting from its rubbery confines at the ends, making it look like a cute bun. Now that the wafting afro was gone, her entire face fit that happy, wholesome smile. "Betsy," he said again, as though that one word was enough to convey a whole new language of meanings. This time, "Betsy" meant "Good girl, this is the real you. And I like the real you..."' That was what that "Betsy" meant. Then, he said, "Betsy" again.

This time, it was like a question. A simple request. "Hmm?" she answered. Her breath nearly fogged his glasses. He hoped that wouldn't happen to break the glamour before he could get her to a compliant and agreeable state.

"Betsy. You do everything for everybody, but what is it that you want? Is it sex, just for you?" *Hope not, hope not, hope not,* he thought. But the question had to be asked to settle the issue once and for all.

"Nah." She smiled. "I don't even much like it anyway. I just want…I really want…" She drifted off, eyes glazing a bit as she searched her heart for the true answer. Bringing her focus back to the nice, young Elvis Costello man with his crazy eyes and big old glasses, she found her answer. "I really want to golf. Be a pro. And teach golf. I want to live near a golf course and play every day." Her reply was spoken like a mantra—as though she had said that so many times deep within her soul so that when she finally spoke the words, they were like a prayer. Or a wish. Her heart's desire.

Yeah! No sex, no sex Hurrah! Jacob was ecstatic. This, he could help her with. In fact, it would solve many issues all at once. The pieces now fit together perfectly. He could just kiss her for helping him with the solution. But no. That might bring up the thought of sex, and he did not want to go there with her. At all. He considered his next words very carefully.

But first, he gestured behind his back to the three old men and Enj. It was the universal sign for money—thumb and forefingers rubbing together. His body blocked that image from Betsy, but the men saw.

Or at least Enj did. He understood the cue. He mouthed the word *money* to the men, who began pulling items out of their pockets, looking for some on their persons. When Enj made the wizards human, he had left the contents of their togas alone, expecting the miscellaneous items to find homes someplace in the new clothing arrangements. Arthur came up empty, having giving his pile of cash to the waif just earlier. But Demetrius and Albert still had their wads of hundred-dollar bills. They quickly handed them over to Enj, who palmed them into Jacob's out-stretched hand. The young man took a quick look at the amount now in his possession and after a mental *holy shit,* began talking softly to Betsy. It was a pleasant tone that brooked no argument.

"Betsy," he began, "what's been holding you back all these years are two things. First…" He broke his gaze, bringing his hand toward hers. She looked down and saw the most money she had *ever* seen at one time in her life. Automatically, she reached for it. He began peeling off the bills and one by one placing the money in her hands. With each sentence, he handed more over to her until the cash had filled her cupped hands and was falling to the floor.

"First," he said, doling out the dough, one, two, three, "you needed bank. Big bank. Which is why…" Four, five, six, the bills kept on coming. "You turned into Honeysuckle, right?" She nodded. "Well, now…" Seven, eight, nine. "You can just be who you are. Betsy. Hanging out at the golf course and trying to make the professional cut. But you can't exactly stay here, can you?"

She shook her head "no," thinking of how Lola May and the other people who had controlled her life for so long wouldn't take kindly to her leaving town without paying them their cut of this trick. Way back in the far reaches of her mind was Betsy yelling to herself, *No way are those fools gonna get a percentage of this!* Ten, eleven, twelve, he was still laying the bills into her hands. "So, Betsy, you are going to leave town and drive far away from here. Here's all the money you need to do that. You are going to play all the golf you want. You got any friends or family who need to know where you are going?"

"No," she said softly, sadly. "The closest things I have to friends or family are in this room. They said they adopted me." Her eyes filled with tears. Jacob reached up and with his thumb, gently wiped her eyes dry, before their connection was lost. It was all in the eyes, and he didn't want anything to interfere. Not even tears. Although they helped him in his overall strategy. "It's fine, Betsy. You're fine, Betsy. They are your family now. Because they are going to help you with your second problem."

Betsy felt the weight of the money in her hands. She even heard a few bills land softly with a slight whisper on the crusty carpet. It was a beautiful thing. It even felt warm her hands, which had been so cold and empty for so long. What problems could she possibly have at this moment when so much had just been given her? After all, she had this lovely, enigmatic Poindexter kid, who was probably her new best friend. And cash. And her car. And this new faux family. At this juncture, life couldn't be more perfect. "You said second problem. What's my second problem?" she asked quizzically.

"Betsy, it's such a small one, so easily remedied. You will play all the golf you have ever wanted. And you will teach. But what you need are students. And here are your first students." He stepped aside, breaking the eye contact, gesturing grandly at the three old guys. The men straightened visibly, tucking in their clothing and trying to smarten up as best they could. Arthur patted his beard down, while Bert smoothed back his long, flyaway hair. Demetrius pouted, looking dolefully at her, deciding that the odds of her taking them under her wing was long at best.

"Them?" she said, looking dubiously at them. Jacob placed his hand on her arm. She looked down at him and then into his eyes again. Their gaze caught as he locked her into his glamour once again. *All right*, she thought, *I guess it's all right.*

"Well, really, it is their money they have given you…a new lease on life, as it were. The least you can do is take them on the little drive out of town and to a few golf courses. Somewhere far away from here. Maybe pick them up a few bags of used clubs. Take them on as your apprentices. You know, just for now."

"Should I really do this?" she asked her Svengali.

"Oh absolutely," he replied, taking her arm and picking up her bag. He led her to the door, nodding the old men to follow him. They scurried behind, quickly scooping up the fallen $100 dollar bills, not wanting to leave the protection of their new teacher. "Only, I want you to take them far away from here for obvious reasons."

"Yes, Lola May knows my car; if I am in town, she'll come find me. And not in a good way."

"So you see, you have to go far, far away, with your new students. Head north. Way north. California. Past the Bay Area even. Find some quiet backwoods community with lots of golf courses. Get yourself hunkered down where the bright lights of Vegas would never look for you. Then play golf with these guys as much as you want. You know some golf courses in California like that?" He continued speaking, lulling her into cooperation, as they headed out of the dismal room and towards the stairs to the parking lot.

Betsy replied, "Oh, I know a lot of vacation golf courses like that. Nothing fancy and not luxurious, but good ones, well maintained. There's some up in the high country."

"Fine, fine. Head there. Now. Before your Lola May finds out you stiffed her."

By then, they were down the stairs, and into the parking lot. She led them to her car and unlocked the doors with her key. Before she could object, the old men clambered into her car.

Enj sternly addressed the men in the car. "You guys behave. Do exactly what she tells you. Because if you don't, I will find out. You just got a pass on annihilation, but don't think I won't come back to do the job if you make another mess of things. Got it?"

"Oh absolutely."

"Most assuredly."

"You can count on us!" These were the hurried replies.

"And check in with your cell phones. Remember, I can find you wherever you are."

"Also, careful with her car. No food or drinks while she is driving. And close the door with the handles only. No touching the door panels or the windows," Jacob added, feeling rather protective of his new friend. After all, it was his fault that the three stooges were cramming themselves into her pristine vehicle, which she already admitted rarely had passengers. He would feel terrible if Betsy's car suffered some sort of damage from them.

His orders were met with enthusiastic nods all around as Betsy climbed into the driver's seat. She handed Arthur the bag to hold as he was in the front passenger seat and the backseat was full of the other two ex-wizards. He patted it like it was a puppy, smiling happily at her. Betsy rolled her eyes at him, started the engine, gunned it, and then took off as quickly as she could, knowing her departure would be reported by the motel manager to her madam. She headed south out of the motel parking lot so as to confuse her would-be pursuers. As she rounded the corner, out of sight of the motel, she turned north, toward the high country of Lake Tahoe, California where peace, quiet, and golf courses abounded.

Enj and Jacob stood near the place where the car had just been parked, watching them leave. They didn't take their eyes off the car until it was completely out of sight. Then they turned their attention to the magic above the motel. Jacob saw misty gray, moving nearly uniformly above and around the building. Enj saw that the magical Band-Aid consisting of the three wizards' essences somehow deflated the bubble of tension. It had flattened, and the magic began to move a bit more fluidly. Although not quite back to normal, it was much better than before. He said to his friend Jacob, "I think that did it," After a few more moments of scrutiny, he was satisfied with the results. "Shall we report in?" he asked his human brother.

"What? So you can say you saved the day and impress your girlfriend?" Jacob taunted.

"Shut up, Fearless Fly. By the way, nice spectacles," he added for emphasis.

"OK, Justin Bieber. Let's go. Do you know how to find your way to Home Base, or will all that hair get in your eyes?"

"You win. Let's go."

"Weak. Very weak."

"Listen, I just shot my wad being pissed off at not one, but three Supreme Elder Others; I am a bit worn out right now," Enj whined.

"Whereas all I had to do was test my theory of annihilation and seduce a six-foot-tall hooker, all at the same time."

"You didn't seduce her. You wouldn't know how. Besides, it was me that took away their magic. Not you. Maybe you need some further instructions."

"OK," Jacob agreed. "Maybe I should just get lessons from you after you try and hook up with your sister, sicko."

With a poof and a whoosh, they both became their old gargoyle selves again. Just a brief flash of light in the motel parking lot. Could have been caused by a passing jet or perhaps a bit of lightning. Nothing to see, really.

The motel manager was staring down the road, watching the classis BMW fade into the line of traffic. He had little interest in a small flash of light in the parking lot as he was focused on trying to figure out which direction Honeysuckle had gone with her tricks. Usually, she just stayed put until the job was done. Looked like they were going to party elsewhere. He never even noticed the transformation of the creatures in broad daylight.

The magically camouflaged gargoyles rose in the air and prepared to head back to Home Base. Their wings lifted them up above the motel, just missing a landing airplane, full of eager Vegas partygoers. Those in the plane who had already began their Vegas trip by drinking heavily on the flight took one look out the window to find two monstrous creatures flying by the tip of the wing. The nondrinkers, disbelieving their very eyes, all separately concluded that the glare was much too much, playing tricks on the eyes. Most everyone began pulling down their shades, vowing to take it a little slower on the partying for a while. If they hadn't been deafened by the roar of the engines and the grinding of the landing gear, they would have heard the conversation of two gargoyles, winging their way home: "Shit for brains" followed by "Hooker lover."

Even if they had heard, no one would ever tell. After all, what happens in Vegas stays in Vegas.

Like High School Again, Only Not

The drive took them off the main four-lane highway to a winding two-lane road that snaked up the low hills surrounding the mountain meadow. They were headed to the abandoned golf course, the one curiously called The Beast, then The Dragon, yet was incongruously designed with an American Indian motif. This was the doomed and ambitious development project that had failed.

It was built at first with such promise. Initial lots selling at top dollar, the first home buyers purchased the choicest lots with the best views and the most opulent homes. Now all were empty. Upside down in financing, most homeowners left the sad and abandoned place, losing their dream homes in a short sale or at an auction on the courthouse steps.

The golf course investors gave up maintaining the grounds and facility. First, a few hardy investors tried to hang in and continue operation. But after the strange event of the standing stones all disappearing one night, everyone was just too spooked to stay.

That was where Christina and Sleeping Guy were headed. The closer they got to the golf course, the surer she was that Ben was there. She could just almost feel him as they neared the abandoned course.

It made sense that he was there. He had played golf in this area before, back when he could thoroughly enjoy losing himself in the game. He even told her that was where he felt the most peace and contentment. He had liked the area so much they once had visited a local realtor looking for retirement homes, partially to placate his wants. Christina and Ben had a deal between them. Ironically, Christina had picked the current house they last lived in, the one where all of this magical madness had occurred, and he got to pick the next one. And if it happened to be up in the mountains on a golf course, then so be it.

Of course he would head up here. He knew the area, and it had once been a source of fun and happiness. What a pleasant respite from all of the recent drama they had been through. The last time she had seen Ben, he had ranted at his family. He had railed at them for his inability to protect them in the current situation with the Others. He could not fathom why they were so eager to join this insane world of fairy tales that could actually kill. And so he left in rage and frustration. Maybe by coming back to this place, he would find some solace, some way to dampen his anger. "Although we all deserved it," she muttered to herself.

They pulled into the empty golf course. Weeds grew up in the cracks of the concrete. They maneuvered around the larger clumps breaking through the pavement.

"Deserved what?" Sleeping Guy asked gazing at the tall grass where the fairway had grown over and the encroaching sagebrush crept unchecked onto what once was the putting greens.

"His wrath," she answered, shutting off the engine. She removed her sunglasses and tucked them into the pocket of her blouse.

"Ben's? Nice guy Ben? Wrath?"

"Yup."

"Are you telling me he is a hothead too? I thought Marissa was the only one. What kind of volatile family are you?"

"You love us. We are the biggest, best thing that ever happened to you."

"Maybe. I'll reserve judgment until I see how this little caper turns out." He was still pouting over her chastisement regarding his (liberal) use of *medical* marijuana. That still stung.

It was quiet near the clubhouse. Built to resemble a giant Indian lodge, it sported totem-pole columns with painted Indian symbols on the support beams. Beside the parking lot was a large pond with an enormous bronze statue of a hunter in full Indian regalia, headdress and all, poised and ready to loose an arrow at an imaginary prey. Possibly the prey was The Beast that the name referred to. It was still baffling to her why they didn't name it Teepee or Chief Shoshone or Wampum Golf Course, or something more in line with the design. Nope, it was just The Beast. Maybe that was how it felt to play it. Like a big beast stole your ball at every turn. *Who knows?* she shrugged.

Due to lack of aeration, the once crystal-clear pond was now bright green, choked with algae. The algae had climbed its way up the body of the statue and dripped heavily off the metal arrow. It was as though the green plant life was working steadily to pull the big bronze man down under the surface of the pond. Nature was having a good time undoing all that had been so meticulously designed by man.

This was a sad and eerie place. The quiet was unnerving, so much so that the sound of their shoes crunching across the lot seemed to echo across the course. They headed to the clubhouse to refer to the course map still affixed to the outside wall. An elaborate wood carving of all eighteen holes was their point of reference. It too bore the ravages of neglect—cracking already from exposure. "Let's find the place where the standing stones were and work outward from there," she suggested. He ran his hands over the map, as though reading it by Braille.

"There." He pointed. The stones were on the edge of the course past the tenth hole. They looked to see the most direct way to get there. They would have to cross several of the old greens, which were choked with brush and tall grass. "Let's get going," she said, anxious to get the inevitable confrontation over with.

It was a slog of a trek. Most of the grass was about knee high, and choked with sticker weeds. The areas punctuated by brush caught and tore at their clothing. Christina was dressed in her designer outfit, still in her human form from the diner, but her jeans, boots, and long shirt helped to keep the injuries to a minimum. Sleeping Guy was taking the bigger hit from the hike. His jeans kept most of the brambles from scratching his legs, but his arms were bare. More important, he was only wearing flip-flops on his feet. Soon, stickers and burrs were catching between his toes. The thin rubber sole provided an inadequate cushion at best for the rocks that attempted to push through and cut his feet.

The sage brush was unforgiving in the way it resisted their efforts. Still, they persisted, Christina knowing that the more difficult it seemed to reached their goal, the more likely magical creatures were about. The resistance was a form of magical barrier, barring most humans from entering an area once they felt it. Sleeping Guy was certainly feeling its effects.

"Dude—ma'am," he corrected himself, knowing this family was a touchy bunch about names. Although they never referred to him by his real name, he thought, a tad hurt by that. Except when they really wanted something.

"What?" Christina asked pushing a big branch aside, only to have it snap back in his face.

"How can you be sure this is the right way? I mean, it looks so impassable, like even when we get to the stones, like it would be totally uninhabitable. So I mean, shouldn't we go in another direction or something?" He panted slightly from the exertion. She stopped and faced him.

"Close your eyes," she directed.

"Fine. They are closed. Now what?"

"Breathe slowly, in and out, through your nose, not your mouth. Good. Now stand very still and relax. Open your hands a bit as though to let the air touch your palms. What do you feel?"

"Nothing. Itchy, I guess. Makes me want to scratch all over." He opened his eyes. "Do you think we ran into some poison oak?"

"No, it's not poison oak. It's magic. We are passing through a wall of sorts, meant to keep people like you out."

"Magic is scratchy? I don't think I like it."

"You just aren't tuned into your Fairfolk side. If you were, you would feel it like I do."

"What's it feel like to you?"

"Like I am coming home" She smiled at him, knowing for good or for bad, her mate was near. "Let's keep going this way." In a way, she felt like a kid again. The halls of high school came rushing back to her: that moment of excitement and dread when you know that that guy will be at his locker, right where you always see him, excitement that you may catch his eye as you pass by, thereby being rewarded with a brilliant smile meant only for you. Cue the birds singing, bells chiming. Or you feel dread because he just may look up, see you, and dismiss you for someone better right behind you. Crickets chirping, sadness, and heartbreak abounded. Could go either way.

Only in this case, there were no halls, no lockers—just sagebrush, thorny weeds, and a woman who only faintly looked like she did when she was human, accompanied by a sloppy, messy-haired, tattooed kid, cussing his way through the overgrown jungle. She looked down at her sweaty clothes, getting messier by the minute from the hike. She was sad that she wasn't that beautiful young girl he was once so enthralled with. Gone was all of that, with just the truth remaining to bond them. Or not.

Yep, she thought. *Could go either way.*

Like Swans and Wolves

They both felt it at the same time. Their reactions, however, were quite different. The man paused. Sensing her before he could see her and sniffing the air in an almost feral way, he knew she was nearby. The elf with the large green wings was literally halted by said wings, their expanse furling back, scooping the air behind him to drag him backward into a stop. "What?" he asked them irritably. They were mute, of course, being wings and therefore limited to nonverbal communication. So he looked at the man for an explanation.

"Damn," was all he would say as he began scanning the area around them.

"Oh," Seen said. He tried to feel as well as see the magic around him. It had suddenly taken on a rather energetic glow, amped up and sparkling. That could only mean one thing: someone from the Family was approaching. They had that sort of effect on the magical essence, leaving their fingerprints as it were on the filmy fluid. Ben had his own tracings in the magic. This one had all the markings of the mother, Christina. "But she never leaves Home Base," Seen said aloud, mostly to himself.

He scanned the general vicinity for her. They were in a small meadow adjacent to the abandoned

 257

golf course known as The Beast. Ben used to call it
The Bitch because of the level of difficulty of play.
The trolls loved this area, having inhabited it for
quite some time now. It had plenty of space to hunker down and meditate. And there were the necessi-
ties of important bridges and train trestles, giving it
all the comforts of home. Now that humans had all
but abandoned their hopes to develop it, the Fairfolk
had come back to reclaim their home.

Ben liked it there. It suited him. There was quiet
and serenity that only an alpine region could provide. The air was crisp and sharp, piney. Even the
water tasted different. It had a brittle coldness to the
tongue that was refreshing. And the Fairfolk here,
the trolls, and lately Seen were his kind of people.
Sure, none of them weren't human, but he liked
their particular lack of guile. These were not the
plotters and schemers bent on testing and twisting
the fates of lesser beings like the Others did. They
did not endlessly maneuver to destroy those who
either by accident or design upset their carefully
spun worldview.

These guys were in fact utterly uninterested in
such stuff. They lived totally inside their heads, relat-
ing to each other only in the sense that they could
together mull over new words or phrases that were
abstractly amusing. They were the equivalent of
geeks, who had little interest in relationships. They
didn't judge or punish and were just happy to take
you as you were. Even if you were a magical human
who once peed on one of them. They were, in short,
a no-pressure kind of crew.

But now, pressure had just entered the arena.
He could feel her presence even though he hadn't

yet seen her. She was just there, beyond the shrubby scrub oak trees that hung low and heavy. The crowns of those trees lay nearly on the ground, branches meandering lazily, parallel to the ground before shooting upward to the sky. There. She was right behind one of the branches, with Sleeping Guy trailing noisily behind her. Seen followed Ben's gaze and spotted her and the home caretaker as they emerged from the shrubbery.

Seen waved enthusiastically, excited to see her. His wings nearly slapped him on the head for being so stupid. If they could have talked, they would have reminded their owner that she wasn't there to say hi to him. She was there to finally confront her husband.

She meekly waved back at Seen, happy to have at least one of the two welcome her. Her shy gesture died as she approached her husband. So much depended upon what would happen next.

Seen and Sleeping Guy greeted each other, having met once before. They nodded in acknowledgment of each other's presence. Sleeping Guy could actually feel the charged atmosphere between husband and wife. He watched Seen adopt this dopey, sappy look that spelled, "Aw shucks, let's see if they kiss and make up." At that point, Sleeping Guy took charge.

"Nothin' to see here. Nothin' to see." He put his arm around Seen's smaller shoulders, carefully threading it between the elf's body and his wings. "Let's jam and leave these two alone to catch up, OK, buddy?"

The elf had hoped to witness an epic reconciliation between the two. Some final chapter in the saga of the Family. The world *should* know what the outcome of this story they all had been living. He assumed it probably was his job to hang around to remember who said what. But when he looked at the caretaker man and saw him waggling his eyebrows meaningfully, he had another thought. *Oh. Oh!*

Realization dawned on Seen that perhaps the couple did not want an audience right at the moment. He had become so accustomed to hanging around the Family and being the fly on the wall that he had forgotten that sometimes it was best to give them privacy.

"Right," the elf said to the young man. "Let me introduce you to my peeps."

Seen was real proud to finally be able to say he had peeps. He couldn't wait to show them to S.G. He led the youth back the way he had originally come, anxious to introduce this human to a bunch of talking, wise-cracking, brilliant, and sometimes farting rocks.

Rock, Paper, Scissors

It was a rocky start. They were both awkward and tongue-tied, neither knowing how to break the silence. Would they begin in anger, blame, and recrimination for each other's actions?

You abandoned me!

You forgot me.

You left our children when they needed you most.

You indulged our children when they needed that least.

You got us into this mess.

You won't help us out of this mess.

And mostly, *I need you,* were the key talking points they had both rehearsed in their heads, waiting for this inevitable moment. And yet they both wondered if any of these points would get them further to their goal of resolution and absolution.

Yep, those were the high minded and lofty thoughts running through the couple. Those thoughts were, however, punctuated by baser, meaner ones. Simple word declarations of war that started with:

Selfish bastard.

Self-absorbed bitch.

Thoughtless mother.

Heartless father.

Along with, *You look shot* and

You look like a Beverly Hills housewife on a bad camping trip.

Which led to the further accusations of *shallow* and *cold.*

In short, they had an entire four-course therapy session, going through the fifteen phases of anger and grief without uttering a single word. After much fidgeting, toeing the scrubby ground, and avoiding eye contact, Christina felt that she had had enough of silent arguing. "Did you get my wine? You look tired. Are you all right?"

"Yes. And I'm fine." He shrugged. Shrugging was his body language for, "No, I am not fine at all," and "I am lying."

"I see," she said, knowing he wasn't OK at all.

"How are the kids?" he asked staring at a spot in space over her shoulder. Acting like it didn't really matter to him how they were, when he so badly needed to hear they weren't harmed by his defection.

What could she say? So many things... *They are in a state of panic trying to keep your whereabouts secret so as to save your ass? They feel lost and rejected by you, wondering if your leaving was their fault? In spite of everything, they are growing and changing and becoming great big mature people without any of our help?* or *They still need and miss you like I do?*

Instead, she said, "They are OK. Marissa is in charge now, and the both of them have a lot on their plates. They..." She paused, trying to say neutral, pleasant things, treading water when she felt like drowning.

She couldn't stand it anymore. This pretense, when they never played that way in their marriage, was making her crazy. "Oh shit, Ben, it's been terrible without you. We have all been barely holding on. Especially me." And then she said those big words, the life-changing words that stop every argument dead in its tracks. "I am so sorry." For the first time, she looked straight at him. And he her.

The mask of stillness that he had carefully wore slipped just a little. Little lights of vulnerability leaked through the edges, making his blue eyes bluer somehow. His mouth took a tiny tick as paused, and then carefully said, "For what exactly are you sorry?"

This question made her the tiniest bit mad. After all, she had just blurted out an apology for her part of this mess. That was huge. And now he was quizzing her to see what exactly she's sorry for? As though it was some sort of test? She didn't exactly like having to account to him like a recalcitrant child. On the other hand, she had done some bonehead things. She took a deep breath and willed herself to be calm. Setting aside her annoyance, she ticked them off on her fingers.

"Well, for one, I was feeling old and useless. Going to Other School with the kids made me feel young again. That was selfish. Two, I loved using magic. It was fun. It made me feel powerful. That also was selfish. Three, our kids are at an age when they usually should leave the nest. This way, we could still be together sharing the big secret about Fairfolk. Also selfish. I just got caught up in the excitement and glamour of it all. But mostly, number four, which really should be number one, I just said the other things first because they came to mind…"

"Christina. Number four."

"Right. Number four, which is really number one. I am **so sorry** I forgot about you in this whole process.

I let my wants and my selfish needs just roll all over what you wanted or needed. I mean, you have always taken a backseat to what the rest of us want. You just try and figure out how to fix things for us. But you never get to do what you want. This time, you really didn't want us to get involved with the Others. But we did anyway. I am so sorry I forgot about you."

She looked at him long and hard. His expression was hard to read. Maybe he was processing her "I'm sorrys" and needed time. So she added, "Because when you left, I realized that forgetting you was to forget the best part of all of us. Life has been beyond crappy without you." There. She did it. She gave it her best shot. She looked hopefully at him.

This helped the situation to an extent. Somehow a big bomb had been defused. And yet, there was still something small and hard in his look—as though he had to be absolutely sure about something and she hadn't quite given it to him yet. There had to be another bomb silently ticking somewhere else that she hadn't yet defused.

This made her the teeniest bit madder still. "Well?" she asked.

"So yeah," he replied, taking a totally different tack. He wasn't ready to get to the heart of the matter. Afraid really of what she would do should he give her the ultimate choice he had in mind. He continued as though she had never made any of her heart-wrenching admissions. It was suddenly as though he was just having a conversation with an acquaintance. You know, just catching up.

"What happened was I was just, you know, hanging out, on my own, thinking about stuff…"

Stuff? she thought. *He sounds like an awkward teenager talking to some girl, instead of his wife, who he had abandoned.* The silent anger within her began to simmer as he blathered on.

"…when I ran into these trolls. Well, actually, heh, heh, I literally peed on them. It's a funny story really, I—"

"Are you fricking serious?" Christina interrupted. She was incredulous. "We are talking about our entire life right now, and all you can talk about is peeing? Really?" She rubbed her forehead as though to forestall a massive headache. It wasn't working. Inside, she was shaking with some sort of toxic mix of emotions, and he had reverted to a fifteen-year-old, talking about body functions. It was too much. The anger was now full blown and right there on the surface ready to burst. Either that or her head was exploding. She wasn't sure which would go first. "I don't even know you anymore," she concluded.

He was ready with a sharp rebuke. In fact, he was ready with a whole bunch of sharp rebukes, things that had been on his mind for a long time now came bubbling up to the surface and spewing out.

"You don't know me? Really? Cause that's very funny. *I* look the same. *I* am just a regular guy, and *you* don't even look like my wife anymore. You've magiked yourself into your favorite image and likeness. All the flaws gone until my wife, the real Christina, is gone. And now there's just some bizarre facsimile standing here. So let's just say, I completely know who I am. You'd best look in the mirror and in that pool of water you love so well to see the truth of who you are." He began pacing in his agitation, two steps away, one step back, as though he never could be too far from his orbit with her as the hub.

Subconsciously, it made him even madder that he couldn't just leave.

"There," she said waving her hand upward as though to erase herself. "Is this better?" Gone was the designer clothing, and there stood the old Christina—white-haired, tall, curvy in a good/bad way, and clothed in a pair of jeans and a T-shirt. She kept the boots, as these probably would have been her fashion choice anyway owing to the comfort factor. Overall, not the best of fashion options, but at this point, she didn't give a shit about clothing.

The old Christina standing there, slightly breathless from her change, gave him pause. He stopped and looked at her. This was the woman he really wanted. "Can you really go back to this?" he asked.

This was in fact the heart of his question. Who would give up magic and power and the ability to change your very looks if you so choose once it had been given to you? Well, he had concluded that he could. But could she? And that was the main issue between them. Would she sacrifice once again? Only this time to save her marriage?

"You *like* this?" she asked incredulously. After all those years she had spent trying to diet and exercise and whittle away the extra poundage, moisturizing the wrinkles into submission, he actually didn't care if she looked like this. It actually kind of pissed her off. Even more.

"Sure. It's all I have ever wanted. Look, these guys back there are great." He gestured behind him toward where Seen and Sleeping Guy stood with the troll clan. They were watching the confrontation between husband and wife with great intensity. They were, however, far enough away not to hear what the two were actually saying. So, although being on display kind of annoyed him, in the big picture, it didn't really matter. What mattered most was how his wife would react to his proposal.

"They were just what I needed for the time being. They don't really like using magic, except when they have to change into rocks and such, so that doesn't really count. And they don't judge. They are simple and relaxed. No pretense. Just Fairfolk who love a good story. And they like me. They get me. They even honor me for my storytelling."

"And in these stories, who exactly are the bad guys?" she asked, in a tone that said, *I know who you made the bad guy and, thank you for making me the evil queen in your little fairy tales.*

"Others," he answered truthfully. "The Others are pure shit, and we are stuck in the middle. They are the true bad guys."

"And what about our children? You realize that one of them is now Supreme Elder Other. Does that make her pure shit? And your son, he is an Other a very powerful one trying to figure out another way to deal with Fairfolk besides blowing them up. Is he pure shit too? Because as I recall, they took on those jobs primarily to save your ass from being blown away." Her voice took on a wicked deadly tone that only a mother defending her children could use.

Small lesson for warring couples. Never make it a fight about the children because it can get pretty ugly right quick. He spared no time in retaliating.

"And you let them be in charge. Put them right out on the firing lines while you did what, run away? Hide? Scry?" He stretched the word *scry* out, taunting her. This had definitely gotten ugly.

She looked at him, suddenly shutting down her feelings. It was too hurtful right now for her to think they could resolve anything. "Yes," she said. "That's exactly what I did. I hid in my room, spending every waking moment using all the talents I had looking for you, worrying about you. Scared to death for you. While you hung with the guys, scratching and laughing over campfire stories. And peeing, apparently. You know what? I'm done here." She brushed past him, heading off in the direction of the last sighting of Sleeping Guy and Seen.

He had no choice but to follow her in the direction of his friends. The mere proximity of her seem to pull at him, dragging him always to trail in her wake. Besides, there was nowhere else to go. All he could think of was the child's game, rock, paper, scissors. Tit for tat, blow by blow, each had taken a turn being paper or scissors, winning the point, only to be bashed in the next round by rock. 'Round and 'round it went until nothing was resolved except the admission on both sides of tremendous hurt. Too much was expected of the other when they were bound by the rules to be either rock or paper or scissors and nothing else. Each continued the silent war as they both headed in the direction of the troll clan.

Arguing one's point always sounds best when one tries them out on oneself. After all, you are the injured party and you are also the mediator. It only stands to reason that you find your own points a) brilliant and b) utterly, irrefutably right. This is the place the couple found themselves in when they arrived at the troll camp. Christina headed straight to Sleeping Guy while Ben made a wide berth around her to the edge of the group.

Seen was introducing the clan to a very wide-eyed Sleeping Guy. He had never seen walking, talking cavemen, and to him, that was exactly what they seemed to be. Their features were mere approximations, roughly formed as if chipped from rock. They all possessed craggy foreheads, deep-set eyes, and strange slashes of mouths as though an artist had just begun to sculpt them only to drop his tools after losing interest.

And yet, they spoke so eloquently. Their words were brilliant, descriptive, and full of follow-up questions about the Family. Details were what they were looking for. *What does the house smell like?* was one of the weirder questions. But also, they were fascinated by the relationships among the members.

You see, Ben told the tale all in black-and-white. There were good guys and bad guys. But as Seen retold it, the humans possessed an entire range of feelings, a spectrum of both good and bad behaviors, making it impossible to determine good versus evil as well as how exactly the story would end. The one thing they all agreed on was a happy ending. They all wanted a happy ending to this epic story, one that would sustain their group meditation for a long damn while.

Fred took a look at the two who were decidedly not acting like a happily reunited couple. She asked, "Excuse me, but exactly when will there be a happy ending?"

This made the group leave off their discussion about television and focus on the somber looking husband and wife. "Let's not talk about this for now" Ben said, busying himself with the task of cleaning the ashes from the fire pit.

"S.G., let's go." Christina with the sheer force of a look, got her driving partner to begin ever so reluctantly walking with her toward the golf course barranca.

Sleeping Guy cast a mournful look over his shoulder at the trolls that said, "*Now don't you feel sorry for me?*"

Seen rushed to his rescue. After all, he was one of the badass heroes in the stories and it was his duty to help resolve this little snag in the plotline. "Wait. You can't go yet. It's getting dark. Too dark to see your way back to the golf course."

"Not for me," Christina said waggling her magic fingers.

"Oh definitely no," Ted said. "We know what happened the last time you tried to light something up. You actually blew up an entire forest. Obliterating it completely while you laughed insanely at the wreckage." Ted was very proud he had remembered that part of the narrative so well. "We certainly can't have that here. Too much attention called to ourselves."

"Oh really? That's what I did?" she said dangerously to her husband. Ben shrugged his shoulders, continuing to rake the ashes from the big pit. Perhaps he smirked, just a little, but only to himself.

"Well, at any rate, it does get dark early around here, and we have a nice campfire with some fresh-caught venison. They have a very interesting way of hunting, you know. They set themselves up as boulders near the tastiest green plants. Then when just the right-size deer come along they simply wait until it gets closer and closer. Then boom! They roll over on it, bashing it successfully to kingdom come!" Seen was delighted to share that little tidbit with Christina and S.G. Such interesting local customs.

The troll clan instantly adopted their rock forms as they did a mini-meditation on the phrase *kingdom come.*

Medieval in origin they postulated. *Indicating that everyone would someday, in the next life, possess their own castle and keep.*

But if that's so, one asked, *then why don't they just do themselves in so as to move along to their kingdom come?*

Interesting question, another said. *Perhaps it relates to earning their—*

"Hey, hey, snap out of it!" Seen said. *Jeepers, they do this all the time. The minute they hear some interesting turn of phrase, they just firm up and hunker into their own little mind-speak.* It had been happening so often that Seen could almost hear them think-talking. It was a whispery sort of sound, like a soft breeze interspersed with the murmurings of an odd word now and then. If he stayed much longer, he might just catch on to their mind language, but for now, he needed backup to help calm Christina down and make her stay.

The troll clan, in unison, unmolded themselves into their more-or-less human forms. The sound was of gravel crunching under car tires, all squinchy and grating. S.G. could not believe what he had been seeing. "This is way cooler than fairies," he said.

Christina sighed as she watched her driving companion make his way back to the trolls, patting them to see what their formerly rocky skin actually felt like. He was fascinated by their metamorphosis. In turn, they inspected his tattoos, demanding explanations for each one.

Feeling far less brave at the thought of traversing the brushy undergrowth, which was growing ever more shadowy as the day wore on, she rejoined the group, pondering her next move. *One thing is for sure,* she thought. *I am staying far away from **him**.* She fished in her pocket, playing with her cell phone, and realized there was no coverage in the area. *So that's why we haven't heard from Seen,* she thought—that and the fact that they treated him like a rock star. For that matter, they were acting like S.G. and Ben were the bomb too. *Everyone but me.*

Well, maybe she should tell them her side of the story and they might start treating her like a princess too. *Two can play at this game,* she thought. "Who is a woman in this group?" she asked, not seeing any clues to help her separate the sexes. A few largish ones shyly held up their hands. "Good," she said. "Now which one of you would like to hear *my* version of the story? It's for girls only. It starts with a dark and stormy night—and a *sacrifice,*" she added for color.

"Ooh, oooh! I do! I do!" the girls all cried.

"Fine," she said. "But this story is for girls only," she warned. "Thems that are, come on over here." She led them to the far side of the field, snubbing the males entirely. A few male trolls looked wistfully at the group of girls now arranging themselves around Christina as they all had done the first time Ben regaled them with his version.

"Never mind them," Ben said, getting their attention again. "I bet this tattooed guy, we call him S.G., or sometimes, Kenneth, can tell you a tale or two."

"Maybe he can start with the origins of his many names?" Ed asked.

Well, that was just fine, Ben thought.

Trolls are such story whores that any new tale would do. Although it would be so nice to get the woman's point of view on the "Absolutely Most Epic

Saga Ever" (as they had been calling it). No matter. When all the fuss of human and Other contact died down, they would have a nice quiet millennia or two to share all of the juicy details with each other.

Christina found a wide, flat boulder to sit on. Before she actually sat on the boulder, she inquired of the girls, "Say, this isn't anyone, is it?" She was referring to her seat, the bog rock.

"Oh no!" Someone giggled. "But even if it was, it wouldn't mind."

"Really?" she asked. "Because I am so not sitting my ass on someone's face. OK?" They all giggled some more.

"She swears just like Rockstar Ben said so," one said.

"Wait. Did you just call him Rockstar Ben? He told you he was a **rock star**? Oh, we have **a lot** to straighten out. Get comfy," Christina said, arranging herself on the rock. The girls all hunkered down around her and one by one assumed their bouldered state.

It was easier for Christina to tell her tale when they were like that. It was almost as though she were talking to herself. And we are all so much more eloquent when talking to the most appreciative audience of all: our own egos. So she began to tell the story of a mom and a lost baby gargoyle and being punished for all of her good deeds. The day drew to its end, and dusk crept into the meadow.

She spoke of rules being broken and children lost to another world and then losing herself to the dour world of elves. At this point, there was a teeny bit of squirming, as the trolls all thought that Seen wasn't the last bit dour. That was the only slight judgment made about her narrative. A few night stars peeked out from the gloom of the dusky sky.

She told them of war and dragons and bonding. She told them of humans in between worlds and not belonging anywhere. Then she told them of the triumph of those same humans, The Family, as they were called, by assuming leadership of the Fairfolk in the form of Supreme Elder Other. She told them most of all about how love—simple human love for each other—vanquished even the most powerful magical foes. And that the simple but powerful force of love drove them past many obstacles and always toward each other. They were all better and stronger for it, and that without love, they were just pale shadows of themselves.

It was full-on dark by the time she was done. It was then she realized that this story wasn't over. She had to finish the chapter, not with anger but with love. Failing that, at least she would finish the chapter of Ben and Christina with kindness.

"Shit, shit, shit," she concluded her story. "There's something I gotta do." She got up stretching her legs, stiff from sitting so long, and made her way back to the campfire, now lit and peopled by brooding males, roasting a haunch of venison.

"Now do we get our happy ending?" Fred asked.

Brilliance Is as Brilliance Does

"Yeah, so, as it turned out, we, in fact, saved the entire city of Las Vegas through a combination of my brilliant ideas and Enj's mad magical skills." Jacob, the human, concluded the long and colorful saga of Enj and Jay, super sleuths and magical mayhem healers in the land of lust and lights.

He was terribly pleased with himself as he sat in the chair opposite Marissa's desk. She listened intently while doing her usual nervous buzzing about the desktop. Enj stood behind his friend, focusing upon picking some invisible smuts off one of his talons. He was feigning disinterest but was in fact on pins and needles waiting to see what Marissa would say. *She looks hot today,* he mused. *All in black—a little black dress, with tiny white roses tucked into her hair.* And that hair, long and loose and flowing everywhere. It was so long that it caught on the barbs of her wings. Occasionally, her big green wings would shake themselves free of the locks, causing her to temporarily flutter out of control. After she shot a withering look back at them, they resumed their normal flight across and around the top of the desk. Her hair was mesmerizing as it wafted around her when she zig-zagged across the span of her desk.

Her feet also consumed his interest. They were so tiny and almost always bare. Marissa learned early on that spike heels tended to dangle and then fall off while she was in flight. Cute, but impractical. So despite her many chic outfits, she elected to be barefoot. It was one less distraction to deal with while she sped through the demands of the day. And as usual, there were many things to do on this day.

"Multitasking," Jacob called it, as she listened to his narrative while continuously checking the email and the cell phone. When she wasn't fixated on one of the screens, she was working terribly hard to avoid looking at Enj. Suddenly, being around him made her feel uncomfortable, antsy. *Must be all the magic he carries,* she thought. *It's making me edgy. Or edgier,* she corrected herself.

Because truth be told, she had been completely unhinged when her brother, or brothers if you counted her sort of adopted pal Enj, had left for Vegas. She was surprised at how badly she missed them. She realized that they were her source of emotional support as she dealt with the day-to-day needs of the magical realm. They kept her somehow in emotional balance as she had feelers out frantically searching for her dad and now her mom, in the midst of all of her other usual demands. The job of Supreme Elder Other was a bitch. And now her plate was just a little fuller. Bob had been a big help. Her mom had been right in picking him as a replacement. He was pretty good at keeping the most annoying Others out of her hair. And he was great at sauntering into her office, hopping up on her desk in his kitty-cat form and basically allowing his mere presence to bring some semblance of calm into their space just when she needed it.

But the fact was she felt like something had been missing since her two boys had left. And she was lonely. So lonely that she contacted the fairy queen Eedle and her consort Otib to inquire about their well-being and of course to hear the latest about their baby. Their little fat, bald Buddha of a fairy child, who had been left to his own devices with only sentry lizards as nannies, was a handful.

Hummer was a strange, smiley little imp, who caused all sorts of trouble in the fairy clan. All in the name of good fun. The lizards, having grown very large by absorbing magic from the baby, were bonded to the little boy. They protected him from most dangers and, best they could, covered for him when his latest caper was discovered.

Eedle and Otib had a lot on their plates. It was bad enough trying to keep a fairy clan in line. Mischief and laziness were fairies' middle names. But then to be constantly watching, well running, well flying, actually, after their fat boy as he ventured in the world outside the safety of the clan was almost too much for the two of them.

Marissa's reaching out to them reminded her of the value of true friends. They were of course delighted that she chose to scry them for a visit. But it saddened her as well, since their life had moved on, and as much as they loved her, they really hadn't a spare minute to listen to her woes. *Yep, it's lonely at the top*, she thought. *But now my boys are home. I just wish I knew why I don't feel the way I thought I would now that they are home. In fact, I actually feel more nervous now that they are here.* This naturally pissed her off. They were about to get a somewhat positive response from her. That was the best she could do, since their very presence was unsettling her day.

"Actually, in part, you guys did pretty good. Possibly very good. I mean, I always had faith in the brilliant theories of my brother-bear, but it is actually nice to see it works when put to the test." She smiled at her brother, relieved that at least something in her crazy world had been resolved. Yet, there was so much more to the story that was troubling.

"A shame though, about the Supreme Elder Others. You know, I always thought there was more than one of them. It was the way he, or rather, they, sat in that big throne of theirs. Sometimes, he would be sitting upright, all business, and other times, slouching as though he didn't give a shit. Also, there was one that had to be a little goofy. Sometimes one of them would really think outside the box, and other times not so much. I thought that maybe Jacob was right in thinking the job made you a little crazy, and that we had a slightly unhinged, bipolar supreme leader."

"You mean tri-polar." Enj spoke up, looking her in the eyes for the first time since he came in the room.

Marissa stared back at him, puzzled by his slight "deer in the headlights" stare. Shrugging, she said, "Ooh funny. Yeah, I get it. Tri-polar." She switched gears a bit, honing in on some of the finer details of the tale. "Now are you sure that this reformed hooker will take good care of the old guys?"

"She's not really reformed," Jacob corrected. "She's just retired from the business now that the geezers have the bank. Hopefully, she will become gainfully employed as a golf pro now that she has the time to work on her game. By then, the old boys should have found some way to be useful to her. They are nothing if not resourceful."

"Turning into a pro golfer? Easier said than done," she told her brother. "The way Dad tells it, that's every golfer's dream. Very few get to any sort of competitive level." She looked down, momentarily distracted by the buzz of her cell phone. She dropped down slightly, stepping on the answer bar with her tiny bare foot. "What," she declared.

"Sorry to interrupt your confab," Bob said from the other room. "I was just wondering if anyone wanted anything, you know, coffee, tea, bourbon, and maybe a nice rack of raw beef ribs for the boys?"

"Eeuw, gross," Marissa replied. "And I know what you are doing." *Nosy Bob, testing the temperature of my office.* "If you must know what is happening, come on in. You'll find out anyway, so let's give you the details while they are fresh."

This was, of course, exactly what Bob wanted. He couldn't wait to come in and see the family dynamic in action. *They are so entertaining,* he reminded himself for the millionth time.

The man, Bob, opened the door to his boss's office. Then he carefully shut it behind him. In the merest blink of an eye, the cat, Bob, hopped up into the remaining guest chair. He sat, tail erect, facing the boys on his right. The man Bob suddenly appeared where the cat had just been. He too sat upright slightly facing the boys. "Which would you prefer?" he asked, smiling. He rubbed his hand through his spiky hair, making sure it was still artfully arranged in a state of studied disarray. No matter what form Bob was in, he always had the same smile—slightly feral, big and sensuous. It bordered on a smirk, as though he alone was in on a big joke and you, sadly, weren't quite there yet.

Both Enj the gargoyle and Jacob the young man were in awe of his style—to change so quick like that without a pop or a bang or even a flash, almost liquid in the moment of transition. And with such economy of effort.

"Smooth," Enj said.

"Show-off." Jacob sulked, wishing he had swagger like this dude. Plus, the guy's hair was good. Crazy good. It took a long time to work your hair into that state of hip messiness, Jacob knew from firsthand experience. He was definitely feeling hair envy at the moment.

"Nice glasses," Bob said commenting on Jacob's new retro look. This made Jacob feel marginally better.

"I like you better as a cat," Marissa said. "But…" She held her hand up, as though to halt his transformation back to the feline state. "We might actually need your opinion on a few matters. And for that, we need you verbal."

"Cool." He shrugged, settling into the chair. "Fill me in on the latest in the stomach-churning, roller-coaster ride of the Family. And I will tell you what calamities you have just set in motion."

And so Enj took a shot at the story. He began his lengthy, overly detailed (especially the part where they had to take the "perps" unawares—this was when they all rolled their eyes at the gargoyle's colorful colloquialisms) in his accounting of Las Vegas and the Supreme Elder Other(s). Bob nodded sagely as Enj and Jacob each told their version of the tale. He said nothing until they had wound down to the end. When they were through, all three looked at him for his reaction.

He crossed his legs and then uncrossed them. He sat forward in his chair, elbows on his knees, contemplating the plain wooden floor. He sighed to himself. Then he rose, stretched, and said, "I would love to meet this hooker. Do you have any idea where she went with her new sugar daddies?"

"That's it?" Jacob said. He was speechless. His brilliant idea, tested and found to be correct, would change everything in Otherland. "Hello. I just saved Las Vegas from annihilation, and all you can say is that you want to meet the hooker?"

Bob gave the boy a good long look before responding. "Look, man, I get that you are smart. We all get that you are smart. If you want, I can go back to my desk and print you a goddam banner that says 'Jacob is the smartest guy on the planet.' Except that wouldn't be true now, would it? Because if you were the smartest guy on the planet..." Bob stood, placing his hand not unkindly on Jacob's shoulder. "You would know exactly where these loose cannons are so we can keep track of them. Because, my friends, magical creatures or no, those three stooges and their hooker-keeper could still cause us a butt load of trouble."

"It's cool, Bob," Enj said placating the tattooed secretary. "It's covered. We basically know where they are headed. I mean, we told them to go underground, stay away from populated areas, find some out-of-the-way golf courses to hunker down in northeast of here."

"Oh fine. You mean in the mountains, like Lake Tahoe?" Bob asked, becoming agitated at their sheer stupidity.

"Well, yeah," Jacob said. "It seemed like Betsy knew the area and the golf courses, and it was way off the radar screen of any of her Vegas cohorts. We wanted her to disappear for a while with the guys. We have it handled, Bob," Jacob repeated with emphasis, as he watched disbelief flash on the man's face. He tried again to convince Bob that everything was all right. "Look, it's all fine. They have their cell phones and are required to check in with us. Totally copasetic, OK?"

Marissa sighed, understanding Bob's distress. "It is so not copasetic. That is the general area where we think Dad is." The two boys looked blankly at her.

"So? It's a big place," Enj said.

"Not so much, Enjie" she said, using the name that would irritate him. After all, she was irritated, and she might as well have company. "The common denominator is golf. Dad loved to golf, and so does she. It stands to reason that they are in the same vicinity. Possibly right now. There must be no cell coverage there because both Mom and Seen haven't checked in, and that's not like them. So let's review."

She ticked off on her fingers, her wings began twitching like they wanted to buzz someone's head. She had other ideas and wanted to stay hovering over the desk. Consequently, she began bobbing up and down, her head and her wings in conflict with one another. This set her hair wafting again, dislodging a few of the tiny roses. Only this time, it wasn't mesmerizing. It was dangerous. Supreme Elder Other Queen Marissa was pissed.

"One," she said, "Dad is AWOL. Possibly involved with a very nice, unsuspecting troll clan. And now they are up to their necks in this little drama. Two, Seen has gone missing. Three, Mom has gone after him and Dad. To date, we haven't heard a damn thing from her. Oh, and she took Sleeping Guy with her. Like he really needs to be involved in all of this stuff? His tiny human head will probably explode.

"Four, some deranged hooker and three defrocked master wizards are bumbling around in the same area. So, five, you have sent our old bosses and yet another hapless human into a very large shit-storm where there likely is no way to get ahold of anyone. The sheer magic alone if any of them chooses to use it is bound to attract the Others who have been hunting for our father. Others that Bob and I have been working very hard to distract, confuse, and otherwise misdirect. You have now put a huge blinking light over that entire area that says, 'Other hunters—Come on down!' Now, do you see the dilemma?"

"Hmm," Jacob said, thinking cap on. He refused to think that he had screwed up that badly. After taking a few deep breaths and staring off into the corner of the blank, white office for a moment, he finally broke the very tense silence in the room. "I know what we need," he said.

"What? Another gig? Because I have just about had it with this one myself," Marissa said, hands on her hips.

"Baby. I'm going to get Baby." More silence ensued. Silence abounded as they all looked blankly at Jacob, waiting for further elaboration.

"Because the wine valley needs its own dragon?" she questioned drily.

"Nope. Because you and Bob are going to fly the friendly skies of my very own dragon. We are all going up there to sort this out. It's time we all took a field trip up to the Sierra Nevadas."

Every Fairytale Needs a Dragon

It wasn't hard for Jacob to make contact with Baby or "Bay-Boy," as he was currently called. Bay-Boy and he were almost psychically linked owing to the imprinting that occurred at the tiny dragon's hatching. (The dragon's name had morphed over time owing to his involvement with other dragons and their general disregard for the details of human speech. Also, he had literally grown out of the name Baby. Jacob thought that *Bay-Boy* had a cool ring to it. And it was a nod to the East Bay Hills in which the dragon currently resided.)

Bay-Boy was innately in tune with his Mommee and vice versa. Imprinting is what dragons do the moment they hatch and is something that a dragon remembers his or her entire long life. It helps the young dragon understand who family is and is not, despite long absences from one another. The young man and the dragon had a bond that would last forever despite their changing circumstances and physical appearances.

Scrying him was almost as good as speaking to him on a cell phone. Actually, it was a much better option than a cell phone. As if a dragon could manipulate such a thing. Probably wouldn't be worth the trouble, as dragons have a tendency to scorch anything that is remotely frustrating. They would burn though a lot of cell phones that way. So scrying it was.

The birdbath in Marissa's office was a handy method of reaching out to loved ones. So this was what Jacob used in contacting his favorite dragon. He thought hard about the ever growing Baby, his dragon almost from the moment of hatching. As the dragon had developed, he had changed in size, shape, and demeanor. But he always remained Jacob's baby. Never far from his thoughts.

Baby, or Bay-Boy, or even Bad Boy, as Jacob sometimes liked to call him, was now quite a sight. Fostered by a mother dragon and her little daughter, he had learned well how to hunt and fight and hide from humans. He lived quite nearby tucked in a corner of the East Bay Hills, in a large plot of public land set aside as a nature preserve. He and his adopted sister resided quite comfortably amid the large herds of deer and the remote creeks. She preferred the rocky streams and large green pools that dotted the waterways, while Bay-Boy needed the great open space to practice his aeronautical skills. Their current abode had both terrains, so neither felt any need to make a change of venue.

Momma dragon had done her job raising and training her little charges and had since flown the coop. Not unusual for a mother dragon to teach her fledgling all that she knew and, if she was young enough to mate again, leave to join the dating game one more time. The biological imperative to mate and continue the species far was stronger than that of nurturing the young.

It was sketchy business being a dragon. Between mating battles and questing knights intent on rescuing damsels, life was terribly unpredictable for the big beasts. And now, the shrinking habitat made it difficult to actually find another dragon with which to propagate. This required frequent mating whenever dragons were available. That was what the mother of this duo intended to do.

Older mothers stayed with their young until they died. At that point, she would offer the ultimate sacrifice and allow her young to feast on her remains. In fact, that had happened to Bay-Boy's real mother. He had done his job well and had dutifully eaten his mother after her passing. He was not only nourished by her body, but he literally ingested all of her accumulated knowledge. Her experience as well as the experience of all other dragons in her lineage was definitely food for a little dragon's thought. Generation after generation had eaten and therefore obtained the knowledge of generations before them. It was a nifty way of imparting vital dragon lore with a species that had a notoriously unpredictable life-span and shaky parenting skills. So, young Bay-Boy completely absorbed all knowledge his true mother had. This had provided the young dragon a wealth of information to ensure survival of both him and his sister.

Since their current momma still had a fire in her belly to party she left the two adolescents as soon as they could fend for themselves while she looked for a mate. She had an ulterior motive for leaving them as well. In this highly unusual case, she had the notion that by leaving them to survive together, it might provide an even stronger bond between the two, a bond that just might supersede the usual ritual of males fighting over the choicest females prior to choosing their favorite to mate.

In this case, the choice might have already been made, thus saving her girl child the potential embarrassment of not being the one chosen. So far, it seemed to be working. The two young dragons worked as a team at survival. And they appeared to be enjoying each other's company tremendously.

Currently, both dragons were napping. Being of the greenish/bronze type, they blended quite well into the murky shadows of the dense forest. Having recently fed, they were quite happily bedded down by a cluster of boulders bordering a deep pool. The splash of the water as it filled the pool helped mask their noisy breaths as they snoozed. In the unlikely event someone came upon them, they always employed the smallest bit of magic to conceal their whereabouts. Just a touch had them looking like messy mounds of dead brush, replete with thorny brambles and bright-red poison oak leaves—the perfect disguise made to ensure a solid and undisturbed naptime.

Only this nap wasn't meant to be. An interruption to dragon downtime had begun. A call was coming in. The normally placid pool began to ripple. The water's reflection, which had previously been mirroring the canopy above, began to change. What once was a green and black patchwork of trees checkered by the brilliant blue sky, changed to pure white ripples on the surface of the water. From the shimmering white grew the image of a young man in a room with pale, blank walls. Details became visible as the white walls fairly glowed with magical essence. It gave a slight halo effect to the young man. He appeared to be scanning the area, looking to find his dragon. As he studied the piles of rocks and brambles beyond the water's edge, he just barely recognized the sleeping giant he had long ago called Baby. Next to the giant dragon was a much smaller one, cuddled up under the crook of Bay-Boy's tiny forearm. The cozy couple and their magical disguise didn't fool the man in the pool. He spotted them right through their camouflage.

"Hey, Bay-Boy!" the image called out from the water. The voice sounded tinny, far away, barely audible to anyone else, yet for the big dragon always recognizable. The dragon murmured sleepily to himself, "It's Mommee." At which giggling could be heard behind the man in the watery reflection.

The young man turned and stared fiercely at the noise behind him. It quieted down, as he repeated, "Seriously, man, get up. We gots places to go, people to see."

Bay-Boy woke with a snort, quickly checking his surroundings for the source of the noise. His adopted sister stretched and unwound herself from him. "What is it, Bay-Bay?" she asked sleepily.

This time, the face in the water chuckled. He chided the big beast, "Hey *Bay-Bay*, Mommee needs you. Get your ass up!"

Bay-Boy finally saw the image in the water, Scurrying to unlock himself from the sleepy embrace of the female dragon, he sat up, clumsily pushing the smaller dragon out of the view of the water. "Does Mommee need me?" he asked, all business now.

"Yeah, I need you to give my sister and an Other a ride up to the mountains. My mom and dad may be in trouble, and we need to get there quick."

The dragon was confused. "But your sister isss Supreme Elder Other," he said, stretching out the "s" sound to a hiss. "Othersss can do as they please. They can magic themselves anywhere they want. Why do you need me?"

"Because, if you take them, they won't have to use any magic. There's already too much where we are going. We need to keep their whereabouts on the down-low. Got it?"

"Too much magic?" the female hissed. "Will it be dangerousss for my Bay-Bay?" She nudged her big head into the sight of the man in the pool.

All out guffawing could be heard in the background behind Jacob. Somewhere in the white room behind the boy, a voice sang out, taunting like a five-year-old in the schoolyard, "*Bay-Bay's got a girlfriend...*"

Jacob once again stared down the unseen voices in the room behind him. After more giggling, the noisy rabble finally quieted down. He turned his attention back to the couple. "No everything should be fine. I got it under control—" A snort could be heard in the background. "Seriously," he emphasized to the dragons, yet somehow directing his comments to the audience behind him as well. "It's all good. I have a plan; I just need your help for a little bit."

"Okay-dokay," Bay-Boy said, trying out the new human phrase Jacob had taught him the last time they hung out together. "I'll do it. Where should I meet you?" he asked. This time the little female was the one glaring. She stared hard at her Bay-Bay cocking her head slightly, waiting for him to process her irritation. "Oh," he said. "I mean *we*—Where do *we* meet you?"

"She comes with you? Everywhere?" Jacob asked, curious that Bay-Boy hadn't told him of this new development.

"E-hev-rywhere-ah," the female emphasized, breathing in a fiery, annoyed way. It sent ashy ripples across the water, breaking up the images for a bit. When the water settled down, Supreme Elder Other Queen Marissa was in the frame, seated on her brother's shoulder. She thought it was time to check out Bay-Boy's new squeeze for herself.

Bay-Boy sneaked a look at the female and then guiltily at his Mommee. He felt bad that he hadn't shared this new development with his pseudo-mother. He had felt protective and private about his unusual relationship with the female. Unusual, it was, and yet, it worked, despite the high degree of dragon unconventionality. Bay-Boy squared his scaly shoulders and flared his wings just a bit in a show of machismo.

Testosterone duly noted, thought Jacob. "Well then, see you at Other Home Base. The both of you."

Jacob stared in surprise at his Bay-Boy. Marissa hovered slightly behind her brother, studying the girl dragon. The female stared back at the Supreme Elder Other in defiance. After a bit of stony silence, Marissa declared to her brother, "This one's in love." Turning to the female, she asked "What's your name, little girl?"

The female blinked. Names are tricky things. Not to be shared unless you are with family. Otherwise, names have power. Names are magically important. A name invoked in a spell can reach out across the span of miles to impact its owner. The more closely related a name is to some aspect of its owner, the more effective the magic is over it. The Others created this rule for dragons in an attempt to better control them from afar. They had lots of Fairfolk to manage and this seemed to be a good way to keep this highly mobile and well-dispersed dragon population under control.

A dragon mother didn't offer a name to her offspring unless she knew it reflected the dragon's personality—which could take some time to determine. And even then, the dragon could elect to change it to something even more personal. The female looked at her fellow dragon for confirmation. He nodded to her and said, "Remember? They are family. And she isss Supreme Elder."

"Hmmm," she said blowing smoke across the water. "Okay-dokay. But only because my Bay-Bay tells me to. I am 'Low-lost.' Lost because that's how I felt before I met Bay-Bay and low because that's how I fly. Low because he flies high and I always go low."

"Euuww, sounds dirty," a voice called out of the water, its owner hidden by Jacob and Marissa.

"It does sound dirty," Marissa agreed. "And not very girly. I think you look like a... a Lola. That's who you are. Lola," Marissa decreed, thereby changing her name for all eternity. After all, when you are named by the supreme leader of your community, you basically have no choice but to accept the title. Graciously.

Which is what Lola did, after rolling her eyes dramatically at her Bay-Bay. He shrugged his big scaly shoulders, his wings drooping in submission. "Okay-dokay." She sighed, sad to lose the special name her boy dragon had given her, however awkward it was. "I am now called Lola."

"La-la-la Lola!" Bob sang out, happy to sing a bit of an old rock tune. Even Jacob smirked at that one.

"Low-los-uh, Lola and I will be there sssoooon" Bay-Boy said, effectively signing off. The last Marissa and Jacob saw was the waddling backsides of the dragons as they left the grounds beside the pool and headed for open space, preparing to fly to Other Base Camp.

Bay-Boy didn't need directions. He could almost feel the energy of the young man, Jacob. His essence acted as a beacon to direct him to Home Base. And as usual, Bay-Boy would fly high, and Lola would be low, right under him, right where she knew she belonged.

"And now for the temp help," Marissa said. "Hey, Bob, where is that damn paintbrush thingy of Mom's?"

"A paintbrush? I dunno. Her office maybe?" Bob replied, uninterested in wherever her thought train was going. He slouched low in the guest chair, his fingers steepled against each other as he pondered what was to come. He was currently thinking how logistically difficult it would be to land a couple of dragons here at Home Base. Between the mass of grapevines and the tiny hilltop big enough only for the barn and a small parking lot, that didn't leave much clearing for beasts.

"Bob. My assistant Bob. The man with large hands and a quick step. Please take yourself to Mom's office posthaste and get a paintbrush. Not a big one, a little one, or else I can't hold it up. Got it?" she asked.

He blinked uncomprehendingly at her, wondering *What nefarious plot has she come up with now?*

She sternly reminded him, "Also, I actually mean for you to do this now, Bob."

"We have company coming, Supreme Elder Other, supreme Madame. I am tad bit worried about those dragons. Not a lot of landing room and a lot of combustible material for them to—"

"Paintbrush. Now, Bob."

Never one to disagree with a determined boss, he gave up his concerns for the moment. "Righto," he said as he slipped out of his chair and headed off down the hall to Mom's place.

"What's with the paintbrush?" Enj asked, curious about the convoluted workings of Marissa's mind.

"I have to get a couple of temps to take my spot and Bob's while we are away trying to resolve the missing parents and their associated dramas. Just doing a little old-fashioned scrying, that's all."

"With who? Vincent van Gogh?" Enj asked, with emphasis on the artist's name. He was always so proud to show off his knowledge of human lore and legend. That particular artist had been the subject of a TV documentary late one night. He had watched it as a youth, a lonely boy gargoyle, hovering outside the family room as Christina tuned in the show. It was kinda cool the way the guy painted what he felt. Very much like how Enj operated these days—emotionally centered rather than objectively driven. Yet another thing that separated him from his fellow, logical gargoyles.

"Oh we are so clever. Really how your **tiny brain** can hold so much useless data is really beyond me. And so suave the way you pronounced his name 'van goff.'" Marissa teased Enj for his smarmy artist reference.

"Tiny brain? Excuse me" Enj said staring pointedly at the tremendous size difference between the girl fairy and himself. "I mean, really. If you are going to throw stones, you'd best not be standing inside such a TINY glass house."

"Oh, shut up." she sneered, irritated that he had so quickly gotten the best of her.

"One paintbrush posthaste, and fairy-sized to boot." Bob breezed back in delicately handing over the fine brush. Marissa took the thing in both hands, allowing for the size difference and flew over to the birdbath. She dipped the brush in, fully submerging the tip and then flew quickly back to her desk, dripping sloppily all the way across the floor. The men leaned away from her, avoiding the spray.

Once she got back to her desk, she swabbed her note pad, drenching the page from top to bottom. Carefully placing the brush across the wet page, she began to hum a little tune. Her wings had her bobbing in time to the tune as she watched the wet page for signs of contact. Little ripples started to dance across it and then faded as the paper melted away into a blur. Soon, a fuzzy image began to take shape where the paper had once been. At first, there was simply a riot of colors—deep greens, burgundy reds, and shiny blues. The colors soon formed a pattern as the image came into sharp focus. An enormous leafy design filled the page with one shiny, cat-like eye squinting, right in the middle of the leafy picture. The eye widened in surprise. Then it blinked. Then the image said, "Whoa! Marissa, you scared me!"

"Sorry to disrupt you, Aunty Berry. But I am pressed for time."

"It's fine, honey. You just startled me. It's not often my canvas turns into a scrying pad. I almost fell of my scaffold when my current masterpiece sort of melted away in one spot." She giggled, backing away slightly to reveal Madam Berry, the elf artist.

Her hair was its usual mess, carelessly piled on top of her head, wayward tendrils escaping the loose knot held only by a wet paintbrush. Her berry tattoos shone brightly across her impish face. Up close, tiny wrinkles could be seen etching her cat-like eyes. They were the only thing that belied her true age. Everything else about her was youthful and timeless and decidedly not stodgy like the rest of her elf clan.

This was why she painted in her home alone and apart from the rest of the elf clan and was also the reason Marissa contacted her. Alone and trustworthy, the fairy could be sure she wouldn't be accidentally overhead by any of the nosy elf group. "So, baby girl," one of her pet names for Marissa. "Where's Mom? I usually hear from her by now."

"Well, she's MIA."

"That sounds ominous. Or fun. I can't tell which," Berry said smiling at the image of the fairy bobbing in her painting.

"That's what I have to find out. So I have a huge favor to ask you. Ginormously huge Aunty. But if you really love me you'll come here."

"Oh dear. Please don't tell me I have to go to the place of Creepy Others to meet with you. Oooh, no offense meant to those Others that I love, like your family and that dear gargoyle Enjie."

"Hey!" a voice called out sharply. "No Enjie. Contrary to what SHE says, my name is not, not, not, Enjie!"

Berry squinted into the pad searching for the owner of the voice. Ignoring his outburst, she greeted him warmly, "Well, I can't see you but I know it's our dear Enjie. How are you, darling? Kissed any cute girls lately?" She winked. She resumed her conversation with the girl. "Tell me, honey, what's up? Why a meeting?"

"No, I don't want a meeting exactly. But I do want you up here. I need for you to fill a chair or two while I am gone finding my wayward parents and saving the world."

"Saving the world is my job," Jacob reminded.

"Oh, that must be darling Jacob," Berry cooed. She especially liked the young man—so smart and very elf-like in his fascination with understanding how to get things done without magic. Lots of elf girls took a shine to him once he had relocated his pet dragon far from their homes. He had become a bit of a celebrity to them. And he was a rule breaker. Something all elves are drawn to despite their rigid set of mores.

It was so tempting to see what happened when the rules went awry. And Jacob and his little family certainly had broken quite a number of rules in the Fairfolk realm. Hence, he was considered, in retrospect, quite delicious by the youth of the clan. Sadly, most of the older generation, however, aside from Berry and her sidekick Find, couldn't stand the boy or his family.

"At any rate, as I told your mother, you can count on me. Even if I have to go over the hill for a bit. But be advised of two things." Berry became very serious. "One, I will come, but I would like it if Find could be with me. It might give me courage when dealing with the likes of those other Others. It's just that the rest of them with their togas and their weird shiny faces just creep me out."

"OK, but—"

"And two," she continued as though Marissa had never interrupted. "Whatever I do, I am positive I will break some important rule or tradition or what-not. Just don't hold me accountable, OK?"

"Aunty Berry, don't you even want to know what I want you to do?" Marissa smiled at her favorite aunt and her quirkiness—very un-elf-like and very refreshing. It wasn't often that Marissa had someone agree to a task without arguing or whining or even flat-out disagreeing with her.

"I understand plenty. You and your mom are in trouble and need me. I have to come to you in a big hurry to help. Whatever it is, I am in."

"I love you!" Marissa answered, giving her aunty the full wattage of her beautiful smile. She fairly glowed at her mother's dear friend.

All of the men in the room stared in wonder at the infinite tenderness and tremendous warmth from their boss. Each one secretly wanted to be the recipient of such warmth. Although for different reasons, they all wondered at how great that must feel. It is a universal desire that all abused children have in desperately wanting to please their tormentor. Marissa just brought out that sort of yearning.

"Yes," she continued, unaware of the effect she had had on the gentlemen present in the office. "Bring Aunty Find. Between you confusing the hell out of the Others and Find scaring the hell out of them by threatening invasive health procedures, you will have all the bases covered."

"And what bases exactly are we covering?"

"Why, you and Find will be running Other Home Base while Bob and I are gone."

"Really!" Berry said, her tattoos fading a bit at the thought of such a daunting task. "We won't be blowing anyone up, will we? Because I am pretty sure neither she nor I could **ever** do that."

"Exactly," Marissa said. "Now you have my permission to magic yourselves into birds or wind or lightning bolts. Whatever it takes to get here right away."

"Give me a few to find Miss Find. She's probably setting a bone or dosing someone with tea. Once I locate her, I will make sure we both get to you as quickly as we can. Oh and, Marissa?"

"Yes?" *Uh-oh,* the fairy thought. *Here we go.*

Berry squinted hard at the blank walls surrounding the tiny fairy. *How cold and unfeeling it must be to work there,* she thought. "Your office looks a bit drab. Any chance I can spruce it up while you are gone?"

"Uh, sure," she said with some trepidation.

"Great!" she called, already maneuvering down from her scaffolding. Her face had left the pad, and Marissa was staring at the messy interior of Berry's art studio. "I'll be sure to bring my paintbrushes," a voice called out from the pad.

The group looked at each other, quietly assessing the elf's last few words. Bob snickered. "Well, there goes the neighborhood."

* * *

It wasn't a long journey to reach the Livermore Valley. It stretched out east of them, past the hills on the eastern fringes of the San Francisco Bay Area. Brown and gold were those hills, dotted by thick trees and underbrush that were vigorously establishing their roots deep under the dry and rocky ground in search of fresh water. Verdant green and gold, the colors of the earth and the vegetation, flashed under them as they flew out of the nature preserve that the young dragons called home.

Trendy neighborhoods claimed the territories at the tops of the hills—the ones that provided the best and most glorious views of the Bay Area. Hot, dry air billowed up from those hills, rising under their wings, helping them along in their journey. They swept through thermals as the hot air was being pushed up the slopes of the hills. The warmth was welcome. Dragons love the heat and appreciate the extra aeronautical help of warm and buoying air. Typically lazy flyers, they prefer their wings to maneuver them rather than to actually work hard propelling their bodies forward.

Soon, they reached an area of flat, dry land transected in perfect geometric shapes. Farmland. The vegetation in those carefully cultivated squares was deep green and in sharp contrast to the wild lands adjacent to them. Those had a dry, arid look to them, while their neighbors sported the dense reds, purples, and greens of carefully watered crops. The biggest crops in this valley were either the silvery gray color of olive trees or the deep reds and greens of grapes.

Bay-Boy carefully searched those grape regions, sensing where he should go to find his Mommee. He was close; the dragon could feel the magical aura of his Jacob. It was a tingly energy that resonated within him, like a happy silly tune that looped endlessly in your head. The tune went like this, *"Mommee, mommee, almost here, mommee, mommee, very near..."* It was quite clear that no dragon had ever crafted a successful tune. That just wasn't their forte. But what they could do was find their mother. And that is just what Bay-Boy did, while humming his silly song.

His senses honed in on a large barn-like structure perched at the top of a rise. It was surrounded by vineyards with not a lot of open space in which to land. There was just enough space in what would be a parking lot for one dragon but not two. Bay-Boy opted for the parking space. Little Lola chose a less conventional landing spot.

Even Others Have to Dodge the Doody

It's not often when staying at Other Home Base that one has to be reminded that the ordinary sometimes supersedes the magical. But then there are the sentry birds. They eat, they fly, and their flight path often corresponds with the Others in the residence. In a word, sometimes even magical creatures have to dodge the incoming. And that's just what everyone in the barn did—ducked and ran for cover into the private offices as the enormous flock of crows careened in from the open eaves as soon as they spotted the two dragons. In great panic, the entire flock attempted to make its way into the barn.

A noisy, cacophonous crowd of slightly drunken birds, fully gorged from eating very ripe grapes, suddenly panicked at the proximity of the smoking, fiery beasts. Full tummies and terror spell just one thing for birds: massive pooping.

This kind of activity simply doesn't do indoors with Others in skimpy togas and other variations of scanty clothing. Shrieks could be heard throughout the building as everyone ran through the labyrinthine hallways, careening into each other like billiard

balls in an attempt to avoid the panicked flock cours-
ing through the hallways.

Inside the Mari's office, the commotion in the
hallways heralded the approaching dragons. The
group in the Supreme Elder's office, however, was
safe from bombardment as long as they stayed
inside. Marissa sighed, having a good mental picture
of what probably was taking place outside their door.
Bob looked at her eyebrows raised in a question. "Do
you want me to go out there and clear the birds out?"
He knew that in his kitty form, no bird in its right
mind would be in the same place as he. It would provide a way out for the group should they need to exit.

"No, not yet," Marissa replied. "The dragons are
close, but not quite here yet, right, Jacob?" she asked
her brother for confirmation. He nodded, feeling
that they were perhaps right above them but hadn't
quite landed yet. That was what he felt anyway.

Soon, they all got immediate confirmation that
the dragons had in fact touched down. There was a
very audible crunch from the rafters up above. But
it was a heavy, whoomph sort of feeling, as though
something very weighty had just displaced a lot of air
right above them. "Crap," Bob said "One of them is
on the roof!" Bob flung open the door to the inner
office and then in a blink, fluidly morphed into his
big bad kitty form. Wherever he went, the birds flew
away. And the birds were absolutely everywhere. The
group followed close in his wake to the big doors
that led to the hilltop outside.

Bay-Boy greeted them at the barn door, snort-
ing and snuffling at them as he waddled toward his
Jacob. He head-butted the young man as a friendly
hello. His head, however, was the same height as

all of Jacob, so his greeting resulted in the human hitting the ground hard. He skidded a bit before scrambling up to greet his now very large dragon. "Never show you are hurt," and "Always walk it off" were his dad's favorite sayings to Jacob when he was playing sports. The same applied when greeting a dragon. Never show weakness. Dragons, even your own dragon, really hate that.

Brushing the dirt off his hands, he patted his Baby on the cheek. "Looking good, Dude!" he greeted his personal dragon warmly. In return, Bay-Boy smiled, resembling a prehistoric alligator with his spectacular array of six-inch-long teeth. This was about eye level to the young man, so he got up close and personal with the dragon fangs, and sadly, up close and personal also to the dragon breath, which smelled quite similar to a hot, musty, Porta-Potty.

Trying hard not to fully breathe in dragon miasma, Jacob noticed some bit of unsightly gristle lodged between a few canines. "Ooh, man, you got a little something-something right in there." He reached in and as gingerly as possible, tugged at the offending meat scrap. It popped out in the young man's hand, smelling quite foul. He shook it to the ground, mashing it into the dirt for good measure. "Been in there awhile, has it?" he asked, wiping his hand on his jeans. "Eesh," Marissa said. "Boys are so gross."

"That is why I need to be near you alwaysss." Bay-Boy smiled, ignoring Marissa, his two shining eyes on his human mother. He was greatly relieved that the irritating slug of meat had finally been removed. "You have nice small handsss."

"Steady now." Bob laughed. "That might be fighting words in some circles."

"They are not so small," Jacob said regarding his own hands as though for the first time. " W e l l , compared to mine they are fairly tiny," Enj teased holding his mammoth hands next to Jacob's. They clearly weren't exactly the same size.

"Your hands are no bigger than mine. It's your brain that is tiny." Jacob fired the first salvo in yet another war of insults.

"You guys are such losers. Now I have some big meats," Bob interjected holding his hands up for comparison. "And you know what they say, the bigger the hands the bigger the—"

"Oh please!" Marissa had had enough. She flew up to the roof of the barn where the female dragon was precariously perched. The beam showed some very long crack lines as it barely could withstand the weight of the big beast. This was the source of the large whoomph and the subsequent crack that they had all heard. While the boys were handling weighty issues regarding comparative male anatomy, she had to handle the more pressing one of, say, potential roof collapse. "Get down from there!" she called up to Lola.

Lola wriggled the scaly talons of her foreleg in a shy sort of greeting. She looked down to the very crowded space below. And said, "There'sss no room for me."

"OK, I'll handle this. As usual!" Marissa hollered to the males below. Now being very tiny, one might think she would not be heard amid the male banter. But she was the Supreme Elder Other and had a special tone of voice that they all could hear. No matter what. Oh wait. Maybe that was a special gift that Marissa the teenager had always had. *She who shall be obeyed.* At any rate, she used that voice right now. "Bay-Boy, make room for your girl."

With a start the dragon looked up and then behind him to the endless rows of lush grapevines. "Really?" he asked just to be sure.

"Yeah. Really. Hurry. This roof could go at any time," she called down.

"OK," he replied dubiously. With a shrug to the fellas, he backed up to the nearest row of vines and swung his tail wildly. The nearby grapevines were swept away, crushed under the moving tail. Suddenly, there was room for two dragons.

In a surprisingly delicate maneuver, Lola dropped to the earth, sweeping fluidly over them as she touched down next to her favorite male dragon. If she could have made a curtsy, she would have. It was a smooth move. No one was knocked over in the process. She settled her long tail delicately in between the remaining standing rows of grapes, folded her wings neatly behind and smirked proudly, letting loose a few wisps of smoke from the corners of her mouth. "How do you do?" she politely inquired of the Supreme Elder Other.

"Well, now, isn't that a nice change," Marissa said flying over to more closely inspect this little (relatively speaking) dragon. "Manners. What a concept." Marissa shot a glare in the direction of the men. Then she gave the full wattage of her smile to the little female. "I think I am going to like you, Miss Lola."

"Wow. News flash. Stop the presses. Marissa likes someone," Enj said, under his breath to Jacob.

Bob smirked. "Good one," he whispered.

Jacob smiled, still patting Bay-Boy's scaly cheek. The heat was fairly radiating off the big creature, so his pats were fairly delicate so as not to burn his fingers.

Marissa glared at the men and then dismissed them with her back. Her wings flicked rudely at the gentlemen. "Only Marissa could manage to curse at someone with her wings," Enj whispered. He was, as usual, in awe of the fairy's abilities.

"It's a gift," Jacob said, proud of his sister's badass style.

Lola smiled at the Supreme Elder Other in a big way, foul breath wafting out between her rows of massive teeth; she was ignoring the men as well. "Only…" Marissa flew a bit higher out of the smell zone. "You really shouldn't grin like that. Too toothy. Not very ladylike. Very earthy smelling."

"Ooh," Lola said, clamping her mouth shut. "Do I smell like butt-air? Bay-Bay says only dragons like the smell of each other's breath. But to everyone else, it smells like a far-ette, yes?" she inquired of Bay-Boy for confirmation. The male dragon nodded.

Bob interjected, "Everyone is fine, fart smells notwithstanding. Now can we get down to business? I really hate that we are all out here with no sentry birds to tell us that someone is coming up the drive. It would seriously suck if some hapless wino drove up right now to see whatever the hell drunk-ass people see when they come upon a group like us."

"Well, I am not a drunk-ass, but I see you all just fine," a new voice called out from among the vines.

"Fine or Find? Find? Funny pun," another voice replied from deep within the crop of grapes. "I bet if we think of it, there is a myriad of puns related to the word *find*. Like Find day for a find or—"

"Enough, my friend," Berry chuckled gesturing for her pal, the queen of corny jokes, to come forward from the rows of lush grapes. "We can pun all day long after these *fine* people leave on their mission of mercy." Berry held her hand out, helping Madame Find, the healer, out from the leafy rows.

As usual, you couldn't help but notice how different the two elf women were from one another. One was bright, colorful, and very petite, with leafy decorations all over her face and arms. The other was stockier, almost mannish, and dressed in a long, drab tunic. The multitude of bulging pockets in which she stored her potions and medicinal teas for every kind of malady, gave her an overall lumpy appearance. Find's face was round and flattish, her hair a tumbling mass of black curls that never stayed in the thong she tied it back in. The riot of rebellious hair and the large catlike eyes were in fact the only features the two women had in common—that and their happy smiles as they greeted their favorite new Others: Marissa, Enj, and Jacob.

Dragons were momentarily forgotten as the family greeted the only elves besides Seen who had ever welcomed them into the clan—also, the only ones who actually smiled in public. Berry hugged her two boys, that is, one young man and one large green gargoyle, whom she referred to as her own, while Find more sedately, but not without considerable warmth, regarded Marissa, asking politely about her health.

Marissa sat happily on the healer's shoulder, swinging her feet like a child. It was almost as though the weight on her shoulders had been lifted by the mere presence of the two older ladies. Even the fairy's leathery wings seemed happy, gently fanning Find's nut-brown neck. That was their way of showing great affection without making actual contact. After all, Marissa's wings still had tiny sharp barbs on their tips, making even gentle contact nearly impossible without bloodshed.

While the happy reunion had been taking place, Bob was conferring with the dragons, explaining that he and Marissa were to be passengers on the flight to Lake Tahoe. Lola was asking the most questions of Bob about how heavy he was. She even dipped her neck down for the man to climb aboard. He slipped his leg over her neck, tucking his body in between her wings, taking care not to get in their way. He hunkered down on is perch while she prepared for flight. Standing straight, she rolled her shoulders, flexing her wings experimentally. Sensing an inherent problem, Bob quickly hopped to the ground before her wings bashed him on the head.

Then Bay-Boy got involved, making some comment to the tattooed man. He nodded and then tried mounting the neck of the larger male dragon. Fortunately, this time, there seemed to be more room for his seat on the dragon's shoulders. And yet, when the bigger dragon's wings began beating, they seemed to have the potential to cut the man's legs on the down sweep. Dragons also have nasty barbs on their great leathery wing joints, and they were just a tad too close to the man's legs for his comfort.

Bob leaned down and spoke in the dragon's ear. Wispy smoke leaked out of the beast's mouth as he considered this latest suggestion. Then he nodded. In a liquid second, Bob was a cat perched high up on the dragon's back. Bay-Boy beat his wings experimentally to find that the cat was safe from any unintended harm. Kitty Bob jumped down from the dragon's scaly back, landing as Bob the man. Straightening his tousled hair and tucking his T-shirt into his jeans, he approached the chatting group, which had been amiably speaking all at once, filling each other in on the happenings outside of each's realm.

"Houston, I think we have a problem." Bob interrupted the group, causing all conversations to come to a screeching halt.

"What?" Jacob asked, irritated that his epic theory, now proven, of how annihilation could in fact be avoided was yet again interrupted.

"We won't fit comfortably on the plane." Bob gestured back to the smoky dragons. A halo of haze seeped around the two great beasts. Even at rest, they always seemed to be spewing something—smoke, acid sweat, or some other vile thing. They were perpetually surrounded by a miasma of relatively unpleasant gaseous smells.

"Sure you fit," Jacob, the mastermind, protested. After all, he had figured it all out. Plan A was to have them ride with Bob as human taking care to keep Marissa the fairy on board through the windy currents. Failing that, plan B was to have Bob as kitty ride while Marissa hung on somehow. So it was all handled. But Bob, as usual, had to throw his two cents in and wreck every well-laid option. Jacob and Enj could accompany them in their gargoyle forms.

"How is this OK?" Bob asked. He went on to explain. "The whole point is to use the dragons for transport so we don't add any more misspent magic to our destination. But I am too big in my usual human form to ride either one of these juvenile delinquents. And as a kitty, I don't A) have any way to hold on, and 2) have you actually sat on one of those guys? I mean their skin is actually smoking hot! I for one am not getting my furry kitty undersides burned

311

to smithereens by those supernova supersonic trans-
ports. And you can bet your bony ass that our Queen
Supreme Elder Other Marissa sure as hell won't be
burning her most gracious and beauteous bottom
on them either."

"Wha—? Whose bottom is whatsit?" Marissa said,
breaking off her confab with her favorite elf aunties
at the sound of her name.

Bob appealed to his superior. "Marissa, go over
and touch those guys. They are smoking hot, and
I don't mean attractive. They are actually burning
temperature-like hot. What the hell do we do with
that?"

"Huh," she said, running her tiny hands over the
scaly skin of Bay-Boy. She looked accusingly at her
brother. "You didn't tell me they were going to be
this warm, did you?"

"Well," her brother said, stretching out the word
until it incorporated his large sigh. "Maybe this
could be plan B …so…Bob is too big to ride like a
guy so he has to be a kitty. And if he is a kitty, someone can hold him. In fact, I will hold him while I ride
Bay-Boy. As a guy, I am actually shorter than Bob so
theoretically I could fit better on Bay-Boy's back…
hmm," he said while pacing around his big dragon.
He walked the perimeter of his dragon, evaluating
the problems of flight and razor-sharp wings.

Bay-Boy kept his body completely still during this
evaluation. For that was what he felt his mommee
wanted. However, it didn't stop his head from tracking the boy's every movement. It snaked all around
until it had nearly made a complete circle following Jacob's path. An intense crick in his neck kept
him from completely swiveling around. Dragons are

flexible but only up to a point. The young man finished his evaluation by stating, "I think I can ride him as a human, holding Bob in one arm. But I am going to have to lay back, almost reclining. And I need a seat or saddle of some kind to keep me in place and prevent me from contacting the heat of his scales. Other than that, I think it could work."

"Oh, and where are we going to find a saddle for a dragon?" Enj asked. Normally, he had his friend's back on things, but this one was pretty hard to figure.

"We are in Livermore, aren't we?" Jacob asked his friend, incredulous that he hadn't had faith in this plan of his.

"Yeah, and last I checked, they are fresh out of dragon saddles," Enj carped back.

"Oooh I get it!" Marissa said, breezily flying into the men's conversation. "Livermore is more than just wine country. It is cattle country."

Enj blinked his liquid green eyes at her, uncomprehending.

She snapped her tiny fingers in front of his beak-like scaly greenish nose. "Get it? Cattle? And who runs cattle? Cowboys. And what do cowboys need?" She smiled, attempting to connect the dots for him. After all, it was so obvious to her.

"Seats for their dragons?" Enj asked, still not getting it.

"You need to watch more TV. Old movies, Westerns, really. There are such *huge* gaps in your knowledge," she said, dismissing him. Turning to her brother, she understood exactly where he was going with this. And she had an idea or two of her own to help embellish things. "So, Jacob. Can you get your bad self over to downtown Livermore? Find a saddle shop and buy the biggest saddle you can find. Tell them you ride a Clydesdale or some such gigantic animal and need a huge saddle. They'll help you. Oh and also" She flew up to his ear whispering her final instructions. Jacob smirked and nodded in reply.

"Sure." He smirked, looking pointedly at Bob. "I'll run inside and dodge the bird shit to get a cell phone and a credit card. Then I'll head down the hill to call a cab. But wait. If I am riding Bay-Boy whilst carrying Bob the cat, how are you getting up to the high country?"

"Easy," she said. "Enjie will hold me."

Jacob arched an eyebrow at his sister, who was trying very hard to act nonchalant about being in such close proximity to big, bad Enjie. He spoke conspiratorially to her and her alone. "I thought you were pissed off at him."

"Well, I was, or I am, er, well, not really," she lamely replied. Her wings were fairly buzzing in agitation.

"You are so not cool," her brother chided.

"Cool about what?" she bristled. She spun about his head, missing his hair by millimeters.

He held up his hands in submission. "Not a thing. Sore subject, you two." Changing the subject for the sake of peace, he added, "Listen, I am off on my mission. Back as soon as I can!"

As Jacob headed into the building, he found himself literally going against the tide. He quickly grabbed what he needed from Marissa's office and headed out the back door and down the hill to catch a ride to town.

Like it or not, the remaining Others, Others-in-training and miscellaneous Others in residence had enough of dodging the panicky birds and their effluvia. Out they all trooped, all one hundred of them, an outraged mob, at the end of their ropes.

If they could safely mutiny without suffering annihilation, they would gladly do so. Right now. But since none really wanted to be blown into oblivion, they all marched out with the united intent to sternly complain and disagree with "thems that are" in charge. Jacob muscled his way through the throng. It didn't really take much of an effort as they were powerful magically but pathetically wimpy as faux humans.

The androgynous bunch of pallid toga-wearers marched as purposefully as they could muster while barefoot onto the gravel flat top. Whereupon they all stopped so as to avid pokey things hurting the bottoms of their feet. Yet, they still felt outraged and united in their general discontent. Some were even sporting bird bombs on their previously pristine togas. They were feeling positively testy. All in all, not a terribly effective mob. But it was the best they could do in facing down Supreme Elder Other Queen Marissa and her retinue.

Marissa all but smiled at the approaching throng. But she didn't, so as to avoid letting them know how cute they looked all riled up. Besides, she had plans for them. *They are here in the nick of time,* she thought.

"Good thinking!" she called out to them in the most approving of tones. She met the throng of toga-clad ninnies, flying right up to the front of the group. Those in the front stepped hastily back to avoid contact with their superior. Marissa pretended not to notice.

The rest were confused by her praise. After all, they were there to confront, not to get along. This momentary confusion was exactly what Marissa had been going for.

"She's got them right where she wants them," Berry whispered to Find.

Her friend nodded and smiled, approving of the little fairy's crafty manipulations. "A born leader," was Find's quiet reply. Marissa continued addressing the tepidly angry mob.

"No, I mean it, truly," she continued. "It's like you all read my mind. And I really like it when I don't have to repeat myself. So this is good. Very good." She began flying above the mob, hovering and tracking each of them. All eyes followed her path as she looked at them, one by one. Just a touch of glamour was all that was needed to work this crowd.

They had in fact never seen anything but the angry, stern side of her, so any emotion that was even a hair off the threatening side was absolutely riveting. And since she added a touch of warmth, those whose eyes she actually caught and engaged felt as though they were basking in warm, delectable honey.

It wasn't really as much glamour as it was Marissa *being nice*. Shockingly addictive. Those in her gaze immediately forgot about being mildly outraged. The rest felt their mob mentality fast eroding and eventually knew they would have to capitulate without comment. Marissa had won, yet again.

"So which of you is the toga maker?" she inquired sweetly.

A tentative hand shot out from their midst. "I am, ma'am. And I don't even use magic. I just makes them is all. Looks at the size of them and just knows what they needs. Even sews pockets in for the new telly-fonee-thingy. By my own hands. Yes, ma'am," said a meek and rather aged voice.

Good god, thought Marissa. *How long have we had that one? He doesn't even speak the King's English much less understand contemporary stuff!*

"Well then," she said flying right up to the voice in the crowd. She found a tiny, aged man so wrinkled and bald it was as though the very concept of a hairy, vital youth had fled from him millennia ago. He had sad, droopy eyelids that barely held up the multiple folds of tired skin above his eyes. As he looked up squinting slightly at the hovering fairy, it looked as though his forehead wrinkled into a million smiles. He grinned hugely when he spied his leader. All three or four of his teeth shone brightly in his decidedly gummy pink mouth.

Sewing was his lifetime vocation. And, being a tailor of sorts, he just loved her sense of fashion. Hence, he loved her with all of his heart.

"Lovely outfit," he complimented his supreme leader with the enthusiasm of a teenager at a rock concert. "Me, the toga maker, hasn't seen something like that **ever**. So pretty and smooth and so little of it!" he said admiringly. "Only...I wonder if one should have one's feet and legs so terribly exposed. Perhaps you are wearing sleepwear? If so, I can makes you something very nice. No magic, just a little bit of cloth and lots of teensy stitches. I can still sew, you know," he said proudly making a slight whistling sound through his remaining teeth.

Marissa hovered over the tiny man, absolutely spellbound by him. He was the real deal. He positively exuded glamour despite his decrepit appearance. This was a natural gift. Plus, he was talking about doing something for her that involved fashion. "I love this guy," she said aloud.

There was a collective gasp from the once-angry mob. "I didn't think it was possible!" one said.

"I want her to love me too!" someone in the group whined.

"Me too!" another added.

"Hey!" Supreme Elder Other addressed her troops, slightly offended. "I have a nice side. You just have to know how to get to it. Now," she said circling the group again. "This guy, the toga maker said the magic words for me. That's right, *fashion*. He dangled the concept of fashion in front of me. And I like that. Just like I loved how you all came out when I needed you. Because I, well, we have a real emergency on our hands. A fashion emergency."

The group began murmuring among themselves, wondering just what kind of emergency she meant. Could it be the bird-stained togas? Or perhaps she just needed a new frock. Maybe it had to do with those togas out of regulation—that is, without pockets to hold the dreaded cell phones. Everyone had an opinion on the matter.

"Here she goes," Enj said speaking softly to the elves. "She's about to mess with their heads."

"How do you know that?" Berry whispered to the big green gargoyle.

"It's that certain tone she has. Doesn't matter what she says exactly, the message is that she's the cat and they are the mice."

"My, aren't we tuned in to our little queen?" Find said to Enj. She cocked her head and evaluated the two. Not much hope for them as a couple, considering the tremendous size difference. But, hey, this was the Family and they had broken so many other taboos in the Fairfolk realm. What was one more?

"Aw come on. I mean, I work with her, you know! It's just a matter of getting used to her ways," Enj sputtered to the very savvy ladies.

"Uh-huh," was their collective response. They weren't buying his "aw shucks, ma'am" story for anything. He had a thing for the fairy. It was written all over his huge, scaly face.

"I wonder if she knows." Find asked Berry.

"Should we tell her?" her friend replied.

"No, you will not!" Enj said furiously whispering to the women. "She will totally kill me if she knows."

"Knows what?" asked Berry coyly.

"Oh never mind. You women are all the same." Enj stomped off toward the dragons. The reptiles were terribly bored with the mob and the chatter. They began walking around in circles, further smashing vines, in order to create a nice space to hunker down to nap until they were needed.

"So anyways…" Marissa rolled her eyes at the elves and Enj who were having a rather distracting conversation on the sidelines. She wasn't exactly sure what was being said, but she just knew it was about her. (Furtive glances were being made in her direction.) If she could only be a fly on the wall to hear what was being said. *But no*, she thought, *flies are icky and eat rotten things, so no, no fly on the wall.* Sighing, she returned to her restless and terribly confused mob. It was time to give them a job.

"Kids, listen up. We need to sacrifice—" Gasps were heard through the mob. Someone fainted, and others began inching away from the Supreme Elder Other in the hopes of making a hasty escape. "No. No. Not **that** kind of sacrifice. You are all so silly." She smiled. They sighed, tension fleeing the hilltop as fast as it had arrived. Starting out the way she did made them not even care one whit about what she might ask of them—as long as it wasn't the "Big S," which was her plan all along. Because she was about to get them to do something really embarrassing and downright icky.

"Volunteers?" The toga maker's hand shot up again. He was more than happy to bask in her glow yet again. "Good," she said. "Because I need you to be in charge of this job. The supervisor, as it were."

"Well, miss, I don't-es know about being in charge. I am old and know little about magic and such anymore. You see I am as old as—"

"Doesn't matter. You are the perfect guy for the job!" Marissa turned her attention to the two dragons lazing among the vines. "Lola! Get Bad-Boy up. We need him right now!"

Lola's head jerked up with a snort. A fresh stream of smoke came out in tiny puffs as she heaved herself upright. Bay-Boy, who had been dozing while propped up on her, fell over in a heap. This woke him up enough to see that Lola needed him. Waddling after her, he approached the crowd of Others. As he moved forward, they in turn moved back. He followed them. They edged backward again until the back of the mob was flat up against the barn. Nowhere else to go.

"So this is my issue," Marissa said loud enough for all to hear. "We need my stupid brother to actually ride Bay-Boy, masterful and magnificent big dragon here." (She flew up to his nose, her arm sweeping flamboyantly to include the enormity of the dragon. She looked for a moment like a magician's assistant, adding color and flourish to some tired trick.) "This big guy needs to provide a safe and comfortable perch for him. Oh, and he will be carrying a passenger. Bob."

"What, who, what?" Bob emerged from the vines, brushing dirt out of his hair. At the sound of his name, his interest was piqued. One could only think that he had taken a brief break from all the hoopla to catch a few zzz's as a cat. When one spends most of one's life as a cat, one does tend to pick up certain kitty habits. Frequent napping was one of them. "I am not riding that thing. I already told you he's too hot."

"That is where all of these fine Others come in. Bob, don't look at me like that in front of the children. I have this handled."

"Yeah, right. The last time one of you guys said that, we were up to our necks in issues."

"Patience and faith, Bob."

"Hmmph," he snorted in reply.

Slight Nudity / Sun Block Required

"So, my stupid bro—I mean, my learned brother is out attempting to find a saddle with which to use on our brave Bay-Boy. See how very long and lithe our grown-up dragon is? Yet he really isn't that wide in the belly department, so I think we can make something off the shelf out there work." At this point, she was primarily talking to herself, working the details out aloud.

The toga maker followed her bobbing flight path, reviewing and analyzing the girth of the big dragon to better understand what she wanted. He began sizing up the creature just like he would any Other needing a new garment. He began speaking his thoughts as well. "Ah, a saddle, like a horse and his rider. But whats we really needs for the saddle, for the comforts and protection of both horse and rider is a—"

"Blanket!" Marissa and toga maker both said it at once. She rewarded his brilliance by flying right up to his wrinkly, happy forehead and laying a big fairy kiss on his papery skin. The old man ignored her surprising behavior. He was already preoccupied planning the design and execution of a dragon blanket.

He began looking around as if to find such a thing lying about at Home Base. "Well, I am not sure I have enough toga fabric on hand for such a big project, but I do have an idea."

With that, the frail old man unwound his own toga and laid it carefully on the ground. Oblivious to the fact that he was now completely naked, he studied the flattened sheet, evaluating how many of such togas he would need to order to make a blanket.

Sadly, he was the only one unfazed by his most elderly nakedness.

"Sheesh," Bob said.

"My eyes, my eyes!" Enj cried, arms waving wildly as he faked sudden blindness.

Find stared down the big green gargoyle. "Haven't you seen a naked man before?" she whispered. Enj squinted, trying to determine if he had ever seen one *so old*.

"Yeah…but…" Berry said, mesmerized by the strange sight of so much sagging skin.

"Get a grip on yourself!" her friend admonished. Find rolled her eyes at her Berry, who obviously was having a hard time coping with the vision before her.

The old man stood before the throng, hands on his hips, and toothlessly barked as best as his reedy voice could, "Well, go one with yas! I need more fabric. Layers and such. A lot more than just what's here!" The stunned group didn't move an inch. "You. You. You! All of you, strip down to your unders forthwith!'

"You heard the man! Strip. Now." Marissa used her big voice, the one she inherited from her father and employed in times of duress. It did the trick every time.

The group of Others, regrettably for the rest of the group, hastened to comply, dropping their togas to the ground. Sadly, most Others preferred to go commando under the toga, so this was a definite TMI situation.

Now, since the human form adopted by the Others was meant to be only a reasonable facsimile of a human being, their privates, sadly, followed suit. They certainly functioned in all ways that private parts need to function, but it was as though the intricate details—the nooks and crannies as it were—had been left out. It made them all look like Barbie and Ken parts, if Mattel had thought to include them. Mere suggestions of what they should be. Lumpish and waxy and altogether lacking the specifics that are required for the human undercarriage. It made them all seem fascinatingly horrible.

There were a few who had had the foresight to include interesting and unique details to their human anatomy. Protuberances, for example. But let's not put too fine a point on this, shall we?

Those who had privates actually resembling actual people parts somehow seemed less nude—earthier—which fit in better in the richly detailed landscape of the verdant hillside. The rest were, well, shiny and eesh. Creepy.

It was much more than Supreme Elder Other Marissa could stand. It offended her delicate sensibilities. She decided to break up the freak show and go indoors. Her psyche needed recovery time. And the elves, similarly horrified, seemed to need a break from it all as well. The boys, she figured, could fend for themselves.

She then turned her attention to the two female elves. Quietly, she whispered, "Listen, while they are all getting nude for a good cause, we have a job to do. It's time I took you on a tour of the place. I will give you the basics to run this operation. Which, by the way, includes giving these weird naked Others useless jobs while we are gone to keep them busy and out of our hair."

"Well, that's no problem," Berry said, happy to be distracted from the increasingly fleshy mob. "I have been thinking of adding a little color to the place. Every time you scry me, your office seems so cheerless and sterile. Perhaps we could put some on painting duty," he suggested.

"Fine, fine," Marissa agreed, "But first you need to organize a cleaning party since the birds have had quite a good time defiling the place."

"Ick," was the response from the two older women.

"—and after that, you can reward yourselves with some of my favorite wine. It is cellared, by the way, under Bob's old desk." That at least, softened the distasteful task immediately ahead of them.

She led the two elves into the barn and left the crowd in its growing stage of nakedness in the able hands of the toga maker. The last word that could be heard as the barn door closed behind the fairy and her new subs was from Find. "You know, now that they are naked, maybe I could administer some simple medical exams prior to clothing them again. Oh, no, nothing too shocking, mind you, just a brief check-up. Well, maybe they would have to bend over a little…"

"That will scare the shit out of them." Marissa chuckled.

"Speaking of shit…" Berry could be heard as they began negotiating the bird-littered interior. The barn door firmly shut as the fairy gave the elves their final instructions.

The toga maker was in his glory. The sheer scale of such a large project was a delightful change, from his usual boring, cutting, hemming, and pocketing flat spans of cloth. This, in contrast, needed to be pieced together like a patchwork blanket. And it required multiple layering in order to provide insulation from the obvious heat that the dragon bodies gave off. Finally, all must be done with a certain style and flair. Well, that technically wasn't necessary, but he was working for a true fashionista, and he meant to please his Supreme Elder. Exciting to say the least.

He quickly formed the naked mob into groups. Some were directed to lay the togas out, piecing them in such a way as to form the proper size. Other Others were given the task of sewing the pieces together. The toga maker always had a ready supply of needles and thread, which he recovered from his multi-pocketed toga.

He handed the needles out and watched as the Others attempted to thread them. Those who were successful in doing so probably had some previous sewing skills. They got the job of stitching. The ones who failed were sent indoors to the toga maker's cubby to retrieve whatever cloth was left inside. They were given the task of cutting the scrap cloth into smaller strips. Those strips were handed out to each Other to use as a loincloth of sorts. This was greatly appreciated by the group, as it was a sunny day and on those parts that hadn't been exposed in a great long while, severe sunburn was entirely possible.

Soon everyone had a task, and under the direction of the toga maker, each was sufficiently diapered for propriety's sake.

Patient, they were as the dragon blanket slowly took shape, layered, stuffed for protection from dragon skin, and deftly embroidered here and there with magical creatures. It shone brightly in the afternoon sun.

They even brushed off the worst of the bird dung, but those more permanent stains became somehow part of the elaborate embroidery. A small splotch became the eye of a dragon, whereas a streak was turned into the flames erupting from a battling male dragon. The old toga designer was delighted to supervise, cajole, and even work on the blanket himself to add important flourishes to the emerging design.

Which was what they were up to when they heard the unmistakable crunch of tires on gravel. The entire group froze momentarily. Panic may have ensued along with liberal and highly unnecessary uses of magic, had it not been for the quick thinking of Bob and Enj.

"Huddle!" Enj cried to the dragons. They curled up together in the tightest knot of scaly dragon flesh possible and plopped down among the vines. Enj joined them behind the rows of lush grapes. Only the tops of the dragons were visible. Bob grabbed the largest portion of the partially stitched fabric and threw it over the pile of dragons, hiding most of the wings. And whatnot.

A cab finished its drive to the top of the hill, stopping in front of the barn. The mob, thankfully now dressed in loincloths and such, parted, making room for the vehicle. Nervous glances all around as Enj lay low among the vines and Bob approached the vehicle. Jacob, having accomplished his task, got out of the backseat, holding a large plastic bag. Whatever was in that bag looked big and bulky.

The cabdriver popped the trunk, and its lid flew up as though it couldn't wait to disgorge the huge thing crammed inside. The young man dropped the bulky bag on the gravel and proceeded to heft the huge saddle he had bought out of the trunk of the car. Jacob shot a glance at Bob and smiled nervously at the cabbie. "Everything OK here?" he asked looking at the nearly nude throng of Others, fidgeting, and the large mound of something in the vineyard covered in sheets. (*Dragon*, he reasoned. *Very close and snuggly dragons*, he amended.)

Bob replied, "Fine as wine in the summertime. Now why don't you pay this guy so he can go and pick up drunks on down the road." Bob hoisted the big saddle out of the trunk and set it aside, away from the path of the cab. He squinted at the big plastic bag. "What's in there? I am afraid to ask." He pointed to the bulky package.

Jacob smiled. "A little present for you. A travel case, as it were." The young man opened the top far enough for Bob to peer inside. It was a large and very stylish cat carrier. The exterior canvas had a chic double "C" pattern all over it. Of course, Marissa would go for couture even with a cat carrier. "A Coach for your coach," Jacob quipped.

"It is way too girly for me," Bob complained.

The cabbie got real quiet at that little exchange. After a moment of watching his fare smirk at the tattooed guy and the tattooed guy scowl back, he just couldn't help himself. "I don't get it. Some girl had you buy it for *him?*"

"Sure. Sure. Kind of a joke, that's all. I mean, look at him. You wouldn't expect this guy to travel in a box like that, now would you?"

"Wait. He is supposed to fit in that box? What you gonna do? Shrink him or something?" the cabbie joked. After all, when confused by your fare (that hadn't actually paid you yet) best to be jolly and jokey until actual money changed hands.

"J.K. Just kidding," Jacob said, fishing in his pockets for cash. "Now, uh, here's a little something extra for you. Maybe you shouldn't tell people about all this up here. We're kinda private people, you know."

The cabdriver took a long look at the situation. Up to then, he had barely focused on the ghostly pale, strange people, nearly nude and looking very creepy. They in turn were trying very hard not to look at him, preferring to watch the big white sheet covering god knows what in the vineyard. He had just about seen it all in this wine region—yuppies, winos, farmers, bikers, you name it. But this was a first. He had no idea *they* had made it to Livermore Valley. "Hare Krishna's," he said to Jacob. "They better not be begging for cash in this town," he growled.

"Nah," Jacob replied. "We keep to ourselves. Just trying to do some organic wine growing. Like that compost heap over there." He pointed to the slightly squirmy mound. He was hoping that the cabbie wouldn't question a) why the compost heap was moving and/or b) why it was covered with sheets. The cabbie squinted at the bizarre scene all around him. Truth be told, there was so much strangeness on a huge scale to see that he couldn't really take in such insignificant details as a jiggling dung heap.

Jacob looked around, assessing the situation from the viewpoint of the cabbie. Yeah, it really did look like some sort of spiritual commune, with these weird, frail people dressed in Jesus underwear, busily sewing sheets together.

He didn't know what the cabbie thought of the white-sheeted hill in the vineyard, but he figured the power of denial probably kicked in with this guy and he would either, ignore it or craft some weird rationalization as to why it was there. The story would have nothing to do with dragons or fairies or any other Fairfolk. That's just how humans operate—in total denial of what they see. Anyway, Jacob was counting on just that.

The radio in the cab squawked, attracting the driver's attention away from the immediate scene. The call of a fare, especially from a winery, was like a siren song, promising much money and big drunken tips. Besides, the cabbie had just gotten a nice fat wad of hush money from the kid, so he probably wasn't going to get any more green here. He handed the kid his call card. "You just remember my number when you get your Buddhist winery up and running. I'll pick up your drunken customers and take care of them good." His comment was said more like a warning than a suggestion.

"Sure," Jacob said smiling agreeably.

"Oh. One more thing," the cabbie asked, friendly now that a deal had been struck for future fares. "Just so I know in the future, what are you going to call this place, once it is open for business?"

"The winery you mean?" Jacob asked, stalling for an answer.

"That's easy," Bob said, wiping the saddle oil from his hands on his torn jeans. He approached the cab-driver and Jacob, having heard the tail-end of the conversation. "The winery will be called 'O. FU.'"

"What's that supposed to mean?" he cabbie said a trifle loudly, sure now that he was being messed with.

"O.FU stands for Others in Funny Underwear. Perfect, doncha think?" Bob smiled in that sly feral way that he had. He loved when a joke was funny whatever way you look at it.

The cabbie had had enough. He turned his back on the strange cult, got in his cab, put the car in reverse, and scrubbed his tires all the way. As his tires crunched their way down the drive, he began to feel better, less irritated and edgy like he felt up on the hill.

Definitely a PR problem up there, he thought. *When they open, they better offer a ton of free wine to get people past the weirdoes running that place. O.FU, my ass,* was the last he thought about that place. In fact, the whole scenario seemed to slip his mind as the day wore on. The only way he vaguely remembered the fare was the fact that he came home with a lot of money that day. Some kid, he recalled had over tipped him. That was all. End of story.

Reality Bites

"Round two," Fred whispered, acting as guest commentator for the group as she watched the couple by the edge of the trees. The husband and wife had moved themselves away from the trolls and their friends to try yet again to resolve the thorny topics of anger, abandonment, and lust for magical power, which had led to bitter estrangement. In short, they were talking about their marriage. The fire cast the two with larger-than-life shadows, flickering wildly against the black scrub, providing an ominous setting for their little drama.

They had been at it for a while now. Christina had on her human form as she gestured broadly to her husband. She seemed in the middle of a long and dramatic story. Seen was interpreting their body language, having studied this family closely ever since contact was made by them with the elf clan. He knew just exactly what was transpiring between the two. Although he could read their actions, unfortunately, he had no idea what it all meant. Relationships in general were baffling to him because of his lack of experience in anything interpersonal.

That was where Sleeping Guy came in. In the first place, he had had enough interaction with this family to know what was going on. And, sadly, his entire life had been punctuated by a string of failed relationships, so he knew what all that body language portended. Between the two of them, along with Fred as color commentator, they gave a running translation for the troll clan about the state of the (dis-)union of Christina and Ben.

"I'm pretty sure she just said that she was a reasonable person who had no choice but to follow the path she had been given," Seen said, watching her as her story came to an end. Ben just looked at her, then gave a bitingly short reply.

"He's not buying it," Sleeping Guy explained. "It's all bullshit to him. The bottom line is that she got into the glamour of your world and she blew it."

Christina's shoulders slumped. She seemed somehow to shrink into herself. "Wounded. He wounded her," Seen translated for the fascinated group. "And pretty soon, she will get irate. Ah, yes, here it comes." They all watched as Christina seemed to rise up, her fury making her seem grow larger than she had been previously. Her shadow bobbed wildly against the brush, emphasizing her extreme agitation.

"Has to be about the kids," Sleeping Guy explained. "She never gets that pissed unless she is defending her kids. She probably felt that she had to go wherever the kids were so that she could keep an eye on them."

They watched as Ben dramatically looked around as though searching for something. "He doesn't see the kids here. He's wondering if she was so intent on watching them, then why did she abandon them to be here? I am just guessing at this one," Seen apologized.

"No, I think you are right," Sleeping Guy replied. "Look, she...yes. You were right. She just pointed at him. She said she left them so she could find you, I mean Ben. She left them so she could find Ben. She was desperately worried about him."

"Oooh, that might work," Fred said helpfully. "Everyone always likes it if someone is worried about them. It makes them feel wanted and, well, not alone. That might get through to our Rockstar!"

Fred liked this game of human watching. It was going to give the troll clan millennia of fun-filled meditating. Most important, it was about relationships, something trolls paid very little attention to, which, in her opinion, was a big mistake. *Just look at the interesting drama that relationships offer!* "Question," she said, addressing the two relationship experts, one a solitary elf with giant leathery wings and the other an unattached human male. Clearly, they were the experts in the matter of love and relationships. "Is the one who scores the most points the winner of this game?"

"No. Just the opposite," Sleeping Guy sadly answered, remembering his own many breakups and battles. "If they score enough hits, they just blow up the whole relationship. Too many hurts to get past. At this point, you can only hope that someone becomes reasonable and stops being a douche."

"Oh," was the disappointed collective response from the troll gathering. They really wanted this thing to work out. After all, it was the stuff of epic sagas playing itself out right before their very eyes. And most epic sages have really happy endings. Well, except for the ones where there is mayhem, havoc, and annihilation. Other than that, they all turn out happy. Pretty much.

"Pardon," Ted said. "Can you explain the meaning and possible origins of the word 'douche'?"

"Forget I said it. Substitute 'dirt bag'. You gotta hope someone stops being a *dirt bag*, OK?" Sleeping Guy had been around these guys long enough to know how off track they became over any odd turn of phrase, much less slang.

"But dirt bags are nice things," Fred was dismayed. Imagine thinking a bag of dirt is a bad thing. After all, most of the time they are wearing one if not several bags of dirt.

Sleeping Guy gave her a long look. Fred interpreted it to mean the conversation was over. She telegraphed the message to her fellow trolls to *pipe down. Pipe down, a phrase of probable nautical origins meaning...Shhh!* The rest hollered in the most firm mind speak way they had, thereby stopping the idle meandering of one of their own.

"She's turning away. Either she has run out of things to say or she is ashamed. Hurt." Seen was a little lost here. This juncture required the knowledge of relationship nuances, and he had no history to relate to. Sleeping Guy stepped in.

"Both. She feels all of the above—hurt, confused, unsure. Otherwise, she would be talking. She always talks when she has something to say. And at this point, she is on overwhelm. He has made his point. She is wounded and totally over being mad."

"She's not mad anymore...That's good, right?" asked Fred.

"Not necessarily. If she is too hurt, she will turn off. Walk away. Eventually, she will shut down, just like Ben. And then they will be done for good."

"But I thought if she wasn't mad, then that's progress. No?" Fred was terribly confused. "After all the opposite of love is hate. And if she is done hating him, then she might love him."

The group watched momentarily in silence. Christina had turned away from Ben, quietly wiping the tears from cheeks. Occasionally, she was seen to discreetly touch under her nose in an attempt to stem the flow from it. Ben was staring off into the trees, studiously avoiding her. Yet neither was ready to walk away. Yet.

After a time Sleeping Guy turned to Fred, in answer to a question that she had asked a few moments ago. It had taken him some time to decide the right answer. Now he had it. One of those light bulb life moments when you learn deep wisdom. Too bad when he applied it to his own life, he realized the sad truth of his own doomed relationship with Marissa.

"Actually, the opposite of love is not hate. It is apathy." Apathy.

Apathetic. Which was the way Marissa had treated him this entire time. Neutral and unaffected by his subtle advances. Unfazed and uncaring. "Damn," he said, commenting on what he now realized was the impossibility of a relationship with Marissa and his yet again failed love life. He sighed. Another let down.

"Wait. Something is happening." Suddenly, Seen became very excited. The group held their collective breaths as they watched Ben first look over at Christina, noticing for the first time that she had been silently crying. Her despair seemed to trigger something in him as he approached her from behind. Firmly turning her to face him, he placed one hand on her shoulder and the other at her cheek, as though to wipe away a tear.

"Tears" Sleeping Guy stated. "A woman's secret weapon."

"Yeah, but she's not sure," Seen began again, familiar with that particular body language. "She is trying to brush off his hand. But look, he just grabbed hers. And he is refusing to let it go."

"What is he looking at?" Sleeping Guy now, out of his element, failed to see what fascinated Ben so about Christina's hand.

"Oh, I know. I know!" Fred said, her voice rising in her excitement. It was all about the epic story. The one she had almost committed to heart.. "It's the ring. Or the mark of the ring that had been burned into her skin. The Mark of Sacrifice. That's it! All he needed was to be reminded of her tremendous sacrifice to the family to know the depth of her feelings. Right?"

Fred was delighted with herself. She really was getting the hang of this human relationship thing after all. The group of trolls had just had this conversation silently, mentally, reluctant to speak aloud themselves. They felt somehow there was an important connection between Fred, Seen, and Sleeping Guy that they were loath to break with their chatter. They had no qualms, however, about telepathically hammering Fred with their questions. She had assumed the job of verbalizing for them. After all, it was just Fred and she could use a little yelling at now and then. Being a rowdy troll teenager and all.

"Or maybe he is reminded that she made a giant Sacrifice and ended up in Crazy Town and therefore cannot possibly be responsible for her actions," Sleeping Guy drily added.

"Either way, it doesn't matter," Seen said, smiling. "It reminds him that she is indeed in need of his love and support. That for all she has been through, she is not whole unless *he* is there to love and protect her."

Seen resumed the play-by-play action. "Yes, they are smiling, and no, it doesn't look like it but they are. They just somberly head-nodded each other. That's a good sign. It's one of their secret signals they make to each other. It either means, 'I get what you said,' or it could mean, 'I hear you.' It also might mean 'I love you.' Whatever this version of head nodding, it always portends an accord of some such has been reached between the two."

"OK, what's he saying now?" Fred asked. She was fascinated at Seen and Sleeping Guy's skills at reading people. *Imagine not even being able to read their minds and yet understanding the inner workings of these human-like magical creatures. Amazing! I really want to learn this mad skill,* she told herself.

Shhh was the collective response of the group as they mentally chastised her. No one really cared one whit what skills Fred desired as long as she continued to ask the questions they were so longing to ask themselves.

Silly teenagers and their presumptuous ways, thought one.

Shhh! was the nearly audible response from the collective.

"Wha—Hey!" Fred was just about to take on the group of gawking trolls and their superior tones, when she noticed a changed between the humans. Rockstar Ben was asking something of Christina. It stopped the woman right in her tracks. She was looking away, as though the answer was just there among the trees. He was still holding her hand. She pulled away. "Oh no!" Fred wailed softly. "Is it all ruined?"

"What has gone wrong?" Seen wondered aloud.

Sleeping Guy stared, fascinated, at the couple. "Wait," the young man said. "I don't think whatever he said really blew it. I know a brush-off when I see one. And this is not it. He just, I don't know, maybe asked a serious question, and she needed a minute to figure out her answer. I think it—Yes!" he said pleased that he was right. "Yes! She is OK with it. Whatever it is. They are in agreement."

The group watched as Christina nodded solemnly. Ben folded her in his arms as though they had both just crossed a very arduous finish line and an exhausted hug was the best they could manage.

"So we get our happy ending after all?" Fred asked.

"I think so. Wait, yes. See they are retreating to the brush in the woods. And no, you cannot follow them." Sleeping Guy anticipated the group-think at this point. It wasn't terribly hard after all since they seemed to surge toward the couple, in an attempt to follow them. "They need privacy. And if you traipse along with them, you will undo everything that just transpired here. So halt your nosy selves." Sleeping Guy admonished them.

Admonishment was entirely unnecessary as the couple seemed to abruptly change their minds about retreating into the brush. Almost in unison, they turned their heads sharply, as though startled by a sound from deep within the woody growth. They froze, just as deer do, before deciding to flee some approaching danger.

But these were humans, humans who possessed magical powers and thus were pretty tough characters in a fight. So they didn't startle and flee. Instead, they remained very still. The group, just a short distance away was just far enough from the couple to be unaware of the type or origin of the noise that so abruptly halted Ben and Christina's progress. They all watched in silence, waiting to see what or perhaps *who* might emerge from the deep growth.

Eventually, they all heard the approaching sound. It was a thunderous crashing noise. The sound of a very large troll, perhaps, blundering about? Or maybe a crazed gardener, slashing his way through the underbrush. A wayward bwana on a misguided safari? But no, it was just a man.

To be more specific, a very old man with a long white beard, tied together under his chin into a stringy ponytail. His shoulder-length hair wafted around his head, sprouting like wings from under a baseball cap. He wore beige Dockers, with the waistband nearly under his ribs. His shirt was collared, but snagged from its recent conflict with brambles. The man held a golf club aloft and swung at the brush like a machete. Clearing a path for himself. His gaze was low to the ground as though he was searching.

"Dear, oh dear," he was heard to mutter. "If I lose another good ball in the dark, she will just kill me!" Then looking up, he noticed the couple at the edge of the clearing. "Oh. Hello" he said, politely. He took another look at them, squinting to get a better view. He took off his cap and, then concentrated on the couple, his gaze never leaving the man and the woman. Finally, a spark of recognition flashed on his face. "Oh my stars! Out of the frying pan and into the fire!" he exclaimed loudly.

Ooh, good one! The trolls collectively thought, sighing with pleasure, savoring the nuances of that particular turn of phrase. They immediately melted into their favorite meditative poses. And accordingly, a huge knot of boulders suddenly appeared where the trolls once stood.

"A thousand pardons," he apologized. Ducking back into the brush, he beat a very hasty retreat.

"Didn't that guy look familiar?" Ben asked Christina.

"Give me a minute, and I'll tell you where we have seen him before." Christina thought back, turning the mental rolodex in her mind.

She had just about got it when Seen shouted, "Ye gods! That was the Supreme Elder Other, and you've just frightened him!"

Sleeping Guy Wakes from a Long Nap

She emerged from the brambles like a tiger, brutally muscling its way through the thick brush. She was a vision, bursting through the brambles—the image of an angry mother, protecting her young. Her brood as it were, followed meekly in her ferocious wake, preferring to let her take the lead through this—literally—very thorny situation.

Her sheer power and size made the scratchy bushes look feeble and inconsequential. She stepped long-legged and masterfully, taking in her surroundings as she approached, sizing up potential threats. This Amazonian woman, with dark burnished skin and chiseled cheekbones, looked more like sculpture than flesh and blood. Her hair was pulled back in a tight, low bun, giving her a timeless, regal look. Honeysuckle saw all of the magical creatures before her and was unfazed.

Taking inventory of the presumed threats to her charges—cavemen, frozen in their tracks, so still they looked like stony statues; an odd man/bat, looking like one of Santa's elves with terrifying green wings; and people, three random people looking like they just got caught with their hands in the cookie jar. Well, two did. One, a young, badly tattooed guy with long, thin hair didn't look guilty at all. He just stood, staring at her, the woman from the jungle, powerful and muscular under her strangely modest pants and shirt. The tattooed guy looked agog at the vision of this very ferocious, very tall woman.

Jesus, Sleeping Guy thought. *She should be wearing some sort of Betty Rubble outfit—all torn and animal skin-like. But actually she is wearing attire suitable for a day on the golf course. How odd.*

Which, in fact, was what she had been doing. Golfing. In the dark. With neon balls. Undisturbed, aside from her motley crew of students (the three wise guys, as she referred to them), and up to then having a heavenly time practicing the art of golf on this abandoned course, until the Idiot One lost yet another ball.

Worse than anything, he came back empty-handed and blathering about trouble on the other side of the hedge row. *Hedge row, he thinks everything green is a hedge row. Idiot,* she reminded herself. *It's a barranca not a hedge row.* She sighed to herself for the millionth time, *Oh well. He may be the biggest idiot of the three. But he's my idiot. And something scared him. So whatever it is I shall kick its ass.*

Only "it" was actually this random assemblage of life forms, from the fantastic (rock people and let's not forget bat-thing-guy) to mundane (grungy student). She decided to take on the weakest thing and work her way up to the bigger ones later. She made a beeline for the gangly student. "Shut your mouth!" she barked. "Flies are coming in."

With that, Sleeping Guy's jaws snapped closed. He had in fact been absolutely stunned at the vision of this Nubian tigress ever since she came crashing through the greenery. He couldn't take his eyes off of her. She was amazing and strong looking and tough. And yet, her mouth, that generous full thing, trembled a teeny tiny bit, as though this was all for show. It was like deep down inside there was a little, scared girl who needed comforting. And he seemed to be the only one to notice this crucial fact. "Oops. Sorry," was his only retort. Hard to think on the fly when face-to-face with a goddess.

As she drew closer to Sleeping Guy, there was something almost chemical in their reaction to each other. If looks could be audible, the ones that suddenly shot between the two sounded like "Zoing" and "Boom" and "Yowza!"'. Her reaction to this grungy, hippie guy was curious. The closer she got to him, the calmer she felt. Her intense protection mode seemed to ebb away as she regarded the thin, lean guy. *I just love his voice. So deep and melodic! Like a TV announcer or a DJ at a classical radio station*, she mused. Taking a better look at him, she thought, *Why he doesn't look so bad close up, she thought. Just a little scrawny. Needs some protein powder and a good workout plan, and he would be buff. Just like his voice.* Her fix-it mode had kicked into high gear, as though she was already making plans for this dude.

If Sleeping Guy only knew her reaction to him, he would be deliriously happy. As it was, he felt completely in awe in her presence. "A goddess has just walked into my life," he murmured to no one in particular. She chuckled at him, feeling like somehow, even with cavemen and bat-like-guy, everything was going to be OK.

And that was the true and best use of glamour. Sleeping Guy had it all along. He just needed the right woman to bring it out in him. His melodious voice was the first clue that he possessed the mad skill of glamour.

"Can you explain what all this business here is about?" she asked rather awkwardly. This chill guy had completely thrown her off her game.

"Well…" he said looking at his surroundings for inspiration. He didn't want to scare her or blow her mind with the news that fairytales were legit. He just didn't know the right way to gently guide her though this. He decided to soft pedal the whole situation. "It's kinda hard to explain. See, these Flintstone guys are real. And we just don't notice them much because we choose not to see them for what they are."

"Oh" she said. "So these guys…" She gestured toward the more outrageous looking of the crowd. "…are part of the fantastical realm that humans, in their deal with magical devils, choose to ignore. You mean like that?"

Sleeping Guy smiled broadly at her—which involved tilting his head slightly up because of the small height difference. That is, she was a tad bit taller than he. It was kind of thrilling and tantalizing for him. To contemplate a large, full-sized woman instead of wasting all of his affections on a miniaturized flying buzz saw (Marissa). A welcome change indeed. "So you know about magic?"

"Why, sure. Saw it for myself in Vegas. Had my boys here with me." She turned towards the wooded expanse and hollered loudly, "Boys, come out here properly and be polite. That's right. I'm here; you don't have to be scared." She turned back to Sleeping

Guy, explaining, "They are a tad skittish, being new at the human form and all. I take care of them," she announced proudly. "They are like my little babies. Well, old little babies, newbies nonetheless, to the human game. And I am teaching them what's what about life. And golf."

"That just sounds so kind of you. Like you are some sort of benevolent benefactor, right?" Sleeping Guy smiled hopefully at her, secretly praying that he hadn't overdone it.

"Yeah," she answered, considering the change of image. *Wow, from dominatrix to benefactor! I like that.* She mulled this new image over and decided that benefactor was just fine. *Perhaps Golf Goddess and Benefactor,* she amended.

While this mental thought train had been occurring, Sleeping Guy just couldn't take his eyes off of her. He took a chance. He went for it. "I guess we should start over." Holding his hand out for a proper shake, very nervously, he stated, "My name is Sle—er, no. My name is Kenneth. And you?"

She looked down at his outstretched hand. It shook just the tiniest bit, betraying his nervousness at meeting her. *Oh, how sweet.* She melted.

"Betsy."

"For real?" he asked.

"Yeah," she cooed, smiling genially at the timid guy.

"Wow, what a name. I love it! You know, kinda retro, like the kind they had in fifties TV shows. Or the movies. The black-and-white ones."

"Well, exactly!" She was so excited that someone got it. "My momma loved the old movies. You know, the sweet ones where everything turns out fine in the end. Happy endings were what she wanted for her kids. So she named me Betsy. After a big movie star in the old movies."

He thought about that for a minute. Then from deep within, in an answer to her comment came bubbling up from the depths of his soul. He had no idea what he said until he said it. It was, of course, to two people experiencing glamour to its fullest, a perfect answer. "If it were me, I would make sure all your endings were happy ones."

Well, it was perhaps, awkwardly said, but she put it down to youth and inexperience. The bottom line was that he liked her, all nappy-haired and sweaty from a late afternoon on the links. He overlooked all of that as though she deserved to be treated special. Like a princess. A goddess golf princess with happy endings.

I'd like to give him a happy ending... Her thoughts had made a slight swerve into the lust zone. Somehow, she felt sure that he wouldn't mind. She looked down, belatedly realizing that the whole time she had been cogitating the endless possibilities of hooking up with this man, she had been shaking his hand. Abruptly, she broke contact, noting that both their hands were just a wee bit sweaty. She smiled sheepishly at him. He smiled right back at her.

"What is happening?" Fred whispered to Seen. The trolls un-bouldered themselves and returned to their fleshy forms. It was to better hear what was going on. Hard to pick up nuances in speech with rocks in one's ears. They gathered closer to the elf, not wanting to miss the teeniest nuance of his answer.

"Well," Seen drew out his reply, "I am not sure. But since whatever it is I surely have had not experienced it, then by process of elimination, I would say they have fallen in love."

"I told you there would be a happy ending to this story!" Fred cried out, delighted that fairy tales in fact did sometimes come true.

Never Underestimate the Power of a Woman

The camp had grown considerably in the last few days. First, it had been only trolls. Nice, quiet, meditative trolls. Then a magical human arrived, peeing in their midst. A sort of urinary baptism leading to a new life of excitement for the clan. This was soon followed by an elf, a wife, and a hapless college student. And if that wasn't enough, the latest additions involved three somewhat bumbling wizards, who apparently had recently lost their magical abilities, leaving them in a perpetual state of confusion, seemingly powerless to deal with even the simplest of dilemmas.

Which was why all the trolls heartily approved of the latest addition to the camp— somewhat terrifying dark-skinned woman of Amazon proportions. Human to be sure, with little to no magical skills (other than glamour, which she only used on the college student, in quite liberal doses. And vice versa, by the way). But so innately powerful and strong. The perfect addition to an epic tale unfolding in their midst.

Such a noisy campsite. But delightfully so, the trolls thought. For once, they were in the thick of story, rather than the passive audience of one. There were so many fascinating idioms and turns of phrases they hardly had time to meditate on one before another would come flying out from left field ("Left field"—a sports reference of Western culture, with which they were currently in love; this meant that they used it often, to the annoyance of anyone who wasn't a troll).

Such a romantic campsite. Between the human mother and father and their attempts at the healing of their recent estrangement, and the odd union of pale scrawny white boy and large, copper-skinned Amazon woman, night times took on a decidedly randy tone. The couples, on a regular basis, would nocturnally got off to their own private locations to "commune," as it were, so the atmosphere positively reeked of bonding. And pheromones.

Such an interesting campsite. Little Fred (well, "little" by troll standards) became the constant interpreter between Seen and the wizards and the human contingent. She had evolved into the human expert, rivaling even Bert in his knowledge of human culture. She patiently explained to "the boys" (as the wizards were referred to) what was happening in the love and romance department, while Seen explained everything else of relevance that did not involve human interrelationships. He was admittedly out of his depth on the relationship score and needed help – even if it was from an inexperienced troll teenager.

Such an informative campsite. The trolls had become positively stupefied on a regular basis by the marvelous stories all had to share. Most days and nights, one would find them frozen in delightfully awkward rock-like poses, meditating on yet another tasty chapter in say, the adventures of "the boys" in

Las Vegas, as told by the old gentlemen themselves and then re-storied by Seen.

As it happened, Seen knew quite a bit about Las Vegas, having Googled it often. (*Google* was a perfect way to while away the day at Home Base whilst acting as secretary to Supreme Elder Other, Marissa. The days were long and the job slightly tedious. The Internet was a great way to stay informed about humans and find out nearly anything of interest to them. Las Vegas became a personal favorite as Other operatives had for a time noticed a great deal of magical activity there due to the wizards on vacation). He felt it was his duty to stay informed on such matters of relevance. And now, it made him the resident expert and quite valuable in the eyes of the trolls.

Vegas, baby. It was the closest thing to magic that humans had. Well, besides sex, but that was out of Seen's purview so, he stayed with being the expert of the bright twinkling lights of sin city. And his knowledge was greatly appreciated by the trolls.

This is how it worked. The trolls would be stretching and stirring, waking as it were from a long group think, when someone would happen by, usually one of "the boys," muttering something as simple as "Wakey, wakey, little boulders." This would throw them into spasms of mental chatter: *Wakey, wakey, a British reference of encouragement for one to awake from sleep.*

Ah yes, but usually reserved for small children…

So they think we are children?

No, it is a means of expressing affection, perhaps reserved for family members…

Ah, are we then a family? Or perhaps we have the potential to actually be a family…

No, they refer to us a tribe—a loose coalition of bonded individuals, united by a common cause...Actually... (This usually came from Fred, who generally liked to express the same theme in a variety of ways.) *I believe it is a reference to an invitation to crossbreed. An interspecies comingling to make a true family. Yeesh!*

They would generally all respond, giving the teenager a rather stony look—which was easy to do, as they had become boulders again. Fred really did like to put a romantic spin on most everything.

Consequently, potty stops became somewhat problematic. There simply was too much to process and dwell on coming from so many directions. All day. And sometimes, all night.

Such a happy camp. Well, except for Fred, who frankly was a little tired of this trollish obsession to think about every little thing to near death. After having discovered her knack for interpreting human behavior, she hungered for more than simple meditation. She wanted action. She wanted, in fact, to be the story and not parse the story. So Fred was a bit on the outs with everyone. She stayed mobile and tactile, preferring her living silly putty looks to her sparkly granite mode. She wanted to get out and do more, experience more. She wanted to live among people who didn't freeze like a perpetual game of red light at the drop of a hat.

So she began to hang with the human, Betsy. She liked Betsy. When the large woman wasn't cuddling with Kenneth (Fred liked to call him by his real name. It made him more human somehow than just referring to him as Sleeping Guy, more like a person and less like a thing. So, Kenneth it was.) Betsy was herding her boys, the three old gentlemen around, teaching them golf and trying to keep them out of trouble.

Betsy had her hands full. The old wizards were like billiard balls, always banging into one another, invariably causing one to career off in some direction that would ultimately end up in jeopardy for them all. Betsy could use a wing woman. So Fred was it.

Fred usually was assigned to Arthur. Arthur was a handful to be sure and needed more minding than the rest. He simply had no sense of danger. Everything was fascinating to him—be it a dozing rattlesnake or a curious skunk, it all seemed simply charming and needing to be investigated. That was where Fred came in. She grew to be very skilled at redirecting Arthur away from the danger. "Oh, look…" she would start. "See those shiny metal tubes with wings? Kenneth says those are air-planes way up there. People are actually in them."

"But they are so tiny," Arthur would say, having forgotten about his intense desire to befriend a scorpion. "Do they have some master wizard shrinking them to fit in that tiny craft up there? Or perhaps they have all been turned into mustard seeds for the duration of the flight. But then…" He would pause, musing to himself. "Do they have weaponry against passing eagles? I mean we wouldn't want to be eaten by a bird of prey being the size of a mustard seed, would we? But, no…" Arthur was perplexed now. "They have no magic. So does an Other magic them for the duration of the flight and then magic them to forget after they have grown back to size? That's against the rules, you know"…

And so it would go, Fred, gently taking Arthur by the elbow, moving him out of harm's way while he had full-blown conversations with himself about the mystical properties of humans. Truth be told, Fred often had similar musings about humans herself. She certainly would like to get her blocky hands on a Google-thing like Seen had at Home Base to ask those questions.

And when nothing could dissuade Arthur from literally jumping off the cliff to see if he could still fly, she would use the ultimate troll ploy. She would suddenly expand her proportions and freeze into a very large boulder, making the previous pathway to disaster now impossible. She had gotten quite good at this game. She had recently expanded her rocky self to the size of a small retaining wall, in order to thwart Arthur yet again from steeping off the cliff and into certain danger.

Fred had developed an array of tricks to herd, protect, and otherwise babysit the old gentlemen. She had become a very good babysitter. In return, she had Betsy's friendship. This was such a change for the once escort, as other women were never considered friends, only rivals and competitors.

Fred being Fred certainly wasn't a rival for anyone's affection in camp. Kenneth barely registered her presence, having only eyes only for his Nubian queen. *But really,* Betsy thought, appraising her new friend's appearance, *with a bit of sprucing up, perhaps involving hair gel, I could make something of the girl. Maybe. Maybe not. Worth a try.* She considered. *One thing's for sure, she needs to blow this pop stand and find another posse, where the pickin's are better. Because here the odds are good, but the goods are definitely odd!*

Very soon, Fred had her chance to branch out.

On a frosty, cool morning, as the more pliable of creatures stirred themselves awake, Seen was the first of those to be up. He discreetly moved off to the trees to take care of urgent business, when he felt something in the air. A strange tingling, as though the magical net that surrounds us all had grown fingers and was poking him in order to get his attention. "Huh?" he said, looking everywhere for some sign that something magical was amiss. The invisible fingers poked him under his tiny, weak chin, forcing him to look upward. "Oh dear!" he cried with alarm when he saw what was in the sky.

Morning routine forgotten, he hurried back to the camp to first find Ben stirring the cold ashes in preparation for a morning fire. "Big magic is coming!" Seen whispered frantically to the man.

"What big magic?" Ben said scanning the campsite for signs of trouble. If the Others had finally found him and decided to annihilate him for being a renegade, he was not going to let them hurt anyone else here. He was in the "'protect by fleeing from my friends and wife" mode, and was quickly deciding which direction to flee.

"No, no, sir," Seen stopped him. He pointed up. "The big magic is up there." He refined his direction, pointing to a spot low on the horizon. Ben squinted but saw nothing.

"Look again," Seen ordered. OK, so he looked and still saw nothing. Well, except for a tiny ripple, blurring a part of the tree line, like heat waves from a very hot bonfire. All heat, but no smoke.

"Don't you see it?" Seen asked. He was incredulous. How even the most basic of creatures could not see what he saw was astounding to him. He always saw the magical net that surrounds all of us. He didn't even have to try anymore. It was just there.

It was usually a swirly, misty sort of affair, fluidly and (mostly) placidly sifting around all objects in its path. Until something came along to disturb it. Then it grew thin, as though a great bubble was forming under it, stretching it to its limits until it collapsed in a catastrophic way.

This time, it was not thin or threatening to blow it. It looked, well, excited. Happy even. The swirly, misty energy usually was pale—at best, pastel-hued. Now something large was flying toward them. It was still too far off to see, but the magical net was telling all who could perceive it that some big shot was coming. In the wake of the flying blob was the mist, bright and sparkly, as though the incoming blob was feeding it, making it more substantial. And very colorful. Big magic was on the way.

Now, Ben could see that something was flying in. Whatever it was, it looked ominous. "Tell the rest of the camp to be ready. Something is about to happen."

Seen roused the rest of the sleeping group and told them to assemble by the fire pit. The three wizards tumbled out of their tents, hair and beards askew and clutching what appeared to be nightshirts. Their white, spindly legs quite possibly hadn't seen the light of day in a fair millennium or two and were not a welcoming sight.

"Oh for gods sakes, go back and put some pants on," Betsy admonished the men. She too was setting her clothes to rights after hastily putting them on. All of them had that thrown-together look.

Most everyone looked confused, especially the trolls, who, while milling about in their pliable form, were ready at a moment's notice to go into defensive mode. This meant turning back into rocks. That was about the biggest thing they had in their bag of tricks, and they, needless to say used it often. Even if it wasn't always appropriate. All eyes were on the horizon as the big blob drew near.

As it neared in the morning light, the big blob became two and then three blobs. An ominously colorful sight for all to behold.

Fight, Flight, or Turn to Stone

Turn to stone.

The last is exactly what the trolls did. You have to forgive them. It's how they roll. By now it was a reflexive action taken as a form of defense. They had, in fact, every intention of providing protection for their non-stony compatriots. That is, if you define defense as turning into a large set of rocks for their friends to hide behind.

Which was, in fact, what the wizards did. They scurried behind the troll clan, anxious to be out of the way, should those blobs mean trouble. It stood to reason, they thought, as they were more a hindrance than a help in a fight. Best for all involved if they stayed safely out of the way. After all, you wouldn't want someone to accidentally trip over them in the midst of a fight, now would you?

But not the rest. Seen, Christina, Ben, and Betsy stood their ground in front of the wall of trolls. Kenneth was there as well. Perhaps standing just a hair behind Betsy. But he was there for moral support nonetheless.

Soon, it was apparent that two dragons accompanied by a green gargoyle were fast approaching. If Ben and Christina didn't know better they would have assumed that a pack of Other hunters had found them. After intense scrutiny involving ferocious squinting, Ben heaved a big sigh of relief, stating, "It's OK. We know this crowd."

Immense tension left the group. Even the boulders shrank a bit in their postures. Shoulders collectively dropped and relieved sighs were heard all around.

"Can we unfreeze?" Fred asked, halfway unfrozen—just enough to ask the question.

"Sure, honey," Christina said. "Don't be scared. That big gargoyle is my adopted son."

"Oh. You mean Lord Enj, the great and powerful trickster gargoyle who is a misfit among his own kind?" Fred asked for clarification in the context of the epic saga she had just heard. Twice.

"Who's a misfit gargoyle?" Enj softly landed, smiling briefly at his human parents and flashing a scowl at the troll who had insulted him.

"Hi, Mommy. Hi, Daddy," called a voice from in between the digits of Enj's caged fingers.

Never Underestimate the Power of a Woman—or Four, Five If You Count Reptiles

"Sup," said Jacob, trying to look cool on his saddle atop the big dragon. The dragon riding definitely was chill, but he had done it while clinging onto a designer travel bag for Bob. Way too girly for cowboy Jay. So he resorted to gangster lingo to offset his metrosexual accessory.

"You found us," Christina said.

"How?" Ben inquired.

"Just following the love," Bob explained.

"It was your sparkly magical net." Enj clarified.

Ben couldn't help but smile at his kids. They sure knew how to make an entrance. It seemed like it had been so long since he had seen them in the swamps. Back then he was angry and fearful for their safety. He was just plain tired from perpetually looking after them and worrying about their mom. And yet, they all seemed to have survived, maybe even thrived without him. This was a bittersweet moment to be sure, one that was filled with the knowledge that his family didn't quite need him in the way they had used to.

Caretaker Dad was over, it seemed. Now his role was what? Loving Observer Dad? Occasional Safety Net Dad? Casual conversation Dad?

None of that mattered for now, as his heart was very, very full. Marissa flew up to him, throwing as much of her arms as possible around his neck. Even Jacob lost his momentary coolness. Hopping down from Bay-Boy, he reached his hand out to shake his father's. Having none of that, his dad pulled him into a bear hug. Jacob didn't resist.

Neither did Enj. He enfolded them all in his large embrace, framing the much smaller, in comparison family, with his wings.

"Would you stop smothering us?" a muffled and irritated Marissa said. Enj's wings were fully engaged in the affectionate embrace. Unfortunately for the little fairy, this meant temporarily cutting off her source of fresh air. Considering she was the only female involved in the huddle this meant inhaling a veritable cornucopia of ripe man smells, from campfire (Dad), to brimstone (Jacob), to briny reptilian (Enj).

She decided to hone in on the briny reptilian. "Enjie, as usual, you smell like ass."

"Would you please put on your happy face, Miss Manners? We are in the company of new friends. We wouldn't want them to see the real you quite yet, now would we? And by the way, my name is not Enjie."

What's up with them? Betsy whispered to Kenneth. After all, her man had just recently successfully translated the body language of Christina and Ben without the benefit of hearing the couple's words. Surely with a few verbal cues, he could decipher the nature of the relationship between the giant green gargoyle and the diminutive blue fairy. Kenneth shrugged, telegraphing, *Not sure yet.*

The group untangled. Strangely, despite the fact that the odd couple was bickering, the two remained physically close together, as though they were somehow attached, keeping them in close orbit of one another.

It was the arch of the eyebrow that tipped Betsy off—not Marissa's, but Christina's. A mother can hear it in her daughter's voice. It's a tone. A certain female frequency that says, "Despite the fact that I have just reamed you a new one, I really do care for you. And you me. This is part of our game." Christina had never heard that tone from her daughter before. It sounded so very grown up for her little girl. She did the eyebrow arch as a dawning realization overtook her.

She did what every self-respecting mother would do at that moment of understanding. She burst into tears. "You are all grown up!" she wailed.

"Ooh, Mommy is leaking!" Lola squeaked to her mate, a dragon equivalent of whispering, "She must be broken. Do we eat her now?"

Lola really was trying to get up to speed with dragon-human etiquette. Eating one of them would certainly speed up the process. This was the only thing she could think of doing. After all, her Bay-Boy had told her that when their mommies grow weak and died, that the baby dragons must eat them. Having never seen her own mother leak like that before, she concluded that this was some mysterious part of mommies, a ritual before dying perhaps. Which was possibly followed by consuming the mother?

It was all so confusing, this strange family her boy dragon had amassed. Her partner shook his head in the negative. "No-ah. These girl humans leak like this sometimes. I think they are just a little broken, not dying."

"Oh." Lola was saddened by his response. She really wanted to get hep to the interspecies relationship thing. The quickest shortcut was to eat someone. Sadly, this was not to happen. Yet.

Betsy looked at Christina, who was looking at Marissa. Eventually, Fred got it. She began smiling in a sappy, gravelly way. Lola squinted her jewel-like eyes, sensing the electricity between the gargoyle and the fairy. She looked at her Bay-Boy and felt the same spark. "Ahhhs," she said. "And I didn't even have to eat anyone to understand." She was very proud of herself at her ability to make the love-connection without the use of blood and gore.

Bob was the only male able to be currently on the female channel. He watched very carefully as the nonverbal clues were bandied about. *Old news, impossible love story, blah, blah, blah,* he droned to himself.

"How is this new news?" Bob said. He was straightening his clothes out from his transformation, clearly over this topic. "They have had the Jones for each other forever, man."

"Huh?" said Ben, looking from Enj to Marissa, unsure which one to be annoyed with. "I thought you didn't er, egg. You told me." He appealed to his daughter who hovered in the air, horrified by her parents' reaction to her and Enj's bickering.

In her haughtiest manner possible, she replied, "Euww, pullease. Not relevant and none of anyone's business! New subject stat!" She saw the blank stares from the blocky trolls and decided that this was enough personal discussion for now. After all, she was Supreme Elder Other, in spite of her parentals. She redirected the conversation to the pressing issue at hand. What to do with Renegade Rockstar Ben. "Can we please say our hellos and then get down to the business at hand?"

And so began the worrying conundrum of what to do now that they had found Dad. The children of Ben and Christina realized that finding their parents was easier than they had thought it would be. This naturally concerned them all. They had discovered their parents through series of hints, clues, scrying, and just plain magical forces, having been drawn to them like magnets.

Since it was, in the end, less difficult than they had thought to find their parents, they knew it was only a matter of time before the Other hunters found them. Annihilation of Ben would be the end goal of those hunters. To them, Ben had the unfortunate label of "Rogue/Renegade Other."

Now protocol would require that they clear all annihilation with the Supreme Elder Other Marissa. And therein lay the essence of the conundrum.

Funny thing about rules. They seemed damn inconvenient when applied to your own situation but perfectly reasonable when applied to anyone else. This was Marissa's dilemma. She would have no problem whatsoever hunting down and, er, well eliminating any rogue Other, except when it came to her family. After all, those other guys ran to the strange side of the spectrum and one running around with magical powers and no supervision was a scary thought. But her dad was another story altogether.

From all accounts (and the trolls were more than happy to tell and retell their part of the story as they met and interacted with Ben), he had no real interest in using or overusing his magical powers. Her dad just seemed to hunker down and assimilate well with these Fairfolk. And they loved him—even called him their own rock star. Marissa chuckled at the thought of her dad being called a rock star, but it kinda fit anyway. They adored him, and he seemed very happy with them.

Especially with Mom by his side. She was, by all accounts, dreamily ecstatic to be reunited with her husband. He even made his own fires the hard way (no magic at all). So it seemed that he hadn't caused a bit of trouble requiring Other intervention.

So for a plethora of reasons, objective as well as emotional, annihilation of Dad was not appropriate—including how totally not fair it would be to Mom or the trolls or the rest of the family for that matter.

But surely something had to be done. Enj and Jacob, with their successful attempt at a "faux" annihilation in Las Vegas, presented a good option, something to make it seem like Dad had received the ultimate punishment for going rogue without the actual mayhem and bodily destruction. But how to do it? That was the endless topic of discussion, a.k.a., arguing, around the camp.

Time was running out. Find and Berry could only manufacture so much in the way of distractions for the Others before open revolt would occur. After that, they would all come looking for them.

Fred fretted. She hated the feeling of discord within the camp. All of this endless discussion did not feel like happiness and contentment. It brought up tensions that did not in any way further the epic story of the Family and their living happily ever after. She was on the verge of becoming distraught. She could not bear to see her favorite characters in the most epic story of all time in the throes of constant verbal conflict. It upset her. It grated on her. It was fingernails on a chalkboard for her.

Finally, she had had it. At the campfire, well not really a campfire, but by the glow of rocky trolls having recently been warmed by dragon fire, she spoke up. Loudly. "Hey."

She was ignored. So she spoke a bit louder. "Hey!"

Shhh, the trolls admonished mentally. They were trying to glean bits of verbal gold from this angry chatter. Fred was interrupting their thoughts. Again.

"No! Not shush. I will not be shushed any longer. *Heyyy!*" she said a bit more heatedly than she should have. It did get everyone's attention though.

"Good. You are all quiet. Now that I have your attention, I shall tell you a story…"

Fred Tells a Story

She began by taking a deep, cleansing breath, as though to fortify herself until the story's completion. In truth, she took a deep breath to calm her nerves. She didn't have the power of glamour to calm this rowdy bunch, but she had a hell of a lot of stories under her belt—and historical knowledge. And if this wasn't an epic moment in history, then she didn't know her granite from gold. The deep breath was designed to center and prepare herself to tell the tale that would move their spirits into a place of harmony and cooperation.

The trolls immediately hunkered down in an interesting variety of boulder shapes—seated positions for comfort's sake. Everyone else took the hint, sitting together in various clumps—a mom and dad here, the odd couple there—like two piano keys snuggled up together, ebony and ivory, and an odd assortment of compatriots, accompanied by two dragons and a kitty version of Bob, ready for a long sit. Or nap. Depending on how interesting this story was.

"Once upon a time in a land not far from here,"

Ooh, the trolls sighed in happy contentment. A real story…

"Ahem" was the gentle admonishment, by the normally good-natured Fred. Gentle soul or no, this was going to be the tale of her life, and she would brook no trollish interruptions, mental or verbal.

"Once upon a time in a land not far from here, there was a king and a queen who lived in a castle high atop a very windy hill. He, like all good kings, was strong and kind and very, very patient. She, like all good queens, was wise and loyal and devoted to her family. Though salty-tongued, she was kind and loving to her family.

"Sadly, the royal pair lived a pale and shadowy existence, having been magiked long ago into believing they were simple creatures. As a result, they lived a plain, humdrum sort of life that only those who do not believe in magic can have. It was a life of quiet desperation as though each knew they were capable of so much more.

"For, tragically, they had been charmed into thinking they were average people, not real a king and queen. That their house wasn't a castle, but just an ordinary house. That their life together in that house on the hill was boring and unimportant. In short, they were cursed into thinking they were and always had been just plain humans..."

"Aww" was the collective sigh. *So sad, just people,* they all thought—except for Bob, who was purring at this point. After all, he liked ordinary people. He found that ordinary people could do very extraordinary things.

Ordinary people can actually be kind of cool. Just look at Christina, Ben, Jacob, Marissa, even Kenneth, Betsy, and Noel, all human and all playing very important roles in this saga...

Fred continued,

"But somehow, deep in their hearts, they knew they were special, different from simple human beings. That they and their children possessed great power. After all, they had two children who behaved like real-life royalty: a true prince and princess in their thoughts and deeds. They were fierce. They were brave and adventurous. They were kind and wise for their very young years. They were characters larger than life itself. The kind you meet in fairy stories. And that is fitting.

"For their very special children, the prince and princess, fearlessly and bravely launched themselves headlong into the world of Fairfolk and not only survived, but they thrived. They prevailed against forces of danger. They overcame magical creatures much stronger and larger than themselves. They even fought an epic battle, besting an evil fairy queen, who was bent on destroying the magical realm for her own nefarious purposes.

"Soon, all magical creatures deferred to them, knowing how vital those children were to the very survival of the magical race called Fairfolk. Because of their bravery, those two children, the prince and princess, led the Fairfolk into new directions of thinking and living. They helped them see the human world with new and accepting eyes.

"They changed the way magical creatures viewed humans. And their parents did the same. Fearlessly, the king and queen offered sacrifice in their own ways to keep the royal children safe. They even challenged the Others, a thing that few Fairfolk ever had the courage to do. And they too survived and led.

"Soon, it was understood by all that they were all true magical royalty."

"You mean rock stars," Enj said. Currently Marissa was sitting in the palm of his hand, unconsciously patting his scaly palm as she listened to the tale, swinging her legs gently like a child at play. *What a treasured moment*, he thought, gazing down at her. *She is so enraptured by the story with such an open, sweet demeanor, so—*

"Ouch!" he said, as she slapped his thumb. Pointing at Fred, she bought his silence with an icy glare. But really, he didn't mind at all. He knew it was just Marissa acting tough. She really didn't mean it. So much.

"In time, the entire Fairfolk realm knew of the charmed king and queen, their royal children and their powers to change the magical world with only the strength of their love. Because, everyone in our world finally realized what their kingdom truly was. The magical world finally understood the rightful place for the king, the queen, the prince, and the princess. They were the undisputed rulers of their special realm.

"Yes, they, in fact, this family, the king, the queen, the prince, and the princess and even their closest friends were the rightful rulers of The Kingdom of Happy Endings!"

"Awww!" The trolls sighed in their gravelly, rocky way. Small pebbles were heard pinging to the ground as the trolls shifted in unison, squirming in delight at Fred's story.

"Really?" Jacob asked, elbowing Seen out of his dopey, happy (and possibly sleepy) stupor. "You buy this?" he asked the elf.

"Oh, absolutely. Look how you have made my life so much better. And everyone else around you as well. And you have done it, mostly without the use of magic. That is power. True power."

"Anyway...despite their Kingdom being one of happy endings, sometimes, hard work was required to achieve such a thing. After a very hard time filled with trials and tribulations—"-

Tribulations—an antique reference to...

Fred glared at the trolls, staring them into submission. All literary references, idioms, and other jargon would be parsed at a later date. Her stony gaze made sure of it.

"After a very hard time filled with trials and tribulations, everyone in the royal family was exactly where they were meant to be, each with their own happy ending. For you see, their strange power to create happiness affected all who were in their kingdom.

"The mother and father, the king and queen, now ruled in a land filled with loyal subjects, their subject's fealty was rock-steady." She giggled at her own pun. The troll clan liked how she lumped them in with the king and queen.

How very interesting and fun and exciting, and whatnot! Rock-steady, tee hee!

Fred gazed at Betsy and Kenneth, working to include them as well...

"They even had their own brave knight—a woman of generous proportions. Such a fearsome and beautiful warrior with her brilliantly hued consort. And not one but two dragons, bonded to the family and breaking all dragonish rules for the sake of love.

"They and the knight and her consort, protect the creatures of their realm judiciously and with great care. In return, the creatures pledge to care for and serve them, heralding an unprecedented era of joy and peace."

Betsy and Kenneth blushed at the official title, which somehow seemed to cement their relationship into something better than either had hoped for.

Bay-Boy smiled proudly at his little charge. Lola took this opportunity to raise her tiny forearm in question. "Does happy endings have anything to do with butt-air? Because if ssso, then I already have done that. Ahem."

Bay-Boy attempted to clarify. "No, you haven't eaten your mother yet and do not know about knights and kings and queens and fairy tales. These are stories of old-ah. 'happy endings' mean snuggling and cuddling and '*special flying*.'" Bay-Boy emphasized "special flying" by arching his massive brow.

"Ooh, that!" She giggled. "Then happy endings means something good good goody!" "Yup," he replied slightly embarrassed at her less-than-cool response.

Struggling to keep this crowd on track, Fred continued

"There were also three wise men, full of child-like wonder at this new kingdom. Their wisdom, although somewhat curious and strange, seemed to be of great import. They may yet carry the power of insight into the great and glorious future that this kingdom will experience. They are important to this kingdom. They are necessary in a mysterious way. They are special..."

"Yup, special. You can say that again." Betsy gazed at her boys. "Arthur, stop picking your nose!" Always on the watch for her charges, she saw that Arthur was deep into the story. And when he was totally engrossed, he tended to gross everyone else out with his unconscious habits. He did it all the time—except when he was learning to golf. Not enough hands to accomplish all required tasks. Still, they always cleaned his clubs thoroughly after each lesson. Just for in case.

"But what about the royal children? The princess and the prince?" Marissa was terribly impatient, reverting to a ten-year-old for the duration of the story. She presently had a bad case of the "what about me's?"

"The prince and princess possessed great powers of their own. Powers too great to remain in the Kingdom of Happy Endings with the king and queen, their loving parents. Their powers were required in other regions of the magical realm. They were great leaders in their own right and were compelled to use their special magic where it is most needed.

"The parents, with full yet saddened hearts, knew that it was time for their children to establish greatness and Happy Endings in the far reaches of the magical realm. They, in short, *kicked them out of the nest.*"

"Ulp" was the gulp from one of the trolls, ready to pounce on that delicious phrase. The "Ulp" resulted in one of the other trolls stepping on his rocky foot as a prohibition to going down that particular thought trail. At this point, none of the troll clan wanted to get off track of the story. It was going so well. And they were actually in it. Fabulous! And one rocky foot stepping on another had its own type

of ouch—enough to stop the thought train that was for sure.

"The children's tale is yet to be finished. But to be sure, the princess is now a great and wise leader of the greater magical realm, reigning with a tender heart along with the wisdom of her brother. And, she has the love of her life, her consort, to guide them through...

"Uh-huh," Betsy said. "I knew it!" She nudged Kenneth while nodding sagely at Enj and Marissa. Concurrently, Enj dropped his hand, thereby ending his perch for the little fairy. Marissa, in turn, became very busy bobbing on the air, rearranging her hair, checking to see if anything was in her teeth by the sheen of Jacob's glasses.

"Dude, just fess up," Jacob said to Enj. If a large green reptile with wings could blush, he was doing so at this moment. Pink (embarrassment) and green (skin color) make the color of ruddy brown, which presently was the hue flushing across his cheeks and down his neck. His wings at this point took a powder, curling away from his shoulders as though they had never seen him before in their lives.

Silence abounded. In order to break the awkward moment, Jacob asked, "So what about me? I mean the prince? I mean, isn't he all conflicted and such by his human versus his gargoyle self? So where is his happy ending? And who does he get to hook up with? Sorry, Mom," nodding to his mother. She shrugged in reply. Hard to chastise your grown son for wanting the same things she did.

"Well, the fair prince has his trusty best friends, the gargoyle and the special elf. His epic story is yet to be told. They remain by his side for his journey, and

who knows who else will join him? His happy ending will come. Of that, I am sure. For now, he is at peace, content in knowing that great things are ahead for him and that all will turn out well in the end."

At this point, Fred blushed furiously, realizing that she had just spent the entire time telling the story while staring into Jacob's startling blue eyes. She looked away, a flush of embarrassment spreading across her generic and putty-colored features.

"And Bob?" Kenneth asked. After all, Bob had, in the past, scared the pie out of him, and he would rather not have his own happy ending marred by the presence of the huge and powerful cat-of-death—the very cat who had in the past threatened to give permission to the dragons to have Kenneth flambé for lunch.

Bob smoothly transformed from lounging kitty to cross-legged man, all tattoos and piercings in their proper places. He replied, "Dude, I told you. I am into recruitment. That's my gig. Can't do it around here; you are all committed, as it were. I am heading back to the Bay to carry on as usual."

"...Everyone has a special place to be their most happy and to spread their love. Bob will be where he is most needed. The Kingdom of Happy Endings may not be the best place for Bob, the colorful feline. His place is near the prince and princess to keep watch over them and offer occasional guidance. That may be where his happy ending will best be found.

"So, in conclusion, can you all stop bickering now because you are interfering with my own fricking happy ending!"

Then, lamely, she added,

"The End..."

Sentimentality Comes in Many Forms

It was quiet at first, as the group contemplated the story, more specifically, their particular roles in the story as told by Fred. The supreme Elder Other Marissa was the first to break the silence. "I really have only two things to say about your fairy tale. Well, three, but let's stick to the two for the moment." Marissa was speaking to Fred while hovering. Her flight path was a sort of spiral trajectory around the young female troll, causing poor Fred to swivel her head most uncomfortably in an attempt to keep up with her superior. Marissa was sizing this one up. Literally.

She ticked off on her tiny blue fingers. "First, I love how you had all of us spellbound by the simple purity of your story line." Marissa was in fact, using some of the jargon she had learned during her stint in college. (It was a very brief stint, resulting in her being outed by said Kenneth here and thereby preventing her from attending any more human institutions of higher learning. However, some of the more fanciful terms did stick. She trotted them out for show as often as she could. This was as good a time as any.)

"Second," she continued with her list. "You need a makeover."

"Oh I totally agree with you." Betsy stood up and joined the two girls. "I'm thinking with a lot of hair gel to calm all of that." She gestured to the unfortunate poufy mass of hair at the top of her head. "And then some clothes. Glitzy, and with sparkles, I think." Betsy was harkening back to her Vegas days when sequins were the required fashion statement.

"What are you—part fairy?" Marissa asked the largish woman.

"Now, do I look like I roll like that? No, I certainly do not think so. Not even for pay. I am and always have been strictly dick-ly, as they say." Betsy was a trifle insulted.

Ooh. The trolls sighed, finding a real gem in the largish woman's jargon. This one was priceless. They could hardly contain themselves. Though Fred was still focused on the buzzing orbiting fairy, so she was not quite as spellbound as the rest.

"No. Not *fairy*. I don't even use that word in a negative sense. I mean fairy. Like people my size. With wings. And bad fashion sense."

"Well, I like that much better. But who says sequins are bad fashion sense?" Betsy was confused. In her world, sequins were much preferred to the chilly and highly uncomfortable straps and leather arrangements she used to wear for work. But that was long ago. Now she wore khaki pants and collared knit shirts. She was proud that it spoke to a sense of conservatism that had never been a part of her life before. Still, she did miss the sequins.

"Sequins maybe," the fairy conceded. "And Spanx. But we'll talk more about that later. Anyways...my third point is, after your makeover, how would you like a job working for me? I need a new secretary."

At this momentous statement, Seen went from content to crestfallen. Oh, he didn't care so much about the makeover part, although he often thought how marvelous it would be for him to have such a thing, Imagine, looking like a normal human—or a normal anything for that matter. After all, he was the only creature besides Marissa with hybrid gargoyle wings. Marissa seemed to carry it off better than he, probably owing to her keen fashion sense.

What upset him was his being summarily fired from his job as secretary. Just like that. No warning or anything. Being with these guys was *his* happy ending. And she just eliminated his job. *Happy ending, my green wings,* he muttered bitterly to himself.

I knew it! His inner psyche finally spoke up. *It was only a matter of time before they kicked you to the curb.*

What are you talking about? Seen adopted a perplexed and annoyed expression while his inner turmoil churned.

Oh come on! I told you I am your only true friend. See how quickly she dumped you for the new flavor of the month.

Marissa, while bobbing and floating in her assessment the ungainly girl, noticed Seen's tragic expression. "Oh, don't get your knickers in a bunch," she retorted.

A collective gasp of delight came over the trolls as they began to contemplate that delightful turn of phrase. But then, Ted asked timidly, "Can we?'

Marissa rolled her eyes. "Go ahead. Rock on. I've got some business to conduct here. But be alert. I may need you later. Fred, you stay mobile please. We need to talk." The girl troll nodded meekly at her superior.

Smiling, the group, sans Fred, hunkered down for a nice long analysis of many things just said, including knickers in bunches and strictly dick-lies.

"But what about my happy ending?" Seen was emboldened by the truth of the story and felt it was his turn to demand some answers.

"What about it?" Marissa was annoyed. *So little faith, this boy has.*

"Well, where do I go if I can't work as your secretary? You said I was very good at it. Many times, as I recall." His tone was slightly wheedling. His voice was tight.

Marissa thought that just maybe he was going to cry. Highly out of the ordinary for an elf. Especially an elf guy. It nearly killed her that he was sad. Not when everything was about to turn out perfectly great any moment now.

"Seen, listen. You were great at that job. But think for a minute. What was the first thing we did when there was trouble? That's right. We gave you a *promotion* and sent you out in the field. And you did great by the way. Well, except for the part about not checking in and all, but I understand how you were in overwhelm mode.

"Nonetheless, I feel like your promotion still stands. You will not be working as my secretary, but as my personal administrative assistant. With a new desk. And a computer. In my office with me. Until of course I temporarily kick you out because you annoy me.

"Now don't you think Fred would be great working the desk outside *our* office?" She emphasized the *our*.

Fred could barely contain herself at the thought of running with these big dogs (*big dogs was a colloquial reference to—*) *Ooh stop!* She admonished herself. "Google. I have heard about this Google from Rockstar Ben and Master Elf Seen. He lives in a box on the desk and has knowledge of all things. I so very much want to work for you and to learn how to talk to Sir Google. Or Sire Google. Lord Google?" Fred was trying so hard not to offend, not knowing what the customs were in addressing an all-knowing creature that lived in a box on one's desk.

Seen, feeling rather smug that his inner psyche was all wrong in this matter, decided to be gracious and helpful to Fred, the New Hire. He committed to help her with this aspect of the job. After all, someone would have to transition her to his area of responsibilities. He might as well start now. Plus, he did like to show off his Internet prowess to anyone who would listen.

"Google? No problem. I know how to access it. I can teach you how to click on Google. I do it every day, me and Google. Yep, Google. We are BFFs." Seen was using his best Internet jargon.

"No need to spell out your profanities. We are all adults here." Demetrius wanted so much to be relevant in this momentous conversation. Right now, the only way in was for him to act like the cool parent, allowing profanities like BFF or whatever to be bandied about.

Bert thought of himself as a bit of an expert on things contemporarily human. Although the term *BFF* was a bit out of his purview, he took a guess as to what it meant. His eyebrows scrunched about his forehead as his presumed meaning began to take on significance. "Oohhh," he said.

Arthur sagely agreed, "Oohh. Yes, I see." Then he added, "What?"

Bert's eyebrows waggled even higher up on his brow, telegraphing the nature of the comment. "Seen here is BFFs with Lord Google. You know, B-F-Fs...On a regular basis now it seems." Now Bert still had no idea what BFF meant, but considering the passing youthful vocabulary in use at the time and the frequency of the use of the profanity starting with the letter F, he had what he thought was the general idea.

"Ah, that explains a lot about the fellow. It's all clear now," Demetrius considered.

"Well, we are nothing if not open about these matters. After all, we are far past the age of stoning one for his or her proclivities. So uncivilized," Bert replied.

"And messy." Arthur hated messy. Unless it meant crumbs from lunch in your beard. That was a good kind of messy. It meant a snack was to be had at a later date. But stoning a person just for having a BFF? That was unnecessary messy to be sure.

"True that." The wizards were in full chat mode. They could go on like that for a very long time. That is until a necessary break was required. Which for old men could be at any time.

"Can you three just stop for a minute. I am thinking Big Thoughts here and really don't want any chatter right now." Marissa waggled her own eyebrows at the wizards, carrying a more sinister threat. They shut down as effectively as the trolls.

"Look, kids. I am quite sure by now that Aunties Berry and Find could use a little help with the troops.

Fred over here would be a perfect choice. And I am thinking that with a little confab with the fairies, that they can help me with my makeover plans for Miss Fred. It's Miss Fred, isn't it, as opposed to mister?"

The ungainly troll nodded.

"Good. Just checking. So yeah, a makeover with the help of my fairy posse. Which yes, probably includes the liberal use of sequins. Well, fairy equivalent of sequins, but sparkly nonetheless. I think I am going to do a little body sculpting myself. You don't mind if I do that, do you, Fred?"

"Oh no, chip away." Fred was positively breathless with excitement. A new job and a makeover. Living at Home Base with all of these legendary Others. With Jacob. Especially Jacob. And Lord Google. An opportunity of a lifetime. Possibly BFF-ing as well. With Jacob. Just think of the stories it would generate!

"Shall I go rocky and let you blast at will?"

"No, I think I am going to use some big magic on you. Then I will fly you to your new home."

"Oh my," Seen cautioned. "Won't that call too much magical attention to us here?"

"Oh, I certainly hope so." Marissa smiled in a very sly way. She addressed the group, "I intend to cause a big commotion. I want the full magical attention of the Others. Especially those hunting for Dad. And when they get close enough, I am going to blow up the parentals."

Some Rules Just Have to Be Obeyed

"But first, I must say, we will be using a fair amount of big magic here and some sort of balance must be struck." Marissa pondered the situation.

What she wanted to do was to orchestrate was a faux annihilation where it would look like she had blown up her parents. She hoped to attract a large number of Other hunters to witness this and report back to Home Base that the deed was done. Finally then, they would stop searching for her dad. He would be safe. And all would get on with their happy endings.

The problem was she would have to expend a fair amount of magic to first attract Others to the area. Then even more magic would be used to make it look like the catastrophic event had actually occurred. Even though she was Supreme Elder Other, even she had to abide by the essential rules of Fair Trade. If they were about to use a ton of magic, then some would have to be given in trade, in order the keep the energy in balance. But who would be willing to give up their magic in trade for what would be expended?

Christina was more than happy to make the sacrifice. If sacrifice was what was needed for her family, then she was all in. Besides giving up magic would resolve another issue she had been working on with Ben.

"It's fine, honey. I am an old hand at sacrifice." Christina was smiling—really smiling for the first time in a very long time. She looked up at her husband for reassurance. He grinned like a kid at Christmas. She gazed back. The look was so full of intimacy that their children were momentarily offended.

Happy at last, her mother approached the small but very in-charge daughter with her hands outstretched, saying, "Take it. Take it all. I don't want one bit of magic left in me. Use it on this darling and charming young girl. Make her as beautiful outside as she is on the inside." Fred blushed, grinning in a gritty manner. She smiled so hard, little flakes of granite could be heard tinkling off her cheeks.

Ironically, Christina was happy at the thought of giving up the very thing that she thought she would love. She actually patted Fred's scratchy cheek. Fred smiled the smile of an affection-starved child. This lighthearted mood was positively infectious, despite the fact that time was of the essence.

"OK. So, Mom. Here is how this is going to go. You and I and, er, him…" She nodded in the direction of Enj, her magical wingman. (The previous mention that she and Enj might have actual feelings for one another made her feel frosty and uncomfortable in his presence.) "…are going to redo this girl just a bit. You give it your all, and Enjie and I will keep things under control. Then we will magic Miss Fred and Bob back to Home Base. Bob, you contact

Noel to come get you and Fred here to take her to the fairies for fashion consulting. Oh, and, Bob?"

"Yeah?"

"Could you supervise the fairies on their fashion makeover? I really don't want her to be bogged down by five million pounds of sparkly crystals. After all, she actually is expected to work for me and can't be looking like a hooker at a drag queen beauty pageant."

"No prob," he replied. "I'll only let them do some accessorizing or some such. I will personally make sure she ends up looking like some badass chic. Intimidating. Like she could scare the shit out of any Other trying to muscle their way in to see you. I'll personally oversee her fashion makeover, vetoing the most outrageous of their fairy design."

"No tattoos, Bob," Marissa warned him.

Bob flatly gazed at her. It was a look of a man who had just had the fun taken out of him. He looked to the sky for a spare reserve of patience. "Really. You are so June Cleaver about the whole body art thing, but OK. Fine. No tattoos. However you want to play is how we go."

"I mean it, Bob."

"Jesus. Now you sound like your mother."

"Low blow, Bob. Not nice." Marissa noted the slight disappointment in her mother's eyes at the insult. She appealed to her mother. "Sorry Mom. It's just that sometimes bosses have to be bitches. No wait. That's not right. What I meant was—"

"Oh, quit digging yourself a deeper hole." Jacob smoothly stepped in to do damage control. "Let's just focus on what is to be done. The way I see it, you guys have plenty of magic to do whatever beauty makeover deal you want on this, er, a, chick. Plus you can see her and Bob home on some magical moonbeam or whatever. And you'll have lots left for whatever else you need if you take all of the magic Mom has.

"Now Enj here is our secret weapon. As long as he participates in the deed, whatever he magiks stays that way. Permanently. As long as the person eats afterward. So hearty meal for all involved, Mom and Fred. That way, you'll stay fixed in your forms. I assume, Mom, you want to stay human after you give up your magic, right?"

"You betcha. Thunder thighs and all. White hair, crazy lunatic aging hippie is the style for me, yessir." Christina was positively giddy at the thought of going back to her normal looks. She paused, her happy demeanor now tinged with a slight shade of worry.

"The only thing about my giving up my magic to do this is, well…"

"What?" Enj, Jacob, and Marissa cried out in unison, exasperated that just when they had a possible solution to this mess, their mom was going to cast doubt on the plan.

"Oh it's nothing. It's just that I want to have at least a little magic left in me to scry you. I mean, I assume Dad and I stay here with the trolls and, well, the rest of the crew and you kids go back and run the show at Home Base, right?" Head nodding all around.

"So how do your father and I get in touch with you if we need to?"

"Mom, it's very simple." Jacob was in full charge now, having figured out all of the little details.

"So you give up all of your magic to placate the needs of the magical net. We get to use that magic of yours to redo Fred, plus to send Fred and Bob back to Home Base in a very flashy way. Meanwhile, Dad still has his magic, and he can scry with you at will.

"Don't forget that we are on the Internet as well. Just say the word, and we will get you set up somewhere with a new cell phone, and even—when you have a place to live—a wireless laptop. Technology is a wonderful thing," he concluded. Sometimes, just sometimes, he sounded a trifle condescending to the folks. But they didn't really mind. After all, it was his master plan. And he was in charge of making it work.

"Ahem," Kenneth said, sheepishly holding up his cell phone. "I still have my phone and charger. So until we set up shop somewhere, we can always go into town and buzz you."

"Perfect," Marissa said, regarding the former Sleeping Guy with new eyes. He seemed more together somehow up here with this motley crew. And he certainly had technical skills that no one else did that would serve them later. She was suddenly very glad he was on this team. Plus, it seemed like there was a zingy, happy thing between him and Betsy. *That's nice,* she *thought. Even he gets a happy ending. Maybe Fred's story is true after all....*

"Well, that brings up a good point." Ben had been mulling over the details of this plan and had a bit of input of his own to add. "I think I know where we would like to set up shop. And I know where you should in fact stage this big blowup. You see, I have always wanted to own a golf course. You know, design it after some of my favorites. The way I see it, I have a built-in construction crew with the trolls here. And a *semi* pro golfer to give lessons." Betsy blushed at the compliment.

"I even have a site manager to talk even the most stubborn planning commissions into agreeing with us." Kenneth was given the nod at this job. Finally, he had the title and the respect he had always wanted. His scruffy, skateboard college days had just ended in one fell swoop. He had a girl and a job and magical creatures around him. They even liked his ability to use glamour to influence people. So far, he had only used it on Betsy (with great results). But with a little coaching, by perhaps the three wise guys, maybe he could develop it as a mad skill. To help with the building and running of a real golf course.

"So if none of you really mind, I assume we can use the flamethrower lovebirds snoozing over there to blow up what remains of this abandoned golf course. Then maybe I can buy it on the cheap and make this happen for all of us."

Ben was finally happy. He had his wife back by his side and a big project to work on. His kids were nearby if they ever needed him. He had his pals around him, and they liked him for who he was and not for how much magic he had. And he even had a little magic left to use in emergencies.

He and his wife had just become empty nesters. Although their empty nest was anything but. Having a big crowd to manage would be the very thing to help them adjust to life without the children.

"Exactly, Dad. I was thinking that the dragons could simulate a lightning strike, set off a pretty big fire around here. We can contain the biggest spread by situating the blast between the streams and the water features of the golf course. It still will be impressive, just not dangerous.

"Hold on, kids. Remember, this is my big idea." Marissa flew toward Jacob forcing him backward with the force of one hand. The conversation had really careened away from her as head honcho. She was feeling a tad irrelevant at the moment.

"Yeah, your idea, after Jacob and I figured out how to fake annihilation," Enj said smirking at his pal. Jacob smiled back, thumbs-up.

"OK, right. Silly me, what was I thinking?" Marissa hit her head with the back of her hand feigning abashment. "You big bad boys have it all figured out. But what you don't have is a sense of timing. You see, we have to get Fred back in time to fill Aunties Berry and Find in on the caper. They have to hold off the Others from coming here until just at the moment of annihilation. I want the Others to witness it, not be in it. As much as I dislike that bunch, they are, in fact, my responsibility. I just don't want any of them to see the dragons do the deed, nor do I want to needlessly waste my Other operatives in the actual blowup. I may actually need those guys at some point."

"Spoken like a true boss," Betsy said, nodding. "They may be a gnarly posse but they are your posse and you gotta watch after them." She smiled at her old boys, her family, having the same feeling about these old coots. They smiled back.

"What's a posse?" Demetrius asked Bert.

"It's means a group, I think," the wizard admitted. "Or possibly a derisive term for a female's reproductive body part. Posse. Yes, I think that is what it is."

"Oh dear, was this some sort of slight?" Arthur asked. He definitely did not want to be thought of as a woman's anything! Certainly not anything below the waist. Eyes involuntarily shifted downward at said girl parts (on various females in the group), then upward, as the gentlemen attempted to understand the reason for this verbal slight.

Fred blushed again. True, she was embarrassed by this conversation, but then there was something else that bothered her sensibilities. She felt a different feeling than embarrassment. It was a new feeling. It began to spread throughout her entire body. It made her feel prickly and agitated. Yes, she was feeling the same way Marissa did nearly always, impatient. She was impatient to get on with her new life. All this talk was hindering the process.

"Would we, I mean should we be standing here?" Ted, although reluctant to interrupt, had been prompted by the troll clan. Fred was intensely grateful for the interruption.

The trolls had been carefully listening to the plan and had had been conducting a mental meeting of their own. Ted was now to be their replacement spokesman owing to the fact that Fred was to be relocated. He began tentatively, "I thought possibly, perhaps we could, um, move away from the area of proposed damage. You know, hide out for a while in the troll caves. Deep in the heart of the mountains. Why, we could work on parts of the new building while we are down there! Building and designing and working. Oh my!"

Enj was frankly ready for less talk and more action. "Sounds like a plan. Why don't I do a flyover with Bay-Boy and his girl Lola, and we'll pinpoint where we want this to happen. Then they can hightail it out to the safe house under the mountain. I'll jet to wherever Marissa is. I mean where ever the group is." *Lame, lame, lame,* he silently chastised himself.

"The truth shall set you free, my man," Jacob reminded him.

"Shut the hell up, if you please," was the gargoyle's response.

"Safe house. Hightail. Jet." The little fairy snorted. "Quit trying to be cool, Enjie, and let's get the job done. Oh and, Mom, before you lose your entire mojo, scry Berry and Find and let them know what and who's coming."

Marissa was anxious to begin the makeover of her new secretary. She assembled her crew. Mom was to provide the fuel. Enj was to add a little extra magic, and Marissa was to do the body sculpting. Fred just wanted to get it over with.

Beauty Must Suffer
Part II

It had to have hurt. Just because trolls assume a rocky shape doesn't mean they can't feel anything. They knew, for example, when they had been peed on. That felt wet and sticky. But to be magically blasted by a tiny blue fairy, a big green gargoyle and a mom had to be intense to the nth degree.

It was decided after all, just to be safe, to have Fred in her rocky state in order to do the deed. They suggested that while undergoing the redo she contemplate pleasant things, such as happy endings. That was the best they could come up with as a substitute for anesthesia.

And so, in her bouldered state, Fred endured. Enveloped by a blue green aura of light, heat and sparks, she clenched her fists until they hurt. She closed her eyes, grimacing from the glare and throbbing pain. She ground her teeth until she felt crumbly bits in her mouth. She didn't shout or cry out. She kept repeating, *This is my happy ending*, and *I want this; I really do.*

It felt like fire. Like pieces of her were literally melting away. A thousand million prickles of bright magic picked at her, chipped away at her, molded her, and essentially shaved away thick, rocky layers to reveal the young woman who resided within.

She knew when it was nearly over just before they stopped. Suddenly, she felt lighter, as though her frame had dropped the enormous weight it had been carrying. It had. She was a mere shadow of her former self. The bright glare, visible to her closed eyes, faded to a pleasant grey.

There was a gasp. The sparkling blue- green light faded to a dull glow around the girl. The group was amazed at the sight. She was a true beauty. The young woman before them was stunning.

Well, to be perfectly honest about things, there were a few flaws in the picture. First of all, her dark hair still had a wiry, coarse look to it. It stubbornly remained an unruly mass that resembled a lion's mane more than silky tresses. And her dress, or shift, or boxy bunch of rags that she had been wearing didn't exactly fit anymore. One sleeve had slipped dangerously off the shoulder and drooped down her arm, giving her an unintentionally sexy look. However, her body was tall and lithe, her skin was pink and glowy and her large blue-gray eyes sparkled. "How do I look?" she asked the group.

Betsy and Marissa exchanged a look. A very knowing look. "She'll do. A few sequins and she'll be fine." Betsy was determined to add some proper glam to the girl.

"I think a corset. You know leather, with a jean skirt, right?" Marissa was inspired by the sexy biker babe style.

"Nice." Betsy nodded in agreement. "But with sequins. Lycra tights and Jimmy Choo heels."

"Ooh, trashy couture. I love that!" Marissa agreed. "But the hair is still, uh you know."

"Tell me. I have had hair issues all my life." Betsy gave Fred a nudge in camaraderie over follicle challenges.

The gentlemen were sure at this point that the women were speaking a foreign language. They were unable to follow anything that had just been said. But the women all understood each other very clearly. Even Fred nodded knowingly. While she didn't quite understand the specific fashion references, she got the gist of the situation. She looked hot. And they were going to make her look even hotter. And that was just fine by her.

She had confirmation of that fact not just from the women but from someone else. Someone whose opinion mattered greatly to her. More than even he knew. The only opinion that really mattered to her came from Jacob. Presently, the young man's mouth was hanging open. That's it. He just stared, gawping at her. It was all she needed to know. It made all of the previous discomfort totally worth it.

"Let's get this girl back to Home Base so she can get to phase two of the redo. After the fairies have a go at her, we'll give her a 'what not to wear lesson' when I get home." Marissa was totally satisfied that step 1 had gone well. She exhaled, relieved and happy that Mom's powerful magic wasn't too hard to control.

The group then turned their attention on Christina. Jacob peered at his mom, approaching her carefully as though she might break upon contact. "Mom? You feeling OK? Human-like and not magik-y?"

Christina closed her eyes. She thought about magic. She wriggled her fingers to see if there was any magical leakage. Those in the know stepped out of the way of those hands, having seen the explosive effects of her past handiwork.

Nothing happened. They all sighed in relief. She knew then that she had given all the magic she had to transform the young troll into a beautiful girl—a great gift that was well worth the loss of the power of being a magical creature.

The mother grimaced, letting out a deep breath. Concluding her magical checkup (or lack thereof), she concluded, "It's gone. Really gone. I can feel it. It's like I feel, um…" She was at a loss for words, so they all helped

"Sad?" (Fred).

"Small?" (Enj).

"Empty?" (Marissa).

"Bereft?" (Demetrius).

"Lost?" (Arthur).

"Blind?" (Seen).

"Ineffectual?" (Jacob).

Ben had the right answer. "Back. She feels like she's back."

"That's right." She smiled. A rare look of peace and contentment spread across her face. "Normal. I feel normal again. Thank you my dears for helping me get back to what is important." She smiled at her children and crossed the space toward her husband. "I feel so good."

"I am glad you feel good, Mommy. Because it's really time for us to go. And I couldn't leave if you and Dad were sad." Marissa and Jacob stared long and hard at their parents, as if to memorize them.

After a brief moment of quiet, Marissa sighed, gulping back the beginnings of a sob. "We have to do this thing now," she said.

The group then turned their attentions to staging the scene for what would look like the annihilation of Ben. First, Bob and Fred prepared to be sent off in a great blazing blue streak of light—back to Home Base.

Readying himself for departure, Bob offered Fred his arm, crooking it in a gentlemanly way. With a nod and a wink, they were off. Fred had instructions to keep all Others from convincing Aunties Berry and Find to let them investigate all of this magical trouble up here until she received Marissa's signal (which she was told she would know very clearly when the signal came). Once the signal was given, she was to allow access to the acting Supreme Elder Others. The ladies in charge would feign concern and then pretend to relent, sending as many Others as they could up here to witness the annihilation. As soon as the Others were convinced that the thorny matter of Ben had literally been eliminated, all would return back to Home Base. Eventually, Marissa and the rat pack would join them back there and everyone would be able to live happily ever after (Fred's words).

Perfect plan.

Nothing could go wrong.

Really.

Hanging with the Homies...

Home is really a state of mind. After all, when one travels, one feels like one is "right at home" if the host has gone out of his or her way to make feel comfortable and welcome—which really isn't like home at all. Because at your real home, no one ever goes out of the way to make you feel welcome or comfortable. You are, in fact at home like the chair or the couch is at home—an expected part of the furnishings.

And so when you are at home, no one really does anything in the way of treating you special when you get there, except of course to acknowledge your existence with a greeting or a peck. (Aside from newlyweds, of course. For them, every day is like one long really good date. Their home is a great big romping playhouse. They are really feeling the "at home" thing.)

So to say that Fred felt immediately "at home" at Home Base would be an insult to the way she really felt. She had her own office with a desk, a screen, and a typing instrument that allowed her to communicate with Lord Google, the godlike entity that resided in the box on her desk. Lord Google was at the ready at any time of the day or night to help her understand words, idioms, and whatnot. And best of all, he was insanely polite. He never crept into her thoughts and told her mentally to shut up. He never engaged her in a group think, jamming his opinions and ideas into her already busy brain. He kept his place in the box, speaking only when being spoken to.

And he played with her. He showed her a game. A bright picture of it popped up in the middle of his dispensing information to her latest query. It said, "*Start Here.*" And she moved her bat-shaped arrow as she was instructed using a thing called a mouse, which didn't at all resemble a mouse, more a ladybug or domed-shape beetle. Nevertheless, she moved the thing misnamed a mouse and placed it on top of the *Start Here*, just as Lord Google commanded. It seemed like the polite thing to do, after all of the information he had previously provided her about absolutely everything. So she clicked. A delightful game appeared on the screen.

Lord Google, it seemed, thought she needed a small break from her intensive education of all things new and unusual. He played with her. What a dear and generous thing this lord was! The least she could do was to play with him, as often as he liked. It was a small tribute to the great loads of information he had bestowed upon her. She considered it almost an obligation to do so. Best of all, it was a game with *words*! Her favorite things were words! He made the words do amazing feats. First, there would be a question. The answer was a word. And if you placed the words in the right blanks they would intersect with other words and form a pattern like a hedge maze.

Imagine, words being so versatile that they even formed patterns when placed together!

Lord Google was a very giving information god. He made her feel better than "at home." He made her feel special. They might possibly be BFFs, but no, she was saving that job for Jacob. If he would have her. She would very much like to be his BFF. And with great frequency.

She loved her office even more than Lord Google and her desk. It was beautiful. The once stark, white walls were now covered with vivid murals depicting Fairfolk life—dragons in their hidden lairs deep within the woods; elves, toiling away at their tall work tables, etching, embroidering, and creating all manner of beautiful handiwork for Fair Trade. Even gargoyles in flight, majestically soaring over human cities, unseen by their inhabitants below. Every wall was a new depiction, freshly painted by Acting Supreme Elder Other Berry and her Other painting crew. The painting crew had been given many jobs, such as this one—busy work to distract them from hunting the renegade Ben. It gave the Family time to find each other and resolve their very complex issues.

Soon, there wasn't a bare wall left in Home Base that wasn't covered in a mural. Berry and Find were running out of jobs to kill time. Presently, Find was teaching them how to dye their togas rich and brilliant colors of their choosing. This the Other operatives adapted to easily, since some still had unfortunate red, yellow, and green togas, which needed a little help in the way of color and fashion.

Fred liked what she was wearing today. It suited her personality. Bob had made sure that her basic integrity was maintained despite the fairies predilection for all things gaudy and overdone. He vetoed quite a few of the fairy couture suggestions, insisting that he had final say on whatever they came up with. After much discussion, resulting in a sort of buzzing consternation by the fairy queen Eedle, a compromise was struck. At Bob's direction, Fred wore stressed and ripped jeans and a plain white tank top. It was the fairies' job to complete the look.

And that was where the fairies took over. They braided her unruly hair into a single side braid that fell to the front. In it, they meticulously placed tiny peacock feathers, pin feathers in rich jewel-like hues of purple, green, and blue. Rose quartz crystals were tucked in the folds of the plaits. A few kept falling out as she moved about the room. There were so many in her hair that it didn't make the slightest difference. It made tinkling sounds when she walked. It was a pleasant sound that reminded one of wind chimes lazily ringing on a balmy summer day. It was soothing to anyone entering her space.

But the crowning touch to her simple look was the scarf the fairies had their brown spiders create. Made from spun silver, it hung like a bib on the front of her tank top. Chunks of semiprecious stones, opals, and serpentine and even granite flakes (a tribute to her roots) clung to the silver fabric. It looked like liquid silver but itched like a mother. However, experience had taught Fred that beauty must suffer. She liked the little brown spiders so much she hadn't the heart to tell them how scratchy it was. Those spiders did take some getting used to, but all in all, they were very sweet creatures.

After they scampered up her arms and legs (a few dropped from the ceiling to adjust from above), they would quickly move off, so as to minimize contact. The little creatures had learned from experience that their presence sometimes made folk uncomfortable. Having them so close to her allowed her to study them as they adjusted and readjusted the slippery scarf. They actually looked nervous, tentative, as though they really, really hoped she liked the work. Their myriads of faceted eyes seemed to shift and dart, looking up at her and gauging her reaction.

All in all, they seemed very kind. Soon, she didn't feel the slightest bit uncomfortable having them on her arms and legs. Ticklish, yes. Uncomfortable, no.

When they were done, they scurried to the furthest corner of the office in order to get a long view of the fashion statement they had created. They waited expectantly, hoping that they had pleased this new creature.

Of course she would tell them she loved it. Never mind the itchy part. Lots of her old rags and hide dresses were plenty itchy. And stiff. This was such an improvement that a little discomfort was to be tolerated. Too bad about the skin rashes though. Still, she just couldn't hurt their little furry feelings by telling them about that. So she said it was the most beautiful thing she had ever worn.

This was, in fact, true. They were delighted, moving like a liquid streak to their new hidey holes at Home Base, at the ready to make a new fashion motif for their new model. If she liked this style, boy would she like the next thing they had in mind for her! Even grander! They went off to plan something *really nice* for her next time.

Watching all of this was another creature residing in the corner of the room. It rarely moved as it was, for the most part, quite content to laze about, absorbing any stray magical leakage that came its way. It was curled in the corner of the office beneath a mural of a painted tree and beside a faux boulder glowing warmly in the painted sunshine. This creature, so easily camouflaged next to the mural, stretched languidly, having stowed itself in the far corner while the brown spiders did their work.

Despite the fact that it was a behemoth in relation to the spiders, it had long ago learned that a) brown spiders were not food and b) when they were on a mission covering Fairfolk with layers, it was best to stay out of their way. Those little spiders en masse were a force to contend with. Careful or they might cover you in sparkly bits. This creature had plenty of sparkle on its own. Any more would be like gilding the lily.

No, this was a unique lizard, pretty enough without the benefit of crystal drops. It was one of the fairy king Hummer's special lizards that had absorbed a great deal of magical energy while it was babysitting young Hummer during his incubation. Back then, the lizards kept the royal egg warm and safe by huddling around it. In return they became big, rainbow colored and shiny. When Fred visited the Family home and subsequently received the fairy clan as visitors (she being much too large to fit into the bramble that was the fairy's home), the fairies used the big lizards as safe transportation across the field and to the human abode.

They came to the house on the top of the windy hill to size Fred up, as it were, to bling her out, fairy style. One lizard, the very one now at Home Base, took a shine to her. He liked the low thrum of magic that she gave off. Also, she would give him a special treat now and then, which he really, really loved. He became her pet, and with King Hummer's permission, (well, he said yes to everything so it didn't take much convincing), the lizard came with Fred to stay in residence, at Home Base, as her pet and personal watchdog.

She was about to give him that special treat any minute now.

At her desk, while pushing the bulky scarf down just a bit to avoid spoiling her view of the computer, Fred was opening up a charming email, an important message from a place in Canada, offering important vital prescription drugs for some mysterious malady, when—

The door opened. An Other operative peeked his head around the barely cracked door. Determining that no one but the new secretary was in, he took a chance to speak with her. He cautiously entered the room. Fred looked up from her desk

"Hmm?" she asked with a neutral demeanor.

"Well see here, Miss—I am not sure what manner of Fairfolk you may have been. But—"

"Troll. I am a troll."

"No, really? But you are so, so, er…" He was at a loss. It seemed like every time he came in to speak to someone, he fell into a veritable land mine of offenses. It never seemed to go well. And yet, this new one seemed so diffident, so sweet. Maybe this would be the opportunity to get what he wanted.

"I'm so, not-Troll?" she asked helpfully.

"Well, that, yes, but also you are so female. I mean…" Now, he was sputtering. "Trolls are a bit more generic, aren't they?"

"Only if they want to be." Fred was being enigmatic, mysterious. In fact, she was playing with this one. It was kind of fun. Her lizard looked up sharply from his corner. In his tiny lizard mind where ideas have simple frequencies and words don't mean very much, he had a very complex thought. *Will she turn? Can it happen? I do love it when she does...* Well that is as complex as lizards get.

The Other gamely forged on. "Well then. Now see here. We have a situation northeast of here. A huge amount of magical energy is being expended just recently in an area where we have a suspicion that renegade Other Ben may be hiding. He might be there right now. The information is not clear. And yet this must be investigated. At any rate, whether he is there or not, annihilation must occur to balance out this rather large amount of magical energy. It is what we have been taught for these many millennia. Tradition and order must be observed!"

"I see." Fred was unperturbed. *They like tradition and order do they? Well then.* "But of course no annihilation can occur without the Supreme Elder Other's permission. And she is not present." *There! Tradition and order. How do you like that!*

This Other persisted. "But there are the substitutes, the fill-in elf folk. They are here and I know it. The doctor one and the painter one. The two women. The ones that keep us busy with their silly jobs. They can give the permission for us to go investigate and annihilate. They must!"

"Well in that case, I could get you in to see them, tomorrow. Or not" consulting the calendar on the computer, which was actually that fascinating crossword puzzle game. She went on. "No, I guess the soonest is next week. They are very busy right now."

"Doing what?" he exploded. "Tie-dying more togas? Painting the water closets? Decorating the commodes? I insist I see them now!"

"No." Fred said it softly but firmly.

"I insist."

"Not today."

"But I must see them. Even just one of them. It doesn't have to be both."

"Another time."

"Listen, missy. I have been an Other Operative for a very long time. Long before this new regime. I know the rules about renegades. They require annihilation. I know what happens when large amounts of magic are used. It also requires annihilation. I have even participated in annihilation. I know the urgency. You most obviously do not. Now if I have to barge my way into that room over there, I will."

"Are you serious?" Fred rose from her desk and came around to face down the Other. He stepped back just a bit. Despite her gentle guise, she suddenly seemed very powerful. Over in the corner, the lizard hissed at the Other but held his ground, remaining for the moment where he lay against the far wall.

"Do not vex me," the Other warned the barefoot girl in her gaudy scarf and torn blue jeans.

"Well, fine then." Fred spread her arms. She smiled. The Other smiled. Was this a gesture of defeat? Did he win? Well, he certainly hoped so.

But no. Fred spread her arms wide in preparation for a change. In an instant, the young girl morphed into a rocky wall, spanning the length of the room. Incongruously, the necklace hung, intact and quite precariously, off a crag on the wall. A few crystals were heard pinging onto the bare floor.

This was exactly what the lizard had been waiting for. It was his special treat. He quickly scrambled up the wall and perched top of it, barely clearing the ceiling. He hissed viciously at the Other. Inwardly, he was humming with great pleasure. The latent magic of the transformation seemed to absorb right through his scaly belly. Ticklish, but fun. The hissing was just for show.

The wall barred the Other's access to the inner office. His bid to speak with the Supreme Elder Others had been foiled by this impassable obstacle. Cursing softly, he did the only thing he could do. He backed his way out of the office, closing the door rather louder than was necessary.

The lizard got his treat. A warm magical rocky perch to warm himself by. The rock wall smiled.

The computer pinged. It was the signal. It was time.

The Family Goes Out with a Bang

There were tears. Copious ones from Marissa, who did enough crying for the rest of the group. The stern warnings from Ben to his children, cautioning that they all must stay together and protect each other, lent an ominous tone to the farewells.

Christina smiled through her tears. Her heart was alternately breaking and bursting with pride that her children had come so far. "I always knew you were great leaders—every one of you!" She gave her three children, Enj (the adopted one), Marissa, and Jacob the full force of a mother's look, layered with complex and deep emotions. It was loving and yet made them all feel a tad guilty about something. What it was they couldn't say. It was just what mothers do. It's a skill they possess.

The art of loving and telegraphing guilt at the same time—it is intended to keep children on their toes, as it were. She even patted Seen on his arm (the gargoyle-looking one) in a motherly way. Seen's heart missed a few beats at the power of that simple touch.

Christina warned them all about the dangers of not staying together. *So young*, she thought. *Even after all they have been through they still think they are bulletproof.*

This both terrified her and made her proud of their youthful (possibly misguided) courage.

Time was running out. Soon, they had to part. Even the dragons were getting restless, filling their bellies with the necessary gas for buoyancy and flame throwing was a complicated skill. Timing was everything, and the time to leave was now. Actually, the time to leave was several minutes ago.

Shuffling about, lots of "OKs," "I-know-you'll-be-all-rights" and "Don't-forget-to's…" and still no one was leaving.

Strangely, it was the three old gentlemen who took charge. They moved en masse toward the parents. In the act of herding Ben and Christina gently away, they murmured,

"Now, now, it will be fine. They'll stay in touch; they'll stay together." Bert.

"Yes, yes, they heard everything you told them. No, no you haven't forgotten a thing." Arthur.

"Don't you remember? We selected them out above all Others. We chose them well. They are our chosen leaders. They possess all they need to know to accomplish their tasks. They most assuredly know what to do back at Home Base. Tut, tut and shush now; let's move on. Nothing more to say." Demetrius.

The old men were somehow very comforting and for a brief moment, seemed a bit wise.

Reluctantly and with one last long look and a wave, the teary-eyed parents finally turned away from their children and began the trek to their temporary new home.

The trolls led the way, bringing the humans toward the deepest and most inaccessible part of the Sierra Nevada Mountains where the troll caves lay. As they faded into the misty distance, a bobbing, motley crew of creatures of varying sizes, snippets of conversation echoed softly throughout the meadow.

The trolls were fully engaged in the banter, as were the former wizards.

"Well, Ben. What will you call the new golf course when it is rebuilt?"

"Ooh, call it Dragon, after the dragons who are going to make it possible."

"I don't think you can call it that. That was one of its old names. The people previously running it might own that name."

"You can **own** a name? Claim a word as yours? Have it **always**?"

"Owning a name? What a thought. Marvelous! Well then. I claim the word 'Trousers.' It has a lovely sound."

"OK, then I get 'pantaloons.'" The trolls were practically swooning at the word.

"'Pantaloons,' huh, mine will be 'bean burritos,'" one troll interjected. "It is a fast-food item that Ben told me about. It apparently has curious properties besides tasting good. Purportedly, it also fixes the, er, going problem we all sometimes have."

"'Roughage'. Perfectly good word and has the same effect. That one is mine."

"Talk about roughage. Try 'barranca.' Good word and also has fiber." Betsy was getting into the swing of this literal fun fest.

" 'Barranca'? Is that a hedgerow?"

"Stop with the hedgerows. There will be no hedges, hedge rows, or hedge mazes in this new golf course. Am I right, Ben?" Betsy could be counted on to get a bit heated on the topic of the misuse of golf course jargon. On this score, her three wise guys tended to irritate. "It will be 'Barranca,' which means messy brush—a golf hazard, got it?"

And so it went. Such a wordy crowd. Such a noisy crowd. Such a bickering crowd. But they were happy. They were a family. And they were off to their own adventures.

* * *

It was the youth of the family who stood watching until there was no more to see of their parents and their new cohorts. For a moment, they felt a little lost, a little broken, nostalgic for a time when their parents figured as the largest objects in their orbit. Once, all things revolved around Mom and Dad— their requirements, their rules, their world. Now, broken away from that orbit, they each felt a frisson of panic. What is their orbit now? Who would lead them? Who would take care of them? What would they do next?

And yet for a long time now, they had been leading their own lives, taking care of their own needs, and deciding what to do next. As that realization dawned on each one of them, the panic was eased. It was replaced by a new feeling—a strange lightness. Jacob heaved a big sigh, as though a weight had just been lifted. It felt good. It was time to make their own way.

Jacob, once a young teen and now a grown young man ended their nostalgic reverie. The moment had come. He gestured skyward to Seen and his crew. "Come on, you guys. We gotta go."

With a Bang and a Whimper

Jacob, Marissa, and Seen headed to the ridgeline to wait for Enj's return. They watched as the gargoyle flew down to the golf course and club house. He circled lazily over the structure, waiting for the dragons to show up. Soon, two lumbering, flying reptiles glided over from their hiding place among the tree line to rendezvous with Enj. The three creatures hovered in the air bobbing as their wings worked their own ways to keep them together. The dragons followed the leadership of Enj, directing themselves toward the back end of the structure. He pointed there and then just past the structure where a large propane tank stood.

Enj flew close to Bay-Boy and Lola, close enough to pat them on the side of their scaly heads, taking care to avoid their sharp, vertebral spikes. He immediately shrank down to the size of a hummingbird. Buzzing in their ears, he said, "You guys are a great couple. Take care of yourselves, and don't let this get out of hand. You need to be around to make a lot of little Bay-Boys and Lolas." He smiled at them in the gargoyle sense, which when translated to hummingbird, was the tiniest of peeps.

They looked sheepishly at each other then smiled back at their partner in crime. The three of them, hovering and grimacing at each other would be considered a horrific sight with too much tooth. But to them, it was just smiling.

He gave one last bit of advice, "Remember, keep away as much as you can. Try to use the tree line as cover. Blast your fire as far away from you as possible. I'll direct it from there. I'll even add some oomph of my own. Then take off for the troll caves fast. When that propane tank goes up, it will bring a lot of heat and fire with it. I want us all to make it out of here in one piece, Got it?"

"Do not worry, Enj-ah. We can take some heat. We are built for it. But we will leave right away. We will meet up with the trolls and your-ah parentalsss. We will watch over them and will not eat them. Unless it is necessary," Bay-Boy added, not entirely sure what the code of etiquette was on this momentous occasion.

Enj was feeling a little teary. It would be a long time before he saw those two again—or Ben and Christina for that matter. "All right," he chirped. "Let's do this. And kids? Try not to eat Family."

Dry lightning strikes from afar look like a strange flash in the sky. If you happen to be looking in the area that it hits, you might see a bolt of light. But it isn't as distinct as lightening in the night sky—the dark background providing clear illumination of the blue-white light. Daytime does not provide such clarity. All that was necessary to feign lightning (for that is what humans surely would blame the resulting fire and explosion on) was a general flash from the sky to the ground. Fire, of course, would result, and if there was anything flammable in the vicinity, then a very large kaboom would follow. The propane tank was just the thing to provide the fuel. Either way, dragon-and-gargoyle-caused or Other-caused, humans would come to the same conclusion: dry lightning hitting a very unfortunate spot.

As far as Others, an annihilation process looked roughly the same. However, the additional fuel would come from Others, magically "igniting" the renegade Other, thereby destroying him, his magic, and just about anything else in the blast zone.

Only this time, the joke was also on the Other hunters. They would be sent to the very spot that they were told Ben was and would "watch" as Ben's very own children purportedly exact annihilation upon their own father and possibly even the mother, as it was well known that Mad Lavender/Christina had also flown the coop and was no longer at Home Base. Current gossip (well placed by Fred), was that she had gone renegade as well and joined her husband. No one had refuted it, so, therefore, the Others assumed it must be true.

The result would be a twofold benefit. One, they would cease hunting down Ben, as he obviously was no longer a problem, having been successfully eliminated by his own son and daughter. Second, they would be doubly scared of Supreme Elder Other Marissa and her henchman, Jacob.

Any creature who could so easily off her own father and mother must be a terrifying one indeed. She would be one to be obeyed at all costs. This would ensure total compliance with any future orders that Marissa might give, regardless of how eccentric they may seem.

* * *

A large contingent of Other hunters flew cautiously over the bare crags of the mountains, approaching the alpine meadow. They hung back, waiting, as they did when they were close to their prey, surveying the entire area in the low swale beneath them. Floating softly, creating a misty veil to hide their appearance in the sky, they resembled a smudge along the skyline. Like a stray cloud looking for its home, they waited, watching and feeling for signs that a magical creature was about. It felt oddly still in the little valley below, blank, and without the great deal of magic they had been anticipating. It was curiously strange. It nearly made the little smudge drift off in search of another prey. But then they felt it. And they saw it.

First came a burst of magical energy. It was unmistakable. They all felt it. Something had just used big magic. Its location was marked by a flash of light. Then, there was a short pause before an enormous deafening explosion, which was heard and felt for miles around. It momentarily deadened the senses. So much so that they missed the momentary image of two lumbering dragons fleeing and trailing a cloud of smoke behind them. Had any of the Others looked in their direction, they would have seen smoke, from the explosion streaming from the wreck, nothing more.

And in that fraction of a moment of senselessness, they were also unaware of a tiny dot of compressed magic, a large gargoyle, temporarily reduced to the size of a small bird, fly past them to the adjacent ridgeline, away from the explosion and toward the safety of this friends. And in their deafness, they failed to hear a small "Ouch, ouch, ouch!" as the tiny, birdlike creature flew past, shaking his wing hard, in an attempt to shake off the pain of a stray ember that had embedded itself in the thin membranes of his wing.

After a few moments, several Others contained in a smudgy cloud began to speak.

"Do you feel any more magic in the valley?"

"Nope. You?"

"Might be something over on that ridgeline, but it doesn't feel like the renegade Ben. His magic was more of a steady thrum. Over there is like a prickly smoldering."

"Well, that's probably the Supreme Elder Other. She feels like danger all right. Just her style."

"You think she did the deed herself? On her own father? My word!"

"She's a terror all right. Might have offed the mother as well. Goodness!"

"Goodness had nothing to do with it."

"By the way, did anyone see some dragons fly in the opposite direction, away from the explosion?"

"Dragons in this area? Well, I guess I would fly away from annihilation if I were them as well. Nothing terribly unusual about that."

"Still."

"Still what?"

"Doesn't it seem a bit strange to have two dragons in the same area together?"

"Not if one is a juvenile. Did one look smaller than the other one?"

"Er, yes, but—"

"Oh really. Stop seeing conspiracies wherever you go. You need a vacation from Othering. Really, you do."

Sulking, "Fine."

"Well, that's it then."

"Problem resolved."

"Time to head back."

"To Home Base?"

"Of course, where else would we go?"

"I certainly hope they are done with the painting projects."

"And tie-dying. My toga is a sight."

"It certainly is."

"No need to be nasty."

"Off we go then."

The smudgy cloud dispersed like so much smoke, leaving Marissa, Jacob, Seen, and a slightly injured Enj, gathered on the ridgeline, to watch the conflagration burn itself out.

Mission Accomplished. Happy Endings for All...

The four youths stood on the overlook, watching the last of the explosion. From afar, it looked almost pretty—a spray of sparkling lights dancing in the foamy haze at the point of impact, turning the atmosphere an eerie pinkish hue. But, in fact, the scene at close hand was of heat and fire and incessant popping as underbrush caught fire, their sticky plant resins exploding in the heat.

Enj's sore wing was testimony to the power of the blast. It wasn't a life-threatening injury. But it would leave a scar. When healed, it would resemble a green, ropy reminder on his otherwise smooth wings, of a time when they turned all the rules of their magical world on their head.

They watched until the sun set on the wreckage and the light softened to an orangey glow on the horizon. Slowly, it would burn itself out, leaving a blackened crater where there once was a verdant mountain meadow and a mysterious golf course.

In time, the moon rose, casting a bluish light on the foursome. Soon, even the mountainside was dark—all flames extinguished as the fuel was consumed. The fairy paused midair, aware that it was finished for good. She sighed audibly. The sigh caught its own kind of spark and exploded into tears—deep, bitter tears for the loss of a mother and father. The men turned to her – a large gargoyle, a young man, and one damaged elf, all three too large to comfort her in their embrace.

Extreme tears call for extreme measures. The green gargoyle pointed his finger at the fairy and pulled the trigger as it were, unleashing a stream of bluish magic. It surrounded the fairy and then completely engulfed her.

For a moment, it was the brightest flash in the mountains. Just another flash and spark in the fire's aftermath. Nothing to be concerned about, really. When it subsided, a girl emerged. A pretty, auburn-haired girl in a layered tank top and jeans, with big dark eyes, and a faint blue scar on her pink cheek.

Her face was pleasantly round for such a slight girl. Her eyes were enormous and liquid brown, verging on deep gold. The gold matched the lovely blond highlights in her deep-auburn hair, which hung heavily down her back. She smiled through her tears at her family, nestling into her brother's arms. Jacob looked over her head at his friend Enj and nodded.

The gargoyle smiled and, then spread his hands over all of them. For a time, they all were surrounded by his aura—a cocoon of magic and light that was both comforting and binding. When this light faded, the motley crew of magical creatures became three young men and the girl. All human and all able to give their sister, friend, and supreme commander a big, consoling hug. Seen, once a damaged elf and now a wan, thin, gangly young man with a rather owl-ish expression, smiled. He enthusiastically joined the group, hugging them all a bit too tightly, happy at last to have both friends and family.

Seen looked like he had just spent twenty years of his life living in the library—pale and lean, the look of a student on a perpetual all-nighter. He had an awkward, uncoordinated look to him, accentu-ated by his pale, skin and his black hair. His display of emotions reminded one of a lovingly tolerated, slightly annoying, overenthusiastic family pet.

Enj was tall and lanky. He was tan and sported a tousled mop of long brown hair, giving him a surfer-dude look. His jeans were slung low on his lean frame, and his T-shirt was faded and worn. It stretched across his taut chest and shoulders. His green eyes sparkled under the haphazard bangs that stiffly sprang from his scalp, as though they weren't sure what direction they were supposed to lay. His nose was long, aquiline, and slightly freckled. His smile was broad and lumi-nous, contrasting with his tanned skin.

Jacob looked like Jacob always had—medium build, broad shoulders, spiky hair, and with bright blue eyes, just like his dad. His face was all angles, ending in a decidedly square jaw that lent him the very masculine look of the all-American guy. One could imagine birds tweeting and harps sounding at his smile. His heavy-framed black-rimmed glasses were square, accentuating the brightness of his blue eyes, making him look like Clark Kent. As though the glasses, would prevent one from seeing that he truly was Superman.

Enj; the dude, Seen; the geek, and Superman Jacob hugged Marissa, until she could cry no more.

They also effectively cut off her ready supply of breathable oxygen, but why quibble when three guys want to give you love and support?

Eventually, someone deep in the huddle grunted uncomfortably, shaking the overenthusiastic Seen off. He backed away. And they all separated—all, except for Enj and Marissa, who remained in contact by holding hands.

She paused in her grief to wonder at this development. She inhaled his scent, manly, musky, and a little smoky. It was a very nice smell. It was a perfect scent. Fairly intoxicating. It was scent she wanted to breathe for the rest of her life.

Enj just looked at her: Marissa, all that power housed behind that innocent girl's face. Sweet and cute combined with powerful and magical. Enj was simply stunned at the image of him and her somehow bonding—definitely not like brother and sister.

For a brief moment, he felt a strange heat between them. She must have felt it as well because they both quickly stepped apart, pondering this as well as the view in the growing darkness below them. There was a mutual sweaty-hand moment as they dried their hands off on the jeans in unison. Jacob noticed. Seen did not.

"So is it all over?" Seen asked, referring to the faked annihilation.

"Yeah," Jacob replied.

"But did it go like you thought it should?" Marissa asked her brother anxiously, peering into the inky darkness.

"I think so," the brother answered.

"So they are not really gone for good?" the sister pestered.

"Well, if you are talking about the Others, they split the scene soon after it happened. As far as Mom and Dad and the crew, well, I am pretty sure they made it to the troll caves…" he answered, a soft question in his reply.

"Well—" Enj said, staring upward into the night sky. "I guess the show's over. Time to book."

"Yes, I do believe it is over," Seen agreed. "Shall we go back to Other Home Base?"

"Oh, let's not go yet," Marissa asked, her gaze also turning to see the vast array of stars only visible in the high mountains. The night sky was spectacular and wasn't lost on them despite the recent spectacular fireworks of annihilation. "They'll only have about a million crazy things for me to tend to. I'm not ready for that yet."

"I know what you need," Jacob said. "There's only one place to go that will fix what ails you," he added a bit playfully, despite the rather doleful circumstances. "Think, ultimate comfort food. Grease and salty happiness."

She gazed back at him, uncomprehending. Then, a slow smile spread across her face. "Really?" she asked.

"Doctor's orders," he replied.

"But, well, you know, what if we eat, and then…?" She left the question unfinished, looking down at her human self and contemplating the consequences of eating while under the magical spell of Enj.

Jacob smiled. "Then they'll just have to get used to a Supreme Elder Other who looks like she's an eighteen-year-old human girl."

"Them too?" she nodded toward Enj and Seen, now looking like a couple of twenty-something males. "I mean, you know how Enj's magic works—"

"I have effed-up already? Sheesh, I have been human like about five minutes and I broke what rule?" Enj asked the brother and sister. He wasn't quite understanding the brother sister code-speak, but he knew it involved him and his brand of magic.

Marissa chuckled quietly, the kind of chuckle you can only make after having endured something dire and sobering. This was not a belly laugh, rather, it was a wise sort of chuckle, as though she had a very good idea of what was about to befall all of them. "No, you haven't blown it. We were just talking about getting out of here and having a hamburger; that's all."

"Wait, eating? All of us? You don't really mean eating at this juncture. Do you?" Seen asked, wringing his hands. He hated to ruin this somewhat peaceful tableau, but he needed to remind them about eating when they were under the influence of Enj and his powerful magic.

"Wait a minute. I get it," Enj said smiling. Only this time, his toothy smile didn't look particularly feral. It just looked like a nice smile, a sincere smile from a very cool guy. "If we stay this way, then all the better. After all, we still have our magic." He shot a tentative spark from his trigger finger. All appeared to be in working order. "And when we get back to Home Base, we will still be in charge—still kicking ass and taking names. But we will do it as humans. And won't that just fry them?"

"Ah, yes," Seen said, now understanding the ramifications of being a fully magical human in charge of Fairfolk. "Maybe we can show them about how humans have loyalty and love."

Wow, love! His inner psyche chimed in. *First, you have real friends and now, you are bandying the word "love" about!*

Wait…Did you just say I have real friends?
You know I just said it.
But you just now confirmed it.
Yes, I did. His psyche went silent.
Does this mean you are leaving me now?
What and miss what comes next? Not a chance.

Seen felt an unaccustomed sense of warmth. It was peculiar, but nice. He was in fact experiencing happiness for the first time in his life and approval from his innermost self. And that one was a tough one to please.

The "L" word seemed to charge the atmosphere. With that, Marissa began fiddling with her tank top, tucking it in. Enj started rocking on his heels, suddenly engrossed in the night sky. Both were carefully avoiding looking at each other.

"Awkward yet again," Jacob said. "So yeah, hamburgers?" he asked again.

"Isn't that the burnt cow stuff you eat, topped with orange and red goop?"

"You haven't lived until you have had a papa burger from the diner in my hometown. "We, in the family, well, except for Mom…" she said, with a wee catch in her throat. "…who loves rare meat, don't eat our beef raw. You are human now. Gotta go with the program. Humans don't eat beef raw. Get used to it," she declared.

"Come on; we're all going, right now, back to the East Bay for some grub." Jacob smiled at each one of them. He knew if he just kept them fed and safe and together, they would all be all right. First came the food.

"Should we let Enj get us there, or should we magic our own selves?" Seen asked.

"We don't need to rely on Enj to get ourselves anywhere. We all have enough magic within us to manage that," Marissa said and smiled at the gawky and trusting Seen. *Such a good friend*, she thought. Then looking at her men, she thought, *I am so lucky*. Before she got to weeping again, she snuffled back her tears and said, "Follow Jacob and me. We are heading west."

With that, she closed her eyes and concentrated. A burst of white light streaked from the center of her chest, pulling her upward and arcing west toward the San Francisco Bay Area. Jacob followed suit. Soon, there were four shooting stars, low on the horizon, heading out for the best burgers and fries in the Bay Area.

The Posse Gets Its Grub On

It was a small, dingy sort of diner, the kind you can see in Anytown, USA. Only this one happened to be in the town in which they had been raised. The diner was in a no-frills, rectangular cinder-block building with a neon "Open" sign flashing in the window as its only outside decor. Despite its generic look, it was well known for having the best burgers and fries in the East Bay. Long lines of customers, sometimes stretching out into the parking lot, were to be expected on a Saturday night. This night, the line was out of the building and around the building.

People waited. Patiently. Because it was worth it. The heady aroma of burgers and fries perfumed the air. The rich, beefy, fatty smell was layered with the perfume of vanilla milkshakes and warm, melted chocolate fudge. It was the equivalent to an olfactory heart attack in the making. In short, it smelled wonderful outside the building and well into the parking lot. It had the effect of mollifying the impatience felt by those in line. They knew that very soon they would have their turn inside, to feast on the amazingly unhealthy comfort foods that had absolutely no equal.

433

Inside, the diner was spectacularly unremarkable—chipped Formica tables and a menu that had been carved in wood decades ago, adorned the wall. Sadly, over time, the prices for the food items changed. When that occurred, the wooden sign remained unchanged. Instead, a small Post-it note with felt-pen writing was all that was needed to update the menu. It was crudely done, but somehow it added to the kitschy decor. Even the staff was essentially the same. Tips were good, and the owner/manager, a tall, lean, Greek guy, was pleasant.

The manager had the look of a cowboy, with his carefully waxed handlebar mustache. His long black hair was combed straight back and fixed in place with a sort of gel. Put a cowboy hat on him, and he would be ready for the rodeo.

A Greek cowboy was how people described him. And it fit. He had a long, hooked nose that went well with his olive skin. One got the impression that he just landed fresh from the Grecian isles. He always had a smile and a look of recognition, as though he remembered you despite the fact that you weren't really a regular. It was true that he never forgot a face. Nice guy with a remarkable memory for faces.

It was he who led the four young people to table six near the back of the diner, close to the milkshake machines. Those machines hummed and growled as they worked overtime, trying to keep up with the endless orders.

Enj was fascinated with the noisy, busy mechanical beasts that made these wonderful drinks and the serving staff who buzzed back and forth around each other, catching the metal drink cups just before it was filled to overflowing. Never once did anyone bump into anyone else as the staff expertly swerved through the narrow walkway around the ice-cream freezer and milkshake station. It was an amazing choreography of order filling and serving, taking years of practice to perfect.

One of the servers left the milkshake station to greet the diners at table six. Sticky, laminated menus (redundant, owing to the enlarged version on the wall) were handed out.

Then the group got serious about the business of ordering. Another older woman, a seasoned veteran waitress, came over, smiling broadly, displaying her ill-fitting dentures. She looked almost pretty but for the unfortunate dental work and the tired lines in her face.

Friendly, she was, as she took their orders and in no time returned with platters full of papa burgers, fries, onion rings, and shakes. Jacob and Marissa showed the two newbies how to navigate the dressing and eating of these juicy burgers, cooked moist and meaty, to perfection.

All was well, until, alas, a snag was uncovered in the food nirvana that was before them. A slight flaw in the heavenly feast had occurred. The nearly perfect meal was marred by the vanilla shake given to Marissa. She wanted strawberry, made with real fruit, not plain vanilla.

"No worries," Enj said, ever the gallant possible boyfriend. "I'll fix it." With a flourish and a whoosh (Well, he was trying to show off a bit to her), he waved his hand. The cup began to wobble, and then, with a liquid-sounding plop, it righted itself into the strawberry shake she had wanted all along. He had guessed by watching the shake-making process what should be in it and added a plump strawberry decoration for garnish. A personal touch of his own.

Marissa smiled, thanking him sweetly. Seen, however, frowned disapprovingly. "What are you doing?" he whispered. "Do you want to get us in trouble? Busted, fingered?" (He was using all the jargon he could think of. Most of it, unfortunately, had come from Enj.)

"**Collared**, you mean," Jacob, Marissa, and Enj corrected, in unison.

"Relax," Enj said. "We're chill here. Nobody saw it. They're all seriously into their grub." It was true; all the tables in the busy diner contained people intent upon either ordering or eating these monstrous meals. No one cared in the slightest about anything but what was on the table before him or her.

All except for one person: a tall man, lean and wiry, with long black hair and a handlebar mustache, who never forgot a face. He watched them now with great intensity from his station at the cash register. His happy demeanor faded as he witnessed Enj magically fix Marissa's drink.

The four were unaware that he had been observing them, just as he watched everyone who came into his restaurant. He watched to make sure customers were well served and that they in turn behaved. No dining and dashing and no funny business on his shift.

Only the funny business the guy at table six just did was something he hadn't seen in a great while. He was shocked at what he had just witnessed in his own diner. Even so, he had a plan. Once he witnessed the magic and felt its effects rippling across the room, he knew what to do.

Turning slightly away from the eyes of the four young people at table six, he pulled an old, rotary-style phone from a shelf beneath the cash register. It looked like something for decoration, as it didn't seem to have any wires connected to it. But this telephone didn't need any wires to make it work.

He carefully dialed the number he had been holding on to for a while now. An old six- digit number that he knew by heart. 'Round and 'round the dial spun, directed by his finger until the number had been entered. He waited. Then he said into the phone, "Get over here. Yeah something's up. Big-time. I got one in my restaurant right now. Uh-huh. Yeah. Fine. See you soon. And bring the trap. The big one."

Epilogue

OK. So I lied. I mean there was *supposed* to be a happy ending. I was so sure of it. All signs pointed to bliss. But then we are talking about the Family. Nothing they have done has been simple. They never seem to flow in straight paths to their happy ending. They always leave a mark upon wherever they roam. Most of the time that mark is a good thing. Other times, the mark they leave is like a dangerous red cape directing the attention of that angry bull called Fate across the arena. Sigh.

In the shopping list of destinies, almost everyone in this tale has a happy ending—even me. For I am truly happy, here in my solitude, while writing the story of a lifetime. And for me, the story is not yet over, since there seems to be an unresolved wrinkle or two. That's good for me. Possibly not so good for the Family. Possibly very bad for the Family.

They are a handful, that crew.

There is a moral to this story, one that I hope you have discerned. And that is, even very normal people leading very ordinary lives, can have a brush with the magical world. That they too can be sucked into the realm of Fairfolk. This could be wonderful or terrible—perhaps wonderfully terrible.

The point is to be ready. To be aware. And never ever to use too much magic. There is a time and place for magic, and picking the wrong time and wrong place can have disastrous consequences. I'm just sayin'.

So the next time you spy something odd out of the corner of your eye, believe what you see. The next time something flashes through the sky over your head, and for a brief moment you are quite sure it was neither a very large bird nor a very odd air-plane, take heed. The next time your parents warn you about staying away from the canyons past the fences in your yard, because there are "Woozer's," know that they actually exist.

For in those brief moments, the magical world is greeting you with a nudge and a wink. And if you are very brave, wink right back. Tell them you are not fooled in the least and they might as well come on out in the open. For you know what they are and that they are real. And so they might as well come out and play.

Just be very careful of what you eat or drink while you are with them.

Happy hunting.

About the Author

We have had this discussion before. Whatever I may say about myself, I fully intend to confound you with misinformation. Some things just need to be kept private.

All right, I will throw you a bone. I am the Professor. I am Christina. I am Mad Lavender.

And sometimes I am Seen.

I am married to a patient and kind, problem-solving sort of husband. He sighs a lot at my antics. I do have two wonderfully magical children, now grown. Their personalities are strikingly similar to two characters in these books.

I live in a house on a windy hill. Odd things have happened there, which I have faithfully and accurately depicted in my books.

And that is all I will say about that.

S. C. Williams

24323774R00245

Made in the USA
Charleston, SC
19 November 2013